J. D. Davies was ~~...~~ ves in Bedfordshire. He is one of the world's foremost experts on the seventeenth-century navy. His *Pepys's Navy: Ships, Men and Warfare, 1649-1689*, won the Samuel Pepys Award in 2009.

27 DEC 2018.   GREAT PARNDON

Please return this book on or before the date shown above. To renew go to www.essex.gov.uk/libraries, ring 0845 603 7628 or go to any Essex library.

DS12 4005

Essex County Council

First published in 2012 by Old Street Publishing Ltd
Trebinshun House, Brecon LD3 7PX

This paperback edition published 2013

www.oldstreetpublishing.co.uk

ISBN: 978-1-908699-26-8

10 9 8 7 6 5 4 3 2 1

A CIP catalogue record for this title is available from the British Library.

Typeset by Martin Worthington
Printed and bound in Great Britain by CPI Group (UK) Ltd, Croydon, CR0 4YY

For Colin and Wendy Bancroft

First draw the sea, that portion which between
The greater world and this of ours is seen;
Here place the British, there the Holland fleet,
Vast floating armies, both prepar'd to meet!
Draw the world expecting who shall reign,
After this combat, o'er the conquer'd Main.
~ Edmund Waller, *Instructions to a Painter (1665)*

To be ignorant of what occurred before you were born is to remain
always a child.
~ Cicero (106–43 BC)

FAMILY TREE OF THE QUINTONS, EARLS OF RAVENSDEN

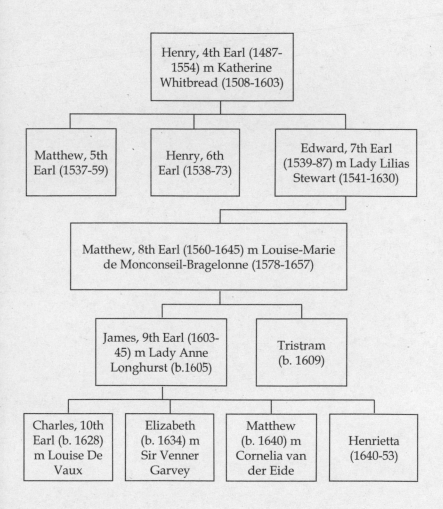

Henry, 4th Earl (1487-1554) m Katherine Whitbread (1508-1603)

Matthew, 5th Earl (1537-59)

Henry, 6th Earl (1538-73)

Edward, 7th Earl (1539-87) m Lady Lilias Stewart (1541-1630)

Matthew, 8th Earl (1560-1645) m Louise-Marie de Monconseil-Bragelonne (1578-1657)

James, 9th Earl (1603-45) m Lady Anne Longhurst (b.1605)

Tristram (b. 1609)

Charles, 10th Earl (b. 1628) m Louise De Vaux

Elizabeth (b. 1634) m Sir Venner Garvey

Matthew (b. 1640) m Cornelia van der Eide

Henrietta (1640-53)

Prologue

Fragment of a letter written by Sir Martin Bagshawe (1616–1665), Justice of the Peace for the Shire of Middlesex. Date unknown; presumed to be February 1665.

...that before his slaughter, the man's flight was as desperate as though he were being pursued by the very hounds of Hell.

My Lord, the last deponent, and the only one actually to witness the murder of this unknown wretch, was Thomas Eden, ostler of the parish of Stebonheath. He states that he was making his way across Blackwall Marsh, alias the Isle of Dogs, by the King's Lane from the Greenwich ferry. Some business had detained him in Deptford, and thus it was dark by the time he approached the chapel of Pomfret; the only building on that entire bleak isle. Eden depones that he was passing by the ruins when he espied two mean creatures, clad in dark raiments, stabbing poniards or some other short blade into the body of a man upon the ground. Eden believes that his sudden appearance as a man on horseback startled the killers, who took flight at once, running off across the marsh in the direction of the Lime House breach. Eden depones that he dismounted and went to the murdered man,

1

who lay upon the muddy floor of the ruined chapel. (This ostler seems a trustworthy fellow, My Lord, not one of those foul, idle rogues who would fall upon a dying man only to steal the possessions from his body, so I think we may value his testimony highly.) The dying wretch gripped Eden's hand strongly, pulling the ostler down to him so that he might hear his parting speech. The strangest thing is Eden's claim that even as his life-blood left him, the man appeared to be mightily content, even smiling, proud to speak the words that he uttered. I know that some men greet death thus, My Lord – witness the example of Vespasian – but it is this man's words that make me pause to inscribe them on a paper intended for such an eminent personage as yourself.

My Lord, Eden swears open oath that the man's dying words were these:

'Twenty captains. Twenty will turn, in the first battle of this coming war. Twenty, true to the old cause. Twenty will join the Dutch and bring down the tyrant Charles Stuart. There will be no more kings in England but King Jesus.'

May God have mercy upon us all, My Lord Percival, if this be true.

Chapter One

Describe their fleet abandoning the sea
And all their merchants left a wealthy prey.
Our first success in war make Bacchus crown
And half the vintage of the year our own.
~ Edmund Waller, *Instructions to a Painter*

The white cliff-wall of France, glimpsed through flurries of bitter February rain, appeared dangerously close. My ship strained in the swell, timbers seeming to protest against the proximity of those ship-breaking cliffs and the subterranean rocks that lurked off them. We were under courses alone, and despite the ferocious tide-race we still had ample sea-room to come off (or so those who were more expert in such matters contended), but I still felt that old dread upon my heart: the dread known only to men who have almost met death in a shipwreck when they sail too near a rocky coast.

Yet if we were close to that ominous lee shore, another was closer still. Spectators upon the shore of France – if there were any such about upon so bitter a day – would have witnessed the curious spectacle of two nearly identical ships, one running as close inshore as possible, the other closing her rapidly from the north-west, sails taut in the strong breeze. A quick count of the gunports cut in their sides would have established that the nearer carried thirty pieces of ordnance, the more distant thirty-eight. Any spectator knowledgeable of naval matters might have contemplated the absence of forecastles and the narrow, high sterns of the two warships and thus identified both as Dutch. For the inshore ship, that assumption would have been confirmed by the horizontal red-white-blue bars flying proudly at her stern. But in the case of the other, he would have been disabused at once by the red ensign with a red cross upon white in the canton, streaming out in the wind: the unmistakeable colours of the Navy Royal of Charles Stuart, second of that name, King of England. The paradox was easily explained by the fact that our hypothetical spectator was gazing upon His Majesty's Ship, the *House of Nassau*, a prize taken during the war between England and the United Provinces of the Netherlands. Or rather, the previous war, for the greatest certainty in the entire world on that February day in the year 1665 was that another was imminent. Perhaps very imminent indeed.

'If he was a man of sense,' said Lieutenant Kit Farrell, at my side upon the quarterdeck of the *House of Nassau*, 'he would by now be making ready to salute.'

I kept my telescope level upon the deck of the Dutch man-of-war. No men were going into her shrouds; no man stood by her ensign staff.

'I do believe he intends to brazen it out,' I said. 'He means to fight, rather than give His Majesty his due in his own seas.'

By time-honoured custom, and perhaps more pertinently by the king's direct orders, captains of His Majesty King Charles the Second's Navy Royal were enjoined to enforce the salute to the flag in the British Seas, defined – entirely reasonably – as extending to the high-water mark of every nation's shoreline from Norway to Spain. Such was stated quite explicitly in my copy of the Lord High Admiral's general instructions, addressed personally to Matthew Quinton, captain of His Majesty's ship the *House of Nassau*. The impertinent Dutch and their continental brethren oft quibbled with this manifestation of what they perceived as Britannic arrogance, the quibbling sometimes going as far as full broadsides, but surely here, in sight of Kent – in waters that were thus as much a part of the king's domain as my native county of Bedfordshire – no Dutch captain would be lunatic enough to deny us our right?

'Perhaps he reckons we will not want the responsibility of being the direct cause of the war,' Kit said.

'In that case, the captain yonder is most certainly steering the wrong course,' I replied. 'Quintons have been starting wars for six hundred years. Mister Farrell, we will clear for battle. And make it abundantly clear to the Dutchman that we are doing so.'

My old friend, to whom I owed my life, nodded in return and passed on the order to those in the ship's waist. A boy ran to the ship's bell at the forecastle rail and rang it lustily. As the off-duty watch began to emerge onto the deck, our two trumpeters took up their position at the poop and began roaring their song of defiance. All along the upper deck, gun crews manned their weapons, hauled on the tackles, and ran out the sakers. Shot, cartridges, rammers and sponges were made ready. Gun captains took up their positions. Several of the men looked up toward me and smiled, for they knew me of old, and I knew them. There was Martin Lanherne, the ship's coxswain and unofficial leader of the ferocious Cornish coterie that attached itself to me during my second commission and had since become my personal following, serving under me in each of my commands. There they were, ready at their guns: men like the giant George Polzeath, the minute John Tremar and the simian Cornish monoglot John Treninnick. Next to them, the unlikely friends they – and I – had acquired over the years, such as the renegade Moor

Ali Reis, the Scot Macferran and the runaway Virginian slave Julian Carvell. If a war truly was to be started this day, I could think of no better men to start it.

'He's responding in kind, sir,' said Kit, his eyepiece upon the Dutchman.

True enough, our opponent, too, was opening his ports and running out his guns. Now he had men in the shrouds, and moving out onto the yards; but the slight turn of his bow toward the *Nassau* proved that he no longer sought to run from us if he could. He was going to meet us, and fight.

'What odds would you give, Mister Farrell?'

Kit weighed the scene before him with the eye of a man far older than his years. 'We've more guns, and heavier – but that gives him the advantage in speed and manoeuvring. On the other hand, we have the wind, and he risks us forcing him onto the lee shore. So if I were placing a bet, Captain Quinton, I'd place it on us.'

I smiled and went down into the waist, moving from gun to gun. 'Well, my brave lads,' I shouted as a fresh shower of rain began to fall heavily, 'Lieutenant Farrell has weighed the odds, and wagers on a victory for the *Nassau*!' A happy growl and some cheering; the men respected Kit Farrell, and they also respected the significant quantity of prize money that such a victory would bring them. 'I'll not challenge that, but let it not be said that Captain Matthew Quinton is miserly with his coin!' Much laughter. 'Well, then! A firkin of wine to the guncrew that brings down any mast of the Dutchman, and a guinea to the man who brings me the sword of her captain!'

The men cheered wildly, stamping their feet upon the deck and waving their fists in the air. I sprang up the steps onto the forecastle, took hold of the foremast shroud and hauled myself up onto the starboard rail, drawing my sword as I did so. There was our enemy, barely half a mile away now and closing rapidly.

'Come on then, you butterboxes!' I cried exultantly. 'Deny the right of our king, would you? Come see how England defends the honour of her flag, my hogen-mogen friends!'

Of course, my performance was for my men, not for an enemy who could never have heard my words. For one glorious moment I imagined myself an armoured knight – why, perhaps even a duke – upon a mighty steed, charging the enemies of my king. Then a huge wave broke over the bow, soaking me to the skin, and the dream was drowned in a torrent of salt water.

As I wiped the ocean from my eyes I wondered what my opponent would have made of a captain who hung over the side of his ship like some deranged pirate, his hair bedraggled by rain and wave, swinging his sword about his head in the teeth of a bitter squall. Even then, all those fleeting years ago, captains – even young gentleman captains but recently sent to sea – were meant to command gravely from their quarterdecks, not play at dukes and Drakes.

On came the Dutchman. The scream of our trumpets reached a crescendo, forming an informal chorus with his. He was within range of our bow chasers now, but there seemed little point in merely toying with them when our full broadside was about to be unleashed –

I squinted my eyes against the rain. Yes, there could be no mistaking it – the foot of his foretopsail was quivering, and the men upon the foretopyard were hauling upon the clewlines. Only a moment later, I knew beyond doubt that he was taking in all his topsails. And at the stern, the proud ensign of Holland was coming down to half-staff. The Dutchman was duly executing the salute to His Britannic Majesty's flag.

She swept past with less than half a cable's length of water between us, our mainyards nearly touching, her men lining her starboard rail and looking sullenly – in some cases, defiantly – toward the *Nassau*. My men jeered and cheered in equal measure, many derisively prodding one or two fingers into the air. The quarterdeck of the Dutchman came level with the forecastle of the *Nassau*, and her captain – a short, bluff old man – raised his hat. I responded by drawing my sword to my face in salute, then shouted out in the Dutch I had learned from my dear wife, 'Quinton, Captain of the *House of Nassau*! My thanks and that of my king for your respect to our flag, sir, although you kept us wondering that you might choose another course!'

My fluency in his tongue momentarily took the Dutchman aback; then he smiled and shouted, 'Uyttenhout of Enkhuizen, Captain of the *Vogelstruis* of the North Quarter Admiralty! Fear not, Captain Quinton, on another day we shall pay very different respects to your damned flag – and take back our ship, there, also!'

As I walked back along the waist of the *Nassau*, past men hauling the guns back inboard, I heard growls of anger and disappointment.

'Be of good cheer, lads!' I cried. 'There'll soon be work enough for all of us!'

'A pox on the work, Captain,' retorted John Tremar in the broad accent of Looe, where his Morwenna raised their twins. 'We'll deal with the Hollanders in short order any day of the year. But I had my mind set upon your guinea and the wine, that I did!'

* * *

We saluted Dover Castle and came to an anchor beneath that mighty edifice. I stood upon the quarterdeck, drinking in the scene. Fishing boats plied to and from the beach of Dover. The packet-boat from Calais slipped gracefully under our stern, no doubt bearing the latest letters of intelligence from the court of King Louis. Further out, one of our larger frigates beat down the Channel; fresh out of the Medway, probably, and eager to join the pursuit of every sail that came within sight from Ushant up to Calais. The pursuit that we would rejoin, once we had revictualled. The purpose and profit of such a mission was immediately apparent. All around us lay the yield of King Charles's harvest of the oceans, the seizures of suspected Dutch merchant shipping that had been going on since the previous autumn, despite the fact that war had not yet been declared. At least a dozen prize ships lay in the anchorage: supposed Flemings, dubious Hamburgers, alleged Swedes, and the most troublesome of all, the Amelanders and East Frieslanders, nominally independent but little more than satellites of the Dutch, just as Jersey and Guernsey are for we English.

There was a cry from the lookout – 'Boat for the *Nassau*!'

I thought I recognised the figure in the stern of the approaching longboat, and raised my telescope. A bluff young man sat there. His head was crowned by the most fantastically vast periwig and an equally monstrous broad-brimmed cap. In his right hand he held a bottle, which he raised toward me in salute.

'Harris?' My surprise was succeeded in short order by concern for proper form. 'Boatswain Ablett, there! A side party if you please, to receive Captain Harris!'

We piped my old friend aboard the *House of Nassau*. He doffed his cap to me and to the ensign, but I sensed at once the reason for his arrival. The paper was there in his hand, having discreetly replaced the bottle. He said, 'Captain Quinton, my respects, sir. I regret that I must trouble you for the use of your quarterdeck.'

I bowed, and signalled for my officers to assemble the crew within the waist of the upper deck. Once the men were in position, Harris unfolded the paper and read aloud the commission in the name of James, Duke of York, Lord High Admiral of England, that appointed him, Beaudesert Harris, captain of His Majesty's Ship the *House of Nassau* for this present expedition. And as Beau read the last word, I ceased to be a king's captain.

'I was as surprised as you,' said Beau as we drank in my – his – great cabin. 'Coventry summoned me from the country. And when I found I was to replace you in this command – you, Matt, of all men – well, it shook me to the core.'

'You gleaned nothing of the reason for my supersession? Is there some discontent with my conduct of this command?' I had a sudden thought. 'Have my prize crews been excessive in their plundering?' I had oft doubted the wisdom of giving Cornishmen, of all the races upon God's earth, the charge of ships containing large quantities of wine and brandy.

Beau shrugged. 'No word at all, Matt. And you neglect the possibility that the duke might have realised at long last that I am a better captain than you, and thus more deserving of this command.' Beau kept a straight face just long enough for my face to flush, then he grinned broadly. 'Not to mention the possibility that he might wish to free you for a far finer ship than this, my friend. Who can fathom the ways of princes?' He took a long draught of his Dover ale, for Beau was ever a thirsty soul. 'In any event, there will soon be work enough for both of us. De Ruyter is at Guinea, taking back all the forts that you and your friend Holmes seized last year, so the whole court, and all the merchants upon the Exchange, are madder than ever for a war. Nothing can prevent it now, Matt. What a magnificent prospect! Glory, victory and honour in full measure for the likes of you and me. God save the King!'

We toasted His Majesty. Given Beau's evidently bibulous mood, a succession of other toasts were bound to follow in short order, so I knew I would have precious little opportunity to transact the business that had to be resolved.

I said, 'I make one request of you, Beau. Once I have a new command – if, indeed, that is what I am to have – I would be grateful if you would release my own following. I will solicit directly for the services of Master Farrell.'

Harris waved a hand. 'Of course, Matt. As long as I receive a sufficient draft of new men once the press warrants are issued, you can have as many of your men as you wish.'

'Kit Farrell is a good fellow, Beau. Depend on him, for as long as you have him. Why, he could teach you more of the sea-craft, as he has with me –'

Beau laughed. 'Oh, Matthew Quinton, how many times have we had that argument? You, my friend, have been seduced by this strange notion that captains of king's ships must somehow know all the arts of the rude tarpaulin. As I have told you many times, that is not fitting for men of our rank. We command by our birth and our example, sir – birth and example. The mechanic craft of steering the ship should be left to those of the lower orders who are born to it.' I sighed inwardly; I should have known better than to give Harris an opportunity to indulge his prejudices. Harris, whose grandfather had been a butcher when mine had been an earl.

'But –'

'Alas, Matt,' Beau continued, 'for all the undoubted rightness of my case, I feel myself out of step with the times. The tarpaulin rules all and the gentleman is cast down, in the navy as in the state.' He finished his glass and poured another large measure. 'You've not heard the news that almost all the old fanatic captains of Oliver's day are granted commissions? "Oh," says Monck, our proud Duke of Albemarle, abetted by those time-servers Penn and Lawson, "these are the men who cleared the seas of the Dutch under our commands twelve years past. Recall them, Your Majesty, and we will vouch for their loyalty!" And our sovereign lord and his noble brother, believing they can reconcile cavalier with roundhead and make us all forget the differences of a quarter-century, are so seduced by the prospect of crushing the Dutch that they ignore the danger. The cavaliers like you and I, whom they have promoted these last four years, are no longer thought good enough, so the turd-chewing rebels emerge from their hiding places and strut quarterdecks again. All this, and yet fanatic plots are reported every day, the dissenters from the True Church grow unchecked, and suspicion stalks the land like a midnight hag. We are embarking upon a great war, and yet dissension eats away at us from within, like a canker. Is this what we endured exile for, Matt? Is this what our fathers fought or died for? Great God in Heaven, is this the England we expected to inherit when our king came back?'

'But –'

Once into his cups, Beau Harris was a mightily difficult man to contradict (and his father had not fought or died in the war, unlike mine; instead, he had made a healthy profit out of selling munitions to both sides). And once so very, very deep into his cups, he was also mightily difficult to stop.

'There are stout cavaliers galore in the realm, Matt, who could command a king's ship. Yes, put good sailing masters under them, men like your friend Farrell, but let them display the innate courage and judgement that is their birthright! 'Tis said at court that His Grace of Buckingham and My Lord Arlington urge such a course upon His Majesty at every opportunity, but thus far they are stymied – presumably by that coxcomb Clarendon, for I cannot believe such vacillation is His Majesty's intent.' I, who knew Charles Stuart rather better than Beau, had a somewhat different perspective upon the matter, but kept my counsel. 'Yet if we have mere tarpaulins in command we risk the security of the realm, let alone making ourselves no better than the Dutch.'

I did not venture the thought that those same mere tarpaulins seemed to have done well enough against the Dutch in the previous war, and that a smattering of men with the experience of winning might not be amiss in the conflict to come.

After an hour or two of such discourse – or rather, of Beau's ceaseless diatribe – I knew the time had come to take my leave. Beau was not insistent upon it; far from it. Evening was falling, and he had offered me one last night in my cabin and my sea-bed. But a ship cannot have two captains, and in my mind, I had already put the *House of Nassau* behind me. I bade a brief farewell to Kit Farrell, upon whom the effective responsibility for the ship now devolved; Kit merely smiled, for he knew full well the deficiencies of Beau Harris and my ignorant young lieutenant, Pomeroy, and was more than capable of allowing them the trappings of command while exercising the real authority himself.

'Perchance we shall sail together again before very long, Captain Quinton,' he said as we parted.

'I have no doubt of it, Mister Farrell,' I said cheerily, although in my heart I had doubt aplenty. A captain without a ship is like an actor without work. Sooner or later the audience discovers a new favourite, and the old one finds it ever more difficult to procure himself a proper role.

My chests were packed by my servants, for I now had my own little entourage of cabin boys: Richard Barcock, part of the endless family of the steward of Ravensden Abbey; Edward Castle, son of a lieutenant of mine in two previous commissions, who had perished during my voyage to the Gambia the previous summer; and Tom Scobey, some sort of cousin to Lanherne. They were all crestfallen, for they knew full well that their employment ended with mine.

I was rowed ashore and took a room at the Salutation, in the shadow of the castle. As the boat drew close to Dover beach, I turned and looked out at my former command, her stern lanterns lit, swinging at single anchor. Other lanterns marked the positions of the prizes, scattered around that exposed harbour. I had an uneasy feeling that I was looking upon the end of the easy war; for good or ill, the real business was about to begin.

Chapter Two

Make Heav'n concerned and an unusual star
Declare the importance of th' approaching war.
~ Edmund Waller, *Instructions to a Painter*

New fashions in houses, new fashions at table,
Old servants discharged and the new not so able,
And all good custom is now but a fable,
And is not old England grown new?
~ Anon., *Old England Grown New*
(popular song of the 1660s)

All war is obscene.

Well, that is what the hedge-preachers proclaim; and usually, I would be the first to reject such womanish ranting. After all, war has been very good to me over the years. Very good indeed, if truth be told. But if we humour the hedge-preachers a while, then the actual means of declaring a war becomes a double obscenity: blood and slaughter dressed up as pomp and theatre. I have witnessed it many times, now

– a man approaching his ninetieth year has witnessed wars enough to rival the entire Old Testament. No doubt it is a consequence of my English birth, for during my inordinately long life my dear land has been war's earthly paradise. We have fought the French. We have fought the Spanish. We have fought the Dutch. Dear God, I am so very old that I can even remember when we fought each other. One of my earliest memories is of a parliamentary dragoon being hacked to pieces in our herb garden, a somewhat unfortunate sight for a five-year-old to behold. That was in the year forty-five, at the height of the great civil war, when King Charles the Martyr's army suddenly and unaccountably decided that the obvious way of staving off its imminent defeat was to launch an invasion of my innocuous home county of Bedfordshire.

However, the first time I witnessed a formal declaration of war was in the year 1665. That twelvemonth began with a fiery comet blazing across our Britannic skies, heralding all kinds of portents to come; or so it was said. Men whispered anxiously of great revolutions in the state, of dreadful wars, of the death of kings. But none foresaw the dark horror in the land that the comet truly foretold, and Captain Matthew Quinton, riding toward the Holbein gate of Whitehall Palace, certainly did not foresee the very personal horrors that would afflict him before the year was out. It was a cold March day, and I had ridden post-haste from Dover after relinquishing my command of the *House of Nassau* to Beau Harris. I was on my way toward a hoped-for interview with the Lord Admiral's secretary, Sir William Coventry, from whom I might learn the true reason for my removal from command and from whom – God willing – I might solicit another. At that moment, out of the gate of Scotland Yard came Garter King of Arms and Clarencieux, accompanied by the serjeants-at-arms, all in the tabards of ancient times. Trumpets blew, drums beat. The many drunks and Bedlam-men in the throng were hushed, or else beaten into silence. Garter unfurled a sumptuous parchment and read aloud the reasons that had induced his Most High and Puissant Majesty King Charles the Second to declare war upon the United Provinces of the Netherlands.

Wars are devious and ravenous beasts: they begin and end with lies, and between times they lap the blood of young men. Indeed, the beginning of this second Dutch war was marked by a remarkably brazen set of lies, even by the standards of those times. The Dutch were manifestly the aggressors, Garter proclaimed, and His Majesty was merely acting in defence of his just rights. (In the Dutch counter-declaration, of course, we were manifestly the aggressors, and they were merely acting in defence of their just rights; which is ever one of the curious things about wars.) De Ruyter was spoiling our ships, and great were the complaints of the East India and West India Companies. Putting aside the rightness of a King of England admitting in public that he was making war at the behest of a gaggle of avaricious merchants, it seemed to me that the Dutch had better cause for complaining of the depredations we had visited upon them, for we had certainly commenced them first; I knew that better than any other man in Whitehall that day, for I had carried out some of those very depredations only the year before.

As Garter concluded his peroration and rolled the parchment, a great cheer went up. The ale-sellers caught the mood, as ale-sellers invariably do, and began to out-vie each other in offering cheap drink with which to toast the new war. The mob toasted the king, the queen and the Duke of York, cried damnation to the Dutch and began lustfully but tunelessly to sing the old songs of English pride and defiance. I even recognised a verse or two of 'Lord Ravensden's Lament', that hoary old panegyric to my grandfather. Yet for all the enthusiasm and royalist fervour, a few dissenting voices could be heard above the throng – even there, in the very seat of royal power. Shouts or snatches of angry conversation, swiftly cried down or pummelled into silence, but there nonetheless:

'God bless the Dutch, who will bring us deliverance from Charles Stuart and all his whores!'

'The comet brings judgement upon the wickedness of a debauched court…'

'Oh for Cromwell, who knew how to wage war better than these cavalier popinjays!'

Thus, and despite all its bitter divisions, England was at war. Yet there was I, a captain of the king's navy, now with no command in this war against our heinous enemy. For me, indeed, it was a war on two fronts, for there was also the ongoing and as yet indecisive campaign being waged against my brother's new wife, a suspected murderess and undoubted French agent. This unexpected matrimony (for the earl was never much inclined to the female sex) was ostensibly to provide the heir to Ravensden that Cornelia and I seemed incapable of conceiving after seven years of marriage; but it had ultimately transpired that this heir was to be sired upon the new Countess Louise by the sovereign lord of virility, King Charles. Thus as I rode into the stable yard by the tennis court of Whitehall Palace, my mind was filled with troubles and ambivalence. I recalled the last time I had been in the palace, the previous summer, when before the king and my brother Lord Ravensden, I had denounced my sister-in-law the Countess Louise as a lackey of King Louis.

'God's fish, Matt,' the king had replied cheerfully, 'if I arrested everyone in England who takes French bribes, I'd have to make the entire country a prison!'

Of course, I did not know then that Charles Stuart would also have had to arrest himself. As it was, my anger had been exacerbated by a recent perilous (and, as it transpired, utterly pointless) voyage conducted at this king's behest, and not even the presence of Majesty could restrain my rage any longer.

'Sir, King Louis knows full well that you have bedded her to give my brother an heir, that our line may continue!' *Because I cannot father children upon my wife.* 'Your Majesty, the French king has wheedled her into your bed by way of my brother's, the better to spy upon you!'

My brother Charles glared at me. The king's change of mood was even more terrifying. He drew himself up. His long, ugly face tightened into a mask. Instinctively, I dropped to my knee in genuflection. 'Majesty,' I gasped, 'I – I beg Your Majesty's pardon –'

'Never,' hissed Charles Stuart, 'never demean Caesar in his presence, Matthew Quinton.'

With that, the King of England turned on his heel, leaving me to bow my way backwards out of the chamber, facing the royal rump. My brother looked upon me with contempt and stayed at the side of the king, his friend. I had seen neither of them since that day. I knew not how I had been granted the command of the *House of Nassau*, but I was certain that it had not been at the behest of my monarch.

I strode across the Privy Garden and then through the endless passages and chambers of the rambling palace of Whitehall, making my way without interruption to a door in the southernmost part of the palace, near to the river and the bowling green. I knocked, entered – and unexpectedly beheld one of the many marvels of that precocious time.

The small oak-panelled room was dominated by a vast circular desk, which comprised a multitude of draws, shelves and boxes. At the centre of it, upon a rotating chair, sat a sharp-looking man of my brother's age, sporting a large but unfashionably light-hued periwig that matched his yellow eyebrows.

Sir William Coventry, secretary to the Duke of York and commissioner of the navy, looked up and spread his hands theatrically.

'Captain Quinton. What think you of my new assistant?'

'I – Sir William, I have truly never seen the like.'

'Indeed not. I believe it is unique in England, sir, if not in the world. Of my own devising, you see,' he said with inordinate delight. 'What is the greatest enemy to the efficient conduct of business in any part of government, Captain Quinton? Paper, sir. The mountain of paper that swamps me day after day in the conduct of the Admiralty. Yet this simple desk permits me to file every piece of paper in a fitting place, where I can retrieve it instantly. Behold' – he reached over and opened a drawer – 'your letters to me, during your command of the *House of Nassau*. And here' – without warning, Coventry span on his chair and reached into a box on the far side of the desk – 'the last muster book of the same, sent in by Captain Harris. With, it has to be said, rather more errors than was the case during your command.' Coventry span back to face me. I did not know whether to gasp, laugh or seek a physician who could clap him up. 'Efficiency, sir,' he said. 'That is what I strive for. Oh, my foes mock my desk behind my back, but this is the future, Captain Quinton. Information – control of it, access to it. He who possesses information in these new, rational times will be a master amongst men.'

'As you say, Sir William.'

The Lord High Admiral's secretary continued to look mightily pleased with himself. I wondered if there were any left at court who had not been treated to a demonstration of the marvellous desk. The odd scullion, perhaps, or maybe a chimney-sweep, but surely no one grander than that. 'So, Captain,' said Coventry. 'You seek me upon business?'

'Sir – my removal from the *House of Nassau* – I wondered upon the cause of it. I hope for a new commission, now that war is declared and the fleet is already assembling at the Nore.'

Coventry leaned back. The rotating chair creaked ominously under his weight.

'Captain Quinton, I am but a secretary.' This was disingenuous; Coventry was spoken of as one of the rising politicians of the realm, keeper of all the secrets of the heir to the throne and many others besides. 'His Royal Highness does not make me privy to all his thoughts, and he did not share with me his reasons for recalling you from your previous command. Nor did he leave any instructions for the issue of a new commission to you before he left to take command of the fleet – for which I leave tonight, to attend upon His Royal Highness.'

'Sir,' I said, 'I am most desirous of another command –'

'With respect, Captain Quinton, so are the three score and more of candidates for command who pester me relentlessly. And of course, the decision by His Majesty and His Royal Highness to recommission many veterans of the last war with the Dutch has greatly restricted the opportunities available to those who have no such experience.' Coventry's tone was curious; it was difficult to tell whether he approved or disapproved of the recall of the men whom Beau Harris had denigrated so ferociously. 'But you may be assured, sir, that I will lay your name before His Royal Highness. As I would with the names of all other solicitants for command.'

Coventry's words were damning. They cut me to the very quick. I cannot remember taking my leave of him and his ludicrous desk. I dimly recall wandering through the maze of Whitehall, getting lost more than once, consumed by my own desperate thoughts. Nothing could make a young sea-captain's name and fortune like a good war, and yet here I was, destined apparently to take no part in this one. Victory, glory, honour, riches – none of it bound for Matthew Quinton. And as the black mood wrapped its tentacles around me, one thought above all turned over in my mind.

How was I to tell my wife?

* * *

Since our return to England upon the king's restoration, Cornelia and I had lived at Ravensden Abbey, the ancestral home of the Quintons in Bedfordshire. This was chiefly of necessity, for I lacked the income to permit the establishment of an independent household. During the last year, though, the arrangement had become increasingly untenable. The relationship between Cornelia and my mother, the Dowager Countess, had ever been, at best, as close as that of mutually suspicious cats, one old and ferociously territorial, the other young and impertinent. The difference in opinion between ourselves and my mother over the matter of my brother's marriage to the enigmatic Louise, sometime Lady De Vaux and now Countess of Ravensden, had created a final and apparently irreparable rift. Mother was seemingly convinced that the lady in question would be able to provide an heir to continue our bloodline, a feat that Cornelia and I seemed wholly incapable of achieving; a brutal truth that brought forth many tears at midnight in our bedroom. My wife, in turn, had been convinced that the Lady Louise was the murderer of her first two husbands and had for good measure done away with the daughter she had borne to the first. Thus affairs had stood before we learned that the marriage had been arranged so that the heir to Ravensden could be fathered upon Lady Louise by the King of England himself, thereby repaying some old and unspecified debt to our family. To say that this revelation had not improved Cornelia's mood is perhaps the grossest understatement I shall record in these journals.

Fortunately, this rift within the House of Quinton coincided with a marked improvement in my fortunes. Firstly, there was the income I had accrued from six months in command of the frigate *Seraph*; secondly, there were the not insubstantial sums of prize money I acquired during that commission and my more recent service in the *House of Nassau*, which had spent four very lucrative winter months cruising the Channel and intercepting mock-neutral shipping. All of this vied in my mind with the dishonour of having no command at the onset of a great war. After all, if Matthew Quinton had prospered so satisfactorily before that conflict was officially declared, exactly what riches might come his way once we were properly and legally engaged in sweeping Cornelia's countrymen off the seas? I had in mind the purchase of an estate in Cornwall, where I now had many friends. That, I calculated, was probably about as far away in England as it was possible to get from my mother and sister-in-law.

In the meantime, however, my improved condition had allowed us to set up home in a respectable and relatively modern four-storied house in Hardiman's Yard, off Harp Lane, far enough from the Tower to be safe if the ordnance store at the Minories blew to kingdom come and far enough from the river to avoid all but the faintest whiff of its dire odour at low tide. It was noisy (especially so compared to Ravensden, which was as quiet as an ancient grave), but then, where in the City was not? Even on a Sunday, when the endless rumble of cartwheels and the clattering of hoofs diminished a little, we were treated to the full glory of the bells of London's hundred and more churches, each of which seemed to keep slightly different time to all the others.

Of course, we were in no position to buy the entire building, nor even to rent it. We had to be content with the three rooms on the second floor, along with a garret room in which we had installed my wife's servant and my own. Conveniently, these were both named Barcock; the eldest grandchildren of the steward of Ravensden Abbey, whose own prodigious brood was reproducing apace. In practice, this new Quinton property had been rapidly taken under the wing of Phineas Musk, the curious and markedly obstreperous steward of my brother's London house, who had accompanied me to sea during some of my previous voyages. Musk invariably slept in one of our rooms when he was too drunk even to get back to Ravensden House upon the Strand; this was often.

I found my wife contemplating the purchase of a tapestry for the wall of our main room.

'Well?' she demanded as I entered.

'No command,' I said miserably, for I had decided that directness was the only way to break the news. 'And no reason for my dismissal from the *Nassau*.'

Her eyes dampened as the prospects of a tapestry receded rapidly from them; but such selfish thoughts never consumed Cornelia for very long. 'No command! What madness is this?' she cried in her native Dutch. She came over and threw her arms about me. 'Oh, my poor love,' she said, reverting to English. 'How can they be so foolish as not to employ you, the finest captain in the king's navy?' She held me tightly; but with Cornelia, holding tended to be a time when she also did much thinking. 'Of course, I see it now – this will be the doing of that Whore of Babylon, our countess.'

One of Cornelia's many great merits as a wife was her ferocious loyalty to me, although this could sometimes be taken to extremes; having taken some time to reconcile herself to my choice of the sea over the more comfortable – and lucrative – life of an officer in the Guards that I had originally sought, Cornelia was now convinced that I was already amply qualified to be admiral of a squadron. (She had some grounds for this; after all, my good friend Will Berkeley, of my own age, was now both Sir William and a rear-admiral.) Unfortunately Cornelia sometimes clung to her prejudices with the same ferocity, and although I had become relatively sanguine upon the matter of the Countess Louise, nothing could shift my wife in her antipathy towards my sister-in-law.

I lifted her face and looked into those bright, damp eyes. 'I doubt it,' I said. 'She could have prevented my getting the *Nassau*, too. As could the king, who had even better cause.'

'The king has been deluded by the bitch's wiles,' she growled.

'I think the king has his own perfectly good reasons to be angry with me, after what I said to him.'

'After all these months, husband?'

'Kings tend to have longer memories than mere mortals, my love. No, I must do what Sir William advises – solicit for a command, along with the rest of the herd, and pray that the Duke of York sees fit to give me some crumb. But all the best Fourth and Fifth Rates are fitted out and gone to sea already ... they will hardly entrust me with a Third ... and dear God, if Beau is preferred to me in the *Nassau*, then what hope is there?'

'Sir William?' Cornelia was momentarily confused. 'Ah, of course, Coventry. The king has knighted him. He bestows knighthoods galore on mean clerks like that, and on avaricious merchants aplenty, yet his worthy swordsmen are ignored.' Of course, she meant just one worthy swordsman. 'So, Sir William Coventry, then, he is the man. You did not offer money?' Cornelia asked. 'Jennens' wife says that Coventry takes money for commissions and warrants. This is your England, Matthew – surely this is how a man obtains office, by buying it? If you are too shy, then I shall approach him –'

'*No*, Cornelia!' I said emphatically, pushing my wife away to arm's length. 'Even if what they say of Coventry is true, I would rather starve ashore than besmirch my honour by paying a bribe for a commission –'

'Oh, honour is all very well,' she said, reddening in sudden anger, 'but will honour buy our food, husband? Will it pay for these rooms?' The tears began, and I held her tightly. I said nothing, for I knew she spoke only the truth; at the present rate and without any further employment for me, our money would probably run out just as winter began. True, we could move back to the abbey, but I dreaded the thought of broaching that option with Cornelia. 'And then I fear for you and my brother, now that it is war between our countries,' she sobbed. 'On different sides. God forbid that you should kill each other. Perhaps that is what the comet foretold.'

Cornelis van der Eide, a notable sea-captain for the Zeeland Admiralty of the United Provinces, had providentially been on hand to save my life during a previous command. We had learned that unlike his good-brother, Cornelis had found no difficulty whatsoever in obtaining a command: indeed, he had been given his choice of several ships, each larger and better than the last.

'I rather doubt that a great star shot across the heavens to foretell the fates of Matt Quinton and Cornelis van der Eide,' I said, smiling to reassure her. 'And besides, for there to be any chance of us meeting each other, I would need a ship, and we now know that the chances of that are slim. Even if I were to get one, these will be truly vast fleets, my love – a hundred ships and more on each side. The chances of Cornelis and I facing each other directly are minute, thanks be to God.'

She looked at me tearfully, then smiled a little. She reached up and kissed me on the lips. Then, slowly and softly, she nuzzled my neck.

'I think,' I said breathlessly, 'that we had better send the Barcocks out for provisions.'

An hour or so later, as we lay naked upon our bedraggled bed, she lifted her head from my chest and prodded me from my exhausted reverie. 'Perhaps this time … I feel it within,' she said softly.

I sighed. Cornelia still prayed that each and every lovemaking bout would make her pregnant, despite the contrary evidence of seven years of childless marriage. I stroked her head. 'Ah,' I said, 'perhaps *that* was what the comet portended.'

She looked at me seriously, then saw my smile and pushed me away. 'I will never stop hoping and praying, husband,' she said.

'Nor I, love, but mayhap one day we will have to reconcile ourselves to the will of God –'

She stared hard into my eyes, and for a moment I thought she was going to burst into tears or launch into another diatribe upon the unfairness of our childlessness or the iniquities of the Countess Louise. But at bottom, and despite her occasional moods and flights of fancy, Cornelia was a deeply rational woman. 'The condition of Matthew Quinton must be truly bleak if he, of all men, is conjuring up the will of God as an excuse for his woes,' she said reprovingly. 'And when all is said and done, who is the predestinarian here, husband?' She clambered out of bed, naked as Eve, and reached for her shift. 'But I almost forgot,' she said, matter-of-fact once again, 'we have an invitation to dinner, three days hence, albeit in Deptford, of all the foul holes this land has to offer.'

'Indeed? Who has invited us?' This was unexpected; most of my friends were at sea, and most of Cornelia's were in the land with which we were now at war.

'A man with one of your unpronounceable English names – Ye Vlin, or something of the sort. A friend of that proud little man who orders you about. The one at the Navy Board. The one with that other silly name. Pips? Peppis?'

'Pepys,' I said. 'Mister Samuel Pepys. The Clerk of the Acts.'

Even more unexpected. Mister John Evelyn, one of the great polymaths of our age, I knew not at all, although he was well known to my uncle Tristram. Moreover, almost all of my meetings with Evelyn's friend Mister Pepys had been in connection with the business of my ships, although I had encountered him at the theatre or occasionally in a tavern. I hardly counted him as a friend; but, I reflected, Pepys was probably the sort of man who would brag mightily if he could attract an earl's heir to a dinner company. And with no commission in prospect, and thus no pay, a free dinner was not to be refused.

* * *

A man may be in only one place. This is one of the immutable truths of the human condition, but it was a damnable inconvenience to me in that year of 1665, when I often found myself needing to be in two – or three or more – places at once. Being unable to divide myself or to take on divine form and thus be omnipresent, I witnessed with my own eyes and ears only a part of the unfolding of the strange events that transpired in that spring and summer. But young as I was, I already realised that those events demanded to be written down; indeed, it was essential to do so, lest one day others seeking vengeance challenged or distorted the record of all those things, good, bad and desperate, that were done in that time. Thus, as I leaf through the yellowing, legally-attested depositions made soon afterwards by the likes of dear Cornelia, my peculiar uncle Tristram, and the rest, I realise to my discomfort that, for the sake of keeping the flow of my narrative, I must now turn author and emulate that monstrous rogue Defoe, whose *Robinson Crusoe* seems to have been read by every preening jackanapes and idle wench in the realm. What does it say for modern, gin-sodden England that such a slight tale should make a talentless oaf a very rich man indeed? Great God, a man wiles away his time upon an island – is that not the condition of *every* Englishman?

So firstly, I take up and contemplate the account of Phineas Musk: long-time retainer to the Quinton family and more recently my clerk and unlikely guardian during my first commissions at sea. The bald word 'account' does insufficient justice to it; beneath Musk's laconic mask lurked an imagination far outdoing that of my talented young neighbour, the Frenchman Arouet, who scribbles poetry, prose and what he terms 'philosophy' at a prodigious rate. (France being France, of course, he has to write under an alias – Volteer, I believe – but even that has proved insufficient to spare him exile upon our more tolerant shore.) Let us call it Musk's narrative, then: the atrocious spelling corrected, the grammar made intelligible, the obscenities, digressions and tirades largely excised, by an entirely objective commentator, namely myself.

With my brother Charles absent from London for his health (no-one seemed quite certain where), and his increasingly estranged countess withdrawn to her Wiltshire estate, or so it was said, Musk had almost no domestic duties to speak of. Although of course he omits to mention this in his account, boredom was a condition welcome to Musk, for it gave him the excuse to wile away his hours in alehouses, pontificating to all and sundry.

'It's all the fault of the French, this war, just mark my words,' he said authoritatively. 'Think on this. England's a Protestant nation. Holland's a Protestant nation. Between us, we have most of the trade of the world. After all, we're told that's why we're fighting the but-terboxes in this new war: the trade of the world is too little for us two, so one must down. Fair enough, I say.' He took a draught of his ale and looked at the four sturdy craftsman who sat around the table with him. 'But then you've got France, a Catholic nation. And it has its eye on the trade of the world, too. So what could be better for King Louis than for us and the Dutch to blast each other to Hell and back, leav-ing him to step in and pick up the pieces? We fight, but France gets the prize and puts the Pope back into England and Holland to boot. That's what I think, any road.'

A saddler of the Ward of Saint Katherine Cree demurred. 'You see the French behind everything, Phin. I reckon the demons in your nightmares must be French.'

'Aye, well, maybe they are,' said Musk. No doubt he was reflecting upon his nominal mistress, the Countess of Ravensden, who had been exposed as an agent of King Louis, and upon a diabolic Frenchman, a Knight of Malta named the Seigneur de Montnoir, who had so nearly brought disaster upon us during a previous voyage.

'Don't make sense to me,' said a farrier of Cheapside. 'They say King Louis is trying to stop the war. He's sending a great embassy to our king.'

'Flummery,' said a scrivener of Southwark. 'The French have a treaty with the Dutch. They'll come into the war on their side, mark my words. And then it'll be all up with poor old England, when a combined French and Dutch army marches over this bridge, here.'

They sat in an alehouse upon the Southwark shore. Through the grimy window, Musk could see the myriad masts of the ships in the Pool of London, and behind them, the squat, menacing walls of the Tower.

'The French and the Dutch?' scoffed Musk. 'Calvinist and papist? Republic and monarchy – aye, and the most absolute monarchy of them all, at that? Oh yes, my friends, a recipe for a lasting amity, that!'

The argument progressed by degrees to the stage of red faces and the slamming of tankards upon tables. Musk was on the point of walking away to find a quieter berth when he heard his name being called.

'Musk! Is a Phineas Musk here?'

It was a boy, one of those knowing lads of twelve or thirteen who would always run an errand for some pennies or a jug of ale. Musk identified himself and the lad handed over a small slip of paper. The wax seal bore no imprint. Musk tore it open and looked upon the message within: *34. 51. 9. 77. P.'*

'You all right, Phin?' asked the farrier. 'Looks like you've seen one of your froggy demons.'

'Need to go,' mumbled Musk.

'Pay for yer share of the ale, then, yer skinflint whoreson!'

Agitated beyond reason, Musk hurried away and made along the shore toward Lambeth marsh. By the time he reached his destination, close by the river, darkness was falling.

Musk made his way through the ruinous door of a tall, round building, open within to the sky. Broken and burned wood, the remains of galleries, littered the floor, making his passage difficult. Finally, though, he stood upon the remnants of a stage.

'My Lord?' he enquired softly.

At that, a cloaked man emerged from the remains of the rooms behind the stage. His face remained in darkness. In a deep and ambivalent voice he said, 'Do you know me, Phineas Musk?'

The steward of Ravensden House nodded warily; this was a game he had not played in many years. 'Yes, My Lord, I know you now.'

'By what name do you know me?'

'You are Lord Percival.'

'And what would I have you do?'

'You would have me complete the quest, My Lord.'

The man emerged at last from the shadows. 'Well then, Phineas Musk,' said that familiar yet almost forgotten voice, 'we understand each other once more.'

Chapter Three

Come, come away to the temple, and pray, and sing with a pleasant strain,
The schismatick's dead, the liturgy's read, and the King enjoys his own again…
The citizens trade, the merchants do lade, and send their ships into Spain.
No pirates at sea to make them a prey, for the King enjoys the sword again…
Let faction and pride be ow laid aside, that truth and peace may reign,
Let every one mend, and there is an end, for the King enjoys his own again.
~ Anon., *A Country Song Intituled The Restoration* (1661)

A sudden rumble of thunder shook the windows of Sayes Court at Deptford.

'Curious,' said the house's owner, the thin and aquiline John Evelyn, opening a window and looking up to a cloudless blue sky. 'Most curious. Upon a day such as this, whither comes the thunder?'

His friend Lord Brouncker looked up from the adjacent table and the plate of sturgeon upon it, already considerably diminished, before his dainty hand descended instead upon a large slice of venison pie. 'It is a time of signs and wonders in the heavens,' Brouncker said, 'beginning with the comet, and as all know, however much we men of science analyse them and predict their paths, the truth remains that comets bring inexplicable events and disasters. Always have. So, coming as it does in the comet's wake, thunder from nowhere is only to be expected, Mister Evelyn. Although no doubt Captain Quinton's esteemed uncle would disagree, as he disagrees with so many other conclusions of our learned society. Is that not so, Captain?'

I avoided Brouncker's penetrating stare and looked out instead over Evelyn's famous gardens, a veritable English Elysium. 'My uncle has always ploughed his own furrow, My Lord,' I said hesitantly, for defending the frequently indefensible Tristram Quinton was hardly my concern.

Brouncker smiled knowingly. He was pre-eminently a mathematician and scientist, President of the recently established Royal Society, which was how he knew my eccentric uncle, a fellow member and the somewhat unlikely Master of Mauleverer College, Oxford. Brouncker was also newly made a member of the Navy Board, perhaps because the king reckoned that a man who could count might be of some use in the navy, an institution not known for employing the most numerate of men and, perhaps because of that, notorious as a bottomless pit which ever consumed most of the public purse.

Evelyn finally turned away from the window, clearly still puzzling over the mysterious thunderclap. 'Your uncle has not favoured you with his opinion of my book of *Sylva*, perchance?' he asked. 'The praise of the eminent Doctor Quinton would be of much worth to me.'

'Alas no, sir,' I lied, picking some rabbit and anchovies from their pewter plates, 'I regret that he has not.' This, I knew, was not the time or the place for the truth of Tristram's opinion, which was that Evelyn's attempt to persuade the English of the merit of planting more trees was as worthwhile as a fart in the grave.

We returned to the table, where Pepys was engaged in a spirited discussion with Lord Brouncker's brother Harry about the prospects for the impending war against the Dutch. I could tolerate the elder

Brouncker, but the younger was quite another matter: an ignorant, flattering courtier of the worst sort, and one of those rabid cavaliers who would gladly have hanged every sometime Commonwealthsman. He was holding forth at some length about the innate superiority of our monarchical navy over that of the malignant republican Dutch, if only the king had not seen fit to recall so many time-serving verminous captains who had once taken Cromwell's commission. Across from them was Cornelia, who had swiftly made a friend of Mrs Pepys, a vivacious Frenchwoman named Elizabeth; this was unsurprising, for both were foreigners in this strange world called England and both had husbands for whom the navy was the be-all and end-all. The two women were whispering conspiratorially and occasionally laughing indiscreetly. Back across the table from them, Mrs Evelyn, the pious and profoundly intellectual consort of our host, toyed with a morsel of carp, attempting desperately to avoid conversation with Lord Brouncker's exotically dressed companion, a remarkably buxom and ugly actress named Mrs Abigail Williams. It was an eclectic gathering. Having subsequently hosted many such occasions myself, I have learned that one can swiftly sense whether the assemblage of humanity one has brought together is a success; and this was most certainly not such.

A case in point was the conversation upon which the party was engaged an hour or two later whilst launching an assault upon a most splendid dessert table of sugar cakes, plum puddings, jellies and more. Our host's wine was flowing liberally, although Cornelia was speculating on how recently it might have been within the hold of a Dutch prize-ship. Whatever its provenance, it had flowed far too liberally into the gullet of Harry Brouncker, who was now holding forth upon the roguery of Members of Parliament.

'Corrupt!' he blustered. 'Self-seeking, to a man! No sense of honour! The sorts of skulking poltroons who count their pennies and record their worthless miserable apologies for lives in diaries!' Methought both Pepys and Evelyn seemed discommoded by that remark, but I might have been mistaken. 'Men who will not grant the king enough to support his estate,' raged Brouncker, 'nor to wage war properly upon that damnable pack of Fleming butterboxes – ah, my apologies, Mistress Quinton…'

'There is not enough money in the land to fight this war, then, Mister Brouncker?' asked Elizabeth Pepys in her thick French accent, seeking to deflect the explosion that was threatening to erupt from my dear wife.

Lord Brouncker waved a hand, thereby stifling the response that his inebriated sib had been about to venture. 'Parliament has voted two-and-a-half millions for it. With respect to my dear brother, such a sum has never been known, my dear lady,' he said, scowling at his dear brother as he did so. 'And if as all men expect, men like Captain Quinton here drive the Dutch off the seas before the summer's end, just as Monck, now His Grace of Albemarle, and the rest of them did in the last war – well then, we will have a peace treaty that brings us all the trade that they currently have, and we will place young Prince William upon their throne to do his uncle's bidding.' Brouncker nodded toward Cornelia, who raised her glass to him in return. Cornelia had ever been an Orangist, one of those who resented the coup in Amsterdam that brought to power the republicans under her *bête noire*, Johan De Witt; but these monarchist principles had formed initially to spite her glum republican parents and dour republican twin brother. 'Think of Britain as a great eagle, my dear, or a vulture, perhaps. Once the war starts, the Dutch will have to keep up their trade with the outside world. Trade is their lifeblood. Without it, they will perish. But there we are, the great British vulture, astride their only sea routes. They try to run their trading ships through the Channel, and we pounce on them. They try to run them around Scotland, and we pounce on them. All their trade, swept up by our brave ships. Riches beyond imagination for old England, and our king a veritable Midas! Halcyon days, my friends!'

Cornelia bridled and, under her breath, she swore in Dutch with a quite exceptional degree of obscenity. After all, she had been brought up in a Dutch seaport by a Dutch merchant whose prosperity depended exclusively upon the wellbeing of Dutch maritime trade. Consequently Cornelia had learned the ebbs and flows of the Dutch shipping industry before she could walk, and needed no lessons in it from My Lord Brouncker.

Mrs Williams suddenly caught my eye. Quite loudly, she cut directly across the company and said, 'Captain, I have not seen your brother lately. He has ever been a devotee of the playhouses – we miss his patronage.'

'Indeed, Mistress. Marriage has provided my brother with attractions other than those of the stage, alas.' I attempted to make the remark sound as light as I could, rather than expressing my true feelings upon the matter of my brother's condition.

'Aye,' slurred a leering Harry Brouncker, 'but his wife has found attractions other than those of the marriage, too!' His arrogant self-regard and broad smile left little doubt that these 'attractions' were, in fact, his own.

Both of the Evelyns were scandalised, although Abigail Williams grinned bawdily. I frowned at the rogue and began to rise from my stool, despite Cornelia's restraining hand upon my arm and her urgent whisper of *'Nee, betalen geen acht!'* ('No, pay no heed!'). I pushed her hand away. For here was a matter to pursue, by God: I had no love for my good-sister Louise, but for good or ill she was Countess of Ravensden. The honour of my ancient house demanded a defence, or else the exposure of any dishonour that she might bring to it. But Lord Brouncker had gripped his brother's shoulder and was whispering angrily into his ear while raising a hand to me to stay my advance. In that moment, too, a young man whom I recognised as one of the clerks of Deptford yard was admitted to the room by Evelyn's maid, thus distracting the party. The clerk walked up to Pepys and whispered hurriedly to him. Pepys's mouth suddenly gaped, and he swayed. He asked another question of the clerk, who nodded vigorously.

Finally, Pepys turned to the rest of us. Some instinct had made us all fall silent at once. For some reason, in that moment I thought upon the comet.

'It – it was not thunder that we heard,' said Pepys, an unsteady note in his voice. 'The king's great ship *London,* coming from Chatham into the Hope – Sir John Lawson's flagship – oh dear God…'

Elizabeth Pepys ran to her husband's side and gripped his arm tenderly. 'Courage, husband!' she cried.

Samuel Pepys looked at us with tears in his eyes. 'The *London* is no more,' he said. 'She has been blown apart by a great explosion.'

* * *

Barely two hours later Pepys and I were bound downstream with full sail set. We had ridden post-haste from Sayes Court across the fringe of Greenwich marsh to the royal dockyard at Woolwich, where all was frantic activity. Every skiff and wherry the yard could muster was being manned for the long haul down to the outer reach of the Hope, where the stricken *London* was said to lie. But the arrival of one of the Principal Officers of the Navy was as the parting of the Red Sea, every man of that cramped little dockyard falling over himself to impress the mighty potentate that they perceived in Samuel Pepys, who was evidently more than a little pleased to be so received.

Urgently, I looked about the yard. Any of the oared craft would take an eternity to reach the wreck, even with the tide now on the ebb –

But there was one vessel that would suit, moored just a few yards off the wharf: a trim little hull, elaborately gilded, with dainty raised cabins astern and amidships as well as lee-boards after the Dutch fashion. Aboard her, men were making hurried preparations for sailing.

'Ahoy, the yacht!' I cried.

'Who seeks her?' bawled a stout creature upon the forecastle.

'Captain Matthew Quinton and Mister Pepys, the Clerk of the Acts!' I could have sworn the man made to genuflect, but then thought better of it. 'Where's the captain?'

'G – gone up to the Navy Office, my lords!' stammered the man, presumably the senior mate.

'You sail without authority or a captain?' Pepys demanded.

The man was abashed. 'Aye, sirs – to save poor souls on the *London*, if we can!'

Pepys and I exchanged a glance. 'Well then,' cried the Clerk of the Acts, 'you have all the authority you need, my friend – aye, and a captain, to boot!'

A skiff took us out to the vessel, which proved to be the *Mary Yacht*. Thus for the first and only time in my life I found myself in command of what was then still seen as a new and un-English innovation, a royal yacht. Our sovereign lord had fallen greatly in love with sailing during his exile, and at his Restoration the Dutch gave him a gift of the *Mary*, the first of many such craft that would soon adorn the royal inventory. Older seamen scoffed (privately, of course) at the notion of any man in his right mind *desiring to sail for pleasure*, of all the lunatic notions. But as the *Mary* went onto a close-hauled beam reach in Long Reach and I took her tiller from the helmsman while the yacht's practised crew took pride in showing off the skill and speed with which they could adjust the set of her sails, I felt the thrill that appealed so much to Charles Stuart.

Pepys was evidently less of an enthusiast. He clung grimly to the larboard rail, especially when our yacht heeled hard over in the breeze, and proceeded to utter not a word during our voyage, as though opening his mouth to the slightest degree would disgorge the entire contents of his body. I was relieved at this, for Pepys could be something of a pontificator; but his silence allowed free rein to my own thoughts, and they focused above all on two things: what we would find ahead of us, and the meaning of Harry Brouncker's unguarded remark about the Countess Louise.

The first mystery was resolved in short order, for with the wind south-westerly and a strong ebb running, the speedy *Mary* made quite exceptional progress into the estuary of the Thames. There were more ships than usual moored before Tilbury blockhouse and thus obstructing the main channel, for this was where vessels from Amsterdam had been laid up in quarantine because of the prevalence of the plague in that city. Now, with war declared and their time served, they were duly cleared of quarantine, only to be immediately impounded as enemy hulls. With them behind us we veritably raced down Gravesend Reach, and there were still perhaps two hours of daylight remaining when, over toward the Essex shore and the isle of Canvey, an appalling spectacle began to unfold before us. At first I blinked, for in the distance I seemed to see nothing less than an aquatic Calvary: three crosses, protruding above the water. A moment later, I recognised them for the masts of the stricken *London*, still shrouded in smoke from the vast explosion that had destroyed the great ship. It was another mile or so before I could make out the remnants of upperworks beneath the farthest cross. The roundhouse and quarterdeck of the *London* still remained above the surface of the Thames, although no such evidence of the forecastle could be seen. The water around the wreck was full of debris: timber and planking, the remnants of flags and sails, the detritus of all those who had lived and died aboard her. The air reeked of gunpowder, burned wood and burned humanity. All around the remains of the *London* were craft of various sorts, wherries, yawls and the like, as well as a big Levanter. Aboard all of them, men were peering into the waters. Occasionally arms pointed excitedly, and what appeared to be large lumpen shapes were pulled from the Thames.

'Sweet God,' said Pepys, 'the poor, poor creatures. God rest their souls.'

I had no words, for I was numbed by the sight and the awful, overpowering smell. We slackened sail as we came toward the throng of vessels around the wreck of the *London*. One craft stood out from the others, and now it approached us: a yawl flying an ensign far too large for it, a great red ensign which denoted the command flag of an admiral.

The yawl secured alongside, and a sturdy, long-chinned, pock-marked old man of fifty or so hauled himself up onto the deck of the yacht. One of the seamen of the yawl at once pulled down the ensign, sprang onto our deck and hoisted it anew to our masthead. That act immediately deprived me of this command so briefly held, but in the presence of the legend who stood before me, I could hardly demur.

I drew my sword and brought it up before me in salute. 'Sir John,' I said, 'thank God you are spared.'

'Aye, thank ye, Quinton,' the newcomer said. 'We can only reflect upon the seventy-seventh psalm, verses eighteen and nineteen. But one seeks the will of the Lord in vain in such instances, I fear.'

Sir John Lawson, Vice-Admiral of the Red Squadron and captain of the *London* (for in those times, we made do without flag captains and other such extravagances) was a dour man, but I could see the unspeakable shock and grief that lay beneath his mask of godly fatal-ism. A Yorkshireman who was skipper of nothing more than a Tyne collier barely twenty years before, Lawson had been a great fanatic in religion until (it was said) a timely and quite prodigious bribe bought his allegiance to the crown. It was Lawson who brought the fleet under his command into the Thames in the bitter winter of fifty-nine, thereby bringing down the detested rule of the army and setting in motion the chain of events that led to the Restoration. Thus he was a colossus of the times, and even those who now damned him as an apostate and turncoat did not doubt that John Lawson was, in truth, one of England's very greatest seamen.

'I give you joy of your preservation, Sir John,' said Pepys. 'Pray, sir, do you know what happened to cause such a disaster?'

'I know for I witnessed it, Mister Pepys,' said Lawson grimly. 'We were nearing the ship, and she was firing off the salutes due to my flag, when a great blast burst through the forecastle and part of the waist. Most of the force must have gone downward, though. Reckon her bottom blew out, hence how she's settled as she has. But why it happened, only the Father of Heaven can say, as the one hundred and thirty-ninth psalm tells us.'

Pepys and I exchanged glances. In a ship firing its broadsides in salute, there are countless ways in which a spark can ignite in the wrong place; in any ship, there are a host of other accidents that can bring about its immediate, awful destruction. But Pepys and I were realists enough to see that in the fevered circumstances of the time, with men going in fear of the comet presaging the end of days and the country rife with talk of sedition and war, it would surely only be hours before very different explanations were rife in the taverns and coffee-houses of London. The *London* had been blown up by the Dutch, some would say. No, others would cry, surely by the French, the eternal scapegoat of the English! Yet others would inevitably incriminate the fanatics, that faceless horde of dissenters, republicans and the like who many of my cavalier brethren saw lurking in the shadows, waiting their moment to rise up and cut all our throats. And all of that was before one reached the outlying realms of conspiracy and sanity alike, where lurked those who would blame the loss of *London* upon the Jews, the Pope, or Satan, or if they were being especially inventive, all three of those, conjoined in unholy cabal.

Dispirited, I looked out across the scene. The light was dying now, but on the boats slowly circling the wreck of the *London*, men were firing torches to continue their search into the night. A search for –

'Sir John,' I asked, as gently as I could, 'do you yet know how many perished?'

His ugly face was impassive. 'Some dozens were upon deck or in the roundhouse and were untouched,' he said. 'They simply walked off the ship when the boats reached them, for mysterious are the ways of the Lord. But three hundred and more are gone. Aye, gone.' He looked down into the hull of the yawl, still tethered against our side. Laid out upon the thwart was a tarpaulin; only now did I see the hideously burned, shoeless remnants of a man's feet that protruded from it. 'My sister's son John,' said Lawson quietly. 'A promising youth of twenty. He was so keen to serve, to fight the Dutch alongside his uncle. So were they all. A good crew, Quinton, most of them my own Yorkshiremen, but many Scots also. Veteran seamen, for the most part.' He looked back at me, and I thought I saw the shadow of a tear in the admiral's eye. 'A score or more of my own kin have perished here, Quinton.' He was hoarse, almost inaudible. 'Much of my family, wiped out in the blinking of an eye. "For all flesh is as grass, and all the glory of man as the flower of grass. The grass withereth, and the flower thereof falleth away." Thus it is told.'

'Amen,' said Pepys and I as one, although whether the Clerk of the Acts felt as empty as did I, I cannot judge.

Lawson moved away, into the bow of the yacht, to be alone with his thoughts. Pepys looked sadly down upon the remains of the admiral's nephew, then at the increasingly spectral sight of the wreck beyond, looming eerily in the gathering darkness. 'A great loss,' said the Clerk of the Acts. 'All those poor souls – it will be so hard to replace so many choice volunteers. And then one must consider our other loss, of course. Seventy-six brass guns, Captain Quinton. Lord, are we thus fated to fight the Dutch without so great a ship, and so much of our very best ordnance? And the costs – the inventories that will have to be made, and the papers that will have to be written…'

A movement upon the water – 'What is that, Mister Pepys? There? You see it?'

We both strained our eyes. To starboard of the yacht and behind the stern of the yawl, the surface of the Thames was dark, the gentle waves almost indistinguishable from the wood and debris of the

London littering the waters. But then I saw again the little mound resembling some basking sea creature – a dolphin, perhaps, or a seal…

'Boathooks, here!' I cried. Three of the crew of the *Mary* responded at once, and Lawson, his interest aroused, joined us at the rail. The hooks were pushed out, and for a minute or two they splashed vainly in the water. Desperately I snatched one from its bearer, hoping that my greater reach would enable me to hook the prize. Pepys joined me, endeavouring desperately to hold the pole level as I prodded it into the water. But the ebb seemed to be carrying the object away from us. I played out my boathook once more, straining my arms, almost losing my grip upon it as I tried to hold it at its very end –

My hook caught, and both Pepys and Lawson joined me in hauling the object in to the side of the hull. The Marys reached down, pulled it aboard, turned it over upon the deck.

A torch had been brought, and its flickering flames illuminated the face of a young woman, probably no more than sixteen or seventeen. She had a certain beauty about her, hauntingly enhanced by the paleness of death. Her simple clothes were dishevelled, but there seemed to be not a mark upon her. Nor had she drowned, for her features bore no sign of that dread fate.

The colour drained from Pepys's face as he beheld her. 'Lord, Lord,' he muttered, 'the poor girl.'

'Some man's wife,' I ventured charitably, 'or daughter.'

'Too young for the one, and too old for the other,' said Lawson brutally. 'But if she gave comfort to one of my men, perhaps even my nephew there, then may God bless her and keep her immortal soul.' He stooped down and prodded the corpse. 'Killed by the shock, most like,' he said. 'We have brought out another half dozen women from the water. Merely a fraction of those who would have been aboard.'

I nodded sadly. In those times, it was common for women to accompany their men aboard ship in the early days of a voyage. Nowadays, the young – that is, my entire acquaintance – goggle at me when

I tell me of this custom, dead as long as Julius Caesar. But as I recall the memory of that poor girl's corpse, I still ask myself once again – what is more natural and more likely to contribute to the common weal of the land? Forcing abrupt partings between lovers, or permitting them to say their adieus gradually, while giving the abandoned womenfolk some understanding of the wooden world that their men must inhabit? Ah, but we are so much more enlightened in this wondrous age of the eighteenth century, the young cry! We have made such progress! But still I live on, an uncomfortable reminder to the young that the notion of 'progress' is the greatest lie ever foisted upon mankind. And still I remember that young girl who perished in the wreck of the *London*.

Chapter Four

Next, let the flaming London come in view,
Like Nero's Rome, burn't to rebuild it new:
What lesser sacrifice than this was meet,
To offer for the safety of the fleet?...
Then, Painter, draw cerulean Coventry,
Keeper, or rather chanc'llor, of the sea;
Of whom the captain buys his leave to die,
And barters or for wounds or infamy...
~ Andrew Marvell, *Second Advice to a Painter* (1665)

Phineas Musk slipped like a wraith past Apothecaries Hall, then left the bustle of Black Friars Lane and stepped softly into the quiet of Saint Anne's church.

(Words to that effect were penned by Musk, on the vellum now in my hand; but the notion of the lumpen form of Phineas Musk making any movement softly or wraith-like causes my ancient eyebrow to rise a little.)

It was well into the night, and the nave of Saint Anne's was illuminated by only a few candles. When Musk's eyes finally adjusted to the near-darkness, he spied the man he sought, seemingly deep in prayer in a pew away to the right, near to the newly restored rood screen.

Musk crossed the nave and sat next to the supplicant and his crutch; for where the man's left leg should have been, there was nought but a stump.

'Requesting forgiveness of your manifold sins, Sutcliffe?' Musk whispered.

The unshaven one-legged man opened his eyes. 'Merely getting a little sleep, Musk. Begging's a tiring and unproductive trade these days. Men are worried about the war, so they're hoarding their coin.'

'You still beg, despite what Lord Percival pays you?'

Sutcliffe shrugged. 'Keeping up appearances. The city expects to see Lazarus Sutcliffe begging on its streets. Men would be mightily suspicious of a Sutcliffe with coin, Musk – the doors and mouths that are open to me now would soon be closed.'

'And have those doors and mouths disgorged anything of interest to My Lord?'

Sutcliffe, who had once fought off the king's army at Turnham Green, albeit at the cost of his leg, looked Musk in the eye. 'Curious business you and he are engaged upon,' he said. 'Or businesses, rather, for as Noll's shade is my witness, I can't see how the root of this supposed treachery of twenty captains will be found in the whorehouses about the Convent-Garden.'

Musk leaned closer and whispered menacingly, 'My Lord doesn't pay you to ask questions, Sutcliffe. He doesn't pay you to think. And me – I don't like men who question and think when they shouldn't.'

The old soldier seemed unabashed. 'So I didn't lose my curiosity with my leg – it's of no account, for Lazarus Sutcliffe's curiosity is of the silent variety. My Lord should be certain of that, with all the service I've given him these many years.'

'He may be, but I'm certain of nothing, Sutcliffe, least of all an old traitor who was in arms for the rebels.'

'You're a damnable cynic, Musk.' Sutcliffe reached within his grimy buff jerkin and produced a folded sheet of vellum, which he handed to his companion. 'A name and address, then – seems the people you're interested in retired from the whoring trade when the king came back. Very grand, they are now. Must have turned a good profit –'

The west door of the church burst open. Framed within it were two tall drunken lads with the crop-heads of apprentices, bawling out some scurrilous song about Lady Castlemaine's cunny. They looked about the church contemptuously; one spat upon the ancient stone floor of the nave. The staves in their hands suggested they were intent upon iconoclasm.

'Out!' cried Musk.

'*Out?* What, by order of a fat old man and a cripple?' slurred the taller of the youths. 'Fuck you! And fuck your whoreson king –'

Musk shook his head sadly, lamenting the insolence of the times. Then he drew out his two concealed flintlock pistols and levelled them at the youths. Sutcliffe levered himself up with the crutch in his left hand as his right drew out a wickedly long blade.

'Aye,' said Musk, 'by order of a fat old man and a cripple. Out, you fucking piss lickers! Out *now.*' The two youths stared at the weapons in horror, then abruptly turned and fled. 'God knows how many more of them will be out on the streets, smashing windows and cracking skulls, if our fleet happens to miscarry,' said Musk. 'Upon which matter, Sutcliffe –'

The veteran sheathed his weapon and settled back onto the pew. 'Upon which matter, then, Mister Musk. As My Lord requested, I am working my way through all the conventicles from Lambeth down to Poplar, consorting with my old friends among the godly.' Sutcliffe shuffled, evidently seeking to make his stump more comfortable. 'The fanatics and their preachers are most talkative these days. There have been signs and wonders in the skies above Honiton, they say.' The veteran shook his head despairingly; his change of sides had been born of disillusionment with the ever more extraordinary manifestations of supposed godliness that Parliament's revolution dragged in its wake. 'They're most indiscreet in their meeting places, crying that the end of days is at hand, that Jesus will soon reign upon earth with his elect – all the wicked nonsense of Cromwell's times. The treacherous scum even pray openly for a Dutch victory, and as you say, Musk, such an eventuality would bring many more of the malignant vermin out of their holes.' Sutcliffe stared at Musk. 'And yet amid all this indiscretion, and from all those whose tongues have ever been prone to loosen at the sight of coin – as yet, Musk, I can find no proof of this business of the twenty captains.'

'My Lord will be disappointed.'

'Well he may be, especially as the ostler, Eden, seems to have vanished from the face of the earth. The longer we go on with no evidence, Musk, the stronger the likelihood that we face only two explanations.'

Despite his annoyance at Sutcliffe's presumption, Musk nodded. 'Either there is no plot at all –'

'– or 'tis so deeply laid it will only reveal itself in its flowering. And if that is so, Musk, not even Lord Percival will be able to stand against it.'

* * *

At my suggestion, Cornelia and I had decided upon a Sunday's sabbatical from our local parish church, Saint Dunstan in the East, and had decamped instead to the Temple Church, where a new and much cried-up young man was preaching. In the event, this merely proved the folly of depending upon the opinion of the herd, for the preacher in question proved to be one of those prating coxcombs who depend overly upon the rhetorical flourish and the obscure allusion. I found it easy to let my thoughts drift away from his tedious discourse, initially to the unfairness of my lack of employment. The idle days since the loss of the *London* had made me ever more peevish, Cornelia reckoning shrewdly that my brief command of the *Mary Yacht* had made me even more keenly aware of the life I was missing. But the more I thought upon it there in the Temple Church, as the sermon meandered interminably through the denser undergrowth of the Old Testament, the more certain I became of a second explanation for my ill temper. So many good men had perished aboard the *London*: men who should have been sailing out to do battle with the kingdom's foes. Did not Matthew Quinton have a duty to fight in their place, and on their behalf?

By degrees my mind wandered into an absorption of the history all around me, for few churches in London are as redolent of the days of knightly honour as the Temple. We sat but a few feet from the tomb of William Marshal, the greatest knight who ever lived, his effigy shown in armour, holding sword and shield. But I sensed at once that Cornelia, shuffling alongside me in the pew, was not so patient, and not so easily diverted. I also sensed that as the dire experience of this unutterable sermon had been inflicted upon her entirely at my prompting, some recompense would be necessary. Thus as soon as the service concluded, and before she could harangue me upon the iniquities of puffed-up Cambridge men in pulpits, I proposed a perambulation upon London Bridge.

It was a fine day, and much of the city seemed to have made the same decision. The bridge was as crowded as on any weekday. The shops that occupied the ground floors of the tall houses on either side of the bridge were thronged with customers, so that mere amblers like ourselves had to compete for space with the horses and riders, carts and coaches, going north and south in the barely four-yard-wide thoroughfare, little better than a tunnel, that connected the two sides of the Thames. But it was a lively and even joyous scene: shopkeepers bellowed out the calls of their trade, mariners jostled for space with baronets, residents of the bridge stuck their heads out of their windows to ogle the crowd below or to banter with their neighbours across the way. There were only a few dampening voices, the most notable that belonging to a wild-eyed youth who stood upon a footstool in one of the alcoves in the east side of the parapet, naked but for a loincloth, proclaiming loudly that the end of days was at end (and for his presumption, being pummelled relentlessly with rotten vegetables).

I kept my hand close to the hilt of my sword: the bridge was so crowded that it was always a prime resort for cutpurses and their kin. But Cornelia had no such inhibitions, elbowing aside all sorts and conditions with sweet smiles of apology. Such was not rudeness, but a consequence of her Dutch upbringing; for in that largely submerged land, the most crowded upon God's earth, the people perforce survive upon the few tracts of dry ground, and life and death can depend upon one's ability to fight one's way through a dense throng.

'Remember, Goodwife Quinton,' I said, 'our purse is sadly constrained.'

The goodwife in question was ensconced before a milliner's, admiring headwear of a flamboyance that not even Lady Castlemaine would have dared.

'Then may not a woman dream, husband?' she said, smiling. Dour Calvinist parents, who had dressed the young Cornelia in the plainest and meannest cloth despite the family living in a port town which saw some of the most exotic linens in the world pass through it, had achieved an end precisely the opposite to that which they intended: their daughter had become a great lover of finery. 'We will not always be poor, Matthew,' she said. 'When your merits are recognised, you will have commands galore and prize money with them. I merely indulge myself in a little planning ahead of that day.'

We will not always be poor. I offered up a silent prayer to Neptune, Mars and the Holy Trinity alike that she would be proved right.

As we moved on toward the Southwark shore and the gatehouse upon which the heads of traitors were impaled, other shouts of the street reached my ears.

'Chapbooks and woodcuts! News of the atrocities committed by De Ruyter upon our settlers at Guinea! Fifteen hundred men, women and children alike tied back to back and thrown into the sea! Aye, and a true and accurate list of His Majesty's fleet, assembled at Harwich, bound to sea to avenge our martyrs! And an account of the generosity of the city of London in offering the king a new ship to replace the old, this to be named *Loyal London*...'

The shout of a woman at the next stall competed stridently with that of the news-seller.

'Butterbur to guard against the plague, friends! Turmeric, just landed from the Indies, certain to make the childless fertile! Fennel for the eyes...'

The one cry had an ennervating effect upon Matthew Quinton; the other had an invigorating one upon his wife. Cornelia pushed her way through the crowd, making directly for the purveyor of herbs and spices. I knew her mind full well. In our time we had tried each and every supposed remedy for childlessness, and fresh turmeric was no more or less likely than many of the others. I only prayed it would have a less catastrophic impact upon my stomach than the diet of ground coriander to which Cornelia had once subjected me for a week.

Cornelia fell into talk with the spice-seller, an ancient crone with a formless bosom. Meantime I was diverted by a raging argument between a carter, demanding right of way southbound, and a coach driver, equally strident in his insistence upon precedence northbound. Then I became aware of other raised voices, rather closer at hand.

'– to let the Dutch walk brazenly among us?' hissed the spice-seller. 'My husband fell at the Foreland fight, my son's aboard the *Triumph*, and yet you dare show your face among good English folk? You, whose kind blew up the *London* and massacre our innocents at Guinea?'

Cornelia was no meek craven to be cowed by such a harangue. 'Foolish woman!' she cried. 'Do you not know that this tale of Guinea has been exposed for a great lie peddled by some mean-minded Swede, who sought merely to stir trouble?'

'Call an honest English matron foolish, would you, Flemish slut?' This from an equally ugly matron alongside the spice-seller: her sister, by her appearance.

From beneath her stall, the spice-seller produced a bloodied knife and pointed it angrily at Cornelia. I stepped forward, my hand upon the hilt of my sword, but by now a crowd had gathered around us. A crowd that numbered among its ranks several of the burlier shopkeepers of the bridge and a number of apprentices: hardly natural friends to a young Cavalier and his Dutch wife.

'Now, sir,' said one gross creature, his hand staying my right arm, 'what sort of a gentleman draws his sword upon two ladies?'

Before I could shake myself free of his grip and draw my sword – albeit to confront unpleasantly adverse odds – Cornelia glanced at me curiously. Then she turned, held her hands to her face, and began sobbing loudly.

'Oh Lord,' she cried, 'what is to become of me? Oh, is this to be death?'

Her bitter weeping seemed to unnerve the two crones at the spice stall. At bottom, they were women and mothers, and there must have been some shred of sympathy for this young woman who could have been their daughter.

In the moment that her adversaries' guard relaxed, Cornelia ceased her feigned tears and lunged forward, scooping up a handful of pepper from its sack and flinging it into the face of the stallholder, who screamed and held her hands to her eyes. In the same movement, she strode toward the sister and unleashed a punch that knocked the harridan off her feet and into the wall, where she slumped to the ground. Cornelia spun on her heel, gripped the stallholder's knife-hand and pulled it sharply behind her back. The woman caterwauled in agony as her shoulder dislocated; the knife dropped to the floor.

'God save the King,' shouted Cornelia, confronting the astonished mob that surrounded us, 'and God save his nephew, the Prince of Orange!'

I smiled with pride as I stepped forward to her side. Now, at last, I drew my sword, and waved it menacingly toward the mob.

'You heard my wife,' I said, 'and she is as good a subject of King Charles as any man or woman here. So cheer with her, friends! God save the King! God save the Prince of Orange!' The mob complied, albeit with evident reluctance. 'And remember this – be thankful that the Dutch fleet is not manned by Dutchwomen, for today you have seen how *they* fight!'

Despite my bravado, discretion demanded a gentle retreat, back toward the London side of the bridge; but not before Cornelia had appropriated a half-pound of turmeric as recompense for her inconvenience.

'What madness!' she said. 'How prone you English are to believe the wildest rumours upon the least evidence, and to form unconquerable prejudices upon foundations of sand!'

I looked around; rather too many eyes were still turned in our direction. 'Perhaps it would be better, my love, to be a little more discreet in your words. And in your fists.'

She looked at me sharply. 'Are you not proud, then, that I am not a mere damsel to be rescued by a fine knight upon a charger? You know well that I can hold my own, husband.'

'And that, my love, is the very matter of it. Do you not think you will merely reinforce the lumpen brutes in their conviction that all Dutchwomen are she-devils?'

Cornelia grinned contentedly. 'Not all, husband. Only this one.'

It had taken only until our first argument, some six weeks into our marriage, for me to realise just how singular a young woman I had wed: a broken tooth and a bruised eyebrow being the price of that realisation. From the days of her earliest childhood, Cornelia had sought release from the tedium of her parents' house by playing upon the wharf at Veere, where successive shiploads of bluff mariners and itinerant soldiers had taken her under their wing. Thus by the age of five, my wife could swear in six different languages and knew how to cheat at several card games. By seven, she could aim and fire a pistol, a Danish ship's captain having delighted in watching her persistent attempts to raise and level the heavy gun with her tiny hand. At nine, she learned how to gallop upon a horse thanks to a cavalryman who had once charged the Cardinal-Infante's army at Kallo. At eleven, she could hold her genever and *brandijwein* as well as many a tar of Amsterdam. And from the age of twelve, she accompanied her father as an unpaid clerk upon his trading expeditions to the likes of Bruges, Calais, Lubeck and London. Realising swiftly that the bluff mariners and itinerant soldiers were now taking a rather different form of interest in her, Cornelia persuaded her reluctant twin brother, already a topman in the Admiralty of Zeeland's service, to teach her forms of fighting that tended not to reach the pages of the formal manuals of warfare. During much the same space of time, she also reacted against her parents' and brother's staunch advocacy of the True Freedom, de Witt's republican ascendancy, by becoming an even stauncher Orangist: a sentiment that could only come into full flower with her marriage to a follower of the prince's royal uncle, King Charles.

I was proud of my wife's somewhat unconventional attributes, and oft reflected that Joan of Arc must have been cast from a similar mould. But I also recalled Joan's fate, and was thankful that not even England still burned witches.

* * *

Sir William Coventry sat at the heart of his astonishing round desk, a folded piece of parchment in his hand. It was the morning after the fracas upon London bridge. His unexpected summons had brought me from Hardiman's Yard to Whitehall with unconscionable speed; I suspected that a beggar at the Charing-Cross, who was a little too slow to get out of the way of my galloping horse, might have suffered a broken limb or two.

Thus when Coventry presented me with the commission, I nearly snatched it from his hand. 'My congratulations, Captain Quinton,' he said. 'I wish you joy of your command, sir.'

I mumbled perfunctory thanks and broke the wax seal with unseemly impatience. The words were in the familiar form: James, Duke of York and Albany, etcetera etcetera, Lord High Admiral, etcetera etcetera, to Captain Matthew Quinton, captain of His Majesty's ship the –

The room swam away from me, swirling into a myriad of whirlpools. I could feel my heart hammering inside my skull. Dimly, I heard Coventry asking me if I was well. I read the impossible word again, looked at him, looked back at the word, and nearly fainted away. 'Sir W– William,' I stammered, 'there is a mistake, sir. This commission must be meant for another.'

He grimaced. 'A mistake? With respect, Captain Quinton, neither His Royal Highness nor I are in the habit of making mistakes.'

(There was truth in this; both men had a pride in method that was already a byword.)

'But sir, this is a commission as captain of the *Merhonour*! A Second Rate! One of the greatest ships in the navy!'

Coventry shrugged. 'And the oldest, and the most sluggish. She would have been condemned last summer but for the prospect of war. What of it, Captain?'

'N–nothing, Sir William.' I recovered myself, and also the recollection of my duty. 'I am deeply grateful to you, sir. And to His Royal Highness, of course.'

Coventry looked at me curiously. 'You might not be so grateful, Captain, when you learn who has truly been responsible for obtaining this commission for you, nor the purpose that underpins it.' Coventry leaned back into his chair and grimaced. 'These are strange times, Captain Quinton – stranger than you know. For instance, I believe it is common knowledge that I have not always been the closest friend of our illustrious Lord Chancellor. Nor has the Secretary, my good friend. Yet in this matter, we three are in perfect accord, for this concerns the good of a kingdom that is under greater threat than you can imagine. Thus by their command, I send you to them now, at Clarendon House.' Coventry relaxed and smiled. 'You should feel honoured, Captain Quinton of the *Merhonour*. You will be one of the very first men to set foot in the new palace of King Edward.'

Chapter Five

But damn'd and treble damn'd be Clarendine,
Our seventh Edward, and his house and line!…
And that he yet may see, ere he go down,
His dear Clarinda circl'd in a crown.
~ Andrew Marvell, *Second Advice to a Painter*

I rode north and then west in a waking dream. The *Merhonour*. Sixty-four guns, nine hundred tons burthen. Twice the size of the largest ship I had commanded thus far in my career. A crew of three hundred and eighty men. A veritable leviathan upon the ocean – aye, and one of the most famous ships of proud Albion! The *Merhonour* was so very old that she had been built when England was still Catholic and still possessed Calais. Her first captain was an aged bastard of King Richard the Third. She had fought against the Invincible Armada. Rebuilt and repaired many times, she had fought the corsairs of Algiers for the first King James and the Dutch for Noll Cromwell. 'Matthew Quinton, captain of the *Merhonour*!': I was in a transport of delight as I repeated that most glorious sentence over and over in my head. My satisfaction was multiplied by the knowledge that I was not the first of my name to command that great ship. For in the year 1595, she was the flagship of my grandfather, the eighth Earl of Ravensden, in Essex's expedition against Cadiz. I even thought I could hear the old swashbuckler's voice in my head: *'You take good care of my ship, lad!'*

Thus it was an inordinately pleased young man of twenty-five who rode out of the confines of Westminster into Pickadilly, said to be increasingly the most sought-after district of the city: great new houses were going up on the north side, where they were still surrounded by fields. A small herd of deer, grazing contentedly on the edge of Saint James's Fields to the south, watched me curiously as I rode by. It was an idyllic day. Perhaps I should have reflected that the greatest happiness often precedes the greatest horror, but I was oblivious to such dark thoughts.

My destination loomed before me. It would be a truly vast palace, that much was clear; but it was yet newly begun, and only the tall, graceful central block was complete to its full height. Two wings stretched away on either side, but that to the left was barely above its foundations and that to the right was a mass of scaffolding. As I drew nearer, I was treated to the full chorus of hammering, sawing and swearing that attends any work of building in England. But unlike any other work of building in the land, this one was surrounded by a ring of fearsome, red-coated and heavily armed troops. These, I knew, were present day and night, regardless of whether or not the owner was within; for there were many in London who would gladly have burned down this monstrous edifice to one man's ambition and vanity. As I rode through the cordon, I saw not a few scowls upon the faces of those who traversed Pickadilly.

I dismounted at the foot of the half-finished grand stairway that swept up to the door. With not a little pride, I informed the lackey on duty there that this was Quinton, captain of the *Merhonour*, for audience with the Lord Chancellor and the Secretary. He pointed me toward the half-finished left, or west, wing. I struggled across uneven ground made even more treacherous by a clutter of broken bricks and stray timbers, entered through a great hole that would eventually become a fine south-facing window, and heard the Chancellor's familiar, booming West Country voice long before I saw him.

'– and I intend a nursery *there*, Bennet, for when Anne comes visiting with my grandchildren.'

'A splendid prospect indeed,' replied a voice that was deepest Suffolk; but even from a distance, I could detect that beneath the accent lurked several layers of profound sarcasm.

The two men hove into view, and I made my salutations, bowing deeply as I addressed the older and significantly more rotund first: 'My Lord Chancellor.'

Edward Hyde, Earl of Clarendon, bowed in return. 'Captain Quinton.' This, then, was the greatest man in the kingdom after the king; or perhaps the man who was greater than the king, in the eyes of his legion of critics. Charles Stuart's political mentor in exile, the magnificent Clarendon was said to pull our monarch's strings (apart from those attached to the royal member, which were pulled by others) while ensuring that the Earl of Clarendon profited mightily. Clarendon House, this very building in which we were standing, was already by-named Dunkirk House, it being commonly assumed that the proceeds of the sale of that town to France had paid for the Chancellor's grand new residence. Although it was far from finished, nocturnal riots before it were already regular occurrences; hence the ring of armed guards. But that was not the principal cause of the universal hatred of the Lord Chancellor of England. Far from it.

I turned to his companion, a sharp-featured man in his mid-forties. The most remarkable thing about him was the large black plaster stuck across the bridge of his nose. 'My Lord Arlington.'

The newly ennobled Secretary of State nodded. 'Quinton. Good. You've seen Coventry, then. Pleased with yourself, I don't doubt. Relish it, Quinton, for I regret we are to disabuse you.'

I made a conscious effort to avoid staring at Arlington's nose, but it was impossible; which, of course, was precisely what he intended. The plaster concealed a deep scar, inflicted on him by a rebel's sword in an obscure skirmish during our late civil wars, and the Secretary (who had done precious little fighting apart from that once) ensured that his wound was displayed as prominently as possible, thereby bearing witness to his personal suffering and, by extension, to that of all his cavalier brethren. My uncle Tristram confessed that he always had a great urge to amputate the rest of Arlington's snout and replace it with a vast artificial proboscis to outdo even that of old de Bergerac.

Clarendon led us into the completed part of the building, into what would soon be a grand reception room facing west, across the fields towards the miserable village of Kensington. The room was not plastered and the floor was incomplete; the similar state of the chimney ensured that the fire remained unlit, so the room felt almost as cold as the bitter air outside.

We stood, for there were no chairs. Clarendon kept well apart from Arlington; these two loathed each other, and I wondered what great crisis of state, alluded to by William Coventry, could possibly have brought these bitter rivals together.

Arlington took the lead. This was unsurprising, for matters of intelligence were fundamental to his role as Secretary. Arlington was also known to have a sounder grasp of naval affairs than the Chancellor, whose ignorance of such things was a byword: my old friend Will Berkeley once told me that in his hearing, Clarendon asked where Sheerness was.

'I won't dissemble, Quinton – we have no time for casuistry and procrastination. A war creates a mountain of business of all kinds, and we also have to prepare for the reception of the ambassadors of the Most Christian King.' If that was so, I wondered why the realm's two most powerful ministers were taking the time to inspect an unfinished building. But perhaps Clarendon's notorious pride made him unable to resist the urge to show off his opulent new home to his arch-enemy, whose own Arlington House was so much more modest; so modest, indeed, that it is now but one wing of the present Duke of Buckingham's residence upon the Green Park. 'It is no secret, I think,' Arlington continued, 'that not all of His Majesty's subjects hope for the success of his arms in this war against the Dutch. There are still many who are loyal to what they call the Old Cause – to strange fanatic ways in religion, to doing away with kings, to levelling all the orders of society. They wait their moment, Quinton, and many of them think this war is that moment. Here in London above all, the creeping multitude of Ranters, Diggers, Levellers, Seekers, Muggletonians, Quakers and God knows what other strange manifestations of untruth pray for a Dutch victory in the battle to come, for they believe that will trigger a new revolution in this nation.'

'It is possible, of course, that many of these fears are exaggerated, and that the numbers of the disaffected are actually very small,' said Clarendon. Arlington scowled at him; the tension between the two was palpable. 'But as you know, Captain, many are undoubtedly dis-contented with His Majesty's rule on … certain other grounds. Even some of the cavalier breed express dissatisfaction with, shall we say, the moral tone of this age?'

A splendid euphemism for the king's flagrant waste of his time, money and abilities upon a succession of worthless, brazen women, my good-sister included, I thought. Perhaps Clarendon referred to himself, too, for there were not a few cavaliers – Arlington at their head – who would have delighted in the downfall of the opulent and, in their view, overly lenient Chancellor.

'Indeed, My Lord,' said Arlington neutrally. 'Now, this brings us to the delicate matter of command within the fleet. His Majesty the King and His Royal Highness the Duke of York have thought fit to employ many captains and flagmen who served the late republic, a number of whom have not served since the Restoration.' Arlington's tone suggested that this was a policy with which he did not concur, thus confirming Beau Harris's aside to me aboard the *House of Nassau*. 'Some others refused to serve, or were left ashore because their views were believed to be too – irreconcilable, shall we say? But we have to face the possibility that some of those recently granted commissions might not be entirely loyal to His Majesty.'

Clarendon moved to stand by his unfinished window and gazed out over the rough pasture that would soon be an immaculate parterre. 'The King and the Lord High Admiral are entirely convinced of their loyalty,' he said.

Arlington all but sneered. 'Quite. But, Quinton, it happens that we have some pieces of evidence pointing toward an active conspiracy and we, as ministers of the crown, always have to act upon such evidence.' Another furious glance from Clarendon. 'For instance, we have the words of a murdered man, recorded by a reliable witness in a sworn deposition, claiming that twenty captains will go over to the Dutch in the midst of battle. Other whispers to the same effect.'

I stood there, in the midst of the great shell of Clarendon House, unable to believe what I was hearing. Here were all of Beau Harris's wine-born suspicions and night-terrors writ large, but uttered by the two greatest ministers of the crown! *Twenty captains* – God in Heaven, if it were true that would mean no less than a fifth of the commanders in the entire fleet – and if these men were veterans, they had probably been given the best commands, so precisely how large a proportion of the great ships of the fleet, the ones upon which the whole outcome against the Dutch depended, might be disabled by this treason?

'His Royal Highness will not hear of it,' said Arlington. 'He prefers to believe that no true-born Englishman would fight alongside the Dutch against his own people.'

'We pray that he is correct,' said Clarendon, who had particular cause for praising the Duke of York's prescience. 'My Lord Arlington's "evidence" is likely to be nothing more than the tupenny tittle-tattle of the streets, Captain. But ... but as he says, a wise minister should not entirely dismiss such talk out of hand.'

And there was the nub of it, I thought. For all Clarendon's doubts about the tale of a plot, and his evident distaste for Arlington's reading of the evidence, he simply dared not reject the secretary's interpretation out of hand. He was, after all, the chief minister of England, and if this heinous conspiracy proved true and was allowed to play itself out, to whom would the blame cling? Still shocked by the revelation of the potential extent of conspiracy in the fleet, I found myself in a place I had never expected to be: entirely agreeing with the Earl of Clarendon, and praying to God that he, not his rival, had the right in this.

'Well spoken, My Lord,' said Arlington sarcastically, evidently revelling in his rival's discomfort. 'And of course, the wise minister takes precautions. Namely, you, Matthew Quinton, our precaution-in-chief.'

'My Lord?'

'Your loyalty is beyond reproach. That business in Scotland in the year sixty-two, for instance... There are few captains of the navy to whom the Lord Chancellor and I would dare to speak thus frankly, Quinton.'

I looked from one man to the other, and felt a sudden shiver of apprehension.

Arlington moved towards me, his eyes narrowing as he approached. 'It seems to us that this great conspiracy, if it truly exists, must have a leader. There must be a new Cromwell lurking in the shade, seeking his moment. If twenty captains are to defect, we believe they must do so at a given moment, upon a signal from that leader – the hoist of a flag, or whatever it is you mariners do to attract attention.' The Secretary looked me square in the eyes. 'You know Sir John Lawson, I take it?'

'*Lawson?*' I gasped. 'But My Lords, it cannot be imagined that Lawson would turn traitor –'

'He turned traitor before,' said Arlington relentlessly, 'traitor to the Commonwealth that he had served so notably, and I have often observed that treason can be addictive. He was also a good friend to some of the fanatic captains who have been left on shore.'

'But he could have died in the *London*, if he had gone aboard when he was meant to! I was there, my lords! I saw the consequences, as did he! To blow up his own ship, and many of his own kin –'

'An effective way of diverting suspicion from oneself, perhaps. Or else, of course, the destruction of the *London* might have been but a convenient accident which achieved just that end.' The Secretary smiled wearily. 'You see the dangers of my occupation, Captain? Trust no one, suspect everyone – the sad fate of the intelligencer.'

'Sir John is appointed Vice-Admiral of the Red,' said Clarendon, who had averted his eyes during Arlington's peroration but evidently could not bring himself to dismiss it entirely. 'Thus he holds the second command in His Royal Highness's own squadron. A position of considerable trust, Quinton. Imagine the consequences if Sir John went over to the Dutch during the battle, and turned his own ship and others against His Royal Highness himself.'

And there was the other reason why Clarendon was reluctantly going along with Arlington's belief in the plot. For in the Chancellor's scheme of things a threat to the Duke of York was more, much more, than a mere threat to the heir to the throne; it was the potential overthrow of all his dynastic ambition.

The secretary nodded. 'That would be danger indeed – especially if Lawson was seconded in any defection by the Rear-Admiral of that same squadron.'

'Berkeley? Will Berkeley? But he's one of my oldest and dearest friends! He's as true a cavalier as any of us, as are all his family! His brother is the king's favourite! This is madness, My Lords –'

My stomach had tightened and my heart was racing. Was it possible for the plague to be brought on by shock?

I saw at once from the expressions of both Clarendon and Arlington that I had struck entirely the wrong note. Yes, my good friend Rear-Admiral Sir Will Berkeley was the brother of the king's favourite, the good-humoured but utterly worthless Earl of Falmouth; and throughout history, there has been a marked tendency for king's ministers to be ousted from power at the whim of king's favourites. Consequently, the former have ever been inclined to seek ways of pre-emptively bringing down the latter. Here, then, was something else that temporarily united the Chancellor and the Secretary: an aversion to the House of Berkeley and all its works.

'I have been as good a friend to the Berkeleys as any man,' said Arlington, dissembling brazenly. 'But war has a habit of breaking friendships and testing men's allegiances, as My Lord Chancellor and I found through bitter experience.' Clarendon glowered; he had been a noted man on the Parliament's side before returning to the cause of the first King Charles, a fact that staunch cavaliers like Arlington – and, come to that, the Quinton family – had never forgotten. 'But you would know this better than either of us, Quinton. Did not your friend Berkeley spend several years at sea under Lawson? Does not the Vice-Admiral have great influence over him? Is he not courting Lawson's daughter?'

'T – true, My Lords,' I said but those are hardly the ingredients of treason –'

'Probably not,' Arlington said, essaying a benign smile that actually made his wholly malign face seem even more ghastly. 'But as My Lord Chancellor has said, it is the responsibility of ministers of state to prepare for all eventualities – to suspect all. Some, for example, might consider such an eventuality to be the loyalty of a man with a Dutch wife.' He stood unsettlingly close to me and stared into my eyes. My loyalty questioned because of Cornelia? But I could look only at the hideous plaster, and the way it dipped into the deep scar beneath. I shuddered, and prayed that he had not noticed. Then, unexpectedly, Arlington smiled. 'But I would be the last man to do so, Quinton, for I, too, expect to wed a countrywoman of your good lady in the near future.' So he did, and to a woman with a rather better pedigree than Cornelia's: a bastard granddaughter of a Prince of Orange, no less. Arlington stepped away a little and returned to our matter in hand. 'No doubt you will be proved correct, and Admirals Lawson and Berkeley will play full parts in the great victory to come, earning the applause of their sovereign and nation, garnering honour to their names for all posterity, etcetera.' His face hardened. 'But in case it proves otherwise, Captain Matthew Quinton and the great ship *Merhonour* will be on hand. We have prevailed upon His Royal Highness to place you directly behind Lawson's new flagship, as his second. If –'

'If Lawson, Berkeley and others defect during the battle,' Clarendon interrupted, his tone clipped and harsh, 'you will be in position to fight them. If you have to, Quinton, you must sink them. Destroy the traitors. At all costs, preserve the life of His Royal Highness, my son-in-law.'

* * *

I rode toward Hardiman's Yard in a dark, vicious mood, a condition not improved by the travails of my journey. The Charing-Cross was clogged with people, the Strand beyond it little better, and when I finally reached the Lud Gate, a heaving and immobile crowd was jostling to find a way past a great cart that had lost a wheel in the very gateway itself. Tempers were rising, and as they did so, the veneer of a land at peace with itself swiftly evaporated.

'Charles Stuart is nought but a papist and a whoremaster!' cried one voice.

'Rebel scum! *Vive le roi*! *Vive le roi*!' came an answering shout, which was joined in short order by many others.

'Christ will reign upon earth, for the old cause rises again! The comet foretells the death of kings!'

'For the King and the Church!' At that, part of the crowd surged. I saw a flurry of fists, and heard the first clash of steel upon steel. The first scream of pain followed hard on its heels.

Once, I would have launched myself into the fray on the side of the stout cavalier lads, but though little older, I was distinctly wiser. With difficulty, I manoeuvred my horse out of the crowd and made my way up to Holborn Bar, thence into High Holborn itself, steering my horse through the foul hordes of lawyers and their clerks. As I did so, I fell to contemplation of my condition.

My pride in the command of the *Merhonour* had largely evaporated, for I could see only the vision of her standing broadside-to-broadside with Will Berkeley's *Swiftsure*, Englishman against Englishman, friend against friend. Did Clarendon and Arlington really reflect the will of the king in this business, I wondered? Somehow I had been sucked into the blackest place of all, that foul, vicious world which men call 'politics', and I hated it. Clarendon and Arlington had sworn me to silence, so honour dictated that I could not approach my brother, one of only two men who could have steered me safely out of this seething pit; and even if I was prepared to lay my honour to one side, the gulf between Charles and me upon the matter of his dubious countess was surely too wide to be bridged. For the same reason, I could not go directly to the only other man on earth who could have attested to the truth of the great ministers' assertions and set my conscience at ease. King Charles was still unlikely to look favourably upon an approach from the man who had accused him of being gulled into the bed of a murderess in the pay of France.

And yet ... and yet. *Someone* had recommended me for the command of the *Merhonour*; it could not have been Clarendon, who was ignorant of naval affairs and thus eschewed naval patronage, and it would hardly have been Arlington, who was no friend to the Quinton family. I considered the great men of the navy, and discounted most of them at once. The Duke of Albemarle I barely knew, and he was known not to favour young gentlemen captains. Pepys's patron, Lord Sandwich, was almost equally unknown to me. Then there was Sir William Penn, whom I had met at the Navy Board: but he, too, was a favourer of bluff old tarpaulin captains, and was the man most responsible for the recall of all the Commonwealth veterans.

Finally there was Prince Rupert, cousin to the king and duke, but he was anathema to we Quintons, for we blamed him for the death of my father, Earl James, at the Battle of Naseby. On that desperate June day in 1645, Rupert's cavalry swept the enemy before them but then galloped off the battlefield in hot pursuit rather than turning in against the Roundhead infantry. Only one of Rupert's officers had halted his troop's charge in order to fall upon the footsoldiers of the New Model Army; but without support, the ninth Earl of Ravensden and his men were swallowed up and hacked to pieces. Thus the devil was a more likely friend for Matthew Quinton than the Prince Palatine of the Rhine.

Which left one, and only one: the Earl of Clarendon's son-in-law.

At the time of his brother's restoration, James, Duke of York, who would one day reign briefly and ingloriously over his Britannic realms as King James the Second and Seventh, was the heir to three kingdoms and thus one of the most eligible bachelors in Europe. But he had thrown away the valuable diplomatic card of his marriage by secretly wedding one of his sister's maids-of-honour, a plain, witty girl who was eight months pregnant by him when they belatedly reached the altar. How history is dictated by the unanticipated rise of a male member at the sight of an inappropriate woman's shapely leg or bosom! For fate dictated that the royal bedfellow was the daughter of Edward Hyde, the man whom the duke's elder brother had just made his chief minister and Earl of Clarendon. To those who favour conspiracy over coincidence, this was damning: surely the evil minister had used his daughter's charms to ensnare the heir to the throne, thus furthering the nefarious purposes of the said evil minister? Hindsight poured yet more oil onto the flames; yea, an entire ocean of oil. The king's marriage to the Portuguese princess Catherine proved childless, and it did not require too fertile an imagination to conjure up a dark tale of Clarendon arranging a match to a barren queen in order to ensure that his own grandchildren would one day ascend the thrones of Britain. (This they duly did, in the stolid shapes of Queens Mary and Anne; but their accessions required a series of alterations in the state that would have boggled the mind of any man alive in that year of sixty-five, myself and their grandfather included.)

Thus as I rode into Hardiman's Yard and endeavoured to assume an air of levity – of celebration, even – with which to break the news of my command to Cornelia, I conceived a list in my head.

Item – the said Matthew Quinton commissioned through the patronage of the Duke of York, who in our eight years of acquaintance has barely noticed the existence of said Matthew. To what end, pray?

Item – the said Matthew Quinton to do the bidding of My Lords of Clarendon and Arlington, respectively the most hated man in England and the most sinister. Two men known for their utter detestation of each other, yet who seem to have found common ground solely in concurring that...

Item – the said Matthew Quinton to be the principal means of preventing the overthrow of the crown in a great naval rebellion.

Item – the said Matthew Quinton to achieve such ends in a ship so ancient that it was built before its erstwhile commander, the said Matthew's own grandfather, was born...

The ship.

A memory came to me, as clear as if I had been transported back in time to be once again an eleven-year-old boy in the library of

Ravensden. A memory of my uncle Tristram, describing to me my grandfather's own illustrated list of the ships that he had commanded during his long and controversial career as one of the great Elizabeth's sea-dogs.

'There, the *Constant Esperance*, in which he fought the Armada … the *Gloriana*, in which he sailed against Lisbon in '89, and of course his own ship, the *Ark Ravensden* … ah, and the *Merhonour*, in which he sailed against Cadiz. Always an unlucky ship, the *Merhonour*, your grandfather said. Not merely unlucky. Cursed.'

Chapter Six

Dutchmen beware, we have a fleet
Will make you tremble when you see't,
Mann'd with brave Englishmen of high renown,
Who can and will your peacock plumes pull down…
~ Anon., *England's Valour, and Holland's Terrour* (1665)

A row-boat upon the Medway, Upnor Castle to larboard, a chill north-easterly whipping up the muddy water of the river. Most of the moorings were empty, the great ships that secured to them long departed to sea. But one of the greatest of all remained, and lay dead ahead in mid-stream: the *Merhonour*. The splendid stern bore witness to her antiquity. Although a royal arms and cipher had been set up, the new wood and bright paint contrasted with the rest of the decoration, which belonged to Cromwell's time or even earlier. There were not a few coats-of-arms of the Commonwealth set among the elaborate panoply of laurel wreaths and lions that scrolled around the windows of my great cabin, and as we drew nearer I even spotted an 'ER', the old queen's cipher, upon the gunport-lids on either side of the rudder.

Broad in the beam compared to some of the newer ships, the ports along her starboard side were in irregular lines, a tell-tale sign that extra guns had been crammed into her over the years, new ports being cut in the hull to accommodate them. A three-decker, albeit a small one, her great hull towered above us. Some of the older timbers still bore the scars of war: dents from cannonballs or the tell-tale pepper-pot marks of grape and musket fire, most of it probably dating from the last war against the Dutch but some of it, perhaps, going back to my grandfather's day. She was ancient and she was allegedly cursed, but great God, she was mine. I had seen elephants the year before, during my voyage upon the River of Gambia, and my ship reminded me of nothing more than a great old bull-elephant, torn and bruised after too many fights: almost ready for that last journey to the grave-yard, but still with one final fight left in it against the impudent young incomers from a rival herd.

Upon a conceit, and despite the fact that I had been aboard her several times already, I ordered my crew to row me all around my command. We passed beneath the stern and the old-fashioned Jaco-bean windows of my cabin, then down the starboard side. The guns were in, and the ship looked suitably warlike; the masts and yards were up, and although we had but half a crew, men were about in the rigging, making clewlines and halyards shipshape. As I looked up at the wooden wall which towered over me, I felt once again the strange conflict of emotions that had assailed me more than once on the road from London to Chatham. Pride, yes, that this great ship was mine; but with it came doubts that did not merely nag; they gnawed at the very essence of my soul. She was so much larger than anything I had commanded before, and in my blacker moments I wondered whether I might have been promoted far beyond my experience and compe-tence. In ordinary circumstances my responsibilities in commanding her would have been weighty enough, for the great ships were meant to bear the brunt of battle and thus carried most of our king's and our people's hopes of victory upon their broad gundecks. But my secret orders doubled those responsibilities, and doubled them again. For the *Merhonour* and her captain were to be the first and strongest defence against a possible rebellion in the fleet. Upon this ancient ship and her very young captain might depend the fate of the heir to England and ultimately that of his brother, the king. And all of that was before one considered the small matter of the alleged curse.

I looked up and saw a familiar face upon the quarterdeck: Giffard, the lieutenant, raised his hat in salute. He had been stiffly formal at my first coming aboard, and I had not yet managed to take his measure. He was a sour-faced old Jerseyman with skin like leather, one of Carteret's cronies who had led the Parliament's navy a merry dance in the civil war. He seemed a competent seaman, albeit too set in his ways for my liking. His main concern, and indeed mine, was the fact that we were being set out so late, long after the main body of the fleet had been manned with the best drafts of men from the Thames and the east coast. This meant that we would be left with the dregs from the outlying parts of the kingdom: God alone knew when they would arrive and what they would be like. We could not sail until we were approximately manned, and I prayed that the war was not already over by the time we were.

Around, under the bow where the golden lion figurehead roared defiance against the Dutch *hogen-mogen* butterboxes, our implacable foes. Above, the union flag fluttered from the staff upon the bowsprit. And so down the larboard side, with Giffard moving across the quarterdeck to continue to watch his captain's progress. Strictly speaking, he was now the *first* lieutenant, it being a new innovation by His Royal Highness that two lieutenants should be allowed to the greater ships of the fleet; nominally to improve the captain's control of his ship, although we all knew that it was but a ploy to satisfy the insatiable demand for commissions in the navy. How the old seamen of the time roared and ranted against this monstrous innovation, declaring it to be beyond wonder and against all the customs of the service! Aye, and how they would spin in their graves if they could see a modern First Rate and its legion of six lieutenants, tripping over themselves as they scurry to impress their superiors. But then, in the year sixty-five, I had made a recommendation for the vacant post of second lieutenant with little hope of seeing it implemented; there were so many disappointed candidates for office (as I had been until so recently) that I was certain His Royal Highness would soon appoint a brash young courtier or the scion of some great noble house.

My boat came alongside, and I boarded my command. The boatswain, an aged and ineffectual Essex man named Pewsey, piped me aboard, and I was reassured to see that the makeshift side party contained several of my personal following, including Macferran, Treninnick, Carvell and the renegade Moor Ali Reis. Beau Harris had been good to his word and released them once his own complement was made up. The *House of Nassau* was already with the fleet and dashing about the sea on scouting duties, a fact that made me not a little jealous: ordered to sea almost as an afterthought, the *Merhonour* was still very far from being in a fit condition to sail. At least the reassuring presence of my own following made up to a certain degree for the evident inadequacies of the ship's warrant officers. The *Merhonour* had not left her mooring in twelve years, and as her shipkeepers, the standing officers had all too evidently seen their places as sinecures. Pewsey, the boatswain, was decayed and ineffectual; I wished I could lay him aside to put in Kit Farrell or Lanherne, but feared that would not be allowed. Thurston, the carpenter, was seventy-three; Faraday, the purser, was nearly blind; Webb, the gunner, was nearly deaf from too many broadsides, and prayed loudly to Saint Barbara, the old patron of his kind. Great God, we even had a supply of bows and arrows in the armourer's stores that must have been left aboard since my grandfather's day. Old men, an old ship and old weapons: perhaps *that* was the curse of the *Merhonour*.

As I stepped onto the upper deck and raised my hat to salute the ship, Lieutenant Gideon Giffard saluted me stiffly in return. 'Captain Quinton. Welcome back aboard, sir.'

I returned the courtesy. 'Mister Giffard. Still no sign of our men, I take it?'

'No, sir.' I was still having difficulty with his Jersey accent, which sounded like a strange hybrid of French and Dorsetshire. 'There's talk of a hoy coming up the river, though, so perhaps they will be aboard that.' We were over a hundred men short of our complement; without them, the *Merhonour* could never leave its mooring, let alone join the fleet. 'But the new chaplain has come aboard, Captain.'

I went below, steeling myself for an awkward meeting. The fleet was now so large, and both the number and quality of those who wished to minister to its spiritual wellbeing was so low, that naval chaplaincy was a byword for the dregs of the Church of England, and I wondered what sort of mediocrity, dissenter or sodomite might have been visited upon me. The chaplain's cabin lay on the lowest gundeck, almost at the very stern of the ship. Like all the officers' cabins, it was a precarious timber and canvas affair with no natural light, no more than six feet by five, which would clearly be a constraint upon the stocky man who now turned to greet me –

'Francis!' I cried in surprise.

'Captain Quinton,' said the Reverend Francis Gale.

'Great God, man, you should have written – I had no idea you were even thinking of serving at sea this summer.'

Francis, a man of God who was as dexterous with the cutlass as the catechism, had first served with me aboard the *Jupiter* three years before, and after we had exorcised the very personal demons that afflicted him, he had become a close friend. He was made rector of our local church upon my recommendation, but had taken leave to serve with me aboard the *Seraph* during its voyage to Africa. That, he had assured me, was to be the end of his seafaring.

'I have reflected much upon the will of God,' he said. 'I asked him whether I served Him best by tending to the farmers and peasants of Ravensden, or by watching over His servant Matthew Quinton in the dreadful fights to come. And the Lord spake unto me, and he sayeth, "Get thee to sea, Francis Gale, and kill as many avaricious cheese-stinking Dutchmen as come within reach of thy sword." Or words to that effect. Thanks be to God, for his wonders are manifold.'

'But my mother and my brother – surely they cannot be content that you have forsaken your parish duties?' I said. 'Yet again.'

'Your brother has been absent from Ravensden for many weeks. Some say he is at his Northumberland estate, others at the countess's estate in Wiltshire, yet others taking the waters at Bath. He is a sick man, I fear – sick in body and sick in heart, for he now sees the folly of his unnatural marriage.' I shuddered, as I often did when the truth of my situation came to me: that I was but one feeble heartbeat away from the earldom of Ravensden and all the dread responsibilities that came with it.

Francis sensed my concern and raised a hand in sympathetic ben-ediction. He had been an opponent of my brother's marriage, and endeavoured to discover something of the mysterious past of my sis-ter-in-law, the Lady Louise. To no avail, alas; all of the enquiries that he and my uncle Tris had conducted seemed to have ended at brick walls. 'As for your mother, she was sympathetic to the argument that you should have a friend at your back. Besides,' said Gale, 'I think I am growing old, Matthew, and it will be good to fight another battle or two before I allow senility to overtake me.'

I was mightily glad to have Francis alongside me, for I knew from experience how useful he was in a fight. I took him around the ship, along each of her three broad gun-decks, and everywhere we went, the lads who had sailed with us before smiled and nodded greetings, for they had shared much with the Reverend Gale and respected the man profoundly. My own following, those who would volunteer to serve under me in preference to any other captain, now numbered nearly a hundred, and included Bristol and London men from my commission in the *Seraph* as well as my Cornish coterie from the days in the *Jupiter*. But the rest of the crew included a fair number of pressed men, chiefly scrapings from the Thames and inward-bound merchantmen, resentful at being kept from their families and their pay. I saw a few scowls as we passed, and heard the growling speech of a malcontent, hastily concluded when the speaker became aware of our approach.

'...that you've never heard of the curse on this benighted ship? They say every living soul aboard her perished of the plague in the year twenty-five – every living thing save the ship's cat – and they say the ghost of the captain's grandfather prowls the decks, and he'd made a pact with the devil, that he had, just like the captain's uncle –'

Francis frowned and glanced questioningly toward me. I merely shrugged, for there was no privacy upon the decks. So we went up to my cabin, a lavish space that was larger than the main room I shared with Cornelia at Hardiman's Yard: the *Merhonour* had been built as a flagship, and thus had two great cabins, one at the stern of the upper gundeck and one upon the middle, an unusual luxury in a ship of that vintage. For the time being I had the run of both, although the enthusiasm of every idle courtier and nobleman to get to sea and impress the ladies was so great that I was certain I would soon have some pompous nonentity inflicted upon me.

We settled ourselves upon fine oak chairs which had once adorned the long gallery at Ravensden Abbey. My little retinue of Barcock, Castle and Scobey, delighted and amazed to be in service aboard so great a ship, scurried to provide us with tankards of good London ale. Then we two men looked out at the spectacle beyond the stern windows: the storehouses, slipways, cranes and ropewalk of Chatham yard, the distant mass of ruinous Rochester Castle next to the spire of the cathedral. I longed to confess to Francis my other overarching concern, the secret orders given me by Clarendon and Arlington, but my honour prevented it; besides, we had another pressing matter to discuss.

'A curse, Matthew?' my old friend asked, quizzically.

'The tattle of the lower deck, Francis. But they are well informed of my history, even if they have conflated the sixth earl with the eighth.' Henry, sixth Earl of Ravensden, was said to have been a necromancer who had sold his soul to the devil, a story reinforced by the failure to discover a body after his alleged death in a tavern brawl; his satanic visage and unconventional interests had been inherited by my uncle. 'Tristram would never be able to sell his soul to the devil, for Old Nick would rightly suspect he was being swindled. And if my grandfather's shade truly haunts the ship, it has not troubled me with a visitation.'

'But you and I are rational men, Matt. Alas, though, the seaman is not. Indeed, he is the most superstitious creature upon the earth, ever prone to believe in witches, ghosts and the like. If this of a curse is allowed to take hold, and if they identify you and your family with it, who knows what harm it could do when finally we go into battle?'

Francis's words troubled me; I had been inclined to dismiss the legend of the curse, convincing myself that perhaps my crew would never come to hear of it, or else that as creatures of a modern, rational age, they would not be as fearful a breed as their forefathers. I had also never even considered the notion that I might be seen as a living manifestation of the curse. *Foolish boy,* a visitation seemed to whisper.

'Then what can be done, Francis?'

'Naturally I can sermonise upon the ridiculousness of such superstitions – the third letter of Paul to the Romans, verses the thirteenth to eighteenth, will serve the purpose.' He was contemplative. 'But if such fails, I suppose there is one other course left to us.'

'That being?'

Francis smiled and took a long draught of ale. 'For that, Matthew, I need to write a letter. A very long letter. To the Lord Archbishop of Canterbury.'

* * *

'Can't sail with you this time, Captain. Not yet, at any rate.'

Phineas Musk stood a few feet from me in the cramped, oak-panelled hallway of Ravensden House, but he might as well have been a world away. This was the last news I had expected: since my second commission, Musk had been as inevitable a part of my services at sea as wind and tide.

'Great God in Heaven, Musk,' I said, 'think of the pay that a captain's clerk of a Second Rate receives! Think of the prize money that will accrue to all of us in this war, even in a great tub like the *Merhonour*! And all of that additional to what my brother pays you as his steward here.'

For almost no perceptible work, I might have added; even less, now that Earl Charles had largely abandoned our decrepit town house upon the Strand in favour of other abodes.

'Builders,' said Musk uncomfortably. 'Can't trust builders. Your brother wants them in to shore up this place and make good the back wall. Needs me to oversee them. They won't fleece me, trying to pass off any old wattle-and-daub as an honest stone wall.'

'And this must be done now? When the house is barely used?'

'Best time,' grunted Musk. 'Nobody here to disturb, other than me. If it's not done soon, the whole thing will collapse. Although now I think upon it, I suppose your grandfather did say much the same thing to me back in the year forty-four.'

If I was being even-handed, I had to admit that the case for such remedial work was unanswerable. Above where we stood, the sagging ceiling contained two ominously large cracks; the smell of damp and long-forgotten cesspits pervaded the entire crumbling building. Even so, I could still barely digest the news. Musk had become something of a talisman upon my voyages; an obstreperous talisman, admittedly, but I was about to sail into my first fleet battle, and it would be strange not to have his oddly reassuring presence at my side. But there was another and even more troubling strangeness to the whole business.

Musk was many things, and not all of them were entirely reputable. One thing he was not, though, was a liar; at least, not to those named Quinton. Yet I had an unnerving feeling that he was lying to me now.

Concealing my darker thoughts, I clutched at a straw. 'You said "not yet", Musk. Then there is hope that you might join the ship later?'

The old rogue shrugged. 'Can never tell how long builders will take. Law unto themselves, builders are. 'Specially at the moment, with all these great new mansions going up in Westminster and the likes of Lord Clarendon paying over the odds. Not to mention,' he said, brightening, 'not knowing how long this war could take. You might have beaten the Dutch and come back wreathed in laurel before the idle buggers even get as far as the plastering.'

I sighed, for there was evidently no remedying the situation; and if Musk truly was lying, then the lie was as elaborately constructed as Clarendon House itself. 'Well then, Musk, I shall take my leave and ride on to the abbey to say farewell to my mother. I pray that your duties here will permit you to join me in due course, for I sense that a Dutch war will not be complete without Phineas Musk.'

A lying Musk, a cursed ship and the possibility of vile conspiracy in the fleet, cocooned within that evil web named 'politics': as I rode for Bedfordshire, I had to content myself with the thought that surely nothing else could worsen the condition of Matthew Quinton.

Chapter Seven

Grim King of the Ghosts make haste
And bring hither all your train,
See how the pale moon does waste,
And just now is the wain.
Come you Night-Hags with all your charms,
And revelling witches away,
And hug me close in your arms,
To you my respects I'll pay.
~ Anon., *The Lunatick Lover*
(popular ballad of the Restoration period)

There was no landscape more familiar to me. The stream where I had played as a boy. The mill and the home farm. The kiln and the blacksmith's forge. The woodland beyond. The gentle slopes on which the Cistercians had planted a vineyard in the days when England's weather was more akin to that of Iberia than Iceland. The abbey itself, the ruins of the church projecting beyond the jumble of buildings in the domestic range. The wisps of smoke rising from the chimneys into the spring air. Apart from the last few months in Hardiman's Yard, my sea-voyages and five years in penniless exile upon the continent, I had lived here all my life.

Ravensden Abbey.

This was home.

I did not allow myself more than a fleeting acknowledgement of the thought that this might be the last time I ever saw it. Although I had fought in a battle on land and in an action between single ships, I had never yet experienced a fleet engagement. But I knew enough men who had; *never expect you will survive it*, they said, *it's easier that way*. The humblest powder-boy and the greatest admiral are as one when the cannon begin to roar. Witness the fate of Richard Deane, one of the Commonwealth's mighty generals-at-sea. Greater than Monck, many said. Could have been greater than Cromwell, some said. It mattered not a jot when a cannonball literally cut him in two at the Gabbard fight.

I rode into the stable yard, dismounted and handed my steed to my namesake, Matthew Barcock. 'Her ladyship's in the Long Gallery,' he said; he was undoubtedly the least communicative of our steward's inexhaustible brood.

I decided to grasp the nettle at once. Allowing no more than an hour for my dutiful farewell to my mother, I should be able to make Barnet, or somewhere nearby, before nightfall. The sixteen pounds and sixteen shillings a month that would eventually accrue to the captain of the *Merhonour*, and against which I had already borrowed quite substantially, meant that I could afford a decent room in a respectable inn, not the lousy mattress in a shared garret that had long been the lot of Matthew Quinton. An early start would enable me to return to Cornelia before the morning was out, giving the best part of one last day with her before rejoining the *Merhonour* on the following day. Through the inner gate into the pleasant garden that had once been the monastic cloister, up the stairs to what had once been the monks' refectory, remodelled by Earl Edward into a fashionable Tudor long gallery, at the end of which sat my –

Sister-in-law.

The Countess Louise looked up from the small writing desk that had been positioned to catch the best of the spring sun. 'Matthew!' she cried. 'What a truly delightful surprise!'

It was not a delight that I reciprocated. I cursed myself for not having asked Matt Barcock which 'ladyship' was in residence; but then, the existence of this new countess was still so new, and so unsettling, that the possibility of him referring to anyone other than my mother simply never occurred to me.

'My Lady,' I said, hastily recovering myself, 'my apologies for intruding upon you. I had sought an interview with my mother, to say farewell before my ship joins the fleet.'

She was half way down the gallery, between the serried ranks of portraits of dead Quintons, advancing elegantly towards me. She seemed to make almost no footfall upon the ancient floor. Whatever else the Countess Louise might have been, she could certainly act the part of a great and stately lady.

'Oh, poor Matthew,' she said, 'you will be so disappointed. And your loving mother will be too, of course.' Either she did not know how things stood between my mother and I, or else she did and was a consummate dissembler. 'The Dowager Countess departed but this morning. She must have taken a different road to Whitehall, else you would have passed her on the way. She has gone to court, you see.'

This news was almost as troublesome as the presence of this cuckoo in the nest of my ancestors. My mother had not been at court in a quarter-century. My mother despised the court, and all to do with it. My mother being at court was as likely as King Charles taking a vow of chastity.

The Countess Louise was before me now. She was dressed more plainly than I had ever seen her, eschewing jewellery or any colourings. She was not disguised by the scent of expensive perfumes, as she had been whenever else I had met her. She wore only a plain black smock, such as countrywomen wear; one could have taken her for a Quaker.

'In that case, My Lady,' I said, 'I will not detain you…'

She reached out and touched my forearm. 'Stay a while, Matthew, please!' Her touch sent a shudder through my body.

'As Your Ladyship pleases.'

'Louise, as I have told you before, Matthew.' She had a way of staring into a man's eyes for just a moment longer than most people do.

'As you say, My Lady. You are not in company with my brother, then?' They were in company precious little these days, as I well knew, and my comment was intended to sting.

'Charles is unwell. His wounds give him more trouble. Even now, he takes the waters at Bath. And … and he has been distant – the nature of my annuity concerns him…' A delicate euphemism indeed for the pension paid by France to one of its agents! 'But I will not inflict my worries upon you, Matthew. When all is said and done, you have lived with the knowledge of Charles's infirmities for so much longer than I.' She sighed. 'Perhaps you will be Earl of Ravensden very soon, and then you will have no need to concern yourself with me any longer.' She looked at me curiously. 'Although, of course, there are precedents for a man marrying his brother's widow. Harry the Eighth, for one.'

This was monstrous. It was unspeakable. The bitch was proposing that I wed her –

'Not a happy precedent, madam,' I said, struggling with great difficulty to maintain my temper, my dignity and my honour. 'And even if my brother were to die, remember that I am married.'

'As was I, Matthew. Twice, now thrice. Marriages are so … transitory, I find.' Suddenly and unexpectedly, she broke into a wide grin; I had never seen her smile so. 'I jest with you, good-brother. I know I should not, on such a serious matter, but the sight of your face – ah, it is a shame that no-one has seen fit to place a mirror in this room, that you could see your expression!' And with that, she tapped my hand playfully.

I was discomforted beyond measure. I was unused to such subtle and dark humour in a woman: Cornelia was more direct, the women I knew about the court merely laughed reflexively at the jokes of the rakes they sought to bed, while my mother had buried whatever sense of humour she had once possessed alongside the corpse of my father.

Countess Louise stepped past me and looked up at the somewhat fanciful portrait of a man in armour: a long-forgotten Tudor artist's imagining of what the first Earl of Ravensden might have looked like, a century before that.

'I am studying the history of the Quintons,' she said, apparently serious again, 'the better to pass it on to the son that Charles and I will have.'

Which Charles? And the absence of any child after nearly eighteen months of marriage, despite the best efforts of a monarch notorious for his ability to impregnate women in about as many seconds, made the countess's sudden interest in genealogy doubly unexpected; suspicious, even, if one had a mind that was thus inclined.

'You spring from such a great race, Matthew! Such an unbroken record of service to the crown. You must be proud to come from such a line. To have all these' – she gestured toward the portraits lining the gallery – 'as your ancestors.'

'Proud – yes. And ashamed, madam, at the dishonour you have brought to this noble house.'

She shrugged off my jibe, which in truth was entirely unmannerly and peevish on my part; her presence was unsettling me greatly. 'Is it really dishonour to the House of Quinton to have its line revived by a dash of royal blood?' No dissembling, then; but she knew full well that I knew of the perverse arrangement between her, my brother and the king.

The countess moved along the south wall, gazing upon the Quinton portraits. 'Consider our proud English nobility, Matthew,' she said. 'How many great lords are truly the sons of footmen or stable boys, brought in to a ladyship's bed to hatch an heir when the husband's member would not suffice?' She had a way of suddenly lifting her head to emphasise a point; it was not unappealing. 'This matter touches thrones, too. Was not King James said to be the son of Davey Rizzio? Do not many still find it curious that the present King Louis was conceived after his parents' marriage had been childless for twenty years, and at a time when there was about that court a particularly fetching captain of the guard? Legitimacy in great lineages is a moveable feast, Matthew Quinton. Very moveable indeed.'

'Perhaps, My Lady. But for these speculations to have any effect in this place, you must bear a child. A task you have not accomplished with any man in nearly twenty years, and which you have thus far failed to accomplish in eighteen months of being serviced by the most virile man on earth.'

For any lady of honour, this would have been an unbearable insult. Surely it was ample to drive any woman into a paroxysm of tears. But the Countess of Ravensden merely narrowed her eyes for a moment, then smiled. 'Ah, well, Matthew, I know what the court and all of England says about our sovereign lord. Our wits can pun all they like about his mighty sceptre, but I can assure you that His Majesty's performance is, shall we say … over-rated?' She walked to the window and looked out over the parterre. 'Of course, it is possible that by the time he reaches me he is exhausted from his bouts with Barbara Castlemaine – they say the bitch is insatiable. And I am told that he still sleeps with the queen from time to time, for the sake of form and our alliance with Portugal. As is only right and proper.' She turned suddenly and faced me directly. 'Why, Matthew Quinton, I do believe you are shocked! Are you not used to hearing women talk thus? Truly, sir, for all your Cavalier pedigree I think you must be a secret Puritan at heart!'

I was profoundly discomforted, both at the directness of her speech and at the growing realisation that I was being toyed with. 'It is – it is unsuitable, madam. Inappropriate.'

'Indeed? I'll wager it is as nothing to the discourse you have with your friends and fellow captains in the tavern. Seamen are not known as monks or shrinking violets, are they, Matthew? And I cannot imagine your beloved and, I may say, refreshingly forthright Cornelia is reticent upon such matters.'

'You will *not* mention my wife! *You will not –*' I raised my hand to strike her. Rather than flinching, she presented her cheek for the blow, smiling as she did so. I stayed my open hand, closed it into a fist, and brought it back down to my side as my face burned with shame and anger.

'I apologise, Matthew,' she said, with apparent sincerity. 'I have spent too long at court, where the quip and the hurtful jest are praised above decorous conversation.'

'What is it that you do here, madam?' I snapped.

She evidently misinterpreted my question; to this day, I do not know if she did so deliberately. 'I have been studying the papers in your family's muniments chest,' she said, ignoring my rather wider meaning. 'Fascinating, quite fascinating. The letters in French between your grandfather and grandmother – so loving, so gallant! What times they must have had.' I glanced at the portrait of my dearly remembered grandmother and wondered what she, the grand and eccentric Countess Louise-Marie, would have made of this interloper, her near-namesake.

The current Countess of Ravensden continued her perambulation of the gallery. 'And yet, so many unanswered questions. Take the fate of this gentleman, for instance.' She stopped before the portrait of a hard-faced man with a short, pointed brown beard and dressed in the fashion of the old queen's time: my great-grandfather, Edward, seventh Earl of Ravensden. 'An inscrutable face. I am glad that you did not inherit it from him, Matthew – your face is an open book.' She smiled playfully. 'Such an intriguing man, the seventh earl. There are hints in his letters of a falling out between him and his mother, the formidable Countess Katherine – and what a life hers would have been! To have been a nun, and to have outlived all her children…'

Katherine had resolved the problems posed by the dissolution of her convent by taking herself to the bed of Harry, fourth Earl of Ravensden, a coarse old soldier who had warred across France and Scotland in the wake of that other Henry, the eighth English king of the name. My great-great-grandmother outlived all three of her sons, who each became earl in turn, and survived until not far short of her ninety-fifth birthday.

'Katherine seems to have been unconscionably keen for the title to pass to your grandfather,' said the present Countess of Ravensden. 'Why should that have been, I wonder? Earl Edward was such a public figure – Walsingham's rival as the great queen's spymaster, was he not? I have seen hints that Earl Edward was somehow involved in the entrapment and execution of Mary, Queen of Scots. And was there not talk that his own death might have been brought about by poison? Do you know anything of these matters, Matthew?'

Inwardly, I gasped at the breadth and depth of this unsettling woman's knowledge. These were some of the most closely guarded of our many family secrets, and yet her knowledge of them seemed superior to mine. Troublingly superior. For I had read and re-read the same letters when I was a boy of twelve and thirteen, searching for answers to the mysteries alluded to within them; but lads of that age want the whole story, and are impatient if confronted only by fragments which present a puzzle that cannot be solved. Yet my memories of those fading documents were still vivid in my memory, and I knew full well that they contained no reference at all to the legend that my great-grandfather had been poisoned. It seemed a singularly unlikely matter to have been aired in conversation between the Lady Louise and her sickly husband, my brother: so when and how, precisely, had she learned of this?

'No, madam,' I said defensively. 'I know nothing beyond what the letters contain.'

'Louise. A pity, that. I have a mind to enquire further into these matters. I must visit Tristram, at Oxford.' My uncle would welcome such a visitation as warmly as the pestilence, I thought. 'And when I am next at court, I must ask Arlington if the state papers of that time are extant, so that I might learn more.' Arlington? Was my good-sister somehow connected to him? The coffee houses were full of talk that the Secretary was in the pay of France, but then, it is the business of those who frequent coffee houses and inns to denounce the patriotism, competence and manliness of every minister of the crown. 'But there is so much of interest among the more recent documents, too,' said the Countess Louise. She walked to the little writing desk and picked up a small bundle of stained, fading letters; the muniment room was in a part of the building particularly prone to damp. 'Equally interesting are the letters from your mother to your father, and vice-versa, in the early years of the late king's reign. Particularly those from the years twenty-seven and twenty-eight, not long after that king married the present Queen Mother and before the murder of His Grace of Buckingham. How I have enjoyed the account of your parents' wedding, the King and Duke themselves in attendance! Why, it is so strange to think of your poor, bent mother as a vivacious young girl – and the court must have been so glittering in those days, so carefree without the memories of civil war that haunt all those of our unhappy generation!' The countess beamed radiantly at me. When she was in this delightful temper, it was easy to see why men fell under her spell – too easy. 'There are so many other letters. Some from your mother to a young Scottish courtier – a certain Campbell of Glenrannoch. Was he not later a great general during the wars upon the Continent? I think I know the name, my second husband would have spoken of him. Major-General Gulliver was ever eager for reports of the deeds of his own kind. Perhaps you have heard of this Campbell, too?'

'No, My Lady,' I lied, praying that my face did not betray me. *A vivid memory of a Scottish castle being ripped apart by a vast explosion, and of the man who perished within it* – General Colin Campbell of Glenrannoch: a man who had alluded to some secret knowledge that he shared with my mother, at exactly the time of which the countess spoke. That had been not the least of the mysteries revealed to me during my second command, aboard the frigate *Jupiter* in the waters of Scotland, but it had been the most abiding, for it was the only one that still defied explanation.

'Ah well,' she said, 'I did not expect it. An older generation, after all.' She looked up at me. 'It is so difficult to get to the bottom of your Quinton history, Matthew – your brother is strangely lacking in curiosity about his ancestors, I find.' Despite myself, I nodded; that had ever been a marked difference between Charles and I. 'But I have talked to the old Barcocks, and one day soon, I must speak to Musk. So often, it is the ancient retainers who have all the knowledge of their betters' foibles!'

'I wish you well, My Lady,' I said. 'Musk is less forthcoming than most rocks.'

I do not know why I made such a jest. Nor do I know why I was suddenly noticing things about the Countess Louise that I had not noticed before: the delicacy of her hands, the innocent way in which she used them to stroke her hair, the clarity of her skin, the elegance of her movements.

I had to turn my eyes away, to look upon anything other than the alluring creature before me. By chance, the first portrait that my eyes settled upon was that of my father. A poet forced to be a warrior, James Quinton, Earl of Ravensden for one hundred and eighteen days before he perished in glory (and utter futility) on Naseby field, looked down upon me. His face was set in that strangely pained half-smile that I just remembered from my early childhood; an expression that my family said I had inherited from him.

My father's countenance gave me the strength to turn once more to the Countess. 'I shall leave you to your enquiries, My Lady,' I said. 'I wish you well of them.'

'Matthew,' she said urgently, 'be not so hasty. I would ask you much else of your family's history. For instance, the muniments contain some mentions of an intriguing character named the Lord Percival, but I can find no other reference to him. There are hints that he was a friend of your brother, but Charles denies knowing any such person. Perhaps you have heard the name?'

Swiftly and truthfully I responded, 'No, My Lady. The name means nothing to me.'

She studied me closely, as though weighing my answer. This of the mysterious 'Lord Percival' seemed to matter much to her. 'A pity. So many mysteries, Matthew. So few answers.' She lifted her eyes to meet mine. 'But must you leave so urgently, good-brother? Surely you should stay one last night here in your home, the home of your ancestors, before you go off to war? One last night beneath this roof, where so many Quinton heirs have been begotten.'

Before my eyes, the gallery seemed to break apart into a thousand jagged pieces. I felt myself sway. I had never felt so much a stranger in my own thoughts; for somewhere within them, in the darkest place of all, was a voice insinuating that for the Quinton heir to be fathered by a Quinton would set all to rights.

Somehow, I know not how, I uttered the words, 'No, Louise. I must for the road, my wife and my ship.'

I am not entirely certain whether my leave-taking was dignified or not. During the next passage of which I was consciously aware, I was already riding at a gallop for London. By Hatfield my poor horse was all but finished, and I exchanged him for a fresh steed.

I rode into Hardiman's Yard as the dawn was breaking, the light of the sun glinting upon the glass of every east-facing window. I burst into our bedroom, and as Cornelia awoke, sleepy and surprised, I took her more roughly than I had ever done before.

Chapter Eight

Our ships are bravely rigged, and manned with seamen stout,
Our soldiers good will spend their blood to bang their foes about:
They long to be a dealing blows, delay doth vex them sore,
With delight, they will fight, when the cannons loud do roar.
~ Anon., *England's Valour, and Holland's Terrour* (1665)

'Merciful Father in Heaven,' I said to Francis Gale, 'have you ever seen such a sorry spectacle?'

We stood upon the wharf at Chatham yard, between the double dry dock and the boat yard. The cacophony of a royal dockyard in war-time surrounded us: above all, shipwrights were hammering timbers into place on the skeletal hull of the *Victory* in the nearby dry dock, for the huge old ship was being rebuilt at vast expense. The stench of tar, newly forged iron, wet rope and freshly sawn wood lay upon the air. For many used to country living, it would have been a vision of hell; but for Captain Matthew Quinton that day, it was as good a place as any to forget his twin nightmares of a scheming, seductive countess and a battle in which he might have to turn his guns upon friends and fellow Englishmen. I should have known better, even in those days of youthful innocence. A nightmare vanishes with the dawn, but nothing is more certain than that dusk will fall again and the nightmare will return, perhaps bringing its fellows along with it for company.

In front of Francis and I stood a hundred or so creatures who could be described as men only by stretching the bounds of the English tongue. Several were evidently boys; seven had limbs missing; one seemed to be quite blind. A good dozen were clearly well past their fiftieth birthdays, and one appeared to be at least eighty. Some scowled at me, for resentment of their situation and hatred of their chief captor must have boiled within them. Others looked about them in blind terror, and it was clear that they never seen a dockyard before – nor, perhaps, ships, nor even tidewater. Several were praying, though to what deity was unclear. Boatswain Pewsey ran his hands through his white hair and shook his head. My men, the likes of Lanherne, Macferran and Polzeath, walked up and down the ranks, frowning. Within a matter of a few weeks, perhaps even days, we were to face the most formidable opponents upon the oceans of the world, and we were to do so with a crew who would not even qualify as sturdy beggars. Still, it could have been worse, I reflected: the complements of many of the great ships had been made up with soldiers. At least this motley crew before me ought to contain at least a smattering of capable seamen.

'All those who have served in a ship of war before – raise your hands!' cried Martin Lanherne, the bullet-headed coxswain of the *Merhonour*.

No hands went up.

'All who have served at sea, then, in merchants' hulls or fishing craft – trows, barges – *anything* – raise your hands!'

Again, no hand rose from the throng.

'All right, Lanherne,' I said, 'you have flogged it enough, so we may conclude with some certainty that the horse is dead.' I stepped forward, for despite everything, these men were mine, I was their captain, and they needed to identify and respect the font of authority conveyed by my commission. 'Men!' I cried, endeavouring to look and sound formidable. 'Men of His Majesty's Ship, the *Merhonour*! My name is Matthew Quinton, captain of this ship upon this expedition against His Majesty's dire enemies, the Dutch! You should be proud –'

A few of the men began to talk to each other in low, quizzical tones. 'Silence!' cried Lanherne. 'Silence, there, for Captain Quinton!'

'You should be proud,' I continued, 'to serve aboard such a famous ship, a ship that has seen off this land's most implacable enemies, a ship –'

The hubbub did not subside; instead, it grew. Lanherne beat some men with his cane, but it made no difference. My heart sank. I had not even got them aboard the ship, and yet already I had a mutiny on my hands. My boatswain was on the verge of tears, looking out impotently over this rabble that he was meant to shape into an honest crew.

'Where did Pett say the draft came from?' asked Francis Gale.

'Western parts, the last places to send men in. Not Cornwall, that's for certain – Lanherne would know his own kind – but there were meant to be men from Cumberland and Westmorland, and yet others from Wales.'

'Ah,' said Francis, 'Wales. That will explain it, then.'

'Francis?'

'They can't understand a word you're saying, Captain. And Cumberland men being able to understand Lanherne's Cornish lilt? Unlikely, I'd reckon.'

'God's teeth,' I groaned, 'and this is the King of England's navy?'

The chatter grew louder, and Lanherne, never usually a man lost for words nor for a means of convincing others of his authority, looked at me in desperation. I had nowhere I could look, other than upon the rabble before me. My prospects of gaining glory in battle, or even of fulfilling my mission to prevent treason in the fleet, were evaporating before my eyes.

I glimpsed two familiar forms approaching from the direction of Commissioner Pett's house and the dockyard gate. One was the black Virginian Julian Carvell, the other his bosom friend John Treninnick, the bent, shambling Cornishman who, like my new crewmen, could not speak a word of English. Between them was a stocky young lad of perhaps fourteen, distinguished by the reddest cheeks I ever saw upon a boy. He looked familiar, but I could not quite place him.

Then the strangest thing occurred. Treninnick suddenly stopped and stood stock still, apparently listening to the chatter from the mob in front of me. His face suddenly broke into the broadest of smiles – a truly terrifying sight, for he was one of the ugliest men I ever knew – and he ran forward, gabbling furiously. Several of the nearest men of the draft grinned, jabbered at him, and embraced him in their arms.

'Lanherne!' I cried. 'What in the Lord's name is happening here?'

The coxswain smiled. 'The Welsh, sir! They can understand Treninnick, and he can understand them! The Welsh and Cornish tongues are but two sides of the same coin, after all. I can pick up some of the words, but it's too fast for me – not for Treninnick, though!'

I exchanged relieved glances with Francis Gale.

'Then get him to translate, man!'

Thus Lanherne translated my words into the rudimentary Cornish that he knew, and Treninnick converted them into a more fluent version that was evidently intelligible to the Welsh. It transpired that in turn, several of those from north Wales spoke a dialect not dissimilar to that of the men of Cumberland, and were able to translate to them. The question of who had served in a king's ship before was asked again, this time in a tongue that the men could understand; now a score of hands were raised. Another two dozen or so had served at sea in some capacity, or else upon the river trade of the Severn. Thus half the draft used the sea, and barely fifty were entirely landsmen; it could have been worse, I reflected, albeit not by very much.

In one respect, the sudden emergence of a conduit for conveying my words to the Welsh and vice-versa only made matters worse. Treninnick's enlightenment of the monoglots as to their new status, as crewmen of His Majesty's ship the *Merhonour*, exacerbated the resentment that seemed to simmer in the ranks; especially, I noted, among those gathered almost as a phalanx around one short, swarthy creature with a great grey beard, such as had been fashionable at court in the late King James's time. I sensed at once that this man, whoever he was, might bring us troubles. Treninnick would need to discover more about him and act as my conduit to and from the Welsh, in which case...

'Mister Lanherne!' I cried. 'Tell Treninnick to thank them for me, and to tell them that I will be honoured to serve with them. And I think we will need to promote Treninnick to be a petty officer – a quartermaster's mate, perhaps – so that he may be our interpreter to and from these brave lads!'

The news of Treninnick's promotion was cheered by his old and a few of his new shipmates alike, although I suspected that I had just appointed the only officer in the English navy who could not speak a word of its tongue.

At last, I turned to Julian Carvell and the florid lad beside him. 'Well, Carvell, what is this that you've found?'

'He was lost in the town, sir. Claimed to be seeking the *Merhonour*, although his way of finding it seemed to involve searching every alehouse in Rochester.'

I studied the lad: he had a look and a smell of the bottle about him. 'I've met you somewhere, boy. Before you had the cherry cheeks, I think.'

'Rushell,' slurred the lad. 'Edward Russell. Lord Bedford's nephew.'

A recollection came back to me: Christmas two winters before, and a call of duty upon the Earl of Bedford and his family at Woburn. There had been a sullen, orphaned little brat... 'Edward Russell,' I said. 'I promised to take you to sea with me, when you were old enough.'

The lad swayed a little. 'Uncle wrote to the duke. Of York. Got permission. Should have written to you, too.'

Carvell boxed his head. 'Should have written to you, too, *sir.*'

I sighed. 'Very well, then, young Cherry Cheeks. Perchance you'll have your head taken off by a cannon-shot before the month's out, or else the drink will kill you in much the same space of time. Carvell, get him aboard and get him sober. I suppose we'll have to find some sort of a decent berth for him. Can't have the Earl of Bedford's nephew in a common hammock –'

At that moment, the dockyard bell began to ring. The men's breakfast time was long past, and there were still some hours before the bell for dinner, which could mean but one thing. An alarm. As one, Francis and I ran toward the commissioner's house, on the hill above the yard. Commissioner Pett stood at the centre of a frenzy of activity, despatching men hither and thither. We could see the dockyard gate being closed, turning the walled yard into a fortress.

'Mister Pett!' I cried. 'What is the alarm, sir?'

Peter Pett was a thin-faced, sharp-nosed man with grey bags under his eyes. 'Spies, Captain Quinton! Spies have been arrested in Rochester! Their accomplices might already be in the dockyard. I have ordered patrols – they might intend to fire the yard.'

Having witnessed a fire in a royal dockyard not so very long before, I knew all too well how terrible a calamity it could be. Concentrate incalculable amounts of wood, tar, pitch and gunpowder in one place and then ignite it. Old Fawkes would have thought it a very paradise.

'They are Dutch spies, then?' demanded Francis.

'Undoubtedly, Reverend, though they pretend to be other.'

'What other?'

'One French and one English. But it's known that the Dutchman is a devil who employs many disguises – the French are their friends and enough Englishmen still admire their accursed republic.' This was rich coming from Pett, one of those who had served England's version of a republic with some distinction. 'What is more, Captain Quinton, the good men of Rochester are convinced that these are the villains who blew up the *London*. I fear there will be a lynching before the magistrates have an opportunity to impose order.'

I relaxed. The *Merhonour*, safe in midstream, now had ample men aboard to ensure her own security, and Pett's men ought to be able to secure the yard. What transpired in Rochester was none of my concern, even if it eventually transpired that two innocent men were hanged by a hysterical mob; such things were common enough, for after all, this was England. Thus I made my compliments to Commissioner Pett and intimated that I would return to my ship.

'Very well, Captain Quinton,' said Pett, 'guard the *Merhonour* well, sir – the last ship that my great-great-grandfather built, that she was.' The Petts were a veritable dynasty upon the Thames and Medway; indeed, this Pett was accused at regular intervals of filling every available dockyard post with his sons, nephews, cousins, uncles and so forth. It was even said that the dockyard cats were Petts.

As I turned to leave, Pett said, almost to himself, 'The sheer brazenness of these French, though! The one they have arrested even pretends himself to be a count of France, and yet to have served in our navy –'

I looked at Francis Gale. He looked at me.

Within minutes, and overriding Pett's despairing protests, the great gate of Chatham yard was flung open by the gang of Merhonours who had commandeered it. Through it, on two hastily requisitioned horses, galloped the captain and chaplain of that great ship, riding in fury for the gates of Rochester.

* * *

The hanging party was already on the high, ruinous, grey curtain wall of Rochester Castle, securing the noosed ropes to the battlements. The battered ruin of a vast square keep rose to the sky behind them.

Beneath, a baying mob of several hundred cried out against the Dutch, the French, the Pope, the King of Spain, the Holy Roman Emperor, and – most commonly and most violently of all – against the Earl of Clarendon. Francis and I spurred on our horses, for we now recognised the two men who were just having the nooses put round their necks atop the curtain wall.

'Stop this!' I cried. 'In the name of the king, I order you to desist! I am Quinton, captain of the *Merhonour*, brother to the Earl of Ravensden, *and I command you to stop*!'

Even as we rode into the mob, I could see that my words were having no effect.

The thunder of a pistol going off very close to my right ear made my horse rear in fright, and I had the very devil of a struggle to bring him under control. As I did so, I realised that the pistol had been fired by Francis, who was now riding through the mob, berating them furiously.

'You murdering Kentish whoresons! You apostates! You foul ignorant turd-chewers! May Satan and all his imps drag you down to Hell and boil you in blazing oil for all eternity! I excommunicate you in the name of the Lord Archbishop of Canterbury and all the bishops assembled in Convocation! You hapless bastards! You beshitten beggars! I call down the wrath of God upon you and all your posterity until the day of judgement!'

The sight and sound of a clergyman in his cassock, wielding one still-loaded pistol, swearing like a trooper and riding up and down amongst them – thereby, of course, breaking up the tight bonds of the mob, diminishing its collective will – confused and hushed the men and women of Rochester. On the curtain wall, those surrounding the suspected spies looked down, and at each other, and wondered what to do.

I sensed my moment, and seized it. 'The French gentleman there,' I cried, 'is the most noble lord Roger, Comte d'Andelys, and what he has told you is true – he did indeed serve in our own navy, aye, and as a mere sailmaker's mate at that!' That drew some gasps and not a few appreciative nods from the people of that maritime town; they might have been even more appreciative had I explained to them that his presence incognito aboard my ship was not unconnected to a precipitate flight from France, thereby escaping the wrath of the very great man whose wife he had seduced. 'He saved my life. And on another occasion, so did that other young gentleman yonder. That's Christopher Farrell, my friends, and at this very time you can find his mother and brother up at the Slaughtered Lamb in Wapping. He's as loyal an Englishman as any of you. His father fought for this country in the last Dutch war. And yet you seek to hang him as a spy? Shame on you, people of Rochester!'

The mob was silent now, confused and shame-faced. Those upon the rampart sheepishly withdrew the nooses from the necks of my two friends. Within a quarter-hour, we were safe within the cathedral close, beneath the shadow of England's second oldest cathedral and making free with the house of a sympathetic prebend. Kit Farrell was restored to good cheer quickly enough, hanging or the prospect of hanging being an everyday hazard of life for any denizen of Wapping; he was soon engaged in a good-humoured conversation with his old shipmate Francis Gale. However, it took a considerable amount of the prebend's passable Oporto wine to calm the nerves of Roger-Louis de la Gaillard-Herblay, seventeenth Comte d'Andelys.

'English hospitality!' he cried. 'Aha, they cry, we have a Frenchman amongst us, ergo he must be a spy, ergo we must hang him! What a country! *Mon dieu*, why do I have such a liking for it?'

There had been rather more in the same vein. To divert my old friend, I asked, 'But what is it that brings you to England, Roger? And to Rochester? You sent no notice of your coming.'

'Did I not? I swear I wrote. But I expect the mail was in a hull arrested by one of your English frigates. Or perhaps I forgot to write after all.' Greedily, he drank another glass of Oporto. 'I came with the embassy, Matthew, which rests incognito at Canterbury as we speak. Not as one of the ambassadors, of course, but in their train. I took a fancy to serving at sea this summer. With you, *naturellement*. The former captain of the Most Christian King's ship *Le Téméraire* might be of some use to you in the battle to come, perhaps? So if you are willing, *mon ami*, I shall sail with you in the capacity of a volunteer.'

This was truly brazen! 'A *volunteer*? King Louis has an alliance with the Dutch, Roger. If this embassy fails, as all men expect it to, then we will almost certainly be at war with France as well as Holland.' He shrugged. Realisation came to me at last. 'Damnation, Roger, the good folk of Rochester were right! You *are* a spy!'

The Comte d'Andelys creased his lips in a way that only the French can manage. 'Spy is such an uncouth word, Matthew. And besides, I think King Charles is no fool. Is there not merit in having a French observer or two in your fleet, to report directly to King Louis upon its overwhelming power and thus to convince the Most Christian not to make war upon England at any cost? You should look upon me as a peacemaker, Captain Quinton.'

The audacity of it all still overwhelmed me, but the logic was not to be denied. King Louis was known to be reluctant to declare war upon his cousin at the behest of a swamp-full of heretical republican shopkeepers, and was seeking any excuse he could to avoid his treaty obligations. By choice, he would have preferred England to make peace with the Dutch; hence the great embassy to which Roger had attached himself. The total victory of one side over the other was most certainly not in the Most Christian King's interests, as such a victor might prove a potent threat to his own ambitions. But if the war was to continue – and the hearts of king, Parliament and most true Englishmen were then set upon it – Roger's reasoning that a show of force might give King Louis pause for thought seemed unarguable. Consequently I raised my glass, and the Comte d'Andelys, Kit Farrell and Francis Gale all toasted good success to the voyage of the *Merhonour*.

'Now, my friends,' said the comte, 'I understand that our ship is not actually likely to sail for some days – not all her stores are in, and there is then the matter of towing her all the way down the river to the Nore – that is so, I think?' I smiled and nodded: *yes, you really are a spy, Roger*! 'That being so, I propose that the captain of the *Merhonour* and his goodwife accompany me to the formal state reception for the ambassadors of France.' I bowed, not only for myself but for Cornelia; she had seethed when she learned that my sailing was likely to prevent our attendance at the great event. 'And, of course,' said Roger, 'I would be honoured if the lieutenant of the *Merhonour* joined us.'

'Giffard?' I cried. 'But the man is an oaf –'

Kit Farrell grinned more broadly than I had ever seen him. 'Not the first lieutenant, Captain. The second. Your recommendation bore fruit. I have been commissioned!'

These splendid tidings led to another round of toasting and back-slapping, although inwardly, I felt more than a little perplexed. I had no expectation whatsoever of my solicitation on Kit's behalf bearing fruit; it had been simply a means of getting his name entered upon the Lord High Admiral's book of candidates for office. A bluff young tarpaulin, recommended by a relatively junior captain, surely had no prospect of gaining a commission at a time when every great man (and woman) of the court was pushing the interests of some worthless relation or protégé. If the young sot Edward Russell had been but three or four years older, there was little doubt that he would have been second lieutenant of the *Merhonour* or some other ship.

That question could wait for another day, I decided. In the meantime, there was a somewhat more urgent issue to consider. 'Well then, Lieu-tenant Farrell,' I said to him privately when Roger and Francis turned to converse with each other, 'it seems I must be your teacher again.'

'Sir?' When Kit Farrell saved me from drowning some years earlier, we made a mutual pact that he would teach me the ways of the sea in return for me teaching him to read and write.

'A lieutenant is at once an officer and a gentleman, Kit. You are now a step closer to the divine than you were in your previous posts, as a mere master and a boatswain,' I said with mock solemnity. 'Thus you will need to learn how to behave as a gentleman – though God knows, some of our noblest lords seem to spend a lifetime trying to do that, and failing.' A most delicious thought occurred to me. 'And of course, few gentlemen will ever have had to learn so much in so short a time, for few ever make their very first outing in society in such a manner as you will, Kit. After all, my friend, you don't want to disgrace yourself before the ambassadors of France, most of our royal court, and the King and Queen of Great Britain, do you?'

* * *

'Very well, Gloag,' said the man known as Lord Percival from his accustomed position in the shadow where the basement's single candle could not illuminate him, 'let me see if I understand you. By your own admission, you traded with the gunner of the *London* for four barrels of the king's own powder. In return, you supplied him with old powder, some of it with barely incorporated grough saltpetre.'

'Aye,' growled the Scot, reluctantly. It was difficult for him to say anything else with Phineas Musk standing menacingly behind him. 'No law agin' it.'

(I have edited Musk's narrative even more substantially than usual at this point, excising his lengthy and particularly vitriolic discourse upon the manifest iniquities of the Scottish race during the entire course of its history from Indulf the Aggressor by way of the Bruce and the Wallace to end with the miserable figure of this Gloag.)

'On the contrary, Gloag,' said the concealed Lord Percival, mildly, 'there might be no laws against it in your country, but there are most certainly laws against it in England. Many of them.'

'Many of them,' Musk repeated, directly into the Scot's ear. 'Same king. Different laws. Different countries, Gloag.'

'But I am not concerned with the legality or otherwise of your dealings in this instance.' Percival pushed a paper across the table, the only piece of furniture in the cellar apart from the stools on which he and Gloag sat. 'You have signed this deposition to the effect that you had no dealings with Dutchmen or Englishmen alike to bring about an explosion aboard the *London*. You implicate the gunner of the *London*, who undoubtedly sought to turn a private profit by substituting inferior powder for that assigned to the ship by the Master of the Ordnance, which you then resold at Gravesend to a Dutch factor masquerading as a neutral Lübecker. From this, we cannot deduce with any certainty the cause of the destruction of the *London*, but it is probable that carelessness in the mixing of powders contributed to that sad eventuality. Would that be the burden of it, Gloag?'

'Aye,' said the gross, nervous creature. 'If you say so.'

'Good. That is sufficient, I think. And of course, your admission of treasonable intercourse with the Dutch in time of war would be enough to put a rope around your neck at any time, should I be so minded.' It was impossible to see Percival's face, but Musk knew full well that it would be smiling. 'Remember this, Gloag, and tell all the others of your kind who feed off the embezzlement of His Majesty's naval stores. There will be no more trading with England's enemies. Nothing will be done that diminishes our prospects of victory in this war. And if I hear even a whisper of you engaging again in these old tricks, I will ensure that this deposition comes before His Majesty's Privy Council. They tell me the prisons are particularly sickly these days, Gloag.'

With that, Lord Percival raised his right hand. Gloag hastened out of the cellar, not casting a backward glance.

'Scum,' Musk said.

'Just so. But his evidence is reliable, I think. Bad powder, on a ship with only a few officers aboard, thronged with women and swamped by drink, as the depositions we have taken from the survivors prove… As perfect a recipe for disaster as one could ever concoct, I fear. Thus we can conclude with some certainty that the *London* was not destroyed by some hellish conspiracy, Musk – rather, by the indiscipline of her crew and the greed of one of her officers.'

'Both common enough failings aboard king's ships, My Lord.'

'You have considerably greater experience of that world than I do, Musk. Which, of course, is why I needed your assistance for this enquiry into treason in the fleet.' Lord Percival stood, drawing his neckerchief closely around his mouth, pulling his broad-brimmed hat down upon his head and closing his old-fashioned cloak in front of him. 'Tomorrow, Musk, I think we shall resume our enquiries into the activities of Harvey's conventicle in Barking. A surprising number of sea-officers seem inclined to frequent it, and we have been led to believe that Eden the ostler was a member of it. Our friend Sutcliffe seems convinced that if this plot of twenty captains has any substance, the proof of it is most likely to be found there.'

'Yes, My Lord. But if I may – upon our other matter?'

Lord Percival looked up sharply. The parallel enquiry upon which they were engaged touched both the honour of an ancient lineage and the interests of the king himself; it was a matter at once both delicate and intricate. 'Yes, Musk?'

'I have thought of a way of getting what we need from Anderson, if he truly does hold the records he is said to possess. But it would require the assistance of another.'

Musk mentioned a name. He heard a noncommittal grunt from his shadowy companion. 'If you must. But in God's name, Musk, ensure that she does not complicate matters.'

* * *

Musk and the cloaked figure of Lord Percival left by an alley, emerging finally into the warren of streets behind Saint Botolph's, Aldgate. They turned a corner and almost fell over a miserable, shuffling creature, bent almost double as he painted upon a door. The creature grunted in alarm and fled. The light was poor, and it took Musk a moment to make out the result of the creature's handiwork: a blood-red cross above the words *God have mercy upon us*. He could hear the faint but unmistakeable sounds of people within, several of them evidently children, all sobbing piteously.

Musk said, 'Plague house. The season's starting early, My Lord.'

Lord Percival looked up and sniffed the air. 'Too early. Far too early. And it should never start here in the outskirts and work inward. The worst plague summers always begin that way. Let's away, Musk, before we breathe in the contagion.'

Chapter Nine

Auspicious prince! at whose nativity
Some royal planet rul'd the southern sky;
Thy longing countries' darling and desire,
Their cloudy pillar, and their guardian fire,
Their second Moses, whose extended wand
Divides the seas and shows the promis'd land...
~ John Dryden, *Absalom and Achitophel* (1681)

An unseasonably warm spring evening. The weather seemed to have taken its cue from the comet, and had gone within days from some of the bitterest cold ever known in England to this strange, sultry balminess. The approach to the great white banqueting house of Whitehall Palace was lined with blazing torches. Down the avenue thus created came the great, the good and the (rather more numerous) not-so-good of the court of Charles the Second: among them, a somewhat mismatched party of four. Of these, Matthew and Cornelia Quinton would have passed readily as courtiers. I had purchased a fine new blue velvet coat with some of the proceeds of my cruise in the *Seraph*, and Cornelia had spent rather more of those proceeds upon a billowing saffron dress of satin, adorned with pearls at her bosom, a conscious reproof to her tedious parents and the gloomy Calvinism they had attempted to foist upon her childhood self. Meantime, preparing Lieutenant Christopher Farrell, at our side, for his first court reception, had presented a considerable challenge. His only coat was an ancient buff affair with tar-stains on the sleeves and holes in the elbows. Some hasty remedial work by Mary Barcock, our servant, had converted my third-best coat into something that approximately fitted my rather fuller and shorter friend, but Kit was evidently deeply uncomfortable in it, constantly fidgeting with the unfamiliar lace cuffs and with his sword, also one of my mine, which hung awkwardly from his baldric and constantly struck his calves.

Fortunately, few would have spared even a moment to contemplate Kit, or even Cornelia and myself: for all eyes were upon the spectacle that walked beside us. The seventeenth comte d'Andelys had brought with him what he considered to be a light travelling wardrobe, two cartloads of it, and from this he had produced an astonishing long white coat and matching waistcoat with ruffled breeches.

'Far too ostentatious, of course,' said Roger as we approached Whitehall, 'even for Fontainebleau, but you English expect we French to dress like demented peacocks. One must not disappoint.'

As we entered the Banqueting House, Kit looked about in awe. For a rough young seaman from Wapping, this must have been the greatest spectacle he had witnessed in his entire life, an experience far beyond his wildest dreams. The high, rectangular space of the hall was lit by a thousand candles, many set high up to illuminate Rubens' glorious ceiling portraying the apotheosis of Charles Stuart's grand-father, King James. Courtiers milled around, bowing, laughing and drinking, creating a ceaseless hubbub of conversation. Women curt-sied deeply to great lords, displaying ample acres of white flesh and fanning themselves against the heat. Yet for all the surface bonhomie, the atmosphere was markedly less carefree than usual. The first glance of a courtier is always laden with suspicion: will you prove a rival to me? Will you seduce my woman? But that night, men and women eyed each other even more keenly. Was that bead of sweat upon one's brow merely a natural response to the heat, or the first symptom of the plague? Was that slight cough issuing from Lady So-and-So's throat in fact the harbinger of doom for us all?

Of course, there was another great unspoken concern. This was the very heart of a realm at war, and signs of it were everywhere. Even the oldest and least martial lord had found it necessary to dust down his ancient scabbard and baldrick, and to strut about the room as though he were an English Cid about to repel the rampaging Dutch hoards. And here in that very heart were all the great men and women of England, save those who had already gone down to the fleet. I pointed them out to Kit. There, the bulky and self-satisfied Duke of Albemarle, that General Monck who had restored the king, surrounded by a coterie of young blades. Away to his right, My Lord Arlington, deep in conversation with Sir William Coventry. Suddenly Arlington's eyes caught mine. He must have pointed me out to Coventry, who also turned and stared at me. Then they resumed their discourse, and I prayed they were not concocting some further amusements for me.

'Great God, Captain,' gasped Kit, 'is that not Lady Castlemaine?'

His glance indicated a slender, black-haired beauty about the same age as Kit and myself, with a wide mouth and sleepy eyes, attired in a ravishing and exceptionally low-cut blue robe. She was surrounded by a circle of young gallants, each competing with the others to impress and amuse the king's principal mistress.

'The very same,' said Cornelia. 'The one with whom the king lay, the first night he was back in England. And he has rarely been away from her bed since.' I thought of the words of the Countess Louise: *Of course, it is possible that by the time he reaches me he is exhausted from his bouts with Barbara Castlemaine – they say the bitch is insatiable.* The recollection brought back a pang of guilt, for I had not told Cornelia of my encounter with my good-sister. I had not told anyone.

'She is younger than I had pictured,' Roger observed, 'and thinner. Too thin for my own king, but one can see why yours is smitten.'

'And there,' said Cornelia to Kit and Roger, her eyes indicating a haughty but plain, red-cheeked, black-haired woman in glorious blue draperies, 'is the Duchess of York. Next to her father.'

'Ah,' said Roger, 'so that is your famous Comte de Clarendon, then! The chief minister of England. Well, well. A mean figure, to have so much power – he looks like a mere country gentleman. But then, that is what he was, no? And so fat! *Mon dieu*, he must eat his beef straight from the carcass. We French prefer our chief ministers to look the part. To be cardinals, preferably. Scarlet robes could turn even such a feeble creature as Mazarin into a colossus.'

Cornelia nudged me. Her glance indicated the unmistakeable shape of the my good-sister approaching the Duchess of York and then curtsying deeply before her. A vision clad in pink satin, the Countess Louise was escorted by young Harry Brouncker. At once they fell into an animated conversation with the wife of the heir, perhaps the future Queen of England. My heart sank. Etiquette demanded that at some point during the course of the evening, Cornelia and I would have to pay our respects to my good-sister. And what if that good-sister then deliberately or inadvertently revealed to my wife the meeting that I had concealed from her?

Fortunately, the assembly was then too crowded for us to cross the room, and my thoughts were able to return briefly to rather less alarming concerns. By now, our little group was quite the focus of attention for some of those in our immediate vicinity. Word had spread that the magnificent gentleman in white was a French milord, and even if he was not actually a part of the embassy, he was clearly a man of influence and considerable wealth. It would also not have required too many enquiries for any lady with a mind to it to discover that the glamorous Comte d'Andelys was as yet unmarried. Soon, he had drawn around him quite a little circle of simpering young ladies and, in some cases, their mothers. And when some of the simperers learned that Lieutenant Farrell, at his side, was a true tarpaulin, a bluff low-born mariner – and thus, according to common myth among a certain sort of woman, an inveterate ravisher – well, he, too, quickly attracted his own following of heaving décolletages, much to his embarrassment. I felt for Kit: a consummate master of his trade at sea, here he was the proverbial fish out of water.

Cornelia observed the proceedings with detached amusement. She had long become accustomed to the fact that at court, the happily married are largely invisible, as disregarded as lunatics or the dead. She also seemed not to be affected by the glances and whispers directed at her, but I distinctly heard the word 'Dutch' muttered among some of the more ignorant, chattering women, and saw the scowls of disapproval aimed in her direction.

The dreadful threat to English national security scanned the wider scene once again. 'A poor turnout, husband,' said Cornelia reflectively. 'So many of the best men already in the fleet – the Duke of York and the prince, Buckingham and Monmouth, Buckhurst just gone down to join them... The court is stripped of its finest, and many of the ladies look quite bereft.'

'Just so, my dear, but perhaps it is better thus. Fewer jealousies, less faction. These occasions have lately become nothing more than theatres of bickering and intrigue.'

We were approached by a familiar couple, and as the duty to their rank demanded, we bowed and curtsied. Kit took his cue from me and bowed, but he was unfamiliar both with the action and with his scabbard, which swung up suddenly behind him, almost striking the Marchioness of Worcester who stood a few feet behind us. Hastily I introduced Lieutenant Farrell of the *Merhonour* to Lord and Lady Mordaunt, our Bedfordshire neighbours and old friends of the family.

Mordaunt was a well built man of my brother's age, with a pronounced chin and thick black eyebrows. 'Quinton,' he said. 'Mistress Quinton. Good to see you can still bring the odd Hollander out in public and not be stoned by the mob – that's England for you, after all, tolerant to a fault, even when we're at war with the bloody country.' Mordaunt sniffed self-importantly. 'Glad to hear you've got a command at last, Quinton. Think I'll take a turn at sea this summer, too – precious little else for me to do these days. And I must have a word with you about getting a by-blow of mine onto a ship as a captain's servant. Need to find some sort of gainful employ for the worthless little runt. You've not got a place for him or me on your ship, I suppose?'

John, the Viscount Mordaunt of Avalon. Any man who takes his title from a romantic myth, publicly insults another man's wife and discusses his bastards in the presence of his own tells you all you need to know about him. This noble lord was brother to the Earl of Peterborough, with whom our family had many dealings; indeed, when both of our estates were at a low ebb in Cromwell's time, my mother loaned Phineas Musk to the Mordaunts, whose own steward had been arrested for conspiracy. John Mordaunt was a great man in his day. One of the most active Royalist agents in Cromwell's England, he built up a formidable intelligence network and worked tirelessly to bring about a restoration of the monarchy. But when that day finally dawned, it came at the behest of Cromwell's own lieutenants, not through the efforts of Mordaunt and his kind, my brother among them. Always obstreperous, the increasingly ineffectual Mordaunt sank into a slough of bitterness. He reserved most of his bile for the Lord General Monck, Duke of Albemarle, who had garnered all the titles and esteem that Mordaunt felt should have belonged to him. Thus when he and his wife left us, they took care to give a wide berth to the large circle of admirers and sycophants that surrounded His Grace.

Kit was looking about in unfeigned delight. 'All these great lords and ladies!' he exclaimed. He had been given a momentary respite by young ladies in quest of ravishing. 'A Farrell in the palace of Whitehall, indeed.' He let out a satisfied sigh. 'If my old father could only see me now, Captain!'

I smiled. Christopher Farrell had evidently absorbed the shock of encountering this astonishing new world of wonders into which I had thrust him, and was finding it increasingly to his liking.

'Perhaps he would have hated you for it, Kit, for was he not a Parliament man? But look, all you have yet seen is about to pale. The sun rises, Kit Farrell, though it be evening, for Majesty is among us.'

A flourish from the trumpeters in the gallery above hushed the crowd. All eyes turned to the door, and to the tall man and tiny woman who stood there. Charles and Catherine, King and Queen of England, both stared directly ahead, then began to walk slowly across the hall. A wave of bows and curtsies accompanied their progress. Kit, Cornelia and I made our obeisance; so, too, did Roger, after the more flamboyant French manner. But Charles Stuart, an aloof vision in cloth-of-gold, did not see us, or affected not to, and I felt a pang of profound guilt that my own disfavour might have damned both my wife and my friends. For the king sometimes exchanged a little nod or a smile with a particularly favoured personage: Charles even bowed his head slightly to Albemarle, king acknowledging kingmaker, and smiled broadly at Clarendon, thus dashing the hopes of the many present who wished to see the Chancellor brought down. As for the poor childless queen, she maintained the icy stillness of Iberian court etiquette, not moving her head at all, resembling a statue. Only once did her eyes seem to move and her lips crease into a fleeting scowl, and that was when she passed the Countess of Castlemaine.

The king and queen stepped onto the raised dais beneath the red canopy bearing the royal arms, sat on their two thrones, and at once the reception resumed its noisy course. It was hard to believe that not far beyond these walls, legions of malcontents were contending with a relentless pestilence to see which of them could overthrow the order represented in that room at that moment. Such, at least, was undoubtedly how Lord Arlington saw it; and to my discomfort, every time I glanced in the direction of that insidious figure, he seemed to be staring directly at me.

Eventually the Quintons could no longer avoid their duty, and made their way across the floor to pay our respects to the Countess of Ravensden. Louise had her back to us as we approached, but I thought I heard – or had I imagined it? – her words to the duchess and Brouncker: '...so we agree that all should be done to preserve him, come what may –'

Brouncker seemed to assent but then noticed my approach, placed his hand on the countess's arm and nodded toward us. She turned, smiling radiantly.

I bowed. 'Your Royal Highness. My Lady Ravensden. Mister Brouncker.'

Cornelia curtsied deeply to the Duchess, pointedly averting her eyes from the Countess Louise and her self-confessed paramour, Brouncker. The chubby face of the erstwhile Anne Hyde smiled graciously. 'Captain Quinton,' she said, 'Mistress Quinton. You are not yet gone down to join my husband's fleet, sir?'

'The ship was fitted out late, Madam. But I ache to be at sea under His Royal Highness's command, and to play my part in his inevitable victory against our nation's enemies.'

(Then, I could still utter such sentiments in the presence of royalty and even half-believe them. No longer.)

'Matthew, how unfeeling!' said Louise. 'Poor Cornelia, to have her homeland denigrated so!' My wife was between Scylla and Charybdis: she was perfectly reconciled to the notion of war between her country and mine, but she could hardly launch one of her habitual colourful verbal retorts against our countess in the presence of the heir to the throne's wife. Louise continued, 'Dearest Cornelia, in due course I must invite you and our dear good-mother to come and stay with me at Lyndbury. The country air will be so much healthier for you than London now that the plague takes hold, and you will not have to suffer the barbs of ignorant folk who denounce you on account of the land of your birth.'

Cornelia was rarely speechless; now, she was flabbergasted. 'I … I thank you, My Lady,' she said, her true feelings constrained once again by the presence of royalty. Brouncker's expression of distaste suggested that he did not concur with his lover's tolerance.

'I, too, intend to join the fleet,' said Brouncker loftily. 'Of course, I shall have a place aboard the flagship, alongside His Royal Highness' – a nod and a smile for the Duchess of York – 'and pray that my sword will find gainful employ against the enemy.'

'I am sure, sir, that your presence will be an adornment to the fleet,' I said as sarcastically as I could. Brouncker and Mordaunt, Buckingham and Buckhurst, and several score more of them, all cluttering our great ships… God alone knew what would become of them, and of England, if the Dutch got close enough to engage such august sprigs of nobility in hand-to-hand combat.

There was an awkward silence. I got the distinct impression that all three of them wished us gone so that they could resume whatever scheming they were about; and in truth, I was glad to make my bow and depart before my good-sister could raise the uncomfortable subject of our recent conversation, thus forcing me to confess its existence to my wife.

'To stay with *her*!' gasped Cornelia as we returned to our friends. 'In the castle she obtained by murdering her husband! *God in hemel*, I think I would rather suffer the plague!'

'Perhaps we all shall,' I said, sniffing the increasingly rancid air. 'England's finest begin to stink, my dear, and stench and sweat have ever been known to expedite the pestilence. Perhaps it is all a cunning

French plot – gather all our rulers in one room and keep them wait-ing so long for the Most Christian's ambassadors that contagion takes hold and wipes them all out.'

Indeed, more and more eyes were glancing ever more frequently toward the great doors at the Charing Cross end of the Banquet-ing House; doors which resolutely failed to open. More and more half-overheard conversations seemed to contain the word 'French', preceded by such terms as 'tardy', 'ignorant', or 'fucking'.

At length, even the Comte d'Andelys joined the general humour. 'My countrymen are unduly late,' he said in annoyance. 'I expect the oaf Verneuil has been asleep again.'

'Verneuil?' I enquired.

'The nominal head of our embassy – the Duc de Verneuil. One of the many bastards of Henri Quatre, which of course makes him a sort of uncle to your king. He will be a useful reminder to Charles Stuart of the most obvious tendency he has inherited from his French grandfather, and thus of the consequences of his indiscriminate bed-ding of Castlemaine and all the rest. The little by-blows all grow up, and have to be given titles, and incomes, and estates, and wives, and so on. Damnably expensive business, bastardy.' Roger cast another appreciative eye over the lithe form of the king's mistress. 'Like so many of our *noblesse de France*, and no doubt like the products of your king's loins, the great *duc* is decorative but wholly useless. Take him hunting by day, pour wine into him by night, and he will consider the embassy to have been a great success. His august presence will also divert attention from the other ambassador, Courtin – now he's the man who'll do all the work. Hard-nosed little cur. Parisian lawyer, the sort who'd convince you his mother was the Tsar of Muscovy if the fee was right.' Roger stifled a yawn. 'Ah, at last. Behold, France comes, bringing peace and harmony in its wake – as long as you do what King Louis wants, of course, else we shall rape your women and pillage your land relentlessly.'

Another flourish of trumpets heralded the entrance of the French embassy – and a surprise that drew gasps from several in the throng. For the Duc de Verneuil did not stand alone in the doorway of the Banqueting House. At his side was a minute woman, well into her fifties, clad entirely in black, her garb of choice these last fifteen years. No-one had ever expected to see the tiny woman – Verneuil's half-sister – here, in this building of all the buildings in England; for it was on a scaffold outside one of its windows that her husband's head was cut off. But it was known that she was about to leave England forever to return to her native France, there to face only death and interment with her ancestors in the vault of Saint Denis. Perhaps at last the time had come to close the most terrible chapter in the history of Henrietta Maria, Queen Mother of England.

As sister and brother advanced into the hall, their respective retinues fell in behind them; and now it was my turn to feel the sudden frisson of shock and confusion that Charles Stuart must have felt a moment earlier.

For at the head of Henrietta Maria's train was her old friend and closest confidante during her earliest days in England.

My mother.

* * *

The Banqueting House was ever hotter, ever more fevered. Rivulets of sweat ran down the necks of embarrassed ladies; men mopped their brows continuously and cursed the new fashion for periwigs. Fevered in another sense, too, for such occasions were ever the stage for rumours to be traded, liaisons to be made and plots to be hatched. As our little party circulated slowly through the crowded, noisy room, paying respects to and exchanging pleasantries with Sir This and Milady That, it was possible to conceive all sorts of fancies concerning what might or might not be going on around us. Lord Arlington was engaged in a close, secretive conversation with Lady Castlemaine: what confidences about our sovereign lord might they be exchanging, pray? And there was our own Countess of Ravensden, now deep in discourse with the French ambassador, Courtin. Roger had been precise in his description of the man, who differed physically from Arlington in almost every way and yet somehow gave off the same aura of power and menace. My eyes kept straying in that direction, towards the Lady Louise and her paymaster, and as I watched, I noticed something strange indeed. My good-sister had always appeared to me as confident, even arrogant; indeed, that was how she had been such a short time before, during our brief audience with the Duchess of York. Yet whatever the Frenchman was saying to her was having a marked effect upon the Countess of Ravensden. Her unheard responses to Courtin's words seemed ever more urgent. Her eyes darted toward the king, then toward me, although she seemed to stare through me as though I were invisible. Her expression, usually so serene, so controlled, was imploring and fearful.

Consumed entirely by my attention to the countess and the French ambassador, I missed the fact that all those around me were suddenly hushed. Cornelia nudged me, and I turned abruptly –

To look down.

And then down again.

Cornelia was already deep into her curtsey, Roger and Kit both bowing, as were all the men around us. For directly in front of me was the tiny, raven-like form of Queen Henrietta Maria, my mother by her side.

Belatedly, I bowed.

'Matthew,' the Queen Mother said in her heavy French accent, extending her hand for me to kiss it, 'it has been too long since I saw you last. Your mother tells me you have become quite the seaman.'

'I – I endeavour to serve His Majesty,' I stammered in French. My mother scowled reprovingly; Quintons should answer royalty with confidence, she often opined, for were we not noble when they were merely butlers to some obscure Scots chieftain?

'Your loyalty is commendable indeed, Captain, especially as I am told my son is deeply offended with you.' The minute face was inscrutable. 'But if kings forsake thee, queens shall not. I remember and honour the sacrifice of your father in the cause of my late husband. Above all, I still treasure the words you spoke to me at our last meeting, Matthew, and I will not forget that kindness. Be assured of it.'

'Your Majesty is most kind.'

My thoughts ran back to my previous meeting with the Queen Mother, some three years before, late at night in the ornate and eerie Catholic chapel she had installed in Somerset House: the last vestige of an ancient faith in England, and the faith to which a doting French grandmother had once attempted to convert the young Matthew Quinton. There, illuminated by only a very few candles and in an atmosphere heavy with incense, she had asked me to describe the death of General Colin Campbell of Glenrannoch, whom I had encountered during my expedition to suppress rebellion in the Western Isles of Scotland; the same Campbell whose doings now seemed to be of interest to my good-sister, the Countess Louise.

'I was not close by, Majesty. The castle was blown up by gunpowder while he was within.' I had said what I thought she would wish to hear: 'He must have died at once. There can have been little suffering.'

She had shaken her head. 'A good death in one sense,' she replied. 'But not in another. Colin should have perished in glory on a battlefield, as did your own noble father, not killed by some skulking assassin and a slow fuse.' She sighed. 'But you came to know him, Matthew? And ... did he speak of the time after my first coming to England?'

This was dangerous ground – the most dangerous of all. 'He ... he endeavoured to explain why he had been banished from the court, Majesty. For being – for being –' *For being your lover, Majesty*; but one cannot say such things to the divinely anointed.

The Queen Mother saw my dilemma. Her expression was curious; an admixture of grief and elation. 'I understand, Matthew. And your mother? He talked of her part in those days?'

'Not – not directly, Majesty.'

I do not know if she believed me; I suspect that she did not. But I remember her next words as though she were standing next to me now, this tiny Frenchwoman who had seen and made so much of England's tragic recent history. 'It is best forgotten, Matthew. All of it. We were all young, and the young think they know so much. But in truth, we were merely slaves to boundless folly. And folly has a habit of returning year upon year to revisit those who perpetrate it. Ah, poor Matthew. I pray that you, who are young now, do not have cause to regret the folly of those who were young then.'

Thus had spoken this tiny, extraordinary woman. Three years later at the Banqueting House, her attention had turned from me to her compatriot the Comte d'Andelys, who was lavishing upon her the sort of extravagant flatteries that are considered acceptable by our Gallic cousins. At length she turned back to me, inclining her little head towards Kit as she did so.

'Matthew, pray name this splendid young warrior to me.'

'Majesty, I name Christopher Farrell, second lieutenant of the king's ship *Merhonour* in the present expedition. I owe Lieutenant Farrell my life.'

'Indeed? Then we, too, are grateful to you, Lieutenant.' The Queen Mother extended her dainty hand. Kit, flummoxed at being in the presence of the nearly divine, stooped and kissed it clumsily. Then Henrietta Maria looked at me curiously. 'Tell me, Matthew – I take it your current disfavour with my son means that this brave young man has not been presented?'

'Alas not, Majesty.' The consequences for others of my gross lèse-majesté were a burden I did not bear lightly.

The Queen Mother looked knowingly at my mother, then at me.

'Then that is an omission we shall remedy immediately. Come, Lieutenant – *I* shall present you to my son, the king.'

I thought for a moment that Kit Farrell, as brave and phlegmatic a man as ever lived, was about to faint. But as he collected himself and essayed some mumbled thanks, I became aware of movement to my right ... of the rustle of billowing satin, caught out of the corner of the eye...

Louise, Countess of Ravensden, was hastening towards us, perhaps calculating that if the Quintons were being favoured by Majesty then she, as the wife of the head of the family, should be at the heart of matters. Or perhaps her interest in the mysterious youthful follies to which the Queen Mother had alluded gave her quite another reason for seeking the royal presence. But before she could reach us, Henrietta Maria frowned.

'*Ah, une autre prostituée de mon fils,*' she murmured to my mother, and promptly turned upon her heel, gesturing to Kit to follow her as she made her way toward her son's throne.

Thus rumped in the most public fashion by the Queen Mother of England, Louise, Countess of Ravensden, stood before us: in a room filled with hundreds, a woman entirely alone. She fought back tears, her face a canvas of anger and humiliation. Aye, and of something more elusive, too, but present nonetheless. Deep in my good-sister's eyes was the wild desperation I had sometimes seen in the eyes of a deer at the denouement of a hunt.

Chapter Ten

To all you ladies now at land,
We men at sea indite;
But first would have you understand,
How hard it is to write;
The Muses now, and Neptune too,
We must implore to write to you.
With a fa, la, la, la, la.
~ Charles, Lord Buckhurst, *Song Written at Sea* (1665)

The tow-boats slipped their cables. The ten accursed miles of the winding Medway were done, the marshland and mudflats of Sheppey and Hoo fell away on either side, and ahead lay the sea. We had a light breeze from west by south. The clouds were low and grey, but seemed unlikely to bring rain. We had a light swell, the tide nearly upon the turn. Far ahead, the waterway of the Thames estuary was as busy as ever: four or five big, heavily laden Baltic traders were outward bound over toward the Essex shore, a veritable bevy of fishing craft and coasters thronged the approach to distant Leigh-on-Sea, while what appeared to be a big Indiaman was wearing ship proficiently in the Yantlet channel. Our ketch, the *Bachelor's Delight*, was off to larboard. Each of the great ships had its own tender, and this was ours, a trim little craft skippered by a cheerful Sussex man named Roberts, its name a constant reminder of marital conditions and thus of my recent leave-taking from an emotional Cornelia, who was at least half convinced that she would never see me again. Yet for all that, there was something else in Cornelia's mood, too, something I had never witnessed when setting out on my previous voyages: a sort of impatience, a sense that there was something else she wished to be about. Seeking some explanation for this, I even wondered whether she might be pregnant. Yet would she have concealed such a thing from a man who might be going forth to death in battle, never to see his child?

The *Merhonour* was already under topsails, but now her courses and topgallants fell, and as we passed Sheerness the great ship finally moved upon the sea again. The yards and shrouds sang as the sails strained in the breeze. Upon my command, our vast red ensign broke out at the stern and the matching pennants at the mastheads. White water began to spill from our cutwater as we picked up speed. Roger, Comte d'Andelys, stood a little ahead of me at the starboard rail, looking out toward the bleak ruins of Queenborough Castle. He was making notes in a little book, and I prayed to the Anglican God of the Quintons that if we were ever invaded by the unstoppable legions of Marshal Turenne, they did not make landfall on the hopelessly undefended Isle of Sheppey thanks to the intelligence gleaned by an illustrious member of the *noblesse d'epée* during a cruise aboard the *Merhonour.*

'Should make the Gunfleet by dusk, sir,' reported Yardley, the master; a thin, grey Kentish man who had served as a midshipman on this very ship in the year twenty-eight.

'Very well, Mister Yardley,' I said, a little testily. I was looking about me, and was aware that all was not as it should be. The sails were a little too loose, especially on the fore. There were too many slack braces and halyards, too many slovenly tackles and garnets, too many cables heaped untidily upon the deck. Too many men were standing around, staring aimlessly at their officers and at each other. There were scowls aplenty, and arms folded defiantly. I saw the bearded Welshman, whom I had noted upon the quayside at Chatham. He was staring at me. If I had been a man of superstitious bent, there aboard a ship allegedly cursed, I might have sworn that he was giving me the evil eye. I returned his stare with what I took to be my finest expression of aloof condescension. These are the 1660s, I thought to myself; such idle fancies have no sway in our times. But I felt a sudden chill, even though it was unseasonably humid.

Treninnick ran hither and thither, jabbering in Cornish, pointing at this capstan or that halyard, and occasionally shoved a man or two in the direction he had indicated. I could see Lanherne, far ahead on the forecastle, cudgelling a stout, hairy brute to make his point. Fatally, though, Pewsey – the officer who should have been dictating the discipline of the ship – stood amidships, occasionally gesticulating ineffectually but otherwise merely shaking his head impotently.

I had served long enough as a captain of king's ships, and had thus learned enough of the sea, to be somewhat alike a new pedagogue, suddenly deposited in front of a schoolroom of obstreperous boys. The pedagogue knows the theory of his subject well enough, and has sufficient awareness of his surroundings to realise that his words are having no effect and that he has no control of the class; but he does not yet have the faintest idea of how to regain that control.

With Giffard strutting upon the waist, bellowing orders ineffectually, and Yardley focused solely on the navigation of the ship, I summoned Lieutenant Christopher Farrell to the quarterdeck.

'Damnation, Kit,' I grumbled, 'it's like a rabble at a may fair! What is the matter with this crew?'

Kit was ever philosophical in the face of adversity. 'Any crew of a great ship takes time to come together, sir, and we've had far too little time to mould this one. We have a good, sturdy core of men in the Cornish and some of the drafts out of the river, it's true, but they're only a fraction of our complement.' He shook his head. 'Alas, Captain, we also have a share of landsmen who have no notion of what to do, and another share of pressed rogues who might have the notion but have no intention of doing it. Some of the Welsh, especially, though whether out of spite, fear of the curse or plain ignorance isn't easy to tell.' Kit grimaced; he was a man who liked being about solutions, not recounting problems. 'Despite all Treninnick's good work, he cannot be everywhere at once, so you have Welshmen all over the ship who can't understand a word of the commands they're given. Or claim they can't, at any rate.'

'Like the Bretons,' said Roger. 'Good seamen, but the very devil to command. If God had meant the Welsh and the Bretons to keep their incomprehensible tongues, *mes amis*, do you really think he would have allowed them to be conquered by the English and the French? I think not. It is unnatural. On *Le Téméraire*, I had them whipped if they spoke Breton. "French is the language of the angels, you miserable bastards," I told them, "so in the name of *le bon dieu, Saint Denis et la France*, you will damn well speak it if you want to keep the skin on your worthless stinking Breton backs." Amazing how quickly men can learn a new tongue when they have such an incentive before them.'

'Just so, My Lord,' said Kit, who was adjusting with some difficulty to granting due deference to this man who had once been a mere sailmaker's mate, and thus by many degrees his subordinate, during our previous voyage in the *Jupiter*. 'But even when Treninnick explains matters to them, our battle is not yet done. It seems the men of north Wales detest the men of south Wales and will not work with them, just as the men of Cumberland will not work with what they call a pack of addled Westmorland rogues. Then some of the Welsh will not work with men from the next valley or the next village, and some of the Cumbrians with the men from the next dale.'

'Will not work with!' I exclaimed. 'I am not concerned with their petty jealousies, Lieutenant! Damnation, this is a royal ship! Men work with men at their officers' command, or else it is mutiny!'

'Aye, sir. But surely it can only be mutiny if the men understand the commands in the first place, and in our case, we also have the problem that discipline among the men is – well, is entrusted to – begging your pardon, Captain…'

'Quite, Lieutenant. I take your point.' Kit was learning the discretion of the quarterdeck, namely that one did not denounce a fellow officer in public. He did not need to, of course: it was obvious to all that Boatswain Pewsey was about as effectual as wet gunpowder.

Kit returned to his station in the forecastle, and I went up onto the old-fashioned high poop deck at the very stern of the *Merhonour*, there to be alone with my thoughts. Of course, our problems were chiefly a consequence of our late setting out; most of the other great ships had been at sea for a month or more, and many of them had crews composed chiefly of volunteers from the maritime counties. Most also carried large drafts of soldiers, including some from the new-fangled Marine Regiment raised by the Lord Admiral. I had come to regret my prejudice against completing my crew with soldiers. A troop or two aboard the *Merhonour* would have been doubly useful: for one thing they could easily have cowed the recalcitrants, and for another, one of the first things I had learned in my naval service was that nothing unites mutually suspicious seamen better than the presence of the hated redcoats. Moreover, most of my fellow captains would also have had ample time to exchange any inept warrant officers for better ones; but that option was hardly available to me, for there were virtually no ships left in harbour with which to exchange an incompetent boatswain or an antediluvian carpenter. A raw and fractious crew, then, yet within weeks – perhaps even days – we would be in battle with the

Dutch, and perhaps with some of our own countrymen, too. I looked out across the mud-brown waters of the Nore anchorage toward the distant, flat shore of Essex, and offered up a silent prayer for the *Merhonour* and her captain.

* * *

In ante discessum…

As I contemplate the peculiar paper in my hand, I consider once again the sheer perversity of my uncle Tristram. Dear Lord, even all those long decades ago, in the year of grace 1665, *Englishmen did not make their depositions in Latin.* Well, none but one, at any rate. The same one who would leave it all to his nephew to translate. My pencil annotations are almost illegible now, except in the (many) places where my younger self struggled for the right word, or the right tense, and scored through abortive efforts with steadily mounting degrees of frustration. But I can reconstruct enough of it to establish the sense, albeit by indulging myself a little in the art of Defoe, so inexplicably popular in this fanciful new century. So, then:

The Tudor quadrangle of Gresham's college on Bishopsgate was an appropriately august home for the new Royal Society, and it was here, as the *Merhonour* made her painfully slow way to the fleet, that Doctor Tristram Quinton concluded his demonstration of the Florentine poison.

'Thus let us observe the effects upon the creatures employed in our experiment,' said Tristram in his fluent Latin. 'I would suggest that the hen gives every appearance of being drunk.' The august Fellows contemplated the bird staggering around the stage and nodded sagely to each other. 'The dog has vomited, but seems otherwise unaffected.' A miserable-looking cur glanced up at Quinton and retched another gut-full of black bile onto the flagstones. 'Whereas the cat is evidently dead.' Lord Brouncker, chairing the meeting as the society's president, prodded the erstwhile creature with his foot and bowed his head in concurrence. 'Thus, honoured Fellows, I believe I have demonstrated conclusively that the Florentine poison, named after the mysterious substance recently presented to His Majesty by the Grand Duke Cosimo, is misnamed. Not unnaturally, and given the reputation of that illustrious city as a den of poisoners, I think we all expected this to be the most lethal substance ever known to man. However, I believe I have demonstrated beyond all doubt that this Florentine poison is nothing more than a distilled oil of tobacco, and as my experiments today have shown, it is therefore unlikely to kill anything larger than a cat.'

Tristram bowed his head slightly in conclusion, and was rewarded with half-hearted applause from his peers. Mister Pepys, some sort of connection of his nephew in the navy, was enthusiastic in his approbation, but Tristram recalled that Pepys's knowledge of science was as substantial as his own of the language of Mongolia. Still, at least Pepys had laughed at the drunken chicken. Then Tris overheard Boyle's soft Irish lilt make an exaggerated stage whisper: 'Merciful heaven, two hours to kill a cat ... but tell me, Wren, how's that theatre of yours in Oxford coming along?'

Tristram made to accost Boyle, whom he disliked (both too godly and too chymical for the Master of Mauleverer's taste). Moreover, he had been made particularly peevish by an unexpected and unwelcome recent visitation to his master's lodgings in Oxford by his good-niece the Countess Louise, who seemed to have developed a suspiciously detailed knowledge of, and interest in, some of the more arcane and secret recesses of the Quinton family history. Perhaps fortunately, Tristram's passage toward Boyle was prevented by the timely intervention of Brouncker, who offered his profuse congratulations upon Tristram's most splendid contribution to the advancement of human knowledge, etcetera, etcetera. By the time he had freed himself from the noble lord, relatively few of the Fellows were left. Fortunately, one of these was his old friend Sir William Petty, sad-eyed and increasingly ruddy in the nose, a man whose range of interests was almost as catholic as Tristram's own.

'Good evening, Doctor Quinton,' he said. 'Interesting lecture, but I'd laid a bet with old Digby that the dog would die. Damnably disappointing.'

'Good evening, Sir William,' said Tris. 'Ah well, sir, I condole you upon your loss. But I'd wager my outcome was less disappointing than the fate of your own *Experiment*!' The Master of Mauleverer laughed heartily and clapped his friend on the back.

Petty took that in good spirit, although between anyone other than friends, the jest would have been mortifying. Sir William's several weeks of seagoing experience as a fourteen-year-old cabin boy had unaccountably convinced him that he was the ideal man to design an entirely new kind of ship, especially at a time when a war was approaching and commissions for any kind of new secret weapon were likely to prove exceptionally lucrative. Regrettably Petty's double-hulled ship, the *Experiment,* had capsized in Dublin Bay; but like Tristram Quinton, he was not a man to be abashed by such trivial setbacks.

The two old friends took to talking, and as is ever the way between men of a certain age and older, they soon fell to discussing the illnesses and deaths of those they knew, and then of those whom they did not.

'The mortality rates are troubling so early in the year, particularly in Saint Giles-in-the-Fields,' said Petty gloomily.

'Mortality rates!' Tristram scoffed. 'Not worth the paper they're printed on, Will. Meaningless numbers. Every man knows that half or more of plague cases never get recorded as such – who wants their houses shut up for all those weeks? And the constables and the aldermen connive in it, of course, so that their wards and parishes don't lose trade.'

'Quite, Tristram,' said Petty. 'But therefore, and by your own logic, the *true* incidence of plague must be especially troubling, it being still so early in the season. Yet here we are, the Royal Society, allegedly the finest minds in all of England, and are we putting all our efforts into finding a remedy for the plague? No, we are not! We are –'

'Killing cats and getting hens drunk, Will?'

'Ah … umm … well, perhaps it might have been more revealing if you had tried the Florentine poison upon some poor soul afflicted with the plague.' Petty shrugged. 'But I suppose that would have meant bringing him among us, and we could hardly risk infecting this august body with the pestilence…'

The two friends were passing on to consider the possibility of dining together at a tavern in Wormwood Street when Tristram noticed a rude urchin enter the hall, look around him, settle his gaze upon Doctor Quinton, and evidently decide that the Master of Mauleverer's unique features matched a description that he had been given. He strode up, essayed a perfunctory nod of the head that might or not have been a gesture of respect and deference, and thrust a small, stained, yellow-brown piece of vellum towards Tris.

'A letter for you, Doctor Quinton,' said the boy. 'Directed here from Oxford, according to your instructions.'

With Petty and the boy watching him curiously, Tristram Quinton snatched the letter. It had been so long, and he had lost almost all hope of ever receiving a reply. And with the war, there was every chance that such a reply might have been intercepted by one of the Dutch capers, the small private men-of-war that were already infesting the mouth of the Channel.

Yet here it was; crumpled yet apparently unopened, it was in his hand, safe after its journey from the wilds of Hampshire County in the Commonwealth of Massachusetts, wherever or whatever that might be. The reply to a letter sent many months before in the slim hope that it would find its way to a man who did not wish to be found: one of those many men of God who, deprived of their parishes at the Restoration, had turned their backs on an England they believed to be irredeemably degenerate, instead seeking out distant wildernesses in which to plant the true word.

Tristram broke the seal and studied the words of the Reverend Tobias Moon, sometime vicar of Billringham in the county of Lincoln, who at the height of the civil war had married the local lord of the manor to a younger wife. A very much younger wife. A marriage which seemed to have been literally excised from the parish records.

Tristram read the missive twice over, and frowned.

'Bad news, Tris?' Petty enquired.

'Good or bad, I cannot yet say. But I think you may yet help me discover which, Will.'

'I? How so?'

'You are of Romsey in the county of Southampton, are you not?' Petty nodded. 'And Romsey is no great distance from Dorset, if I recall correctly from Blaeu's maps?' Another nod. 'Then tell me, Will, how I might learn more of the birth of a child in that county. The birth of a female child, in the year twenty-eight or twenty-nine.'

* * *

The afternoon grew murky as the *Merhonour* ploughed inelegantly through the seas, making her uncertain way east from the Buoy of the Nore, then north-east into the Swin. My officers grumbled that we were too leewardly, that if the wind strengthened we were in danger of being pushed onto the West Barrow or one of the other vast and perilous sandbanks that obstructed the broad mouth of the Thames. We were a great slug upon the oceans, complained Giffard; too old, too heavily gunned, too crank, too clumsily girdled, with masts that were too weak and ballast that was inadequately trenched. All that before one considered the not insignificant matter of our diverse crew. I nodded gravely, for even I was aware that we could hardly be described as a greyhound of the seas. My first command, the ill-fated *Happy*

Restoration, had been an ill-sailing brute, but I was then too ignorant of the sea to be very aware of her failings. My subsequent commands had been quite new Fourth- and Fifth-Rate frigates, relatively nimble and speedy. Standing upon the deck of the poor *Merhonour* was akin to being accustomed to riding Arabian stallions and suddenly being asked to mount a carthorse.

As we moved slowly up the Swin, we spied a vast collier fleet coming down the Middle Ground, the widest of all the passages into the Thames. Two or three hundred broad-hulled, deeply-laden craft, bearing the coals from Tyne, Tees and Wear that would keep London warm; perhaps more importantly with spring finally at hand, they would keep the capital's brewhouses at work, too. Escorting them was just one tiny ketch, all that the navy of England could spare for convoy. She saluted us, and her commander reported that the east coast was infested with enemy capers. They had been attacked off Flamborough, losing a half-dozen colliers, and again off the Spurn, losing four more. God be with you, *Merhonour*, he cried as he sailed on. And God be with you, too, I thought: God and the king, who has issued a blanket protection to the crews of the colliers, thereby preventing me doing what I very much desired, namely pressing there and then a cohort of veteran seamen to replace the rabble that presently comprised my crew. The vast fleet passed to starboard of us on the opposite tack, the collier-men's grins being reciprocated by scowls from the Merhonours at our starboard rail. They knew, just as the men on the colliers knew, that the latter would be earning at least twice as much as the king paid, for the manning of the navy meant that the colliers were desperate for men. Conversely, of course, the men of the navy were desperate to get out of it in order to join the colliers, and were deserting in their droves. Supply and demand, I believe it is called.

Once the last of the colliers had cleared us, I raised my telescope and swept it from east to west. We were well into the King's Channel now, with Maldon's river and the Essex shore to larboard. The low cloud and murk had parted a little, and at last I saw the sight I longed to see.

I sent a message below, requesting the comte d'Andelys and the Reverend Gale to join me. When they were present upon the quarter-deck, I pointed dead ahead.

'Behold, the navy of England,' I said to Roger. 'Tremble, Frenchman!'

My friend laughed with me, but the sight ahead of us was more than sufficient to make any foe tremble. Beyond the West Rocks and within the buoy of the Gunfleet, a great wooden town seemed to rise from the midst of the sea. Or rather three towns, each distinguished by the colours of the ensigns at their sterns: blue, nearest to us; white, furthest away; red, in the centre. At the very heart of the fleet lay a great ship, a vast three-deck First Rate, flying at the mizzen a plain red flag, at the fore the red flag with three golden anchors that signified the presence of the Lord High Admiral of England, and at the main the royal standard that signified the presence of a prince of the blood.

'The *Royal Charles*,' I said to Roger. 'The Duke of York's flagship. And see there, the blue ensign at the main? The mighty *Prince*, the colour signifying that she is Lord Sandwich's flagship. To the north, the *Royal James* and Prince Rupert's white squadron. One hundred ships, more or less. Twenty-five thousand men. The most terrible sight upon God's earth, My Lord.'

The comte d'Andelys whistled, and stared in silence at the ever-nearing multitude of ships. Roger was impressed, as I had intended. Although the King of France was building a great new navy as rapidly as he could cut down trees and shape them into hulls, he still had barely half of what lay ahead of us in the Gunfleet anchorage. God willing, this was the instrument that would shortly hammer the Dutch from the seas, bringing victory, eternal peace and an end to dissension in Charles the Second's England. Or else, if the dark tale related by Clarendon and Arlington was true, twenty of these ships would soon be the means by which Charles was swept from his throne, cavaliers like the Quintons would be condemned once more to exile or to death, and England would become yet again a mean, hypocritical, puritan republic, ruled by those who hate the very notion of joy.

As the *Merhonour* entered the serried ranks of the fleet, we fired off our salutes to the flags and were saluted in our turn. Timid souls ashore might have been forgiven for thinking that the great battle had begun; and in one sense, for Captain Matthew Quinton it had.

Chapter Eleven

A man so various that he seemed to be
Not one, but all mankind's epitome.
Stiff in opinions, always in the wrong;
Was everything by starts, and nothing long;
But, in the course of one revolving moon,
Was Chemist, Fiddler, Statesman and Buffoon...
~ John Dryden, *Absalom and Achitophel*
(of George Villiers, second Duke of Buckingham)

The great cabin of the *Royal Charles* was great indeed. A broad and lofty space was made light by a row of stern windows far larger than any I had seen, comfortably dwarfing those of the *Merhonour*. Through the glass, the navy of England lay at anchor, only the occasional ketch or victualler's hoy moving between the recumbent hulls riding the slight swell. Above our heads, the deck was adorned with a work of art almost as lavish as that upon the ceiling of the Banqueting House. Nereides, myrmidons, cherubim and the like surrounded a portrait of our sovereign lord the king, yet curiously His Majesty was shown standing upon what was unmistakeably the quarterdeck of this very vessel, a few feet above our heads. The artist was commemorating one memorable day, five years before. I remembered that day well, for Cornelia and I had witnessed it from the shore, having rushed from Veere to Scheveningen. The restored king being rowed out to a navy that was royal once again; the huzzahs of the sailors; the salute booming out from the guns of this very ship, then named *Naseby* after Cromwell's greatest victory – aye, and the battle in which my father had fallen – but which within the hour was rechristened *Royal Charles*. Cornelia and I had hugged for joy upon the beach, for the return of the king meant that England, with all its boundless possibilities for everlasting felicity, was open to us again.

The turning tide meant that the scene within the great cabin was warmed by a rising April sun. A council of war had been summoned, and as was the method in those times, this was confined to the flagmen and captains of the great ships, albeit with certain notable exceptions. Indeed, it was the first council of war I had attended in my life, and would prove to be by far the most memorable. The broad and sturdy oak table at which we sat was crowded with charts, ship-lists and the like. I sat next to Sir Will Berkeley, Rear-Admiral of the Red, whom I still counted a dear friend, despite the gnawing doubt that the words of Clarendon and Arlington had planted in my mind. The dour Earl of Marlborough sat on my other side and Sir John Lawson next to him; all in all, a line of titled dignity that I envied not a little. Further down the table the well-fed Earl of Sandwich, Admiral of the Blue (our rear squadron), was engaged in a lively discussion about the late comet with his subordinate flagmen, the sad-eyed Ayscue and the jovial Teddiman, who sported an inordinately wide *moustachio* after the Dutch fashion. Across from them sat Myngs and Sansum, Vice- and Rear-Admiral of the White, arguing on some point to do with the ordnance favoured by the Dutch. I cast more than an occasional glance in their direction. Like all the flagmen of the Blue, Myngs and Sansum had been Commonwealth's men, promoted by Cromwell; indeed, the aquiline Myngs was something of a legend for all the havoc he had wreaked upon the Spaniards in the Carribee. But as I contemplated them, and considered the number of erstwhile servants of the late Lord Protector in that cabin, I felt myself shudder. For if some or all of these men really were about to transfer their allegiance once more, what hope did my few cavalier friends and I have of preventing the outcome?

My Lord of Marlborough, captain of the venerable *Old James*, said, 'Good to see you here, Quinton. Knew your father, of course – fought with him briefly in the west in forty-three. Good man. Great loss.' He was something of an oddity among our nobility, this earl; impoverished in lands but serious, mathematical and inclined to the sea from an early age, he had travelled more widely than most of his kind and had but lately commanded the expedition sent east to take possession of Bombay, part of the dowry that accompanied our barren Queen Catherine. History has forgotten him, unlike that self-promoting mountebank Churchill who later took his title, but I know which of the two Marlboroughs I preferred. 'An auspicious assembly,' he said. 'Men with a proven record of thrashing the Dutch allied to some of the noblest blood in these isles. Royal blood, come to that. The hogen-mogens should be shitting themselves, Quinton, for the seas have never seen the like before.'

I nodded, and studied the royal blood that was already among us. Prince Rupert of the Rhine, Admiral of the White, sat at the starboard head of the table, reading over some papers. The incongruous little spectacles perched upon his ugly hook nose gave him the appearance of an eccentric professor, but this belied his ferocious reputation. I was told once that there were still people in Bolton who believed Rupert to be the devil incarnate following the depredations he wreaked upon that miserable place during the civil war, when he had been the most successful but also the most vicious general for the royal cause.

I had reason to share their opinion, for my family blamed the prince's vainglorious manoeuvres at Naseby for the loss of my father's life. It was telling that Rupert had acknowledged every other officer in that room with at least a courteous nod, but he studiously avoided my eyes.

That left one member of the council only: by far the youngest, and also the only one who was not a flag officer or a captain. It was quite impossible to mistake the paternity of this handsome sixteen-year-old youth. The thick black eyebrows, the cleft chin, the sparkling eyes were all the same, but the lad had a straighter nose and altogether a more pleasing face than his father. He was evidently not overawed by being in the presence of all these august seamen and mighty admirals; far from it. He looked about him with an air of magisterial superiority fit for a future king. And perhaps, deep in his heart, that was already how James Scott, Duke of Monmouth, saw himself.

'Well, Matt,' said Will Berkeley, 'who would have thought it, eh? You and me, the new Drake and – well, the new Matthew Quinton, I suppose. I expect your grandfather must have attended countless of these occasions.'

'I cannot imagine he would have had much patience with them,' I said. 'And at least you and I agree better than he and Drake ever did.'

My friend smiled. I looked upon that bluff, open face, so much older than its years (for he was only a few months older than I), and inwardly, I prayed yet again that Arlington's suspicions were misplaced. I had known Rear-Admiral Sir William Berkeley for so long. If he was a traitor, then the very foundations of what I took to be true were shaken.

The door of the cabin opened, and we all stood as one, bowing to the man who strode purposefully to the table and took his place at the head of it. James, Duke of York, was then thirty-two years old. As tall as his brother and with an equally prominent nose, albeit somewhat thinner and straighter than the kingly snout, the duke undoubtedly had the physical presence appropriate to a royal prince. He was the only man in the cabin already clad in a breastplate. He walked in a measured, stately way. His every expression, his every gesture, conveyed gravity. Consciously or unconsciously, he had become very different to his witty, cynical elder brother; and in those early days of the restored Stuarts, many preferred this prince, who seemed more open, more predictable, more straightforward. How different things would be twenty years later, when the long, stern face of James Stuart was imprinted on the coins of the realm.

Behind him hobbled Sir William Penn, the Great Captain Commander. This was a new creation in our navy's history; indeed, to this day Penn remains the only man ever to have held the rank. His appointment to it solved an impossible mathematical conundrum. In 1665, there were five great men qualified to command the fleet or individual squadrons, and expecting to do so; yet there could be only three squadrons. Rupert and Sandwich were given two of them. The fact that the senior squadron, the Red, was given to the heir to the throne at once rendered the equation workable; the Duke of Albemarle could be ensconced in London as acting head of the Admiralty, and thus with no loss of status or honour, while Penn could be appointed to this new-fangled rank and placed in the Duke of York's own ship, for no matter how proud our seamen were that the heir presumptive to England was commanding them, none could deny the troubling truth that the duke had never previously commanded anything more than a yacht, let alone a fleet of a hundred ships. Thus Penn would be the power behind the floating throne, the aquatic *eminence grise*, call him what you will. The fact that this unpopular, unprepossessing, gout-crippled creature would be the true overlord of the fleet concerned not a few, but I had my own very private cause for disquiet at the presence of the Great Captain Commander. For was not he, too, a sometime Commonwealth's-man, formerly one of Cromwell's generals-at-sea?

The duke took his place and bade us to sit. Penn slumped down beside him in relief, and at once elevated his swollen foot. 'Your

Highness, Your Grace, My Lords and gentlemen,' said the duke, 'I greet you all.' He looked around the table and acknowledged each man in turn; Matthew Quinton was greeted with a perfunctory nod. 'What we are upon,' he said, in his measured, formal way, 'is the business of England. Our country's honour and glory lie in our hands. God willing, the issue of this summer's campaign will be a complete victory for His Majesty's arms over the perfidious Dutch. And God willing, we will show to the world the full power of His Majesty's navy royal –'

There seemed to be some sort of commotion beyond the bulkhead. Raised voices could be heard. The cabin door opened. Framed within it was a stocky figure of a man, weak-chinned and tired-eyed, lavishly dressed and sporting a vast periwig that stretched down to his chest.

'Your Grace,' said York. 'You are, perchance, a little lost?'

George Villiers, second Duke of Buckingham, bowed. 'Your Royal Highness. No, sir. I merely seek admission to this esteemed council, as is my undoubted right. I presume that my invitation to join your deliberations was – misplaced, perhaps?'

There was a murmur around the table, but the Duke of York ignored it: he continued to stare directly at Buckingham. 'You are mistaken, Your Grace. There was no invitation. Membership of this council is confined to the flagmen of the fleet and the captains of the great ships.'

This was a barb. All of us present in the cabin knew that Buckingham had demanded the command of a great ship; like Beau Harris, he argued that commands should be given to cavaliers regardless of whether they knew the sea or not. But the king had dismissed his boon companion's pretensions, and Buckingham's resentment had continued to smoulder beneath the surface. Until now.

'With respect, Your Royal Highness,' said Buckingham, with more restraint than he was usually wont to display, 'it has always been the case that the greatest nobility of England are entitled to a place in such councils. It is our role, sir. Consider our very title, you and I – duke, *dux*, a leader in war.'

York was unperturbed, although we all knew how much he detested Buckingham, a close ally of Lord Arlington and thus an inveterate opponent of York's father-in-law Clarendon. 'That may be true of armies, Your Grace, but it is not the custom of the navy. I defer to those with rather longer experience of the sea than my own – My Lord of Marlborough, for instance.'

Marlborough nodded in concurrence; he, too, had no time for the Duke of Buckingham, whom he later described to me as merely the spoilt runt of a king's catamite. 'If that be true, Your Royal Highness,' said Buckingham, whose cheeks were reddening, 'then may I ask why His Grace of Monmouth, who has no flag and commands no ship, is present at this council?'

Before York could answer, Monmouth himself intervened, albeit at the price of a reproving frown from his uncle. 'Why, Your Grace,' said the young man in his pleasant voice, 'I sit here by special dispensation, that I may better learn the arts of war prior to making them my trade. A special dispensation provided by my father, the king.'

Buckingham scowled; no doubt he was thinking that the eldest of Charles Stuart's bastards was unduly indulged by his doting father. 'But I can offer much to these counsels, Your Royal Highness!' he protested. 'My father was Lord High Admiral of England – my father commanded great fleets –'

'Your Grace,' said York levelly, 'you are not your father.'

Buckingham bridled, and the temper that he had barely held in check for so long finally exploded. 'In the name of God, sir!' he cried. 'I am the Duke of Buckingham! Buckingham, do you hear? I demand my right!'

York's face was stern and humourless: very much its ordinary condition. 'Your Grace has many rights,' he said, 'and many virtues. But for you to sit upon this council, sir, would run counter to all the customs of the navy since time immemorial. And I, as the *present* Lord High Admiral of England, must uphold those customs in the name of His Majesty the King, my brother.'

Buckingham's eyes darted hither and thither in desperation. They appealed to Prince Rupert, to no avail. They even settled briefly upon me. Finally, though, even the great duke had to admit defeat. Without another word, he turned on his heel and left the cabin.

York watched him go; still he did not smile. 'So, gentlemen,' he said. 'To business.'

* * *

The council of war proceeded to discuss a variety of matters, the most pressing of which was the rampant desertion from the fleet. We lamented the disloyalty of the local authorities, from constables and tithingmen even to the very lords lieutenant, who either turned a blind eye or actively abetted the runaways. Leave was to be stopped, even for volunteers, we decreed, and the Privy Council written to for an order to the mayors and magistrates; but it would do little good, Marlborough whispered, for this had been the way of our English sea-affairs since time immemorial. Then we proceeded to digest the latest reports from our scouts, one of which was Beau Harris's *House of Nassau*. The Dutch fleet was still within the Texel anchorage, waiting for the ships from the outlying admiralties. All concurred that this was most excellent news, for it meant that the Dutch would have less preparatory time at sea than ourselves. Then there was the equally pleasing intelligence from Lord Arlington's office, namely that as ever, the Dutch were consumed by jealousies between their seven provinces and five separate admiralties, veritably a body politic concocted by Old Nick. Consequently, they had managed to end up with no fewer than twenty-one flagmen, a revelation that prompted much jesting among us about cooks spoiling broth and the like. Evertsen, Admiral of Zeeland, detested Tromp, Admiral of Holland, and vice-versa; both detested Wassanaer of Obdam, the land general placed above them, who was in any case even more crippled by the gout than our own Great Captain Commander. Not even De Witt, Grand Pensionary of Holland and seemingly the only force capable of holding together the ramshackle edifice of the Dutch state, could bring his admirals to love each other. Best of all, by far the most able Dutch commander, de Ruyter, had not yet returned from the coast of Africa. The prospects seemed auspicious indeed, and Marlborough whispered to me that perhaps the comet had foretold disaster for Holland, not for England, God's chosen plot.

The Duke of York looked about him. 'Now, gentlemen,' he said gravely, 'let us not assume from all this that the Dutch will be merely lambs to the slaughter. Sir William, if you will, please explain how we plan to bring the slaughter to the lambs.'

Penn straightened in his chair, a move that caused him no little pain as he adjusted the position of his foot. 'Your Royal Highness speaks aptly,' he said in his soft Bristol accent. 'Those of us who fought in the last war against the Dutch know all too well what formidable foes they are.' The likes of Lawson, Myngs and Ayscue nodded vigorously. 'And it was for that very reason that we had to devise a new way of beating them.' He shifted his leg again, and winced. 'For the first months of the war, as some here present will recall, we fought as we and the Dutch had always fought, division against division, ship against ship, each side charging abreast at the other like knights of old. And the Dutch are masters of that art, for they bested us time and again. So in the spring of fifty-three we sat down together, Blake, Monck, Deane and I. We discussed what we could do to overcome the Dutch. Now, they were all army men, who had fought for Parliament during – begging your pardon, Your Royal Highness – the sad wars in our country. They had fought in sieges, both from the inside and the outside. Thus they knew the potential of artillery, if best use could be made of it.' Penn winced again. 'So we conceived a notion of placing the entire fleet into one great line; aye, a line of battle, divided into three squadrons, Red, White, and Blue. A vast wall of ships, gentlemen, in which almost every gun in our broadsides could bear upon the enemy. Over four thousand guns, firing over a hundred thousand pounds of metal at once – the most fearsome blast in all of history. In the next two battles, we trounced the Dutch, for they had no answer to our line of battle. Their ships have ever been smaller and lighter than ours, and the damage we wrought upon them was most dreadful to behold.'

The Duke of York nodded gravely. 'Thus by my order, gentlemen, we will employ the line of battle as our tactic of choice during the campaign to come. Once we put to sea, we will practice the evolutions of forming our line, maintaining it through such manoeuvres as tacking, reversing it – yes, Your Highness?'

Prince Rupert had clearly been growing impatient during Penn's exposition, and now he began drumming his fingers upon the table. 'It is un-English, this line of battle of yours,' he said in his strong Rhineland accent. 'We should go at the enemy ship-on-ship. Battle at sea should be like a cavalry charge, honourable and inexorable, where the sheer force of the gallop –' The prince was looking around the table, trying to turn others to his point of view, and at that moment his eyes finally settled upon me. In that one, fleeting second, he and I both saw the magnificent, inexorable charge of his own cavalry at Naseby, sweeping all before it; and then riding off the field in search of plunder, leaving my father to die and the Duke of York's father to lose his crown and his head. I do not know what expression was upon my face, but I saw Rupert's change. He halted in mid-sentence, looked back at the Duke, and said quietly 'But if it is the will of Your Royal Highness and of the majority of this council that we fight in line, then so be it.'

'Never witnessed that before,' said Marlborough later, as the council was breaking up. 'His Highness taking up a position and then retreating from it so quickly, that is. And remember, I saw the prince at councils of war twenty years ago, when he was captain-general of the king's army, so I know him well. The most forthright man in defence of an opinion one could ever find, even if that opinion was pig-headed and wrong, as it often was. Perhaps he is getting old. As am I, indeed. Our day is nearly done, I think; it is the time for you young men now, Matthew Quinton.'

I did not tell Marlborough the true cause of the prince's retreat.

* * *

The council came to a conclusion, and after we had been issued with copies of his new fighting instructions, the duke dismissed us. Prince Rupert left the cabin at once, evidently in a vile humour. I spoke briefly with Will Berkeley and we tentatively arranged dinner aboard his *Swiftsure* with Beau Harris, newly come in from his scouting mission upon the coast of Holland. As we were on the point of leaving the cabin the duke said, 'Oh, Captain Quinton. I would have you inform me of the condition of the *Merhonour* and her crew, if you please.'

I excused myself from Will, and turned once more to face the heir to the throne. We were now alone in that cabin, which suddenly seemed a more claustrophobic place. I have observed that princes have a peculiar way of filling any space that they occupy; that is, unless they belong to the present House of Guelph, alias Wettin, alias Hanover, in which case they seem to fill less space than a fly in a cathedral.

York bade me sit, and I occupied the Duke of Monmouth's old place, directly across the table from him. 'So, Matthew,' he said, 'I understand my brother is still displeased with you.'

This was not what I had expected, and I felt myself flush. 'Y – your Royal Highness...'

The duke's upper lip bent slightly; I had known him long enough to understand that this was the closest James Stuart ever came to a smile. 'It is not a matter of concern to me, Captain. His Majesty's affairs are his own. All of his affairs, if you understand me.' And that, in turn, was the closest that James Stuart came to a joke. 'Whereas you and I, Matthew Quinton, have more pressing concerns – above all, this business of the treachery suspected among the captains of this fleet.'

'Yes, Your Royal Highness. As you say.'

'Do you believe it?' The question was abrupt, but he did not permit me the time to answer. 'I do not believe it. Lawson, Sansum, Myngs, all the rest of them – I know these men, Quinton. I have commissioned them, I have talked with them. Yes, they were infected with the contagion of the late times, but I am confident that makes them less likely to be infected with it now.' The duke fixed me with a firm stare. 'However, My Lord of Arlington persuades me that a prudent man guards against all eventualities.' York spoke the name of Arlington with evident distaste. 'He and his agents ashore are making every effort to uncover a plot, if one truly exists. He also tells me that I should make more of the cavalier captains here in the fleet, the likes of Marlborough, Holmes and Allin, privy to this intelligence, for even if my *Royal Charles* and your ancient *Merhonour* stand together, what hope will we have against twenty revolted captains and all of Obdam's fleet? But I will not do so, Matthew. Now, why is that, do you think?'

I was unaccustomed to having princes ask me to explain their thinking back to them, and stammered in pursuit of the right words. 'W – why, Highness, it may be – that is, it could be the case that making more men privy to the secret would make it more likely to be revealed. And – and let us say that the intelligence of this plot proves groundless. Might not needlessly sowing suspicion among our captains weaken their resolve to fight? If they are half-expecting treachery in the ships around them, might they not fight the Dutch less wholeheartedly? Thus we might be defeated by the very existence of the rumour, rather than by any truth in it.'

James Stuart looked at me curiously. 'Bravo, Matthew Quinton!' he exclaimed. 'Men who can comprehend the thoughts of princes so perceptively ought to become ministers to them. Perhaps one day you will be a new Wolsey or Clarendon. Not, I trust, a new Arlington.' There was no love lost between the Duke and the Secretary, essentially because James knew full well that Arlington's dearest ambition was to bring down his father-in-law. Although I dared not state it, I also suspected that this might have had not a little to do with the Duke's dismissal of the notion of a conspiracy among the captains; if that notion originated with Arlington, James would be instinctively disinclined to accept it.

I mumbled some gratitude for the royal praise, but James was dismissive. 'This is our secret, Matthew Quinton. You and I, together with those few whom I trust aboard this ship.' The duke stood, thereby compelling me to do the same, and walked to the stern windows of the *Royal Charles*, looking out over his fleet. 'It is a sad truth that we live in times when Englishmen do not trust other Englishmen. Let us pray that once the cannon come to roar, we shall all find that trust again.'

Chapter Twelve

Good people draw near,
If a ballad you'll hear,
Which will teach you the right way of thriving.
Ne'er trouble your heads
With your books or your beads
Now the world's rul'd by cheating and swiving.
~ Anonymous poem, c.1660s, from a manuscript
at the Bodleian Library, Oxford

Barkstead Parva was a substantial stone house with lofty brick chimneys, pleasantly situated in one of the comparatively rare fertile valleys of Surrey, that miserable desert of a county. A rough heath rose behind it, but the house and its trim little garden would have had ample sun in summer. A pleasant spot; but one that was about to be made most unpleasant indeed.

The steward of Barkstead Parva, a stunted, unsmiling old retainer, announced Sir Venner and Lady Garvey, and admitted into the hallway a small, round man in an ill-fitting periwig and his much younger wife.

Much, much younger, as Deodatus Anderson must have observed at once. And pleasantly pert, with clean brown hair arranged in immaculate ringlets. And elegantly attired in a grey riding-coat with petticoats visible beneath. And, surprisingly, Dutch.

It was fortunate indeed that, as both Phineas Musk and Lord Percival had suspected, Anderson knew the name and, more pertinently, the reputation of Sir Venner Garvey, good-brother to both the Earl of Ravensden and Captain Quinton, sometime councillor to the late Lord Protector, Member of Parliament and one of the most considerable and active men within that illustrious institution; fortunate, too, that Anderson had never actually seen or met the gentleman in question.

'Sir Venner,' said Anderson, a bent, decaying man in his sixties. 'My Lady Garvey. May I present my wife?' A fat woman who might have been beautiful for a few years to either side of 1630 curtsied clumsily. Anderson gestured them through to his parlour, a decent, plain room overlooking the wilderness that is Surrey. 'We are most honoured by your presence in this, our humble dwelling. Most honoured and, if I may say, intrigued at the cause of it?'

Rather relishing the part of Venner Garvey, whom he detested, Musk looked around the substantial modern manor, doubtless erected in place of some perfectly good old English farmhouse that had been torn down to make way, and decided that humble was certainly not the word he would apply to it. (His text, which I have again abridged somewhat, here digresses into a lengthy tirade against such excessive show.) As he sat upon a markedly uncomfortable chair, he also wondered once more at the means by which Anderson had come to be able to fund such a display of humility.

'I will be direct, sir,' said Musk, affecting a Yorkshire accent in imitation of Sir Venner's. (His account suggests that his impersonation was impeccable; I, who often heard it, conceive that it must have been unutterably dreadful.) 'We seek to acquire a property in this vicinity, for those occasions when sessions of Parliament or other business bring me south. Lady Garvey finds that the air of the city does not agree with her, you see.' Keeping up her impersonation of my sister Elizabeth, Cornelia smiled wanly. 'Your name was recommended to me by – well, let us say a mutual friend. He intimated that you would be the man to recommend suitable properties, even if you were not prepared to part with this most delightful seat of yours.'

Anderson took the bait. 'Quite so, Sir Venner.' He looked a trifle embarrassed. 'If it is not an indelicate question, sir, might I ask what price you had in mind for the property you might wish to purchase?'

At that moment, Cornelia leaned over and whispered in Musk's ear. 'Ah. Yes, my dear. Of course. Mister Anderson, might it be possible for my wife to lie down for a brief time? The journey has tired her, and –'

'My monthly pains are especially troublesome,' said Cornelia, bluntly; such coarseness would have been unthinkable in an English-woman, of course, but the Dutch were curious creatures and all kinds of strange behaviour could be expected of them. Musk exchanged a glance of fellow-feeling with Anderson, whose wife rose at once and fussed concernedly over Cornelia, leading her off to the stairs in the corner of the room.

'Lady Garvey will benefit from the rest,' said Musk, 'so there will be no reason for you to remain with her, Mistress. In fact, it is important to me that I discuss certain matters jointly with yourself and your husband.'

Both Anderson and his wife looked at him perplexedly, but neither raised an objection; Sir Venner Garvey was known to be one of the most eminent members of Parliament, a man with powerful connections both at court and in the City, and if he wished to speak to the Andersons together, who were they to quibble? As his wife led Cornelia upstairs, Anderson remembered his duties as a host and summoned his steward to fetch some refreshment for his illustrious guest. He apologised to Musk for the fact that the house was understaffed, the cook, the maid and the parlour-boy having gone into Godalming to buy provisions at market; but Musk already knew that. Indeed, the timing of his arrival at Anderson's door had been determined by it.

The steward brought out some cold salted meats on platters, along with a choice of wine, Madeira and *thé*, the fashionable new drink much favoured by the queen. Musk contemplated the offering and requested some lamb and Madeira. 'You live well, Anderson. Serving the Rump as a commissioner of victualling was lucrative, I take it?'

Anderson's eyes narrowed, and he became more guarded. In some quarters, asking a man what he had done before the king's happy and blessed Restoration was akin to demanding that he enumerate aloud his crimes and his lusts in church upon a Sunday. 'I have been blessed in the offices that I have held,' he said cautiously.

Mistress Anderson returned just then, and must have detected the discomfort in her husband. She sat beside him, and looked upon Musk with a new hostility. 'Ah, indeed. And you, Mistress Anderson – you, too, were blessed in the offices that you held, I think.'

'I – I do not follow you, Sir Venner –' she blustered.

'That was the thing about our rulers in the late times, was it not? Puritans, the godly … call them what you will, they prided themselves on searching out sin in others and castigating immorality in all its forms.' Musk took a sip of Madeira. 'But we know the truth, the three of us here in this room. We know that it was all a sham, nothing but foul hypocrisy and cant.' Mistress Anderson was growing ever more agitated, her eyes darting this way and that. 'We know how ungodly those so-godly great men of the Commonwealth could be, once they locked their bedroom doors behind them. And you know it best of all, Mistress Anderson.'

She was flushed now, and sweating. Her husband gripped her hand. 'Great God, sir!' he protested. 'What is that you *want*?'

'You could provide for every taste, I'm told. You could tell which major-general preferred boys, which councillor of state had a fondness for whips – for you could satisfy every taste, could you not, Goodwife Anderson? Or as you were known at the Protector's court, the procuress-general?'

Anderson stood, his face contorted in rage. 'You scoundrel, Garvey! You filth –'

Musk reached casually within his tunic-coat, produced a loaded and primed flintlock pistol, and levelled it at Deodatus Anderson. 'Ah, well, you see, Anderson, I doubt very much whether Sir Venner Garvey would interest himself in your affairs. And it is time that I desisted from taking his name in vain.'

Anderson looked upon the pistol in horror, and sank slowly back into his chair. '*Who are you?*' he hissed.

'A man who does interest himself in your affairs, master and goodwife. On behalf of others who have even more interest in them.' Calmly, Musk nibbled a piece of lamb. The *faux* Yorkshire accent was gone now, supplanted by his native London speech. 'You see, Mistress, it came to our attention that you were renowned for your meticulous record-keeping. It's said you kept entire ledgers – names, dates, prices, proclivities, all of it. And the identities of the whores and catamites that you provided. How useful that information might be! Why, who knows which of your clients are now respectable bulwarks of His Majesty's realm...'

A slight noise made Musk, Anderson and his wife all turn slightly toward the door from the kitchen. The steward stood there, and for a fleeting moment Anderson smiled, presumably believing the tables to be turned. The moment lasted only as long as it took him to register the presence of Cornelia Quinton behind the steward. Like Musk, she held a pistol in her right hand. Her left held two large leather-bound volumes.

'Well done, Mistress,' said Musk. 'You had no difficulty finding the object of our interest?'

'The opposite,' said Cornelia happily. She wielded a pistol as comfortably as any dragoon. 'It was in the room next to that in which I was left to rest. They did not even think to lock them away – simply had them upon a shelf! *God in hemel*, any common thief could have walked in and wandered off with them. And thanks to the thoroughness of the goodwife, there, each volume is indexed.'

'Well, then,' said Musk, getting to his feet, 'no need to detain this household any longer.'

Cornelia moved to his side; her pistol, like Musk's, continued to point menacingly at the Andersons and their steward.

'You will not escape, sir!' Anderson cried defiantly. 'We have friends – aye, powerful friends!'

'Indeed,' said Musk as he and Cornelia backed toward the door. 'Then ask your so-powerful friends if they have ever heard the name of Lord Percival. Ask them if it is advisable to pursue the servants who do his bidding. Advisable for the continuing good health of any man and woman. And thus, Master and Mistress Anderson, we bid you good day.'

* * *

Ik gilde van het lichen ... writes my dear wife in her deposition, lying upon my desk alongside Musk's. But in English, then, and combining the two accounts before me in the manner of a historian weighing his sources – a Bishop Burnet, say, the greatest historian of recent times (in his own mind, at any rate), although hopefully without that mewling Scots jolthead's propensity brazenly to invent his evidence:

Cornelia shrieked with laughter as she and Musk urged their horses into a full gallop along the lane toward Chiddingfold. She made no concession to ladylike dignity, and sat astride her steed like a man.

'Oh, Musk!' she cried. 'The thrill of it! I think I should become a highwaywoman, like old Kat Ferrers! If only my dear Matthew could see me – could have seen me back there!'

'Most audacious, mistress,' Musk shouted back. 'But why did you take a second ledger? We only needed the one. It is only the one name that we seek.'

Cornelia glanced across at him and grinned. 'You should see some of the names in the second book, and some of the things they like to do! Who knows how such knowledge might be useful?'

The two finally reined in some five miles later, when they were certain that Anderson had not ignored their warning and sent out a pursuit. They dismounted by a stream, watered their horses, and finally discarded the personas of Sir Venner and Lady Garvey; in Musk's case, this meant losing his periwig, a fashion that he had never understood and suspected he never would. He ran his hand across his bald head, hoping to dislodge any lice that might have strayed from their lodgings in the vile adornment.

He and Cornelia sat down side-by-side on a grassy hummock, and Musk opened the saddle bag that contained the ledgers. 'Well, then, mistress' said Musk, 'let us see what Mistress Anderson can tell us.'

Gradually, the thrill of the chase evaporated. Cornelia Quinton looked away, down the torpid little stream, with an intensity that suggested she was trying to spy its destination, the distant sea. As Musk read avidly, Cornelia was increasingly subdued and thoughtful.

'Oh, Musk, do we do the right thing?' she said. 'Suddenly, I know not why, I feel guilt beyond measure.'

'Guilt, mistress? Taking these books can't be a sin, I reckon. The people listed in them and the Andersons, they're the ones who've committed the sin.'

'No, Musk. I mean Matthew. Hiding what we do from him. I feel I have become but an adulterous wife, one of those brazen harpies who lies to her husband as a matter of course.'

As gently as he could, Musk said, 'Mistress, you know My Lord's reasoning upon this – that is, as to why Captain Quinton must not know what we do.'

She nodded reflectively. '*Ja*. His argument is sound, I think.

Poor Matthew has concerns enough without being further weighed down by becoming privy to our business. And even if he knew of it, he would be proud of what I have done here, and in what cause. Of that I am sure.' And of that, indeed, she was entirely right: as I sit here, all these years later, I still feel the pride and love (aye, and something of the alarm, too) that surged through me when I first learned of Cornelia's momentary transformation into a veritable Wicked Lady.

Cornelia thought further upon her condition. 'But if my brother Cornelis could see me… What would he think, Musk? His twin sister, a spy for England and her mysterious Lord Percival, holding a man prisoner at gunpoint!'

Musk sought to distract her from a further descent into guilty self-doubt. 'You hold a pistol most expertly, Mistress,' he said.

'And could have fired it just as expertly, Musk!' said Cornelia. She sighed. 'But my brother would not be proud, I think. He would lecture me on the unsuitability of it all, as he always did even when we were but children and I wished him to teach me how men fight. The older he gets, the narrower his views become, and he can only see Dutch women as meek *mevrouwen*. Even his sister.' She shook her head, lamenting Captain Cornelis van der Eide's limitations. 'Not that he would get so far as such a lecture, for he would already have disowned me for serving England in a war against our native land. My dear brother has ever seen the world in black and white, those two shades only.'

Musk was still thumbing through the ledger, scanning the end-less lists of names and paying relatively little attention to Cornelia's ruminations. Suddenly, he stabbed a stubby finger at one entry. 'Look, mistress! I think this might be the name that we seek.'

He passed the ledger over to Cornelia. 'Yes, Musk, you might be right. So we return to London, then, and to this address?'

'I think we have had enough drama this day, mistress. No, I must lay this information before My Lord, to request his further orders, and he has left town for some days upon – upon the other matter that concerns us.'

'Ah, this so-mysterious "other matter" of yours, Musk. The matter that cannot be confided to a mere woman, of course. Cornelia Quinton will serve to play the part of dear Liz and to wield a pistol if she must, but entrust her with as few secrets as possible!'

Musk shuffled uncomfortably and turned his eyes from her. His thoughts were still partly upon the information in the ledger, and not entirely upon the words he uttered. 'That is not the case, mistress. We seek only to protect you and – well, to protect you.'

'Protect me and – ? Who is the "and", Musk? Who else? It is Matthew, is it not?' She was urgent now, and reached out to grip his wrist tightly. 'Your other matter concerns him. Does it put him in danger, Musk?'

Musk silently cursed himself for his indiscretion. 'No greater danger than he is already in, mistress, aboard a fleet about to sail into battle.' Musk cursed himself again, this time for sounding more callous than he had intended to be.

Cornelia began to cry, and Phineas Musk cursed himself a third time.

* * *

It is customary for flag officers to entertain the captains of their division to dinner, and thus on our last afternoon at the Gunfleet the *Bachelor's Delight* took me across to the *Royal Oak*, Sir John Lawson's new flagship in the stead of the exploded *London*. She was anchored close to the Cork Sand, almost directly off Harwich and Landguard. As Roberts steered me under her stern to the larboard entry port, I considered her as a potential opponent for the *Merhonour*. The odds would not be good, I decided at once, and surely cast grave doubt upon Lord Arlington's confident assertion that the *Merhonour* could obstruct any treachery on Lawson's part and successfully defend the Duke of York against an attack by the ship I now boarded. The *Oak* was brand new, indeed was over a century younger than the ancient *Merhonour*; she carried seventy-six guns; and she had a crack crew of volunteers from Lawson's Yorkshire, a county vast enough swiftly to make good the appalling losses on the *London*. True, I had fought a Commonwealth turncoat in a larger ship once before, but that had been less of a mismatch than any fight between *Royal Oak* and *Merhonour* would surely be.

Thus I was a somewhat troubled man when I went into Lawson's cabin, and my mood was not improved by the sight of my fellow captains, already arrayed around the table. Without exception they were old Commonwealth-men, the likes of Jordan of the *St George*, Clarke of the *Gloucester* and Abelson of the *Guinea*, who was some sort of kinsman of Lawson's. I would have had a more comfortable meal in the centre division with the likes of Marlborough and Beau Harris or even in the rear with the supposedly suspect Will Berkeley. They all fell silent as I entered, exactly as if I had interrupted them in the midst of some treasonous discussion about how to restore Tumbledown Dick Cromwell as Lord Protector. In truth, though, the silence might have been a consequence of my appearance. I had become accustomed to wear my finest attire upon such occasions, and Cornelia had recently insisted that I should purchase a new close-kneed suit for a campaign fought under the Duke of York and in the company of much of the nobility of the realm. Thus I must have been something of a spectacle in emerald-green with gold trim, crowned with a periwig that made my head unique among all those in the room. For in terms of fashion, at least, all of Lawson's other captains were still true to the principles of the godly republic. They were bare headed and wore nothing more flamboyant than their day-to-day buff tunics; thus I felt, and looked, like a peacock among pigeons. It is to avoid such embarrassments, they say, that today's sea-officers cry out, 'ah, we must have a uniform!'

Utter nonsense, of course. In truth, it is so that they can appear equal to the grandees of the army and cut a greater dash among the ladies, who ever swoon away at the sight of a red coat. May God grant that even our idiot Hanoverian masters never concede such an effeminate and un-English frippery as a naval uniform.

As it was, my discomfort increased when I realised that Lawson had placed me next to him at table, reflecting both my rank in society and the fact that *Merhonour* was, notionally at least, his second in the mighty duel to come. He greeted me fulsomely enough, but I prepared for the sort of dinner that must be served in purgatory.

Yet the fare was good enough, when it arrived. Lawson knew how to act the part of an admiral, and his galley supplied carp, mutton, lobster, oysters, together with puddings in profusion. Inevitably, we drank Hull ale, for Lawson had once lived in that garrison city and was stout in its defence during the civil war; stout on the rebel side, that is. Perhaps as a tribute to his adopted home, Lawson seemed determined to consume a prodigious quantity of its product.

The victuals might have been substantial, but that was more than could be said for Sir John's conversation, which rarely interrupted the steady flow of ale into his gullet. He was either one of those men who finds convivial discourse difficult or one of those godly souls who believes such levity to be beneath a Christian man, even a remarkably thirsty Christian man. Quite suddenly, though, he turned to me as I was chewing upon a tolerable piece of mutton and said, 'Well, then, Captain Quinton. Your ship. Well manned, you think?'

I nearly choked upon the meat. Lawson was breaking one of the unspoken rules of naval tables by discussing matters of business; worse, he seemed to have led me into a trap. Of course my ally and superior officer would be interested in the fighting qualities of the *Merhonour*. But so, too, and for very different reasons, would a potential opponent.

I determined upon truth: after all, the inadequacy of my crew would be apparent to all in the division once we weighed, so there was little point in dissembling. 'I have many good men, Sir John. But the most recent drafts are likely to be troublesome. Many landsmen, Welsh and other such dubious creatures. We have had fewer men run than some others in the fleet, but I think that is only because they are less experienced in the ways of deserting a man-of-war. I pray I will have time to mould them into a good fighting crew that can face any foe.'

'Ah, then, let us hope that you shall prove the truth of the second letter of Paul to the Corinthians, Captain. Chapter twelve, verse ten.' My face must have borne the confused expression of a young man whose education had been disrupted by civil war and who had subsequently slept through too many ineffably dull sermons in his local parish church. "When I am weak, then I am strong." A principle that I have ever found useful in my own life.' Lawson finished his tankard and had it refilled at once by his attendant. 'Consider the time when his present Majesty was about to come in. Should I not have been at my weakest, Captain Quinton? John Lawson, as firm a man for the republic as you could find in England?'

I looked about me uncomfortably, for at any dinner table in the 1660s such discourse of the old divisions was considered anathema. 'I do not know, Sir John.'

'Aye, I should have been.' There was not a little Hull ale in Sir John's speech, but there was something else, too; for some reason, this was something he felt he had to say to me. 'But I thought upon Corinthians, Captain, and realised that in truth, I was strong. The king needed the navy. Only I could deliver him that navy without a fight. And so we came to an accommodation, the king and I. Thus here I am today, a knight of the realm and vice-admiral under the heir to England himself.' He was slurring a little, his eyes glazing over. 'Does my story shock you, Captain? Does it smack of selling your soul? Some would say I sold it, you see. Some of my old colleagues, that is, who still hold firm to the Old Cause, without kings or bishops.

John Lawson, bought for ten thousand pounds... But now that we have had five years of kingly rule, would ten thousand pounds be enough to buy John Lawson's soul back again?' The corner of his lip curled a little; it was what passed for a smile upon the Yorkshireman's grim face. 'I tell you this, though, Matthew Quinton. Ten thousand would be nowhere near enough to buy you twenty captains.'

Chapter Thirteen

But, nearer home, thy pencil use once more
And place our navy by the Holland shore.
The world they compass'd while they fought with Spain,
But here already they resign the main.
~ Edmund Waller, *Instructions to a Painter*

Phineas Musk was returning to Ravensden House in good cheer. Admittedly, the matter of the twenty captains was as opaque as ever. Despite Sutcliffe's best efforts, the members of Harvey's conventicle at Barking remained tight-lipped on what, if anything, they knew of the conspiracy. But Lord Percival's other matter was well in hand. Moreover, Musk had consumed a most acceptable rabbit pie at the Vulture on Cornhill, noticeably quieter than usual as the more timid clientele sought to avoid any risk of infection; he had contemplated the merits of several tankards of prime Wapping ale, and found them satisfactory; best of all, Goodwife Marten, cheerily unconcerned by plague and her marriage vows alike, had proved very willing to entertain him for an hour or so. True, he had seen a beggar drop dead in Portsoken and heard those who ran to attend the corpse proclaim in terror that it was the pestilence, but one less beggar was hardly a matter of much concern. Moreover, Musk had never been within twenty feet of the cadaver, so in his estimation the plague could not trouble him. Besides, it was well known that drinking prodigiously was one of the surest defences against the pestilence. Phineas Musk was doubly secure.

According to Musk's account, he thus returned to Ravensden House refreshed and ready to embark upon an arduous round of domestic duties. *Aye, time for a slumber, more like, you mendacious old villain!*

Yet the house was not right. The front door was almost never used, and Musk entered at the back, as was his wont; but there should have been no lantern burning in the pantry, and there certainly should have been no noises emanating from the eighth earl's parlour, which had been sealed up since the old man's death twenty years before. There should have been no noise anywhere in the house, other than the occasional familiar transit of a rat across the floorboards. Musk went to the cupboard that constituted his personal armoury, drew out a pistol and a cudgel, and moved toward the parlour.

Musk prayed that his approach would be silent, but it was the very devil to succeed in this. He was not a light man, and the floorboards of Ravensden House were known for their perverse groans and screeches. And the hall was dark. The front windows were never unshuttered, and the lanterns were unlit. He trod carefully, slowly, toward the door of the parlour.

The room was at the front of the house, to the left as Musk approached it from the rear passageway. The room in which Earl Matthew had died was a grand affair; or rather, it had been grand once, when the earl was in his pomp. Musk had been inside perhaps half-a-dozen times in the last two decades. As he approached the half-open door, though, he could hear furniture being moved within. Musk confesses that a sudden, irrational vision of the irate ghost of Earl Matthew came into his mind, and he shivered.

He cocked his pistol, pushed the door open and stepped into the room.

A prodigiously broad, crop-headed brute of a man spun around in surprise. He held a sheet of paper in one hand and a vicious dagger in the other. He thrust the latter toward Musk, who raised his pistol and levelled it at the other's head. The thief stepped back, contemplating the distance between the two of them and the probability of his being able to stick Musk with the blade before Musk could put a pistol-ball between his temples.

The brute's features seemed familiar. Musk struggled to place him, although recognition came within a few moments.

'Sleep,' he said. 'You're one of the Countess's men.'

'Bravo, Musk,' said a new voice from the dark far end of the parlour; a woman's voice. 'You have a formidable memory.'

Louise, Countess of Ravensden, stepped into the lighter part of the room. She wore plain draperies of brown and grey, a marked contrast to her usual finery.

Musk kept the pistol levelled at Sleep. 'My Lady,' he said grudgingly.

'Come now, Musk – do we really need weapons?' she asked.

'What is it you do here, My Lady? You and this foul ratsbane?'

The countess stared at him innocently. 'Why, Musk, is this not my house?'

Not even Musk could resist both her logic and the law of property. After a moment's hesitation, he lowered the pistol. 'Aye, My Lady. It is your house, by right of your husband. But you have not ventured here before, but for that once with the Earl. You endeavoured to persuade him to demolish it, I recall.'

'Perhaps I was over-hasty,' said the countess. 'Such a fascinating building. So many secrets – and it gives them up so jealously.' She turned to her attendant. 'Sleep, I have no further need of you for the moment. Go to the kitchens and amuse yourself.'

The rogue lowered his dagger reluctantly and scowled at Musk as he passed. With him gone, Musk looked around the room that had once been so familiar to him. The parlour had lain undisturbed since March 1645, but now signs of disturbance were everywhere. Rugs had been pulled up, chairs overturned, cabinet drawers opened. Layers of dust had been upset. The room had been searched.

'You have a curious way of treating your rooms, My Lady,' said Musk, whose lack of deference to his betters was a byword.

She smiled. 'Ah, Musk, I could dissemble and find some excuse – which as a discreet servant, you would of course accept, whatever your inner thoughts. That is the way of it in your station, is it not?' She gave him no time to answer. 'But you are a man known both for bluntness and for your loyalty to the family of Quinton. So I don't doubt that you would write post-haste to my poor sickly husband at Bath, and to Matthew and Tristram for good measure. After all, have you not been part of the little band that has sought to bring me down by whatever means it could?' She stepped before him and looked directly into his eyes. 'No surprise, Musk? What a good actor you are. But the game that you, Tris, Matthew and Cornelia tried to play against me was doomed to fail. Here I am, Countess of Ravensden and bedfellow of the King of England. Perhaps soon to be so much more – with your assistance.' The countess smiled. 'Ah, *now* the actor's mask slips! Yes, Musk, your assistance. That is why I have come here now – to see you. But you kept me waiting, Phineas Musk, so I became curious to see whether this house contains what it is I seek.'

Musk had heard enough revelations for one evening, but yet he sought to recover himself. 'And what is it that you seek, My Lady?'

She turned from him and walked to the fireplace, above which hung a dust-covered portrait of Earl Matthew's father, the enigmatic seventh earl. 'That, I think, is a matter we should come to later, Musk, after I have ensured that you will not betray me to my husband or any other. 'Tis said that every man has his price, so name yours, Phineas Musk.'

'My Lady?'

'What, did you think we would haggle? That is not my way. Note this, Musk – I ask you to name your price before I discover whether or not you have the knowledge I seek. That is how highly I value the transfer of your loyalty to me.'

'You are brazen, My Lady.'

'It is a brazen time,' she said, 'especially for women at our most brazen court. And I learned long ago that demureness and naivety are not characteristics that take a woman far in this world. In this England of ours every man's loyalty is for sale, Musk, even the king's. If you were a street vendor selling loyalties upon your cart, you would mark up the prices, would you not? So let us be blunt with each other. You know full well who it is that I serve, I think, and you know that he can afford to pay any price you name.'

'Reckon the King of France might have a groat or two to his name,' said Musk flippantly. 'But let me give you another case, My Lady. Aye, I'd mark up the price if I had loyalty for sale. But say I was selling a horse instead. I'd not be content with fixing a price, would I, not if it was a favourite old nag. I'd want to be sure any buyer was a fit owner and would treat it well. In short, I'd want to know what that person intended to do with it. So you tell me what you want to know, My Lady, and I'll see if I care to fix a price for it.'

It should have been stalemate, Musk thought; if she met his terms, she must be truly desperate for whatever information she thought he possessed.

She stood by the fireplace, staring up into the blank eyes of Earl Edward. Slowly she turned toward him and said, 'Very well, Musk. On two conditions. First, my friends in France are keen to learn the identity of an agent of Arlington's – although some say that it is actually Arlington himself, using an alias. He is an inveterate enemy of our cause, and the Most Christian's ministers will be most generous towards whosoever exposes him and brings him down. You are said to know London better than any man alive, Musk. You know people of every rank from the court to the gutter. Thus I would have you bring me the true name of this so-called Lord Percival.'

'Odd name, that,' Musk said. 'Lord Percival. Shouldn't be difficult. And King Louis will give old Musk as much as he wants for that one name? You're not really driving a hard bargain, My Lady.'

'Perhaps more so for the second condition, Musk.' She approached him and stood unsettlingly close to him. 'I would have you swear upon oath, upon the Bible and before Sleep as a witness, that if I take you into my confidence and tell you what it is that I seek, you will not then betray my trust to any of the Quintons.'

'An oath is an oath,' Musk said. 'Immutable. Unbreakable. Phineas Musk doesn't break oaths, and he keeps his word.'

Thus it was that Phineas Musk swore not to betray the confidence of what the Countess Louise would tell him to any man or woman of Quinton blood or name, nor to any greater or lesser than a Quinton.

With that resolved to her satisfaction, the countess told Musk what she wished to know. Of the whereabouts of Tristram Quinton, a matter that seemed to be of particular concern to her, he could not enlighten her. But upon her chief matter of substance, Musk was surprised that she should be so concerned with what to him seemed but ancient history. Thus with very little hesitation, he named an outrageously inflated price for what seemed to him a most inconsequential answer.

* * *

A gun fired aboard the *Royal Charles*, and her sails were loosed. Upon that, every ship in the fleet emulated her, the *Merhonour* included, and moved out into the broad channel of the Sledway.

A fleet putting to sea is one of the most wonderful and dreadful sights upon God's earth. Great swathes of canvas billow, ensigns unfurl proudly, mighty hulls turn to seek the best conjunction of breeze and tide. Yet all these years later, it is the sounds that return to me most readily: capstans turning, the groan of protesting anchor cables at the hawses, the creaks of timber straining in water, the strange shriek of wind amid rigging, the thunderous cracking of the sails, the cacophony of ancient sea-songs aboard a hundred ships as crews went about their business. But one ship, and one alone, had no song of its own. My loyal men were dispersed to watch stations all over the hull to leaven the ranks of the lubbers and the recalcitrant; thus no song of Cornwall could issue from the deck of the *Merhonour*, for there were too few Cornishmen in any given quarter. The Welsh could sing, I had always been told, but these Welshmen of ours showed no inclination toward song, and precious little toward work either. I caught a glimpse of my bearded foe, just behind the forecastle and beneath the ship's bell. An observer might have thought him an officer, for men evidently did his bidding and took upon themselves any task allocated to him. I vowed that I would have to come to a reckoning with this creature, and sooner rather than later.

It was a hot April day, with a steady wind from the south-southwest. The *Bachelor's Delight* was to windward, trim and easy upon the breeze. It took us an eternity to take up the station specified in our sailing orders, upon the starboard quarter of Lawson's *Royal Oak*, and to achieve a feeble approximation of close-hauled. We were near enough for me to be able to see the vice-admiral, there upon his quarterdeck, without the aid of my telescope. I was still shaken by his words to me on the previous day, and had spent a sleepless night in my sea-bed, pondering what to do. Lawson knew of the suspected conspiracy, and had made sure that I knew it; which surely meant he had to know of the part that had been assigned to me, to guard against his defection during the battle to come. It was my duty to go at once to the Duke of York to warn him of this terrible new truth. Yet as I tossed and turned, there was a part of me that still urged caution. Lawson had been far into his cups, and after speaking to me of the vast bribe that had won his loyalty, he had turned away from me to talk with Jordan, to his left. When he and I spoke again, it was as though the previous conversation had never happened: instead, he wished to know my opinion of Will Berkeley as a prospective son-in-law. I could hardly offend against the hospitality of his table and the respect due to him as my senior officer by raising the subject again. So had Lawson's mention of twenty captains been merely a strange coincidence, an accountable chance remark by a man in his cups? Or was it a subtle way of telling me that although twenty captains had been offered inducements to desert their loyalty, they had refused them? The admiral's strange remark had no clear meaning, and thus it presented me with no clear course to follow. God alone knew what damage it would do to the fleet's prospects in the imminent battle if the Vice-Admiral of the Red and nearly two dozen other veteran officers were to be summarily dismissed upon the unfounded suspicions of Matthew Quinton. I had a peculiar vision of His Grace of Buckingham installed in Lawson's place, and shuddered at the thought.

I could tell no man on the *Merhonour* of my dilemma, not even my dear friends Kit Farrell, Francis Gale and Roger d'Andelys. The latter two stood with me upon the quarterdeck as we struggled to hold our station on the sleeker and better crewed *Royal Oak*; I could see Kit upon the forecastle, endeavouring through Treninnick to explain to some Welshmen the correct way of tying a bowline knot. I sensed that Francis and Roger knew not all was well with Captain Matthew Quinton. Roger probably suspected the consequences of too much Hull ale. Perhaps Francis sensed there was something deeper, but he was too tactful to pry.

The great fleet stretched away on either side, ahead and astern, in its three squadrons of Red, White and Blue: the entire ocean seemed to be carpeted with stout English oak, rising and falling majestically upon the grey swell. But I took no pleasure in the sight and returned gloomily to my cabin. I lay upon my sea-bed and thought for a long while. I reflected upon a battle I once fought against a Commonwealth captain who had ostensibly embraced the Restoration, only to plot its overthrow and cunningly conceal his true allegiance. Perhaps that example was too heavy upon my mind, too weighty an influence in my thinking about Lawson and his kind. But then, perhaps it was also being given too much weight by the likes of Clarendon and especially by the devious Arlington; and young as I was, I was already learning not always to trust the words of princes and potentates alike. Politics, I reflected; God preserve me from politics. As if such concerns were not sufficient, I fretted about what might be happening elsewhere in my absence. I strongly suspected that something of import to my family was afoot ashore, of that I was certain, but I was in no position even to scratch at its surface. The victuallers that came out daily from Harwich or Bridlington to supply the fleet brought a steady stream of letters from Cornelia, but whereas she was usually the most prolific of correspondents (twenty-seven pages on one occasion during my first voyage), her letters were now inexplicably terse, filling barely one side of a small sheet and revealing next to nothing of her activities. I contemplated pregnancy, miscarriage and a host of less plausible explanations, and found none of them reassuring. Most alarmingly of all, there was almost no mention of the doings of the Countess Louise, or of the fragile health of my brother. The one letter I had received from Tristram was similarly silent upon the matter of my good-sister. Add the strange evasiveness of Phineas Musk, and dark suspicions overwhelmed my thoughts. Above all, I was increasingly alarmed by the reports of plague in London, and concerned for Cornelia's safety. She would have dismissed both my fears and the plague itself in short order, but that knowledge did nothing to lighten my spirits.

I felt the ship rise and fall in the light swell. I heard the groans of the ancient timbers, and for a moment imagined them to be the legion of dead Quintons crying out from their tombs. There even seemed to be one particular timber that creaked with the voice of my grandfather: *Believe.*

Aye, My Lord of Ravensden, but believe in what?

With heart and mind in turmoil, I took a sheet of paper, dipped my quill in the ink, and began to write.

'In the name of God, Amen. I, Matthew Quinton, Captain of His Majesty's ship of war *Merhonour* in the present expedition against the Dutch, being of sound body and mind but conscious of the transitory nature of life and of the manifold dangers of the service upon which I am now engaged, do make this, my last Will and Testament...'

* * *

'The island, yonder,' said Kit, pointing to a grey line upon the horizon, 'is Texel. There, to the south of it, is the Helder, the north tip of Holland. Between them is the Mars Deep sea-gate – the main passage into their Zuider Sea and thence to Amsterdam.'

I studied the low shores, so like those of Essex or Suffolk. It was difficult to distinguish the two land masses from the channel that separated them. Only the occasional tower of a church or windmill broke the monotonous flatness. But as I stared more intently through my lens, I spied another sight: there, behind the Texel shore, rose the very tops of a forest of masts. 'Then that, I take it, must be the Dutch fleet. Lord Obdam himself and his myriad of flagmen.'

Kit studied the sight. 'Only sixty or seventy sail, I'd reckon' – God alone knew how he could make such an estimate at such a distance – 'which means the Zeeland and Rotterdam ships haven't joined from Hellevoitsluis. No surprise, that. We'd have had intelligence of it if they'd put to sea.'

'And that,' said Roger, who stood at our side upon the quarterdeck that day after the sailing from the Gunfleet, 'they are surely unlikely to do while your fleet sits here, between their two contingents.'

'Aye,' said Kit, 'they'll have learned their lesson from the year fifty-three, when Monck was upon this very shore and yet they came out separately. They took the devil's own hammering that day.'

Roger lowered his telescope. 'So if the Dutch will not come out while your fleet lies off their shore, gentlemen, what in the name of the *bon dieu* are we doing? Surely we are in stalemate, with no battle in prospect.'

'It is called blockade, My Lord,' I said. 'The Dutch will not come out, nor, while we hold this latitude, can they go in. And the Dutch live by their trade. Their return-fleet from the East Indies is due within weeks, carrying spices almost beyond value. If we take those ships, and cut off the rest of Holland's trade, the Amsterdam bourse will eventually collapse. Then De Witt and his cabal will have to send Obdam to sea, to attempt to break our stranglehold. Instead, of course, we will destroy him. Either way, the Dutch republic is finished.'

I said the words with a confidence I did not feel in my heart; but who was Matthew Quinton to quibble with the expressed opinion of the Duke of York, Prince Rupert, Sir William Penn and all the rest of the great seamen?

'It does not seem an honourable course,' said the Comte d'Andelys. 'The great ships of England, all her mighty princes and her proud lords, content to prevent the passage of some mean merchant hulls – not fit work, *mes amis*. If this was a French fleet, now, we would force the sea-gate, there, sail into their anchorage and burn Obdam's fleet at anchor. Now *that* is an honourable course.'

'Also a desperately dangerous course, My Lord,' Kit said. 'No more than one ship at a time can pass through the sea-gate – I have sailed through it enough times, on hulls bound over the Pampus to or from Amsterdam. It has grown worse of late, and you'll not find more than three fathoms at the best of a spring tide. You have two miles to run in such conditions, My Lord. The Dutch have forts on both shores, too, and the channels shift constantly, like ours in the Thames, so even our newest charts are probably worthless. And of course it is a lee shore, with all the dangers of coming off it safely again.'

Roger, the former captain of the Most Christian King's great ship *Le Téméraire*, looked at Kit in some puzzlement. 'My sailing master used to make much of that term, especially when we were coming between Bertheaume and Camaret into the Road of Brest. Remind me again, gentlemen: what is this "lee shore" of which you speak?'

Kit and I exchanged an amused glance, tinged with the knowledge that only a few short years before, it would have been Matthew Quinton asking that self-same question.

The grand fleet of England duly commenced its blockade of the Dutch coast. During the next days, we stood out to sea or came closer inshore, depending upon the winds and our frequent soundings, for the shoals in those waters were notoriously treacherous. Our scouts, like Harris's *House of Nassau*, would sometimes dart up almost to the mouth of the sea-gate and fire a few guns in defiance before coming off again. Then we made a grand promenade down the featureless coast as far as Scheveningen, watching the alarm bonfires spring up upon the dunes and listening to the distant noise of church bells proclaiming that the English were coming. Such was our purpose, of course: to spread panic among the honest burghers of The Hague, perhaps inducing them to force De Witt's government into a humiliating surrender. We fired the *Merhonour*'s guns for the first time, albeit unshotted, off the shore near Zandvoort, again to intimidate the local citizenry. Having seen the performance of my truly motley crew upon the yards and sails, I was quite prepared for a fiasco. Yet the battery of the *Merhonour* more than held its own; not quite up to the mark of the truly crack ships like my old colleague Robert Holmes's *Revenge* or Val Pyne's *St Andrew*, but respectable enough. Despite being ancient and deaf, Webb our gunner clearly knew his business. He had decent quarter-gunners under him, and even the most lubberly Welsh generally knew how to fire an artillery-piece: many had fought during the civil wars, or else had served aboard colliers or other craft that carried a gun or two. Some, Treninnick had learned, seemed to have served on ships that might or might not have had formal letters of marque permitting them to wage war upon the trade of other nations. Kit Farrell was too discreet a soul to employ the word 'pirate', but nonetheless, his opinion on the matter was clear enough.

My Lord of Andelys fulminated against the dishonour of all these activities, too. He was all for landing on the broad, tempting beaches of North Holland, marching in triumph into the Binnenhof itself and stringing up the Grand Pensionary of Holland from the nearest tree.

But as the fleet made its serene way upon the North Sea, sailing hither, then thither, and so inexorably wearing or tacking back to hither, the concerns of Captain Matthew Quinton multiplied. True, with no immediate prospect of battle there was equally no immediate alarm over the intentions of Lawson and the hypothetical twenty captains. For good or ill, I had not reported his ambiguous speech at dinner to the Duke of York; thus that particular die was cast. But as that apprehension faded, others sprang forth to take its place.

Quite apart from my troubled thoughts about what might or might not be happening ashore, there was my abiding concern for the crew of the *Merhonour*. Despite their surprising competence upon the great guns, they were evidently still very far from being a fighting unit capable of putting the fear of God into the proud butterboxes. The Welsh continued to be obstreperous; more so now that word of the curse of the *Merhonour* had got amongst them, for there is only one creature more superstitious than a seaman, and that is a Welshman. Pewsey reported frequent fights between the decks; reported them, but evidently did nothing to restrain or prevent them. His sole essay at disciplining a member of my crew came one morning in my cabin when he presented me with that notorious defaulter and likely ringleader of mutiny, Cherry Cheeks Russell. Presumably even the timid

Pewsey reckoned that the management of a thirteen-year-old youth was within his powers.

'Pissing below decks, Captain,' said Pewsey. 'And smoking his pipe away from the tub. At the same time.'

Within the hull, smoking was permitted only in the immediate vicinity of a large tub of water, for obvious reasons; and pissing was permitted nowhere below decks, ditto, or so it evidently appeared to all but some of the more backward landsmen and to young Cherry Cheeks.

I stared at young Russell, who returned me a bleary, uncertain gaze. It was barely the forenoon watch, but it seemed clear he had already been imbibing something rather stronger than the daily issue of small beer.

'Great God, boy,' I said, 'you are a disgrace to the House of Russell. A hopeless sot and addicted to your pipe before your fourteenth birth-day. For the reputation of our English nobility, let us be thankful that a dozen lives or so stand between you and an earldom…' Young Castle and Scobey, standing in attendance behind me, sniggered; they were much the same age as Russell and evidently detested this wayward sprig of a chivalric house. 'Tell me, then, Cherry Cheeks – exactly why is it, do you think, that His Royal Highness's instructions to his captains enjoin them to prevent pissing and defecation below deck?'

'Smells,' said Russell, hesitantly. 'And I didn't def – def – shit. Not this time, anyway.'

'Worse than smells, Mister Russell. Disease. Foul miasmas, bring-ing on all manner of sicknesses. Smallpox, for one. Even the plague that already stalks the streets of London. Why do we have pissdales on deck, Mister Russell? And why do you think God gave ships heads?'

The boy said nothing, and stared down sullenly toward his feet.

'Your orders, Captain?' Pewsey asked.

'Well, then. The law of the sea is entirely clear in such a case, I think. For drunkenness, the loss of a day's pay. For smoking away from the tub, punishment at the captain's discretion. For pissing beneath decks, up to twelve lashes. What do you have to say for yourself in mitigation, Cherry Cheeks?'

The lad shuffled. 'Sorry, sir. Won't happen again, sir.'

'No, Mister Russell, it will not. But it seems to me that your youth stands in your favour and inclines me against the lash.' Cherry Cheeks looked up with relief. 'Nevertheless, punishment there must be, otherwise every man on the ship will do what he pleases.' I seemed to consider the matter. 'Tell me, Boatswain – when you asked Russell if he had done the things of which he stands accused, how did he answer you?'

Pewsey seemed nonplussed. 'Why, he denied it, sir! Despite the word of three witnesses.'

'Ah. Then that denial would have been a lie, would it not, Boatswain?'

'Aye, sir. That it would.' Pewsey caught my gist, and smiled.

'And the navy has an ancient punishment reserved for liars, does it not, Boatswain?'

'Aye, sir. That it does.'

Russell's short-lived relief had turned once again to lip-nibbling anxiety. 'Very well,' I said, putting on what I trusted was my gravest expression and tone. 'Mister Russell, you will be hoisted from the main stay for half an hour with a broom and shovel tied to your back and the entire crew shouting "A liar! A liar!" You will then will spend a week cleaning the ship's hull, directly beneath the heads.' Castle laughed out loud, and I scowled at him. 'I pray that the experience will teach you the importance of cleanliness aboard a man of war, and that your high birth will not protect you against the custom of the sea –'

I had no opportunity to finish my peroration, for a knock brought Ali Reis into the cabin. The Moorish renegade, whose command of languages was truly extraordinary, had set himself to learn Welsh, that he might join Treninnick as an interpreter to that rude race. As yet he had found precious few teachers, and the new drafts, knowing him to be one of the captain's men, generally kept silent in his presence.

'Begging pardon, Captain,' said the Moor, '*Royal Charles* has hoisted the Union at the mizzen peak. The signal for the fleet to form line of battle, sir.'

* * *

I ascended to the deck by the tortoise-stair, the curious old-fashioned private spiral ascent for the captain that only the more ancient ships retained, and saw at once that no battle was imminent. This was to be one of the training manoeuvres that the Duke of York had promised, no doubt to see how long it took the fleet to form into its line.

Kit Farrell had the watch upon the quarterdeck and saluted with a bow of his hat, a gesture (and, indeed, an item of clothing) that was evidently still perfectly alien to him. Alongside him was Yardley, the master, who acknowledged my presence perfunctorily. Along with a small bevy of midshipmen and masters' mates, Francis Gale and Roger D'Andelys completed the complement upon the quarterdeck.

'Well then, gentlemen,' I said, 'His Royal Highness seems to have chosen propitious weather for it.'

We had a warm but somewhat variable breeze from the south west; that, after all, was why we were out of sight of the Dutch shore, lest we were blown onto the butterboxes' treacherous sandbanks. Consequently the fleet was moving slowly west upon the Dogger Bank, roughly between the fifty-third and fifty-fourth degrees of latitude, awaiting a change of wind that would permit us to resume our close blockade of the Texel sea-gate.

I surveyed the scene. The ships of Prince Rupert's White squadron, to the south, were already putting on sail to fall into their positions in the van. Conversely, Lord Sandwich's Blue squadron, to the north, was shortening its sails in order to fall in to the rear of the fleet. Both had to manoeuvre in relation to the Red and the Duke's command flag; thus for the ships in the Red itself, there was comparatively little work to do to take up station. I knew from my many readings of the Duke's fighting instructions (or rather, Penn's, for we all knew the true authorship) that our appointed place was directly astern of Lawson's *Royal Oak*, half a cable's distance from her, with the *Guinea* in the place behind us. An easy task, I thought. We would simply shorten sail briefly to allow the *Oak* to move ahead, then we would come up quite close into the wind to take position astern of her. I said as much to Kit.

'Aye, Captain,' he said. 'That should be the manner of it, indeed. But we will have to be brisk about it, sir. It will bring us dangerously close to the wind, and being as cumbersome as we are, we cannot risk coming closer than eight points to it. The *Oak* is a far better sailer than we are, and the *Guinea* is but a small Fourth, nimble enough to turn upon a farthing.'

Yardley nodded. 'Not certain of this wind, either, Captain,' he said. 'Strange weather altogether, since the comet.'

I ignored the master's pessimism. 'Very well, gentlemen,' I cried, 'let us be brisk indeed!'

Men scuttled aloft. We would shorten our courses and depend upon our topsails alone; with *Royal Oak* resplendent under full sail, that should be sufficient to bring us astern of her. But almost from the first moment, it was evident that our manoeuvre was going badly awry. The main course began to rise toward the yard, but unequally; the men heaving upon the clewlines and buntlines to larboard were evidently far more competent than those to starboard. All were notionally Able Seamen, fit for the yards and tops, but some were clearly more able than others.

'Ah, now this is familiar,' said Roger. 'This is how French ships sail. My officers were quite animated by such things when we first put to sea, and flogged relentlessly until *Le Téméraire* could put out and take in sail more smartly than a slovenly washerwoman hanging her laundry.'

There is nothing more galling to an Englishman than to have his conduct compared unfavourably to the French, and I would have upbraided Roger if our situation had not been so precarious.

The great main course was fast resembling a triangle, rather higher on one side than the other. Entirely ignoring his duties and station as a quartermaster's mate, Treninnick sped back and forth across the yard, trying desperately to make men learn what they must do. If I had ten Treninnicks, I thought, we might still be saved, but not even he could remedy it now. On the fore, indeed, matters were even worse; the course was barely shortening at all. And the *Merhonour*'s rudder, ever stubborn, was coming round at its wonted snail's pace – perhaps I should have ordered more men to assist the helmsman in hauling the whipstaff over –

If we did not turn and slow, and that soon, we might run into the starboard quarter of the *Oak*. Worse, the *Guinea*, a sleek little hull manned by a crack crew of Humbermen, had shifted her sails neatly, come up far closer to the wind than the lumbering *Merhonour* could ever manage, and was already nearly in position, thus rapidly reducing the sea-room available to us.

All that was needed now for an entire disaster was –

'Wind's gusting round, west by south!' cried Kit.

Even if we managed to shorten the courses and hurriedly backed the remaining sails, we would surely collide with the *Oak,* or the *Guinea,* or even both. Yet if we turned away, with the wind as it now was –

'Starboard the helm!' I commanded.

'But Captain –' protested Yardley.

One of my previous commands, and one of my previous crews, might have brought it off. The good old *Jupiter*, or the nimble *Seraph* – how I wished I was on one of their quarterdecks, and not that of this ancient, leaking sea-cow.

The great ship lost headway. With her sails in confusion and her helm as unresponsive as ever, there was but one conclusion. We fell away from the *Oak*; aye, and from the *Guinea* too, and then from the rest of the fleet in their wakes. The *Merhonour* was in irons, wallowing impotently to leeward of the navy royal.

It was a calamity. It was utter, gut-gnawing humiliation. I could sense the eyes of the entire fleet, watching the hapless *Merhonour* in the slough, blinking away tears of mirth and nodding knowingly to each other about the curse on the old ship. Lawson's all-too-apparent wrath, and the scorn of his kinsman Abelson, were but the most adjacent manifestations of our shame. I knew that aboard the *Royal Charles*, the telescope of the Duke of York himself would be trained upon us.

Well, Matthew Quinton, I thought to myself, *you are well and truly blasted now. The king thinks you an arrogant fool, and the heir thinks you an incompetent one.*

Chapter Fourteen

Expect who can the Dutch fleet should come out
Whilst Opdam lies at anchor of the gout?
Perhaps they have no wind and so keep in:
What? Out of breath before they do begin?
~ John Bradshaw, rector of Cublington, Buckinghamshire,
Some Thoughts upon the Dutch Navies Demurr and upon the
First Squadron of the Kings Royall Navy (1665)

'*Sic semper tyrannis,* crieth the righteous man! For doth not the Prophet Isaiah tell us, "I will punish the world for their evil, and the wicked for their iniquity; and I will cause the arrogancy of the proud to cease, and will lay low the haughtiness of the terrible"? My dear brethren, thus shall it be with the tyrant Charles Stuart! Even now, the instrument of our salvation comes to us from the east! The wind fills the sails of the godly Dutch who will deliver us from this unholy Pharaoh – a tyrant who must go the way of his father! Aye, we shall all be as the sixth angel foretold in Revelation, preparing the way for the army from the east that will cleanse the land of fornicating princes and the plague their sins have hatched! Recall the sixteenth verse of the sixteenth chapter, brothers and sisters – "And they gathered them together at the place called in Hebrew, Armageddon"! Aye, dear brethren, Armageddon, the battle to come upon the sea, where the godly will prevail! Alleluia! Alleluia! Alleluia!'

All around Phineas Musk and Lazarus Sutcliffe, the Reverend Jeroboam Harvey's congregation raised their hands to their heaven, crying loud and repeated 'amens'. Almost all the women, and not a few men, were weeping copiously. The eyes of a thin girl close to Musk were glazed over; in trance-like ecstasy, she began to dance. A man at the front, almost at the base of Harvey's makeshift pulpit of kilderkins, suddenly began rolling on the floor of the great barn that housed the conventicle and started speaking in tongues, to applause from those around him. Musk caught the eye of a comely matron attired in a simple Puritanical garb of black broadcloth, white linen collar and hood; she was waving her arms in the air and seemed to be mouthing the words of a psalm. Musk was impressed. Far from being transparent and entirely out of place, as he had expected, the Countess Louise seemed born to the role.

Musk himself cried out, 'Oh, Alleluia! Alleluia, amen!' before whispering to Sutcliffe, 'Sweet Jesu, why can he not have the common decency to speak treason five minutes into his sermon rather than after two interminable hours?'

The crippled veteran murmured, 'Once heard Hugh Peters, that was Noll Cromwell's chaplain, berate us for four hours. And we didn't even fight that day.'

Musk grimaced. 'Ah, Peters … his head is still stuck on a pole at the end of London Bridge, is it not? Proof that justice catches up with malcontents and bores alike. Enough, though. Time to introduce our Israelites to the notion of the Babylonish Captivity, methinks.'

Musk pushed his way through the congregation and reached the very front, directly before the sweating black-clad form of Jeroboam Harvey. The dissenter was still ecstatic from his peroration, his arms outstretched toward his adoring acolytes. It took him a few moments to register Musk's presence. Then he smiled benignly.

'My brother,' he said, 'what is it that you seek?'

'What do I seek? Well, that's a question. To tell truth, Reverend, what I seek is your miserable rebellious arse locked up in the Tower for a few score years.' Musk turned to face the congregation and shouted at the top of his voice, 'God save the King!'

Upon the signal, the doors of the barn were flung open from outside. Heads turned in alarm. Somewhere in the middle of the congregation, a woman screamed. Regardless, two files of red-uniformed militiamen of the London Trained Bands strode into position along the walls of the building, matchlock muskets primed.

Many of the dissenters, and Harvey himself, fell into fervent prayer. Thus at first not all beheld the strange apparition that now strode into the heart of the barn, an unfashionably long cloak flowing out behind him. The man was booted and spurred, but strangest of all, his face was masked by a kerchief.

He walked to the front of the barn, stood alongside Phineas Musk, looked out over the congregation and then spoke in a loud, deep tone. 'By Act of Parliament in the sixteenth reign of his most blessed and sacred Majesty Charles the Second, by the Grace of God King of England, Scotland, Ireland and France, chapter the fourth, it was made the law of this realm that religious assemblies of more than five persons outwith the Holy Church of England be henceforth declared illegal!' The masked figure paused and looked about him, over the terrified faces of the two hundred or so souls in the barn. 'And I see somewhat more than five persons in attendance within this undoubtedly illegal conventicle,' he said sharply. 'However, His Majesty is a most lenient and benign sovereign, and thus has no wish to incarcerate innocent subjects who have merely been led astray by a false and foresworn traitor!' The masked man turned, and pointed theatrically at the trembling minister upon the firkins.

'Jeroboam Harvey, self-styled minister of the Word, by the authority vested in me I arrest you for high treason against His Majesty's most sacred person! We have the requisite two witnesses' – Musk smiled, but Sutcliffe endeavoured to remain anonymous – 'and as an example to these good but deluded people, you will most assuredly hang! Sergeant, take this man!'

As the wailing from the congregation reached a crescendo, Harvey was escorted away, singing the one hundred and twenty-ninth psalm in a broken, nervous falsetto: 'Many a time have they afflicted me from my youth: yet they have not prevailed against me...The Lord is righteous: he hath cut asunder the cords of the wicked. Let them all be confounded and turned back that hate Zion!'

The soldiers began to usher the members of the congregation out of the building. As they did so, the cloaked man pulled down his mask and said, 'Well done, Musk. A most satisfactory day's work, I feel.'

'As you say, My Lord.'

Musk looked away, and again caught the eye of the so-comely broadcloth-clad Puritan matron, one of the last conventiclers left in the building. Musk nodded almost imperceptibly. In return Louise, Countess of Ravensden, smiled slightly and stole one more glance at the unmistakeable face of John, Viscount Mordaunt of Avalon.

* * *

I dreamed of the Countess Louise. She was bound to a stake atop a blazing pyre, and I could even seem to smell the smoke in my nostrils. My grandfather was her executioner, stoking the flames around her. Then she stepped out of the blaze, stepped toward me, bearing balls of fire in her hands – aye, fire –

'Fire!' Dimly, dream gave way to reality, only they were nearly the same. I heard the cries beyond my bulkhead, just before young Castle burst in upon me with the news that there was fire beneath, on the middle deck. Hence the smoke in my nostrils; it was creeping up between the planks beneath me.

Fire: no four letters are capable of creating such terror aboard a man-of-war. For what is a man-of-war but a vast tinderbox of wood, filled to the brim with substances that burn and explode?

I sprang from my sea-bed and ran down the spiral stair from the steerage to the middle gun deck. At the foot of it, I looked astern and saw flames consuming the starboard officers' cabins. The heat struck me as a great wave. For a moment I feared for Roger d'Andelys, who had taken the lower great cabin on this deck, directly beneath mine; but then I recalled that he was still aboard the *Prince Royal*, having been entertained rather too amply by My Lord Sandwich and His Grace of Buckingham, who after his rebuff at the council of war was serving as a volunteer aboard that ship.

Dense smoke made it difficult to make out individuals, but I could hear Lieutenants Giffard and Farrell, who were already barking orders. Some men were sent to draw up pails of water from the pump-wells, others to break open water-casks in the hold and establish a bucket-chain from there to the blazing cabins. At last, Welsh, Cornish and English alike were joined as one: there is nothing quite as effective at bringing men together as the prospect of imminent immolation.

It was no time to stand upon the dignity of my rank. I seized a leather bucket from one of the Welshmen and flung its contents into the conflagration. Smoke and steam stung my eyes, and I retched. Recovering myself, I took another bucket, and another, and another, standing shoulder to shoulder with a desperate band of Merhonours. I was reaching for yet another bucket when Francis Gale appeared at my side. 'Captain,' he said, 'we need officers on deck. Men are jumping off the hull.'

I ran to the upper deck, gulping at the blessed air, feeling the welcome breeze through my sweat-sodden shirt. It was a cloudy night with a choppy sea; a grey dawn was just coming up over the low lands to the east. But the light was ample enough to see some of the Welsh-men struggling with the likes of Lanherne, Treninnick and several other petty officers. I could see the mysterious bearded figure in the midst of them, intoning strange, sing-song words that sounded like an ancient lament. Quite suddenly there was the roar of an explosion, and a tongue of flame spat forth from our hull – the heat had fired the charge left in one of the starboard culverins.

This was the last straw for one man. He suddenly broke free from the throng, reached the starboard rail, leapt up onto it, and stood there for a moment, framed against the sky, before jumping off. I ran to the ship's side. Although the *Merhonour* could have been making no more than two or three knots, there was already no sign of the man. No doubt he could not swim, but even so preferred to take his chance in the water than face the apparent certainty of being consumed by flame, or torn apart when the fire reached the powder magazine. The *Bachelor's Delight* was on our other quarter and thus in no position to rescue him; besides, Roberts was maintaining a prudent distance, closer to the *Royal Oak* than to us, no doubt in case the flames reached the gunpowder barrels in the *Merhonour's* magazine and blew her apart. From his viewpoint, that must have seemed a very real possibility. Smoke was billowing out of the gunports adjacent to the officers' cabins on the starboard quarter. Another of the culverins fired spontaneously, causing another great wail from the terrified men on deck. The destruction of the cursed ship seemed imminent...

'We've had a half-dozen jump, Captain,' reported Ali Reis, part of the small band of loyal men trying to restrain the herd. 'The first of them could swim, so they've got to the boats, but those that followed have sunk like stones. May Allah rest their souls in eternal peace.'

Francis and I went to the stern and looked down upon our three ship's boats, which, as was customary, were being towed behind the ship. I saw that the swimming Welshmen had been joined by others; a few men were clambering out of the lower ports and hauling themselves like apes along the tow-ropes. If the fire had been in the powder store, the captain of the *Merhonour* would have run to join them, but our case was surely not as desperate as that. Or so I prayed.

'Very well, then,' I said, and turned to Francis. 'One thing for it, I think, Reverend.'

Francis and I hurried back beneath decks, fighting our way through the throng of men rushing to the stern with pails of water. The smoke on the lower gun deck was thick, and I coughed as I jumped from the bottom of the ladder. Men were screaming and running about in confusion, believing – not unnaturally – that they would be trapped by flames above them, but there was no time to concern myself with that. Down below to the orlop, to the armourer's store. The armourer, a sullen old Lowestoft man named Oakes, was already at his station and duly unlocked at his captain's command. He handed Francis and I as many flintlock muskets, pistols and cutlasses as we could carry.

Returning to the main deck, I saw the unmistakeable black figure of Julian Carvell and threw a musket to him. The Virginian grinned, as he always did when he had a weapon in his hand. He fell in behind us and joined us on the upper deck, where I handed my armful of weapons over to Ali Reis. He kept one for himself and passed the others to Lanherne, Macferran and the rest of the loyal men. The men loaded and primed their weapons swiftly. As guns were levelled at them, the score or so of panicked, screaming Welshmen fell back from the ship's rails, into the waist of the deck. My men fanned out to surround them.

'Mister Lanherne,' I cried, 'you have my leave to shoot any man who attempts to break out of confinement! And get Treninnick up here to translate that to them!'

'Aye, aye, sir!' came the cry from my coxswain.

'Francis,' I said, 'recite some prayers, or a psalm, or something of the kind. Lanherne and Treninnick will assist you.'

He looked at me in astonishment. 'They're an unlikely pair of curates, Captain, and this does not appear to be a very receptive congregation.'

'Perhaps not,' I said, 'but I think they are god-fearing, all the same – though which god is the question, of course. And I have observed that nothing calms a troubled soul more than the old words of reassurance.'

Francis Gale could not dispute that, for it was the foundation upon which his entire vocation stood.

I returned below. The scene appeared unchanged. Flames still spat from the canvas partitions of the officers' cabins. Steam hissed as water from leather buckets was flung onto the seat of the blaze. Kit Farrell turned and raised a finger to his forehead in salute. Like the rest of him, both finger and forehead were singed and covered in grime and sweat.

'Think we're getting it under control, Captain,' he said breathlessly. 'Lieutenant Giffard has gone below to oversee the drawing of water from the pump wells and the sea. And the beams and planks aren't catching. We've men below keeping the deck above them watered. Thanks be to God that none of the officers seem to have had any powder in their cabins.'

'Thank God indeed, Lieutenant.' I looked about me; there seemed to be a new feeling among the men, a sense of triumph supplanting that of fear. Everything was as ordered as it could be. Relays of men now passed buckets down the line to those at the front, who were being relieved every few minutes and supplied at once with generous tankards of small beer by the cook and his mates. This would have been Kit's doing, of course; yet another debt of gratitude I owed to my friend.

'Do we yet know how it began?' I asked.

'They say it was in the boatswain's cabin,' said Kit. 'Pewsey left a candle burning when he went on watch. Seems it fired a bunch of rosemary he kept hanging there for luck.'

Kit gesticulated toward the hunched figure of the boatswain, who was sitting upon the deck a little way forward. Pewsey was rocking slowly back and forth against one of the timber knees, sobbing and reciting the words of the eighty-third psalm over and over to himself: *As the fire burneth a wood, and as the flame setteth the mountain on fire, so persecute them with thy tempest, and make them afraid with thy storm. Fill their faces with shame, that they may seek thy name, Oh Lord.* So much for his lucky rosemary, supposedly the favoured charm of seamen since Aphrodite arose from Poseidon's lair garlanded in chains of the stuff. I decided at once that there was little point in questioning or upbraiding the man; that could wait for later in the morning. For now, it was only important to ensure that the ship was safe and her crew following orders. With the former apparently assured, it was time to address the latter.

* * *

I returned to the upper deck, and to my astonishment found myself in the midst of a rhetorical disputation.

'Yea, the second epistle of Peter warns us against false prophets, and you are truly one such – yes, you, the bringer-in of damnable heresies, as the apostle tells us – if I but had my sword in my hand, you foul Welsh imp of Satan –' cried Francis Gale in exasperation.

The bearded Welshman was shouting something back to him in his own tongue, a strange torrent of words in which one phrase recurred over and over: *derfel gadarn.* The other Welshmen were nodding vigorously or howling approbation of their ringleader.

I must have worn a puzzled expression, for Francis shook his head violently and cried, 'Ah, Captain Quinton, I am as Elijah was amidst the priests of Baal, one lone prophet of the Lord shouted down by his enemies. And if we are to believe the First Book of Kings, at least Elijah knew what the priests of Baal were talking about.'

'They resist the word of God, then, Francis?'

My chaplain nodded to Lanherne, who had evidently been translating once again for Treninnick and thus for the Welsh. 'The bearded one, there, proclaims the fire as final proof that the ship is truly cursed, Captain,' said the coxswain of the *Merhonour*. 'There is this thing, this *derfel gadarn* – Treninnick calls it a wooden saint, so God knows what it was – which obviously meant much to them. The English seem to have burned it, or him. The old man cries out that the destruction of the ship by fire will avenge the fate of the *derfel gadarn*.'

'Then what is he – the bearded man? Why does he have such power over these wretches?'

'Treninnick has heard some of the others name him as Ieuan Goch of Myddfai, Captain,' said Lanherne. 'Or in English, Red John of some place that might as well be on the moon. He claims to be a seer – in his tongue, a druid.'

'A druid,' I sighed. 'Of course. What else could he be? We need but the Holy Grail, a few forest nymphs and the ghost of my grandfather to give us a full measure of madness aboard this ship. But the *Merhonour* is cursed, as they say, so it must only be fitting.'

I looked around me in despair. I needed a healthy dose of scepticism from a Phineas Musk or a Roger d'Andelys, but neither was to hand. I needed the erudition of Uncle Tris…

Uncle Tris. A boy balanced upon his knee, listening to the wondrous tales of the Knights of the Round Table. Drinking it all in, memorising it all, praying that one day he could be counted among that noble brotherhood…

'Derfel!' I cried. 'One of the seven warriors of Arthur who survived the battle of Camlan! He was made a saint, or so the legend tells us. Lanherne, get Treninnick to ask them if this *derfel gadarn* of theirs is something to do with the same tale.'

Before Lanherne could address himself to Treninnick in Cornish, the bearded Welshman took a step toward me. 'A *saes* who knows of Saint Derfel,' he said in fluent, rolling English. 'Truly the days of miracles have not ceased.'

Francis Gale moved threateningly towards him. 'Damn you, man, I wasted all that time and breath upon you when the ship was in dire peril, *yet you understood me perfectly all the time?*'

The Welshman smiled and waved his arms to no apparent purpose. 'There is no listening more revealing than when a man thinks none can hear him. I think you are a Shropshire man by your voice, priest, so you should know us better than these others do. You are, after all, very nearly one of the *Cymru* yourself.'

Francis scowled: no greater insult can be directed at a borderer than an insinuation that he truly belongs on the other side of it. The druid, or whatever he was, then turned to face me directly. His eyes were black and penetrating, bearing an unsettling similarity to those of the Countess Louise. 'You see, Captain, in the four hundred years since you conquered us, we Welsh have ever found it useful to pretend not to understand you *saes*. Whereas we understand you clearly. All too clearly, indeed. We understood you when the wooden shrine of Saint Derfel, which we had venerated for near a thousand years, was taken to London and burned by your Cromwell – Thomas, that was, not the so-called Lord Protector.' He almost spat out the last word; evidently Ieuan Goch of Myddfai was no enthusiast for Oliver, our late king in all but name. Perhaps that was something I could turn to my advantage.

'Great God, man,' I protested, 'that must have been a hundred and thirty or more years past. How could you claim this fire as vengeance for that?'

Ieuan Goch of Myddfai opened his arms toward the daylight breaking over the Dutch shore. 'The ninetieth psalm of David: *a thousand years in thy sight are but as yesterday when it is past, and as a watch in the night.* In other words, Englishman, we Welsh have long memories.' His voice rose and fell in strange, song-like cadences.

'Long memories and mightily insolent tongues,' said Francis. 'Show respect when you address Captain Quinton, brother and heir to the Earl of Ravensden.'

I raised a hand, for I sensed that this peculiar Welshman required a delicate approach; and if well handled, perhaps he could be the key to securing the loyalty of his countrymen.

'I take it you have never used the trade of the sea,' I said. 'How, then, did you come to be taken up by the press?'

The Welshman grimaced and stroked his great beard. 'I was in Merlin's town of Carmarthen, tending to the sick who still favour the true old healing over these modern charlatans, your so-called physicians and surgeons, such as that creature you keep beneath decks.' Craigen, surgeon of the *Merhonour*, was a feeble Scot whose remedies for all human conditions seemed to comprise bleeding, or sawing off a limb, or both. 'I had the misfortune to be aboard a vessel at Carmarthen quay, tending to a ruptured sailor, when Lord Carbery's press officers swept up the river. They were not discriminating in their choice of men, so long as they made up the number they had been given.'

'You are a healer, then?'

'Healer, bard, seer – all of these things. I am a *dryw* in direct descent from Rhiwallon, physician to the high and mighty lord Rhys Grug, Prince of Deheubarth, and his son Cadwgan. Surely you have heard the legend of the physicians of Myddfai, Englishman?'

This so-called druid was unduly puffed up in the pride of his unpronounceable lineage. I recalled once attending a play with my brother: some part or other of the tragic history of King Harry the Fourth. Charles' friend Follett was cast as some fantastical Welshman called Glendower who claimed to be able to summon monsters at will. His scenes involved much rolling of eyes and emphasising the wrong parts of words, traits that drew hoots of laughter from the usual boorish London audience. It was only now that I realised how well Follett seemed to have researched his part.

'No, I have not,' I said slowly: I had to be careful now, for the wrong word risked marring all. 'But I will deal plainly with you, Ieuan Goch of Myddfai. You can tell me the tales of your physicians and your princes. Indeed, I will appoint you an assistant to the surgeon so that your skills may be useful to us all. And as such, of course, you will be paid better than you are now, as a mere landsman.' Ieuan Goch's eyes flashed at that. I calculated that a wandering druid would depend chiefly upon alms, and the proverbial poverty of Wales would bring him precious little of those. 'But you can also secure for me the wholehearted loyalty and effort of the Welshmen aboard this ship, beginning by assuring them the fire is almost extinguished, so their lives are safe. And do all in your power to quell this talk of a curse. In return, the Welshmen will be esteemed as our equals, and your bards in centuries to come will sing your praises.'

The old man looked me up and down as though he were assessing the market value of a bull. 'You are a strange creature, Matthew Quinton,' he said with a curious impertinence that I permitted to pass. 'Young, yet so much less of an oaf than most of your *saes* brethren. A man seemingly aware of history, yet so unaware of your own, I think.' He rolled his eyes, this strange, unsettling creature, muttered some words in his own tongue, then settled his gaze back upon me. 'There is a Welsh saying, *a fo ben, bid bont*: let him who would be a leader, be a bridge. And indeed, I think you have been a bridge to us in this dealing, so perhaps you will be a leader worthy of our trust.' He looked out, over the ship's rail, toward the other ships within sight and especially toward the distant hull of the *Royal Charles*, flying the royal standard at the main. 'I have thought much upon this war, and have concluded it is meet and proper that we of the *Cymru* should serve the noble prince James, son of the martyr, of the blood of the ap Tudurs and the *mab darogan*, the son of destiny, he whom you call King Harry the Seventh.' *He* had concluded – the towering arrogance of the man! Nothing of obeying orders, or doing duty; yet I would make nothing of it, for after all, he had travelled a different road but still arrived at the place where I wished him to be. 'Very well, then,' said Ieuan Goch of Myddfai, bowing his head to me. 'Let it be so, My Lord.'

'I am addressed as Captain, Welshman – keep "My Lord" for the likes of the comte d'Andelys when he returns aboard.'

Ieuan Goch of Myddfai nodded his head, but his eyes narrowed. 'Be not so certain of that which you cannot see and do not know, My Lord,' he said. With that, he raised his right hand, pressed two fingers to his forehead in an immaculate gesture of salute and turned away, leaving me staring after him in perplexity.

Chapter Fifteen

Wronged shall he live, insulted o'er, oppressed,
Who dares be less a villain than the rest.
Thus, sir, you see what human nature craves,
Most men are cowards, all men should be knaves;
The difference lies, as far as I can see,
Not in the thing itself, but the degree;
And all the subject matter of debate
Is only, who's a knave of the first rate?
~ John Wilmot, second Earl of Rochester,
A Satire Against Mankind (published 1679)

Lord Percival and Phineas Musk emerged from the Lanthorn Tower and found themselves in the midst of a torrential downpour. In his deposition, Musk states that he favoured an immediate retreat back into the dryness they had just forsaken, but his master was intent on pressing on. The vast bulk of the White Tower, one of London's most enduring landmarks, loomed over them as they made their way west through the inmost ward of the city's fortress, passing the ruins of the old medieval palace and its great hall as they made for the Bloody Tower. Musk contemplated the thickness of the walls and wondered whether they could withstand the two terrible enemies that assailed them, the plague and the Dutch.

'You think our friend Harvey spoke true, Musk?' Lord Percival demanded suddenly.

'The Tower and a treason charge can be greatly efficacious in loosing a man's tongue, My Lord. He had the look and the smell of a man desperate to save his body, whatever he might say about his soul.'

'Indeed. He seemed so eager to clear himself and please his audience that it would not surprise me if he subscribed to the Thirty-Nine Articles and turned Laudian within the week. That being so, his confession causes us some difficulty.'

'My Lord?'

'He knows nothing of any plot by twenty captains, Musk, and he knows nothing of the whereabouts of the ostler. That much is obvious. No doubt we could apply the Tower's instruments of persuasion, but I doubt very much if they would extract a different tale from him.' They passed through the gateway of the Bloody Tower into Water Lane, the Traitors' Gate directly ahead of them. The pikemen on duty stood to attention as they passed. 'No, Jeroboam Harvey is a puffed-up malcontent with a fondness for his own voice and a deluded belief in the godliness and invincibility of the Dutch. No more, no less. And that, Musk, creates a problem.'

'My Lord?'

'The fleet will engage within days, so perhaps it is already too late to expose this conspiracy. Harvey was our last hope, unless we can somehow find the missing ostler – Sutcliffe has no other names, no other hints even as to a direction we could travel.'

'If there ever was a conspiracy, My Lord.' Musk's broad-brimmed leather cap disgorged ever more rainwater onto his shoulders.

'Yes … if there ever was a conspiracy.' Lord Percival seemed especially thoughtful. 'I have been considering that possibility, Musk. Think on this. We live in fevered times. Rumour is everywhere, the drumbeat of each passing hour. The king is dead. The queen is pregnant. Cromwell is alive. The Dutch have landed. The dissenters have risen. The papists have risen. Each new tale excites the rude multitude for a day or two, then fades into the oblivion whence it sprang. So why has this one tale been so persistent, Musk, above all the rest? If it is not true, how did it come into being, and why has it gained such credence? Why have you and I spent weeks chasing shadows, when we could have been about other business entirely – notably the business to which you must return tomorrow?'

They came to the Byward Tower and the blessed dryness of the passage through it. Once more pikes clattered against breastplates as guards came to attention. Musk realised he had no answer to Lord Percival's question; none but a tiny and dark suspicion, growing ever greater as each moment passed.

'No, Musk,' said Lord Percival as they stepped out onto the causeway across the moat to the Middle Tower, 'our friend Harvey is not quite the last creature we must interrogate. There is one more.'

* * *

The navy royal of England was somewhat *en fête*. Our outlying frigates had spied a body of ships to northward and made all sail to intercept them. They proved to be a returning Dutch merchant fleet, of which we had received intelligence from Limerick a fortnight before. Hoping to sneak past the north of Ireland and Scotland, then down the Norwegian coast and so through the sea-gates, they had instead fallen directly into our path. The frigates took eight of them: mostly flyboats with prodigious cargoes of wine from Bordeaux and Lisbon, although one was a West Indiaman worth, it was said, some £30,000. How I envied Beau Harris and my former command, the *House of Nassau*, which played a part in the capture!

The triumph was followed in short order by a council of war which took a resolution to sail for England. The Dutch had not fallen into our trap by coming out to fight us while we were upon their shore, the Duke of York argued, so perhaps they would be more tempted to do so while we were back upon ours. Moreover, the one essential without which an English fleet could not keep the seas was in dire straits. Not gunpowder, for we had used almost none of our store; not sails, for we had not been battered by particularly vicious gales; not even men, although our surgeons were alert to any sign of plague or the more usual sicknesses that beset a fleet at sea. No, far worse than any of these. The fleet was almost out of beer.

This grim reality brought forth a mighty diatribe from Prince Rupert during the council of war. 'England is a realm awash with beer,' he cried. 'How is it, then, that the victualler of the navy can find barely enough to keep us at sea for a month? What, pray, is all the money that Parliament voted being spent on?'

It was difficult for any man present to disagree with His Highness's sentiments. For my part, I welcomed the prospect of our return for two reasons: it would give Thurston and his crew the time and resources to repair the fire damage more effectively than they could at sea, while the mails that hopefully awaited us at Harwich might contain news from home to ease the concerns of the captain of the *Merhonour*.

We made landfall between Southwold and Hollesley Bays, and skirted the coast of Suffolk down toward the Gunfleet. I was at the quarterdeck rail teaching Cherry Cheeks Russell how to take a bearing, not without an awareness of the irony of it all; not too many years before, I had been the pupil acquiring the same knowledge. A pupil who, though I say so myself, was undoubtedly quicker on the uptake than my sottish young companion.

'Very well, Mister Russell, we will try again upon Orford Castle, yonder. No, this side, there is but sea on the other. The great brown tower. No, that is Hollesley Church. *That* great brown tower.'

I pointed. 'That is a castle, then, Captain?' asked my reluctant pupil.

'Quite so, Mister Russell. A mighty keep of King Henry the Second, and the best seamark for miles upon this coast.'

The boy looked at it curiously. 'One day, I want to be the lord of a castle like that,' he said, with the sort of determination he usually applied only to the pursuit of a bottle.

I smiled, for the young Matthew Quinton had known such dreams. Indeed, Captain Quinton of the *Merhonour* was still not immune from them; after all, if Will Berkeley, only a few months older than me, could already be a knight, then why not I?

'Well, young Cherry Cheeks,' I said, 'for that to be so, I think you will have to study long and hard. You can spell barely a single word correctly, and your knowledge of the sea-business seems to extend no further than knowing when the cook is about to distribute food and drink.'

The lad shrugged. 'Thought it was going to be all battles and glory,' he said, 'not this tedious sailing.'

I said nothing, for I could hardly admit that I largely shared his assessment of our situation. Indeed, in one sense I envied young Russell. He did not bear the responsibilities of command, and he did not spend many a waking moment wondering what those whom he loved or hated might be doing in his absence. The evasiveness of Musk, the curious silence of Cornelia, the mysterious decamping of Tristram to Dorset: either those closest to me were engaged in some sort of conspiracy of which I knew nothing, or else distance, the loneliness of command and the imminence of battle had overwhelmed my thoughts, blowing up a few disconnected, innocent facts into a giant web of irrational fears. Was that, perhaps, in itself a manifestation of the curse of the *Merhonour*?

'Twenty-two degrees,' said Russell, interrupting my grave-black thoughts.

'What?'

'The keep of Orford Castle lies twenty-two degrees of relative bearing to starboard, Captain Quinton.'

I, too, lined up the ancient keep. 'Dear God, Cherry Cheeks, you are quite right – you have fixed a bearing correctly for the first time! Perhaps we will make a seaman of you yet.'

The lad grinned. A thought suddenly struck me: I had been so consumed by my own concerns, and overtaken by such events as our failure to join the line-of-battle and the fire aboard, that I had quite forgotten to implement the liar's punishment upon young Russell. Pewsey had never raised the matter again; and besides, since the fire he had been relieved of his duties and confined to his hastily reconstructed cabin, pending an eventual court-martial. Perhaps Cherry Cheeks Russell would make a seaman after all, for he seemed to have perhaps the most essential attribute for success in the seaman's ever-uncertain art: luck.

* * *

Hoc loco quo mori miserum esse… So wrote my uncle in his infuriating Latin script. Once more I bring up the ancient vellum to no more than a few inches from my eyes, and attempt to decipher my original pencil translation of more than sixty years past:

This will be a miserable place in which to die, thought Tristram Quinton as he backed slowly up the main street of Chaldon Worgret. In truth, calling this squalid lane a 'main street' was akin to calling our American plantations a nation, just as to call the dozen or so inbreds advancing toward him 'men' seemed to be stretching a point beyond its limits. They had been cowed briefly by the unexpected sight of the two swords he drew when they surrounded him in the one inn of the village – that is, the stinking thatched hovel a few hundred yards away – but ultimately, not even finest Toledo steel could overcome such adverse odds and deter so many lumpen opponents.

'Now, my good people,' said Tristram, 'I am a man of peace. I am a man of science. I am the Master of Mauleverer College in the University of Oxford.'

'Warlock,' hissed a foul, unshaven creature at the front of the pack.

'Warlock!' echoed two or three of the others.

'Not so, my friends,' cried Tristram. 'As I said at the inn, I have merely come to your fine town to learn the truth of an incident that occurred in these parts –'

'Aye, the old Lugg business!' cried the foul one, who seemed to be both a ringleader and to have a better grasp of the English language than the rest. 'Ye've no concern with that, stranger, other than ye'll share her fate! Burning!'

'Burning!' cried the man's chorus.

'My dear friends,' said Tris soothingly, still endeavouring to placate but still keeping his swords extended and occasionally twirling the points menacingly, 'I have no interest in reopening old wounds –'

'And they say ye're a friend of the vicar at Hardingford, that's a Papist!'

'Roger Falcondale is a former student of mine. It may be true that he is a little too inclined to the persuasion of Arminius –'

'And ye talks with a warlock's long words, that we may not understand thee!' snarled the ringleader. 'And ye dress strange, and offer money to tell ye how the Lugg bitch came to burn! And ye tried to get under Jen Cooper's skirts at the inn!'

The mob surged forward menacingly at that. 'That,' said Tris uncertainly while glancing quickly behind him, 'was a mere misunderstanding, my dear friends! I am, as I say, a man of peace, and I shall prove it to you.'

With that, he raised his two swords, plunged them into the soft earth before him, and stepped back, bracing himself against the barn wall behind. With his right hand, he reached within his frock coat – an item of clothing unknown in that part of Dorset until that day – and made much of locating and producing a kerchief, with which he proceeded loudly to blow his nose.

'Warlock!' screamed the ringleader, raising a billhook above his head as he ran directly for Tristram.

In the blink of an eye (or so my ever-immodest uncle proclaims), Tristram reached back into the frock-coat with his left hand, produced a flintlock pistol, aimed it at the ringleader's ribcage and fired. Tristram put the kerchief fastidiously to his lips as the man was blown backwards, a great fountain of blood spouting from his torso as the lead ball flattened and exited.

Casually, Tristram again reached inside the coat, this time with his right hand, and drew out another pistol. He described an arc with it, pointing it at each incredulous face in turn. Then he reached out and plucked one sword from the ground with his left hand.

'Never, ever, assume that you face a right-handed assailant, my friends. Now, let us return to the matter in hand. The Lugg business. The burning of a witch in this place, more than thirty years ago. As I said at the inn, I have an amount of honest coin of the realm – a goodly amount – to bestow upon whosoever tells me the truth of that affair. Or, of course' – Tristram gestured toward the still twitching remnant of the man upon the ground – 'we can conduct matters differently. But remember that I am, as I say, a man of peace.'

Chapter Sixteen

A cowardly spirit must not think to prove a seaman bold,
For to be sure he may not shrink in dangers manifold;
When sea-fights happen on the main, and dreadful cannons roar,
Then all men fight, or else be slain, and braggarts proud look poor.
[Chorus]
A seaman hath a valiant heart, and bears a noble mind;
He scorneth once to shrink or start for any stormy wind.
~ Anon., *The Jovial Mariner, Or the Seaman's Renown*
(17th century)

Cornelia Quinton and Phineas Musk made their way past Saint Helen and Saint Ethelburga, and so out into Bishopsgate. This was ever one of the busiest streets of London, full of coaches, carts and horsemen bound for the north or for the City itself. Yet now it was eerily quiet. The doors of several houses bore the plague-cross.

Cornelia and Musk had taken all essential precautions against infection. Cornelia wore a kerchief around her lower face; concealed within it was a posset emitting fragrances that were held to ward off the plague-bearing miasma. Musk trusted to his pipe, puffing out a cloud of tobacco smoke to repel any noxious air.

'Woe for London,' said Cornelia. 'I pray it does not assail us as terribly as Amsterdam, last year. My brother says a tenth of its people died, and it still rages there.'

'Aye, madam,' said Musk. 'No leveller like the pestilence, that there isn't. I recall the plagues here, back in twenty-five and thirty-six. The former took away over thirty thousand, they say, two of my sisters among them.'

'You had *sisters*, Musk?' Cornelia Quinton had known the steward of Ravensden House for the best part of seven years, but had never actually heard him speak of his family.

'Brothers, too. They've only hanged one of them, far as I know.'

The unlikely pair passed through the square, brooding Bishop's Gate itself and entered the Moor Fields. Those broad spaces were empty of their usual clientele of hawkers, vendors, jugglers and whores. A few stray cattle grazed forlornly; an occasional horseman or pedestrian scurried along one of the paths criss-crossing the fields, hoping by haste to avoid any potential source of infection, such as the man and woman making for a decaying, narrow house almost in the shadow of the Moor Gate itself.

In ordinary times, this building was known for the openness of its door; or at least, its openness to men of all ranks and conditions with sufficient coin to purchase the wares within. Now, though, the door was marked with the tell-tale red cross.

'As we feared, mistress,' said Musk. 'Time to go back, I think. You've done all you could. My Lord wouldn't expect more of us, going into the way of the plague and the like.'

But Cornelia Quinton was to be daunted neither by Musk's entreaties nor by the regulations to prevent the spread of the plague. With barely a sideways glance to see whether or not she was observed, she strode to the door and hammered loudly upon it.

'Have we come so far to be deterred by some paint on a door, Musk?'

They heard steps upon the flagstones within. Someone came up to the door, stopped, listened, but did not move away. Cornelia hammered again.

'Begone, in God's name!' cried a quivering woman's voice from within. 'We're closed for business. Three cases of plague within – may God have mercy upon all our souls. And besides, you'll be arrested –'

'We seek one of the bawds – one of the girls. She uses the name of Lugg, or did when she was at the Spanish dame's establishment in Drury Lane.'

There was silence behind the door; for even in plague-time, a brothel keeper remained alive to the possibility of turning a profit. 'Lugg, you say? And what would you be doing with her?'

Musk nudged Cornelia. 'Constable,' he said, nodding in the direction of the Moor Gate. Cornelia turned and saw three men checking buildings, alleys and outhouses. The bastions of the law had not yet seen the man and woman concealed within the archway of the house further up the street, but it would be only moments before they did.

'Admit us, madam,' hissed Cornelia, 'and we will pay you five guineas at once.' Musk shook his head vigorously and gripped Cornelia's arm, but she shrugged him off. 'Another five if you can show us the girl. And if she is the one we seek, much more to carry her away with us.' There was a silence of calculation behind the door. 'We have no time, madam! Is it yes or no?'

There was a sound of a bolt being drawn back, and the door opened. Cornelia and Musk stepped within, and the door was smartly locked shut behind them.

'Five guineas, then,' said the woman's voice. 'Let's see it, Dutchwoman.'

Seeing anything at all took some moments, for with all the windows shuttered and no candles lit, the hallway was in almost complete darkness. The house stank of decay and a strange, indefinable yet revolting sweetness. Somewhere upstairs, a girl was sobbing.

Gradually, Musk and Cornelia made out the shape and something of the appearance of the creature in front of them. A short, bent woman, it was clear, but it was impossible to tell her age; she wore a mask over her head, obscuring it entirely but for two slits cut for her eyes.

Cornelia took out a heavy purse and handed it to the old whoremistress. 'You're running a mighty risk, Dutchwoman,' she said, opening the purse to estimate the amount of coin within. 'Double risk, indeed – catching the plague or being arrested for breaking the plague laws. Or both. With a war on, they could probably hang you for treason, too. You must want my girl mighty badly, so I think you can't be seeking her for the usual reasons, are you?'

'Show her to us,' demanded Cornelia.

'Another five, you say, just for showing her?'

'We are true to our word, madam.'

'Very well. But remember, I want the money for showing her to you. Don't expect to like what you see, Dutchwoman.'

The crone led Cornelia and Musk up two flights of stairs, and into a small room lit only by two feeble candles. On the bed lay a woman of eighteen years or thereabouts. A face that might have been beautiful only very recently was covered in a foul rash and bathed in sweat. Dried blood stained her nose and mouth. Upon her neck was a swollen purple bubo. Cornelia extended her gloved hand and pulled down the sheet that covered her. The girl was naked, revealing the full extent of the rash; yet more purple or reddish-brown buboes disfigured her groin and armpits. Her belly was swollen and her blueish flesh ran with sweat.

'So now you've seen her,' said the brothel-keeper. 'Five guineas more.'

Cornelia handed over a second purse. 'Now leave us,' she said.

'Leave you? What you going to do with her? Fancy a threesome with a plague victim, do you? Seen all sorts over the years, but that –'

'Leave us!'

The old woman shrugged and left the room, closing the door behind her.

Cornelia looked down at the recumbent body of the girl. 'Nothing can be done until she recovers,' she said. 'If she recovers. The colour of the buboes suggests she's nearly at the crisis.'

'Aye, mistress,' said Musk, 'so it seems. And by the looks of her, recovery will be a miracle. As great a miracle as if we don't catch the plague, you and I.'

Cornelia pulled back the sheet to cover the girl's modesty. 'Oh, you will survive, I think – it will need more than a trifling epidemic of plague to do for Phineas Musk.' Cornelia smiled. 'And as for me ... remember, we Dutch are Calvinists, and predestination is a reassuring notion in such times as these. It is already ordained whether I will live or die, however many plague houses I visit.'

Cornelia knelt down at the side of the bed to pray that the young whore named Lugg, too, was predestined to live. In his deposition, Musk admits that he looked about him awkwardly; he had no truck with predestination, or with any theology other than the preservation of Phineas Musk, and presumably reckoned that remaining longer than was necessary in the room of a plague victim was not especially conducive to that end. Nevertheless, he had particularly good cause to pray for the survival of the Lugg girl. Awkwardly, he fell to his knees and joined his mistress in prayer.

* * *

The fleet was at anchor once again in the Gunfleet, some four leagues off the Naze. A steady procession of victuallers was coming out to us from Harwich, making good the supply of beer to our thirsty fleet. I was in my cabin listening to Thurston, the ancient carpenter. Having effected the repairs to the fire damage, he was now opining that we ought to seek orders to take the *Merhonour* up into the Stour and put her upon he careen, that being the only way of enhancing her sailing qualities to even the slightest degree. I was listening sympathetically, but was firm in my refusal. No amount of careening was going to turn the *Merhonour* into the finest sea-boat in the fleet, and I was aware that orders to sail might come at any moment; not to mention the possibility that the Dutch might attempt a surprise attack. I had no intention of missing what might be the only battle of the entire war with my ship beached and its bottom exposed to the air, for such a fate truly would have been the final proof of the curse upon the *Merhonour*.

Almost at once, my presentiment seemed to be fulfilled. I heard gunfire, first from one ship, then from another, then from more and more. I ran to the quarterdeck, and realised at once that the gunfire was coming from the ships to southward: hardly the direction from which the Dutch would attack. Giffard, who had the watch, had his telescope trained that way, but even without an eyepiece, I could see bunting being set on the southerly ships and their crews manning the shrouds, cheering loudly.

Young Scobey handed me my telescope, and I levelled it at the little flotilla approaching the fleet from the south.

'Four of the royal yachts,' I said to Giffard, recognising at once the headmost as my erstwhile command, the *Mary*. She flew a large royal standard at her masthead. 'But not the king … he would hardly sail without at least a dozen craft around him.'

'We just had word from one of the victuallers,' said Giffard. ''Tis the Duchess of York, come to visit her husband. Yet again.'

'Then we had better dress ship to salute Her Royal Highness, Mister Giffard,' I said.

I did not share with him my true thoughts, which were

dishonourable to the very point of becoming treasonable. We were a fleet ready for war, about to encounter an enemy that might be already at sea for all we knew, and yet we were to be overrun with *women*! We already had enough idle and entirely useless scions of the nobility cluttering the fleet: I was fortunate in that regard to have only the amiable and covertly martial Comte d'Andelys sharing my ship. Yet somehow it had been decreed that we should now also be slaves to the cloying presence of petticoats. I thought upon the poor drowned girl of the *London*, and prayed that was not a foretaste of what might occur if the Dutch attacked while the Duchess and her retinue remained in the fleet. What was the woman thinking of, to inflict herself upon her husband at such a moment?

My one consolation was the reflection that the noble court ladies were certain to confine themselves to the flagship or to the ships that contained the court rakes, the likes of Buckingham, Sedley and Buck-hurst. There was no prospect at all of a woman disturbing the martial preparations of the *Merhonour*.

* * *

A fog had fallen upon London: a thick, swirling miasma that made the plague-ridden streets seem even more ghastly than they already were. As Musk and Lord Percival entered the precincts of Saint Giles-in-the-Fields, a true vision of Hell confronted them. Shadowy masked figures moved through the graveyard, heaving great linen-swathed parcels from the dead-carts and dragging or carrying them to large, newly-dug holes, far wider and deeper than single graves, whither they flung them without ceremony. Other figures were piling the clothes and other possessions of the dead onto bonfires, the smoke and ash drifting across the churchyard while the flames enhanced the hell-ishness of the scene. Musk's original words, lying before me on the fading paper, are perhaps less eloquent than those of a Quinton; but I make no attempt to emulate his brutal descriptions of the condition of individual corpses, too explicit by far for these times that pretend to greater gentility. Even now, my stomach turns as I contemplate his account.

One man stood at the centre of proceedings, a little way from the west door of the modern Gothic church of Saint Giles, directing all. As Musk and Lord Percival approached him they saw that his head was entirely concealed by a leather mask, akin to that worn by executioners; yet another of the ways by which men sought to protect themselves from the foul air that carried the plague. Or so Musk and his mysterious lord assumed.

'Sir Martin Bagshawe,' said Lord Percival. The masked man turned. 'You have led me a merry dance indeed, I think.'

'My Lord?'

'Now, Sir Martin, we are going to talk frankly, you and I. Or rather, you are going to talk frankly. You are going to talk of a killing at the chapel of Pomfret. You are going to talk of the alleged deposition of a certain ostler of the parish of Stebonheath named Thomas Eden – because following extensive enquiries, Sir Martin, I am as certain as a man can be that no such fellow exists, or ever has. You made a commendable job of inventing a life for him, should such enquiries ever be made – even a forged hearth tax return, indeed, to set alongside the forged deposition in his name, and the false report of his attendance at Harvey's conventicle. Impressive, Sir Martin.' Lord Percival pressed on relentlessly. 'Above all, Bagshawe, you are going to talk of a tale about twenty captains of His Majesty's navy royal. A tale, I venture to suggest, that you and other kindred spirits – former Commonwealthsmen all – concocted in order to spread dissension in the realm and especially in the fleet, thereby abetting the heinous designs of those who seek to bring down His Majesty. That is what you are going to talk of, are you not, Sir Martin?'

It was impossible to see the expression behind the mask. 'God's teeth,' he said, slowly and angrily, 'you still concern yourself with *that*? Look about you, man. The city is dying. England is dying. What will there be for your precious fleet to defend?'

Close by, two tiny corpses – children, evidently – were thrown into a pit, with lime immediately shovelled on top of them. No mother wept for them.

Almost in the same moment, there was a commotion at the far side of the pit. A young man, his face disfigured by the plague-rash, limped to the side of the great hole and began loudly to intone the twenty-third psalm. Two of the corpse-bearers approached him tentatively, looking to Bagshawe for guidance. The magistrate gave a slight nod of his masked head, and the bearers withdrew.

'...and I shall dwell in the house of the Lord forever. Amen.' At that, the young man stretched out his arms and fell forward, down into the pit, preferring to await his death-agony with those who had already endured it.

Bagshawe nodded again, and the gravediggers stepped forward to entomb the young man and the dead around him. It was evidently not the first time that any of them had witnessed such a spectacle, or colluded in it.

Evidently shaken, but still in control of himself, Lord Percival whispered, 'No, Sir Martin, England will live. England will always live. But, sir, if you are involved in a treasonable conspiracy designed to bring down the king, then I fear you will not.'

The masked man was silent for some moments. 'That,' he said sadly, 'is not a threat that carries much weight with me, My Lord.'

He reached up with his gloved hands and pulled off the mask. Even the unmoveable Phineas Musk shuddered involuntarily; for the face of Sir Martin Bagshawe was monstrously red and swollen, with carbuncles upon his chin and ears. He was sweating profusely. 'I also have the buboes in the groin and the armpit,' said Bagshawe. 'Two days now. But someone must oversee what is done here, and give orders. Most of my fellow Justices have fled to the country, or else are already dead.'

He replaced the mask before any of his minions could catch sight of him. Then he shook his head, more in pity than denial. 'Very well, then, I will talk, My Lord. I have but little time left for talking, I think. Thus I will give you the truth you seek, to salve my conscience before I join that poor fellow in the grave-pit yonder. Let us go into the church, then, and if you are willing to risk a quarter-hour in the company of the plague, you will hear my confession. But be prepared, My Lord Percival.' Bagshawe's voice was stern. 'It is not as you have said – indeed, it is the very opposite of what you have said. You see, My Lord, we have all been played for fools. Played for fools by a very great personage indeed.'

* * *

As was only fitting, the royal salute began aboard the *Charles*, the temporary floating palace of the Duke and Duchess of York. Each ship in the fleet took it up, rapidly filling the Gunfleet with a magnificent cacophony. The *Merhonour* joined in, firing guns on both sides while specially selected members of our crew lined the rails, waving and huzzaing. I stood upon the quarterdeck, raising my best hat and circling my sword above my head. It was the only fitting way to mark our sovereign lord's thirty-fifth birthday, which was, by happy coincidence, also the fifth anniversary of his blessed restoration to the throne of his ancestors.

There is nothing like a party to raise the spirits of a true Briton, and to briefly drive away fears of curses, plagues and the Dutch alike. I went through the messes, toasting each in turn, all the way along the upper, middle and lower gundecks of the *Merhonour*. Lord, what joy and what a din! Men danced between the guns, Ali Reis the Moor fiddled, and my Cornish friends greeted me with boisterous songs and much undeferential back-slapping. Even the less obstreperous and sullen of the Welsh made merry, for after all, the Welsh had been staunch on the side of the late king during the civil war, and had suffered for it with the blood of thousands. In their own tongue, they sang the strange harmonies of their bleak, rain-sodden land, and a few even raised their wooden cups to honour their captain and their king.

As I passed along the decks, I strove to imprint the memory of every single face upon my mind; for how many of these men would survive what was to come?

Upon the quarterdeck, we officers gathered in our best attire and employed my finest crystal (in truth, Ravensden Abbey's fourth finest) to toast His Majesty, Her Majesty Queen Catherine, Their Royal Highnesses the Duke and Duchess of York, the king and duke's sister the duchesse d'Orleans, her brother-in-law the Most Christian King (this a nod to Roger d'Andelys, who wore an astonishing befeathered creation) and all good success to His Majesty's fleet in this present war. Lieutenant Christopher Farrell fidgeted with his newly acquired and still unfamiliar periwig, the finest that Harwich could provide. Cherry Cheeks Russell, admitted to the august gathering by virtue of his rank, was already considerably fuddled.

It was a marvellous, clear day. Even the fogs and rains seemed to have vanished in salute to our sovereign lord. I left the happy throng momentarily and went over to the larboard rail. The foul plot of twenty captains and the plague ravaging London both seemed so very far away. Surely such an auspicious anniversary and such a happy fleet could only portend imminent victory over the Dutch?

With both that pleasant thought and my glass of wine warming me, I looked out across the waters of the Gunfleet. A skiff seemed to be steering toward us from the direction of the *Royal Charles*. Behind the six rowers and forward of the helmsman sat a woman. As the craft drew nearer, her face became clear.

I heard myself bark an order, although to this day I am not certain how I managed to form the words: 'Mister Lanherne! Side party to receive My Lady Ravensden!'

Chapter Seventeen

I am an undaunted seaman, and for King Charles I will fight:
I'll venture my life and my fortune to defend my country's right:
What enemies ever oppose us my valour with them will try,
And in the Duke's sight, I'm resolved to fight with a full resolution to die.
Anon., *The English Seaman's Resolution; or, the Loyal Subject's*
Undaunted Valour (1665)

My good-sister's tour of the *Merhonour* had reached the main gun
deck. She seemed not in the least concerned that her descent of the
steep spiral stair from the ship's steerage might prove the undoing of
her astonishing costume, all billowing satin with a tight bodice and
short, puffed sleeves. Nor did she seem at all abashed by the significant
display of ankle – aye, even of calf – that her descent necessitated, nor
by a plunging décolletage that left little of her bosom to the imagination. Although our gunports were open for the royal salute and a
blessed breeze aired the deck, it still felt as though we were descending
into an oven. On this deck, as on the upper deck above, bare-chested
or loose-shirted Cornishmen and Welshmen craned their necks

shamelessly to boggle at the sight, and were duly overwhelmed by seas of Celtic lust. Like their captain, they sweated in rivers, yet the lady at the heart of it all seemed utterly serene. And yet something rather less than serene, if truth be told.

'Heavens, Matthew, what mighty weapons!' cried the Countess Louise, stopping before the first gun on the larboard side. She was evidently in playful mood. 'So much greater even than those upon the deck above!'

'Culverins, My Lady,' I said, praying that she would obey the laws of propriety at least once and address me before my crew as 'captain'. I resented her intrusion into our private, male, wooden world, which should have been concentrating entirely upon the imminent battle; I resented the dangerous possibility that any visitor newly come from London might be bearing the plague with them; and I resented even more this devious creature's latest intrusion into the life of Matthew Quinton. Nevertheless, few things give a captain more pleasure than showing off his ship to others, and I found my pride rapidly put my other emotions to flight. 'They fire eighteen pound shot, My Lady. We have even greater upon the lowest gundeck – demi-cannon firing thirty-two pounds.'

As was ever the case below decks, my height forced me to bend low, bringing my eyes almost to the same level as hers. The throng of men, the vast carlings and knee-timbers that supported the deck above, and the crowding presence of the guns, barrels and tackle all around us, forced me to stand much closer to her than I would have wished to be. Thus I could smell distinctly the exotic fragrance in which she had doused herself, strong enough even to diminish the hideous stench of several dozen Merhonours, and noticed things about her I had never seen before – a little mole upon her neck, there...

The Countess Louise closely inspected the nearest culverin, then stroked her fingers slowly up and down along its smooth iron barrel. 'Such length,' she said. 'Such restrained power. And then, in the heat of action ... it ... erupts.'

Her face remained entirely innocent. To this day, I doubt whether the same could have been said of mine, or of those nearby.

We passed along the deck, the sweating men parting like the Red Sea before Moses. Even the most insolent were as simpering babes in her presence. To them she was entirely gracious, the epitome of a great lady, bestowing a smile here and a little nod there. All the while, she kept up a constant barrage of questions, apparently genuinely eager to know more of this entirely male world into which she had stepped unbidden.

'This long pole, then, is the whipstaff, by which the ship is steered?'

'Indeed, My Lady. It is connected to the tiller on the deck beneath, which in turn moves the rudder at the stern.'

'Ah. And only one pair of hands, pulling upon this pole, is sufficient to move it this way and that?'

I stammered a response. 'G – generally so, My Lady, although in heavy seas and high winds we would have several men upon it.'

'I can imagine it – the bucking and rearing of the ship, riding upon a great sea.' She looked about her. 'The door yonder?'

'Admits to the lower great cabin, presently the quarters of My Lord of Andelys.'

'An interesting man, the noble *comte*. Tell me, Matthew, does he spend much time at the court of the Most Christian?'

A strange thing to ask, even for an avowed agent of that monarch. 'I believe not, My Lady. Since his return to France, he has been concerned principally with the restoration of his ancestral estates, which were much wasted during the wars of the Fronde.'

'I see.' She was thoughtful and seemed to be on the verge of asking another question about Roger, but appeared to think better of it. Instead she spied Ali Reis and Julian Carvell before the trunk of the mainmast, and returned the shameless stares with which they favoured her.

'Not only a Frenchman, but a Moor and a blackamoor also! Truly, good-brother, the world sails with you! Tell me, blackamoor, how come you to be aboard?'

I had never seen the eternally confident and cheerful Julian Carvell lost for words, but now he was almost as tongue-tied as a mute, staring down at the deck and shuffling uncomfortably. 'Signed aboard a king's ship in Virginia, M'Lady,' he mumbled eventually, trying and failing to keep his eyes anywhere other than the countess's bosom.

'Virginia,' she said. 'I know of Virginia. My late husband, General Gulliver, had an estate there. I believe he owned a hundred or two of your kind.'

'I did not take kindly to being owned, M'Lady,' growled Carvell, recovering his voice and meeting her eyes impudently.

She eyed him up and down as though inspecting a horse. 'Had I known he owned such as you, I would have endured the voyage and undertaken a tour,' said my good-sister, out-brazening him. Ali Reis and the other lads crowded behind him smirked.

'Now, Matthew, what is this device?'

'The warping capstan, My Lady. And a little way ahead lies the jeer capstan, which we use for lifting guns, yards and so forth. This, the warping capstan, is for the anchors, as is the main capstan on the deck beneath. But as its name suggests, this is the capstan we employ when we need to warp – that is, My Lady – say, if we are entering or leaving a harbour, then oft times we need to secure the ship to buoys or pillars ashore to haul her in or out.'

She seemed aggrieved. 'I know what warping is, Matthew. I saw it done often enough when I was a child, albeit never performed upon machines so vast.'

This was an unexpected revelation. I recalled how determined my uncle and wife – aye, and myself, if truth be told – had once been upon laying bare the life of our countess, which seemed shrouded in such mystery. Yet now, unbidden, she offered up this tantalising clue to her past. 'You grew up near the sea, My Lady?'

'Near enough to it to walk to this harbour or that.' *Which?* But with my men so close on every side, all ears, I could hardly press her. 'Do you know, Matthew, I think that if I had been a man, the sea would have been my trade, too?'

It was impossible to think of a riposte to such a strange remark. All I could venture was, 'We are nearly at the very fore part of the ship, My Lady. You have seen enough?'

'There is more, beneath this deck?'

'Another entire gun-deck, but lower and darker. Beneath that, the orlop with the cockpit and many of the officers' stores, along with the powder room. And lowest of all, the hold. But I fear the heat and stink will overcome Your Ladyship, and the ladders to the lower decks would be too steep and narrow for – for –'

'For my choice of garment.' She smiled. 'If I were dressed as you are, good-brother, nothing would deter me from exploring every inch of the ship. But you have the right of it. I fear my present attire was not intended for such as you have described.'

As we approached the great brick fireplace of the galley, toward the ship's bow, the tenor of her conversation changed abruptly.

'I must obtain for you an invitation to dine aboard the *Royal Charles*, Matthew. Why, it is a very miniature of Whitehall! Most excellent company – Her Royal Highness, of course, and dear Harry Brouncker, my very good friends – Lord Falmouth – and last night we had his Grace of Buckingham with us!'

I recalled another dinner, one that now seemed so very long ago, and vowed that I would do all in my power to avoid being in the company of the loathsome Brouncker and this, his assumed lover. Yet I have to confess I was intrigued by this new proof that, having been rejected by the king, my good-sister seemed successfully to have ingratiated herself with the woman who might one day be queen. After all, what else could explain my good-sister's presence in the fleet, unless she felt an especially urgent need to be serviced by Harry Brouncker?

'My thanks, My Lady. But there is much to do aboard this ship if we are to be ready for battle.'

'Surely the ship will survive without you for the duration of one meal, Matthew?' She studied my face too closely for my liking. 'Why, truly you have turned Puritan in your wooden world, good-brother, as I told you at Ravensden Abbey!' Many of my men were still within earshot, else I would have reproved the insolent harpy. With difficulty, then, I managed to maintain decorum and merely nodded.

As we turned, she said casually, 'Tell me, Matthew – have you heard if My Lord Mordaunt is come to the fleet? I have a matter of import that I wish to discuss with him.'

Mordaunt. Why the devil should she concern herself with Mordaunt? 'No, My Lady. But as you have said, the fleet is full of volunteers, and more come out by the day. It may be that the noble lord is somewhere among us, but that his presence is as yet unknown to me.'

'Ah. But then –'

I heard a message shouted down the hatchway of the stern ladder and watched as it was passed from man to man down the length of the deck. Within moments one of the Welshmen – Morgan, as I recall, who had once been a drover – was turning to me, saluting with a knuckle to the forehead, and saying in heavily accented English, 'Begging pardon, Captain. Signal aboard the flag – flagmen and senior captains to attend the council of war.'

O give thanks unto the Lord, because he is gracious: for his mercies endureth for ever. Yet even as I offered up the prayer of Azariah, my good-sister gripped my arm unexpectedly and urgently. 'Before you abandon me, Matthew, one more thing, I beg – do you know what is become of Tristram?' The Countess Louise's mask had slipped; there was a strangeness about her eyes, an uncertainty in her tone, that I had seen only once before, that night of the great reception at Whitehall. 'He – he promised to supply me with evidence from your family's history. But he is not at his lodgings in Oxford, nor at the Royal Society, and I do not know what has become of him.'

'No, My Lady,' I said sharply, eager to be rid of her and to be at the council. 'I regret I have not heard from my uncle, and have no knowledge of his movements.'

As I escorted the countess back to the upper deck, I thought upon her curious remarks. Why should she suddenly be so concerned to know the whereabouts of Lord Mordaunt and Doctor Tristram Quinton? And in that moment, I came to a troubling realisation. As I had told her, entirely truthfully, I did not know where Tristram was. I had not received a letter from him for many days, and Cornelia's troublingly perfunctory epistles from London made no mention of him. And Doctor Tristram Quinton was usually the most frequent and effusive of correspondents to both my wife and myself. Thus it was with something of an unquiet mind that I was rowed across to the *Royal Charles*.

* * *

The council assembled once again in the great cabin of the flagship. The Duke of York and Sir William Penn were already present as we entered; the duke's face, usually grave, seemed almost elevated.

'My Lords and gentlemen,' he said, 'I will not detain you long. We have had fresh intelligence from Whitehall. The Dutch fleet is at sea.' There was much murmuring: the young Duke of Monmouth grinned broadly, evidently eager for the fight. 'Thanks to Sir George Downing, his Majesty's envoy at The Hague, we know they have orders to seek us out upon our own shore and to pursue us up the Thames if they can. All the way to London Bridge, says Downing.' The fleet's commanders looked at each other. There was more murmuring.

'Impudent rogues,' growled the old Earl of Marlborough. 'The last foreign potentate to sail that far was the Emperor Claudius. I see no reason why he should be supplanted by Meinheer De Witt.'

The Duke of York gave what might have been one of his ambiguous half-smiles. 'Indeed, My Lord. Thus I believe we should disabuse their High Mightinesses, and that swiftly. Sir William?'

Penn, his gout briefly in remission, stood and looked about him. 'The fleet will sail upon the ebb tomorrow morning,' he said. This was urgency indeed! I prayed that my makeshift crew could make the *Merhonour* ready for sea in such an unconscionably short time. 'With the wind remaining thus, north-easterly, there is a danger that if we remain in this place they will trap us with the sands behind us. Therefore, Her Royal Highness and her retinue are to be landed at Harwich immediately, lest the enemy attempt anything upon the yachts.' I closed my eyes in relief and offered up a silent prayer of thanks: the means to be rid of my good-sister had been found for me. 'The fighting and sailing instructions remain as issued previously, nor is there any amendment to the signal book. However, thanks to Downing we have a new list of the enemy fleet. Study it well, gentlemen.'

One of the Duke of York's attendants circulated the simple printed broadsheet headed *Esquadres van de vloot, die onder den Lieutenant Admirael Generael, Heer Jacob van Wassanaer, Heer van Obdam, uyt Texel in Zee sullen gaen.* Later, in the boat carrying me back to the *Merhonour,* I had time to peruse it. There, Obdam himself in the *Eendracht,* eighty-four guns; there, Tromp the younger in *De Liefde,* eighty-two. Seven squadrons, five of Holland, one of Zeeland, one of the Maas, thus retaining their perverse multiplicity of flagmen. The ships generally smaller than those in our fleet, with even the greatest mounting many fewer guns. And so I continued on down the names until I reached the one I sought, in the list of ships of the Admiralty of Zeeland: *Oranje,* seventy-five guns, four hundred and fifty men; captain, Cornelis van der Eide. Thus it seemed I would be exchanging the embrace of my good-sister for that of my – perchance equally deadly – good-brother.

I returned to the *Merhonour* as dusk was falling, to be met at once by an urgent address from Francis Gale. The reply to the letter he had addressed to the Archbishop of Canterbury was finally come, and he wished to act upon its contents at once, before the ship sailed on the morning ebb. I weighed the time that we would lose against the possible efficacy of the remarkable course of action that Francis was proposing, and decided that nothing was to be lost by humouring my friend. After all, I reflected, every man in the fleet from the Duke of York downwards would expect the *Merhonour* to be tardy in sailing.

Thus it was that an hour or so later, with the Gunfleet in darkness, that an astonishing scene was played out upon the deck of the *Merhonour*. The entire ship's company was crowded into every vantage point in the waist and forecastle. Torches and lanterns had been lit and affixed to the ship's rail on both sides to illuminate the spectacle, although it was nearly time for the night watch to be set. I stood upon the quarterdeck, resplendent in my breastplate, best jerkin and hat, alongside Gideon Giffard, Kit Farrell and Roger d'Andelys, all similarly attired.

Francis Gale emerged from the steerage to gasps and murmuring. He was attired in his usual surplice, but over it he wore a vivid purple stole, a garment previously unseen on his person and unknown in any parish church in the land. Upon his head was a square black catercap, a vestment that Francis usually eschewed. The chaplain of the *Merhonour* strode confidently through the throng and pulled himself up onto the main hatch, at the heart of his congregation.

The hubbub diminished. Francis looked around, not speaking until he was attended by complete silence.

'In the name of the Father, and of the Son, and of the Holy Ghost, Amen.'

The crew amened dutifully, if a little uncertainly.

Then came something perfectly unexpected – at least, perfectly unexpected by the ship's captain. Ieuan Goch, standing upon the fore-hatch, intoned the same words in his own tongue: 'Yn enw'r Tad, a'r Mab, a'r Yspryd Glân, Amen.' The Welshmen in the crew amen'd more loudly.

In a particularly strong and confident tone, even for him, Francis began a prayer that was entirely new to every man aboard the ship, her captain included. 'Saint Michael the Archangel, illustrious leader of the heavenly army, defend us in the battle against principalities and powers, against the rulers of the world of darkness and the spirit of wickedness in high places!'

Simultaneously, Ieuan Goch translated: 'Mihangel Sant, arweinydd enwog o'r fyddin nefol...'

I smiled. I still had no inkling of what Francis was about, but it was clear that he had recruited Ieaun Goch to his cause. An unlikely but for-midable alliance indeed, I reflected as the prayer continued. 'Entreat we beseech thee the Lord God of battles to cast Satan down beneath our feet, so as to keep him from further holding man captive.' In the flickering torchlight, I could see men looking curiously at each other, then, spell-bound, at their chaplain. 'Michael, bearer of the fiery sword, carry our prayers up to God's throne, that the mercy of the Lord may descend and lay hold of the beast, the serpent of old, Satan and all his demons, casting him in chains into the abyss, so that he can no longer seduce mankind!'

Roger whispered, 'I have heard these prayers, I think. In Latin, naturally, and cast in a very different way – when our priest in Andelys was dealing with some poor peasant girl, said to be possessed by the devil. But it is the same rite, I think.'

'Rite? What rite?'

He looked at me in surprise. 'A rite of exorcism, Matthew. You did not know?'

No, I did not; but even as I gawped in astonishment at Roger, the purpose of Francis's correspondence with the Lord Archbishop was finally made clear. Only from Sheldon himself, the fount of authority for all naval chaplains, could Francis Gale obtain the special licence necessary to perform such a ceremony.

'Let God arise,' cried Francis, 'and let his enemies be scattered! Let them also that hate him flee before them!'

The sixty-eighth psalm, then, familiar enough to every man aboard for the responses to be uttered lustily. Ieuan Goch's translation ensured a pious and emphatic echo from the Welsh. The psalm concluded, Francis embarked upon the dread climax of the ritual, his voice rising ever louder, his arms and eyes becoming ever more animated.

'We cast thee out from this ship, every unclean spirit, every satanic power, every legion and onslaught of the infernal adversary, in the name and by the power of our Lord Jesus Christ! We command thee, begone!'

Now even the dullest man in the crew knew the purpose of this astonishing communion. Everywhere I looked, I saw tension, excitement and fear writ large across men's faces. The more devout had their eyes closed and were intoning their own prayers. Others urged Francis on, like spectators in an ancient amphitheatre supporting their favourite gladiator.

The Reverend Gale was equal to it all. Arms raised aloft, he circled upon the spot where he stood, speaking with all the authority that an archbishop could bestow, striking down the curse of the *Merhonour* and the dark force that lay behind it.

'Begone, Satan, father and master of lies, enemy to the good of mankind! Bow down before God's mighty hand, tremble and flee as we call on the holy and awesome name of Jesus, before whom the denizens of hell cower, to whom the Cherubim and Seraphim praise with unending cries as they sing: Holy, holy, holy, Lord God of Sabaoth!'

A sudden breeze made the torches flicker. I felt my bones chill; was there truth in all of this? Could that be a sign of a departing malignity?

I chided myself: Quintons should be made of sterner stuff.

Francis nodded to Stockbridge, one of the ship's boys, who stepped forward and presented him with a large phial. Francis took up a brush, dipped it into the phial, and sprinkled a clear liquid over the men nearest to him. Then he stepped down and strode through the crew, purifying every man and every quarter of the ship. Not a brush, then, I realised: an aspergilla, sprinkling holy water to drown any remaining evil aboard the ship. Some men wept. Others raised their hands in supplication to receive the divine fluid.

'Impressive,' said Roger. 'No cardinal could have done it better.'

'Let us hope that it has put paid to the curse of the *Merhonour* – or for the men's belief in the curse, at any rate,' I said, hoping that my rapid breathing and racing pulse were not evident to my interlocutors. 'And that, gentlemen,' I said, looking at my officers, 'we shall have to leave in the hands of God.'

As I turned to leave the quarterdeck, a thought clad in my grandfather's unexorcised voice whispered, *Aye, boy. God, or the Dutch.*

Chapter Eighteen

I see not what your force can do to Penn
In th' Royal Charles with all your ships and men.
Know that the sturdy famous Royal Oak
Fears not your artificial thunder stroke.
But if she should miscarry, we could fell
(If it were lawful) more at Boscobel.
~ John Bradshaw, *Some Thoughts Upon*
the Dutch Navies Demurr (1665)

Noon: the first day of June in the year of grace, Sixteen Hundred and Sixty Five.

Yardley and his mates were already in place upon the quarterdeck, adjusting the Master's quadrant. I brought out a much smaller and altogether more curious instrument that resembled a small golden ball, but which, once unlocked, revealed a multiplicity of dials and gauges. This had been my grandfather's pride and joy, accompanying him on all his voyages across the oceans of the world. I lined up the eighth Earl of Ravensden's dial to the sun, and at the horizon. I read off the numbers on the gauge, then repeated the process as a failsafe. Finally, I consulted my waggoner, examined the chart, and announced authoritatively, 'Fifty-two degrees, thirty minutes north.' I said, 'Virtually due east of Southwold by three leagues. Or thereabouts.'

Giffard, Yardley and Kit Farrell, who had all taken their own independent observations, nodded in agreement, and the *Merhonour* duly had her noon position. This was one aspect of the sea-trade in which I felt increasingly confident, having practised it daily during my previous commands. After some early disasters, such as when lying in the harbour of Messina and establishing to my own short-lived satisfaction that we were several hundred leagues up the Amazon, I had reached a condition where my observations were rarely even a minute or two out from those of the most expert navigators.

Prayers and the noonday observation ushered in a new ship's day, and with it the crew's main meal. But messes had barely begun queuing at the cook's pot when our lookout cried out.

My officers and I all lifted our eyepieces and looked out toward the east, where Prince Rupert's White squadron formed the van.

'The prince is hoisting and lowering the Ancient,' said Giffard. 'The enemy fleet's in sight.'

The intelligence was around our fleet in the blinking of an eye. It was almost possible to sense the new resolve that only the prospect of imminent battle can bring.

I turned to my lieutenants. 'Very well. Mister Giffard, Mister Farrell, I think it is time to clear the decks for action.'

Kit grinned in return. 'Time indeed, sir.'

The distant sounds of trumpets and drums provided evidence that the process had already begun on other ships of the fleet. Now the *Merhonour* joined them, the off-duty larboard watch joining their brethren of the starboard in making the ship ready for action. I had given the same order several times aboard lesser ships, but had never before witnessed it aboard such a great man-of-war. I went below and took in the scene. My cabin was already vanishing before my eyes: the bulkhead that kept me private from the rest of the ship was coming down, the legs were being removed from my table, and my sea-chest was being manhandled into the hold. Roger d'Andelys seemed to have forgotten his lordly dignity and was cheerily assisting the men in demolishing every partition in their way; but perhaps tearing down the structures of the English fulfils some ancient, deep-rooted need within every Frenchman. The men were content and determined, all still in awe of the previous evening's performance from Francis Gale, most convinced that the curse of the *Merhonour* was well and truly despatched to the infernal regions whence it had sprung.

Forward, gunport after gunport snapped open in succession, admitting the bright daylight, and I saw the upper gundeck in all its splendour, to either side the nine bronze culverins that had so impressed my good-sister. Gun captains and their crews were vigorously polishing their weapons, competing with each other to achieve the brightest shine upon their barrels; a strange conceit, as a dull gun will kill as effectively as a shining one, but such things have ever mattered greatly to the English mariner.

I returned to the quarterdeck and levelled my eyepiece once again upon the horizon, straining to spot what the van could already see, irritated beyond measure when some of our own ships passed in front of my lens and blocked my view. There was our scouting frigate, returning toward the fleet with her topgallants flying, the signal that the enemy was in sight. There, behind her – a speck – was that the top of a mast? Another speck, to northward? A moment later, there could be no mistake. Upon the horizon at east-north-east, bearing down upon us, borne upon the wind blowing from that direction, a tiny band of specks grew and merged into a broader band of wood and canvas. The headmost were now recognisable as ships; hulls and sails became distinguishable. Not long afterwards, it was possible to tell two-deckers and three-deckers apart, with reassuringly fewer of the latter than were present in our fleet. Another turn of the glass, and I could just glimpse the unmistakeable horizontal bars, red-white-blue, of the Dutch ensign. Only a little longer and I could confirm with my own eyes the word that had already come back from the scouts of the van: one hundred ships, more or less, almost identical to our strength.

'Well, gentlemen,' I said with as much levity as I could muster, 'it seems Lord Obdam has us at a disadvantage. He has the wind.'

Giffard and Kit nodded gravely. This was dire: Penn's confident plan of battle had been founded on the assumption that we would have the weather gage, upwind of the enemy, and could thus choose the moment and the method of our attack. Yet we had lingered too long at the Gunfleet, in part thanks to the Duchess of York's untimely sojourn, and a strong north-easterly had given the Dutch fleet the advantage. At any moment, the enemy would press down against us and we would have to attempt to form our line-of-battle defensively, into the teeth of the wind and the Dutch.

I turned my glass upon Lawson's *Royal Oak*, alert to any sign of an untoward movement by her, and then upon the other ships commanded by former Commonwealths-men: Jordan's *St George*, Smith's *Mary* and in the distance the likes of Myngs' *Triumph*. Nothing: no unexpected movement out of the sailing order, no putting on or slackening of sail. Nothing. The navy of England remained united.

The glass turned and the ship's bell rang. No doubt like every other captain in the fleet, I stood rooted to my quarterdeck, the telescope at my eye until the socket hurt. Another turn of the glass, another ring of the bell, and still the Dutch stood upon the horizon. Still no English ship made an unexpected move.

'What in the name of Heaven is Obdam waiting for?' I complained in the middle of the afternoon. 'He has the advantage. Why does he not attack?' I did not utter my still darker thought: that any treachery within our own fleet was not likely to reveal itself until, or if, the Dutch admiral made his move.

Roger d'Andelys had come on deck. 'Cowardice,' he said. 'A French fleet holding the wind would be engaged by now. Perhaps the Dutch seek courage in the only way they know, and even now their decks are awash with gin.'

Kit Farrell shook his head. 'Madness more like, My Lord. The longer Obdam delays, the greater the likelihood of the wind changing, or of our fleet regaining the weather gage.'

And indeed, that was precisely what we were endeavouring to do: all through the afternoon, our fleet edged slowly southward and eastward, seeking to restore the advantage to ourselves. The Dutch must have known what we were about, and yet they made no attempt to stop us. Still they refused to engage.

Understanding, when it came to me, was a kind of epiphany. I lowered my telescope, looked at Roger and Kit, and said calmly, 'Not quite cowardice and not quite madness, but perhaps a little of both. He does not trust his fleet.' I thought back to our first council-of-war, to the intelligence that had been presented to us, and felt increasingly confident in my assessment. 'They've had almost no sea-time compared to us, he has a hierarchy beneath him that not even a madman would conceive, and enough jealousies between them to make the House of Commons resemble a harmonious congregation of saints. Obdam has to give himself time to ensure that his fleet obeys his will – and though an east wind gives him the advantage now, it will also cut off his retreat if he loses. So he waits for a still more favourable wind – and to convince himself that his fleet will obey him.'

All of my concern, and perhaps that of the Duke of York too, had been with the possibility of disloyalty in our own fleet; we had forgotten that Obdam had perhaps even greater cause to suspect it in his.

Confident now that no battle was imminent, I went below for a meal of herrings, salt-beef stew and bread.

* * *

Through the evening and night, and then through the whole of the next day, the picture remained the same. The Dutch stood off to the east, some three leagues away, and came no nearer. For our part, we continued to edge further to eastward, especially in the afternoon when the wind came round more to the south-east. At noon we were some four leagues south-east of Lowestoft, eight hours later some seven leagues due east of it. I slept through a fair part of the afternoon on that second day of June, albeit on a blanket upon the deck where my cabin had been, anticipating that I would soon need every waking hour I could muster. Yet sleep was elusive. A man-of-war is always a place of noise and bustle, and when battle threatens, it is doubly so. What seemed to be a herd of stampeding bulls upon the deck above my head turned out to be men rigging the protective canvas 'fights' upon our bulwarks: the feeble barriers that were intended to give the men on the upper deck (the captain included) some protection from small shot if it came to close fighting.

At about midnight I was summoned to the quarterdeck, bathed in the light of our vast stern lanterns and by a sharp moon. Kit pointed triumphantly to our swallow-tail pennant at the maintop.

'Wind's changed, Captain. South-south-west. We have gained the weather gage, sir. And look yonder. One of the Dutchmen is ablaze – probably a fireship that's taken light accidentally.'

Off to the north-east, bright flames lit the horizon. Through my eyepiece I could see a black hull and masts, all alight. Occasionally the hull of another Dutch ship passed in front of the burning wreck, seeming for all the world like a ghost ship upon the fiery ocean of Hell.

'Perhaps they'll do our work for us, Kit,' I said lightly. 'We need only another hundred or so to do the like!'

Dawn broke at four. At once, it was clear to every man in our fleet that the Dutch had awoken from their torpor: Obdam had ordered his ships to tack, and they were bearing down upon us, stemming westward. The signal to form line-of-battle broke out upon the *Royal*

Charles, and I prayed that this time, the *Merhonour* would not be disgraced. I strode impatiently from starboard to larboard and back again, then down to the forecastle and back again, watching as Yardley and Giffard conned us toward the stern of the *Royal Oak* in the van division of the Red Squadron, with Prince Rupert's White ahead of us and the remainder of the Red, followed by the Blue, stretching away astern. This time, I had no cause for fear. We fell in immaculately, half a cable astern of Lawson, who stood at his stern rail and nodded appreciatively.

But in truth, it was the mirror image of the practice manoeuvre. The *Merhonour* was in her allotted place, but faced with a real enemy, many of our other ships had luffed up too far to windward. Rather than an immaculate line, we had little bunches of three or four ships almost abreast, obstructing each other's lines of fire. And all the while, the Dutch approached us on the opposite tack.

It was the first time I ever saw the approach of an enemy fleet, and I marvelled at the sight. I had seen one battle of great armies, that on the dunes before Dunkirk seven years before, and although the approach of the enemy on land is a terrible prospect, it is as nothing to his approach by sea. Soldiers are but men, and thus an army is only as tall as men, with horses, flags and pikes alone giving it greater height. Yet a great fleet fills sea and sky alike with timber and canvas, each of the larger ships carrying more cannon than many an army. Young Barcock and Castle brought me my martial paraphernalia – my grandfather's sword, my father's breastplate, Cornelia's kerchief tied to my scabbard – and as I put on the garb of a warrior, I prayed both that I would be equal to the task ahead, and that the Will stored safely in my sea-chest would not need to be read for many a day.

Now commenced the overture to battle: the cacophony of drums and trumpets as each crew was whipped up into warlike spirit by music, which has accompanied warriors into battle since long before the days of Caesar and Alexander. And now the strangest event occurred. The

Merhonour, the one ship to have had no song when we first sailed from the Gunfleet, suddenly became the only ship of the English fleet to have one. As our trumpeters and drummers paused briefly to take beer and refresh their throats, Ieuan Goch of Myddfai sprang onto the grating of the fore hatch and began a war song of his land. At once, the majority of the Welshmen joined in; I could hear an answering harmony from below decks. The Cornish evidently recognised the tune, too. Treninnick, up upon the main yard, waved his arms about joyfully as he sang along.

'Ah, Matthew,' said Roger d'Andelys, who had turned the crew of *Le Téméraire* into the finest choir upon the Atlantic, 'bravo indeed! A company that can sing is a company that can fight, in all truth!'

He listened intently to the tune, hummed a few bars to get the note, and then burst into a fine rendition of the bass line, despite having to content himself with 'fa-la-la' for lyrics. None apart from the Welsh or the Cornish could sing any of the words; indeed, out of all that mighty and distinctly lengthy air, verse after verse of Celtic defiance, I recognised but one word. It was the name of the last castle in South Britain to have held out for King Charles the Martyr: Harlech.

The first firing began not long after dawn. We heard the thunderous blast of the guns from the van, Rupert's white squadron, and within moments the smoke was across our deck, attacking our nostrils and silencing the war-song of the Welsh. It thinned momentarily, and there were the headmost Dutch ships, clearing Sansum's rear division and starting to exchange fire with our leading ships, the *Bristol* and the *Gloucester* –

'Too far off,' observed Roger d'Andelys, who stood at my side; my lieutenants had gone to take up their stations on the gun decks. 'There'll be but little damage at this distance.'

Roger was right; there must have been six or seven hundred yards between the two lines. The *Royal Oak* opened fire on the headmost Dutchman – nearly our time – *nearly our time –*

There was a sudden roar of gunfire. The hull of the *Merhonour* shook as balls struck it. Several more passed through our rigging, and one tore a hole in the mainsail. In horror, I gazed not at the Dutch to larboard, for still their leading ships did not fire upon us, but away to starboard. There, some three hundred yards away and thus well out of her place behind us in the line, lay Abelson's *Guinea*.

She had fired upon us.

The great marine rebellion had begun.

* * *

As the smoke cleared, I stared angrily across the water toward the *Guinea*, drew my sword and waved it defiantly at the traitors.

We had been betrayed – the poor manoeuvring into line was but a ruse, a means by which the defecting ships could get into position to windward of the loyal – within moments we would be in a pincer between the *Royal Oak* and the *Guinea*, with the Dutch van squadron barely a few hundred yards away and ready to join them –

I felt bile and anger rise in my throat. Once before I had been deceived by a captain and a ship that secretly remained true to the old cause of the republic; now I contended against twenty, with no hope of coming off alive. Angry, afraid and determined, I turned away from the starboard rail, ready to give the order to open fire on the *Guinea* and then to fight both sides of the ship at once. Ready to fight an inevitably hopeless battle to the death against Dutchmen and English traitors.

'We are betrayed, My Lord!' I informed the Comte d'Andelys.

Roger drew his sword and saluted me. 'So we fight Englishmen, then, Matthew? So be it. I shall be neither the first Frenchman nor the first Gaillard-Herblay so to do.'

'*Vive le roi, mon seigneur d'Andelys, et vive la Merhonour!*' I cried, returning his salute. 'Scobey, there! Orders to the Master Gunner –

starboard battery to prepare to engage the *Guinea* upon my command, each gun as she bears –'

Hearing my order, the gun captains nearest me upon the upper deck readied their linstocks -

Hold, boy. Look again. It might have been the breeze, or the incessant gunfire all along the forward half of our line of battle, or perhaps an almost forgotten voice in my head. But something made me turn back to the rail, to look out again at the *Guinea*.

Abelson's hands were raised in supplication. His ship was turning, endeavouring to fall into her proper place in the line directly astern of us. And at once I knew: there was no treachery here. In his eagerness to fight the Dutch, Abelson had given the order to fire even though his vision was obscured by the gunsmoke ruling back from the *Royal Oak*'s broadside. His gun crews had fired into the *Merhonour* by accident. The relief flooded over me like the waves of a spring tide.

I snatched a voice trumpet from Turner, one of the master's mates, and shouted a belaying order to Scobey. A breathless and clearly exhilarated Cherry Cheeks Russell ran onto the quarterdeck at that moment. 'Captain, sir! Mister Webb requests the order to open fire!'

'Are the lower deck ports safe, Mister Russell?'

'Mister Webb swears they are so, sir!'

The consequence of Penn's belief in the line-of-battle, and thus in sheer weight of shot, was that the heaviest guns possible had been crammed into every ship in the fleet, the *Merhonour* included, so that in even a moderate swell opening the lowest range of leeward gunports threatened to swamp the ship. But if Webb swore we had enough freeboard – very well, then –

I looked out to larboard again. The headmost Dutch ships had attempted to concentrate fire on the *Royal Oak*, attracted by her Vice-Admiral's flag at the foretopmast head, but now their stems were cutting through clear water again. In a moment, they would be abreast of us.

'Very well, Mister Russell! Orders to Mister Webb! Larboard guns to fire an entire broadside upon the headmost of the enemy as they bear, then sequential fire by the battery upon the downroll, lower deck first!'

Russell ran off to Webb, and within moments the larboard battery of the *Merhonour* blazed out in defiance, as it had done against the Invincible Armada all those years before. Flame and smoke spouted ferociously from the larboard broadside. The great ship shook from the recoils, the ancient timbers groaning in protest. I felt the timbers strain and quiver beneath my feet, sending shock waves through my entire body. The *Merhonour* was beginning her last battle; and thanks be to God, it seemed it would not be fought against fellow Englishmen.

That first pass of the fleets was my first experience of a fleet battle, and it seemed hellish beyond all measure: the endless roar of broadsides, our own among them; the ever-increasing clouds of acrid gunsmoke; the scream of shot flying overhead, or into the rigging, or into the sea. Our guns blazed away, the crews working almost as automatons: fire, recoil, secure, swab, reload, ram home, turn outward again, aim, linstock, *give fire*! Boys ran to and from each gun as though their lives depended on it, bringing up fresh powder cartridges and more shot from the magazine below. Upon my watch, I calculated that each gun was firing perhaps every seven or eight minutes, and few ships in the fleet would be able to match that. I made several expeditions along the upper deck to encourage the sweating, determined gun crews, nearly dancing between the recoils of the great guns, stabbing my sword at the distant enemy and roaring like an actor declaiming Macbeth.

'Strike home, my lads! Steady your aim, Pascoe! Let the Dutch dogs shit your chainshot, boys! A hit, by God! Fine shooting, Penhaligon's crew! Now, my brave Welsh boys, you'll not let the Cornish outmatch you? *Give fire!*'

Through the smoke I could sometimes spy the hulls and masts of the Dutch ships as their fleet passed along our line. Occasional glimpses of the flags at their jackstaffs and ensigns bore witness to the complexity of the Dutch state: here a ship of Flushing, there one of Hoorn or Harlingen; here a tricolour, there a nine-barred triple-prince ensign. All were intermingled, suggesting that their squadrons were in even greater disarray than ours. Many ships were past us before our gunners were able to lay in a bearing and open fire; when the smoke rolling along the line was particularly dense, some ships were by us before we even knew they were there. For one brief moment we exchanged broadsides with the *Eendracht* herself, Obdam's flagship, but then she was gone into the smoke, her place taken by another. And so it went on for an hour or more, the captain of the *Merhonour* pacing his deck, waving his sword and shouting defiance and encouragement, until at last the entire Dutch fleet was past us.

During the lull that followed I slumped against the starboard rail of the quarterdeck, greedily imbibed a bottle of small beer that young Barcock brought me, and rested a voice made hoarse by ceaseless shouting. Kit Farrell came on deck with Francis Gale, saluted, and reported the situation below decks. One man killed by a great splinter through his stomach – this on the starboard side, and so a consequence of the *Guinea*'s error – and three more wounded, with one more ruptured when he misjudged his grip on the rope he was hauling. I nodded; it was a minimal butcher's bill, although it would not seem so to a newly and as yet unknowingly widowed young woman of Shadwell. Roger d'Andelys had been right, and the two fleets had been too far apart to inflict serious damage on each other. But there was surely worse to come. For now they were nearly clear of Lord Sandwich's squadron in the rear, the Dutch would be able to tack back and thus regain the weather gage.

Kit lifted his telescope to study the scene of battle. 'Captain,' he said suddenly, 'look there, sir. The *House of Nassau* – I can barely believe it...'

I took up my own eyepiece. There, just visible through occasional gaps in the swirling gunsmoke, was our old ship, now Beau Harris's command. There was no apparent fault with the *Nassau*; her masts and rigging all stood, although there were a few shots through her sails, and she appeared to be answering her rudder. But there was something terribly, terribly wrong with Harris's ship, and it must have been immediately apparent to every man in the English navy.

Put simply, the *House of Nassau* was sailing in precisely the opposite direction to the rest of our fleet. She was sailing directly into the middle of the Dutch.

'Why in Hell's fires as he done that?' cried Kit. 'He must have ordered –'

'Harris must have ordered the ship to tack,' I said hoarsely, my voice still fragile. 'Whether because he seeks a glorious immortality or because he does not actually know what a tack is, we might now never know.'

And there, I thought, *would have gone Matthew Quinton, but for the grace of God and the patience of Kit Farrell, so few years before.*

Kit was almost in tears. 'He is a good man – Captain Harris. No seaman, and wilfully ignorant of the ways of a ship, but a good, decent soul.'

'Aye,' I said with a heavy heart, 'a good man, and a good friend.' I put my hand on my lieutenant's shoulder. 'Let us pray that even if he does not have the sense to steer the correct course, he has the sense to surrender before they blow him to oblivion.'

The Dutch fleet swallowed the *House of Nassau* like a great sea-beast devouring small fry. I saw the clouds of smoke and heard the blast of broadsides as she met her fate. As one, Kit, Roger and I raised our swords to attention in salute to Beaudesert Harris, captain of His Majesty's Navy Royal; Francis Gale intoned a prayer; and I felt that emptiness which only the death of a friend before his time can bring.

Roger d'Andelys, who if truth be told was even less of a seaman than Beau, suddenly pointed ahead. 'Look, Matthew – your German prince is turning to starboard. What is he about, I wonder?'

A confirmatory cry from our lookout reached me, and I took up my telescope. Rupert's flagship, the *Royal James*, and the ships ahead of her, had evidently withdrawn their men from the guns and now had them about the yards, putting on more sail as though the devil pursued them. I swung around and trained my piece on the masts of the *Royal Charles*. There was no union flag at the mizzen; no order for the fleet to tack from the rear. And yet that, surely, was precisely what Rupert was doing.

I looked toward the *Royal Oak* to see how Lawson would respond. But the Vice-Admiral remained resolutely set in his course, east by south. Rupert's ships were now starting to come up on the opposite tack, all out of order and in no line of any sort.

In desperation, I turned to Kit Farrell. 'Kit, what in God's name is happening?'

My friend's brow was furrowed. 'Lawson has the right of it, since there is no signal,' he said slowly. 'But the prince has the right of it, too. Tacking from the rear is our only chance of preventing the Dutch weathering us.'

The *Royal James* ploughed by us, a few hundred yards to starboard, the great plain white flag billowing out from her maintop. I could plainly see Rupert, Prince Palatine of the Rhine, Duke of Cumberland and Bavaria, upon her quarterdeck, talking animatedly to his flag-captain Kempthorne. Rupert the bold, whose impetuosity had killed my father. Rupert the truest cavalier, ever unconcerned with the orders – or absence of orders – from his superiors. Once again the prince had taken matters into his own hands and acted upon his initiative, just as he had so disastrously at Naseby.

'Captain,' said Kit, 'if we of the Red do not turn and follow him, there will be a great gap in our fleet. Obdam will most certainly pour through it.'

I looked in horror as the truth of Kit's words became apparent upon water. The White was almost past us now, Myngs aboard *Triumph* even raising his hat to Lawson and myself as he passed. Yet still the Red did not turn – still *our division* did not turn, as it would have to do first according to the Duke of York's fighting instructions and that document's rigid insistence on how the line-of-battle was to be maintained. Why was there no signal from the flagship? If the danger was so evident that young Kit Farrell had noted it, then surely Penn and all the veteran seamen around the Duke had done so too?

Then the most dreadful of thoughts came to me. What if this was the moment of treason? What if Lawson was deliberately leading the Red and Blue away, so that they would not be able to support Rupert? Yet surely that was impossible – he could not have foreseen the prince's manoeuvre. But what if he had acted spontaneously upon this sudden and apparently heaven-sent opportunity to divide our fleet?

The thoughts, and the dilemma, overwhelmed me. I went to the starboard rail and looked down into the waters. To tack, and follow Rupert – perhaps to be overwhelmed by the Dutch and killed by the folly of that prince, just as my father had been? Or to hold my course and fight Lawson if his treachery became apparent, thus to be killed either by English treason or by the Dutch annihilating our divided fleet?

I thought of Cornelia, of my mother, of my poor brother, of Ravensden Abbey, of all I held dear. And at the last, there seemed to be another voice: *Tack, boy.*

I turned from the rail and saw the expectation in the eyes of my companions upon the quarterdeck. Kit Farrell, Roger d'Andelys and Francis Gale stood there, my own three wise men. Yardley, the master, stood a little apart, but he, too, stared at me, awaiting my command.

'Very well,' I said. 'Gentlemen, we will come about and follow the White. Mister Yardley, make it so, if you please.'

For good or ill, once more a Quinton would follow Prince Rupert of the Rhine to death or glory.

Chapter Nineteen

Now, Painter, reassume thy pencil's care;
It hath but skirmish'd yet, now fight prepare
And draw the battle terribler to show
Than the Last Judgment was of Angelo.
~ Andrew Marvell, *Second Advice to a Painter*

Nowadays I am an object of antiquarian curiosity, somewhat akin to Stonehenge or Hadrian's Wall. Children goggle at me in the street. Fresh-faced young sea-officers seek me out, or are told to seek me out, to hear my tales of nearly mythical battles long ago and of the legends with whom I served – Rupert, Holmes, Lawson, all the rest of them. Yet these young men look at me with disbelief when I recount the story of this battle of Lowestoft. A captain acting on his own initiative, rather than waiting for the signal, rather than holding his place in the line? At that, they give me glances that must resemble those cast toward heretics at the stake by the men entrusted with lighting the faggots. For now obedience to the Fighting Instructions is all, and 'risk' and 'initiative' are words as abominable to the average sea-officer as 'court-martial' and 'marriage'. I said as much some months ago to my old rival and neighbour Torrington's boy, insufferably proud at having been made a post-captain at twenty-three (but such wonders are manifold when one's father is First Lord of the Admiralty). He listened gravely, for he is a serious youth, but I doubt that he absorbed the lesson. Still, perhaps after my time young Johnnie Byng will make a decent enough officer, as long as no-one thinks fit to put such a heavy insipid in command of a fighting fleet.

* * *

Having made the fateful decision to tack and follow Rupert, I realised at once that I needed to justify myself to my Lord Admiral. For now I was disobeying his orders twice over: I was falling out of my allotted place in the line without either his order or that of my divisional commander, Sir John Lawson; and, perhaps worse, I was abandoning my injunction to stay in Lawson's wake in case he truly intended to go over to the Dutch side. Yet to me, in that dire moment, the very real threat of Lord Obdam and his mighty fleet, glimpsed from time to time through gaps in our own confused formation, was far more immediate than any hypothetical prospect of a defection by the Commonwealths-men. Surely if they had meant to change sides, they would have done so already, not after they must have lost men to Dutch shot? This was my reasoning, although a dark doubt remained upon my heart.

I called for pen, ink and paper, and to my surprise found that those materials were supplied by Cherry Cheeks Russell, who brought them to me with a strange look of exultation on his young face. I rested the paper on top of one of the quarterdeck sakers and hastily scribbled a note to His Royal Highness.

The only way I could communicate such a confidential message to the Duke of York was by sending either *Bachelor's Delight* or a boat over to the *Royal Charles,* but that would be a remarkably dangerous mission. True, there was a lull in the firing – the Dutch were still completing their own tack from the north-west, and the sound of gunfire between them and the rear division of the Blue had been gradually diminishing as the two fleets drew apart. But any craft attempting to steer from the *Merhonour* to the *Royal Charles* would face the prospect of being run down by almost the whole of the Red squadron as it still beat south-eastward, following Lawson and the *Royal Oak.* After some contemplation, I decided that the *Delight* was too valuable to be risked in such work; she might be needed later in the fight, perhaps, in extremis, as the salvation of men abandoning a sinking ship.

'I need a boat's crew,' I cried, 'and a volunteer to carry my despatch to the duke aboard the *Royal Charles*!'

Julian Carvell, the laconic Virginian, volunteered at once to lead the crew, and alongside him stood Polzeath, Ali Reis and Macferran. Four of my most loyal followers; it would be dire indeed if the boat perished, yet I knew I needed a strong, competent crew to undertake such a perilous mission, and these men were undoubtedly some of the best under my command. But that still left the question of who could be spared to bear the message and deliver it into the duke's own hand upon his quarterdeck.

Roger d'Andelys stepped forward. 'I will take your despatch, Captain,' he said formally. 'A gentle row upon the waters will be most beneficial to my constitution.'

I bowed my head. Roger might play the French fop, but there was no doubting the bravery of this man who had once saved my life upon a Scottish moor. 'I thank you, My Lord, but it will be mightily dangerous work, unfit for a man of your rank – and who knows how I might yet require the services of the former captain of the Most Christian King's ship *Le Téméraire* in this engagement?'

'I will carry the message, Captain,' said Francis, 'for if God will not protect me, I fear there is little hope for any other.'

'Well said, Francis,' I said, 'but I think you will soon have ample business aboard this ship. I fear, old friend, that we will need both your prayers and your sword in the hours to come. And do you think my brother and mother would forgive me if I lost the vicar of Ravensden, so forcing them to present another?'

Cherry Cheeks Russell stepped forward eagerly. 'I'll go, Captain. I can swim – my cousins have thrown me in the lake at Woburn often enough for me to learn how to get out of it without drowning. Don't matter if I get killed, neither. There'll still be enough sots and enough Russells in the world.'

This was unexpected; I had not marked down young Russell as either a hero or a suicide. I half suspected that his intervention might have been brought on by Dutch courage, but the more I thought upon it, the more sense it made. My officers were either too good to be spared or too incompetent to be trusted. On the other hand, Cherry Cheeks had the social rank to be a fitting emissary to the heir to the throne, and if he perished under fire, well, then: as he himself had concluded, he was expendable.

The boy deserved a reward, I thought, but what could I possibly give him? Then it occurred to me. I smiled, and swiftly added a post-script to the letter he was to bear to the Lord High Admiral.

As the boat's crew made ready, there was a shout from our lookout at the mainmast head. 'Captain!' Kit cried. 'Look, sir! Look at the *Charles*!'

I snatched my own eyepiece and levelled at the fleet flagship. There, at the mizzen, flew the Union Flag. The courses of the great ship were loose. She was tacking, and she was ordering the rest of the fleet to tack. Ordering it to follow Rupert and the *Merhonour*.

'My congratulations, Lieutenant Farrell,' I said formally. 'It seems you divined the situation correctly.'

He grinned. 'If the Blue and the centre and rear of the Red tack smartly enough, there should be no gap between us and the White.

We will yet beat the Dutch, Captain Quinton.'

'Amen to that! And with no need to adhere to our position in the line, merely to keep the fleet together, I think there is only one proper station for this ship. Mister Yardley, there! You will steer to fall in astern of the *Royal Charles,* if you please!'

* * *

What none of us knew then was that the confusion over the order to tack was caused by one of those moments of chance and low farce that so often determine the outcome of human affairs. The Duke of York had actually given the verbal order exactly when he should have done, when it first became clear what Obdam was about; but the sailor sent aloft to break out the Union at the mizzen took so long over it that most of the Dutch fleet had completed their turn before the signal was hoisted. Thus but for the quick thinking of Prince Rupert, our fleet and the very future of England might have been doomed by the clumsy fingers of one poor wretch.

As it was, my immediate concern was with the safety of young Russell and my boat's crew. In one sense, the flagship's turn made their task easier, giving them more time to complete their voyage – for after all, the *Royal Charles* would no longer pass by us so rapidly on the opposite tack. On the other hand, the manoeuvring and positions of the intermediate ships was now even less predictable than they had been. My Lord Marlborough's *Old James,* almost as old and cumbersome as the *Merhonour,* slewed around awkwardly and almost ran them down; as it was, the boat could not avoid her wake and pitched dreadfully, so much so that I thought it would inevitably be overturned by the next wave. Through my telescope, I could see Russell clinging onto the wales for dear life. Yet the boat held its course, and I reflected that Polzeath had probably ridden out far worse conditions while fishing off his native Cornwall, Macferran in the waters of the Hebrides and

Ali Reis in the Middle Sea. As for Carvell, who unlike the others was not born to the sea, he had an apparently maniacal disregard for his own safety that seemed almost to guarantee his survival. Thus the boat completed its little voyage, and I almost cheered out loud when it secured to the larboard side of the *Royal Charles*.

Cherry Cheeks Russell later told me that he had found His Royal Highness upon the quarterdeck. The heir to England was in martial attire, clad in half armour and wearing a great broad-brimmed hat; but when he took it off to wipe his brow, Russell said, it was apparent that the hat concealed an iron skull-cap. The Duke was in the midst of a little court of his own, standing next to Sir William Coventry and Charlie Berkeley, Earl of Falmouth. Nearby were Lord Muskerry, a Mister Boyle who was a son to the Earl of Cork, and the obnoxious Harry Brouncker, my good-sister's stud. Incongruously, York's little dog was running about the quarterdeck, as content as if it was chasing a bitch in St James's Park. The Duke of Monmouth stood apart, listening to and occasionally laughing at the merry banter of the courtiers, but maintaining his wonted air of regal detachment.

A little way away, the Great Captain Commander sat upon a chair with his foot raised upon a stool, for Sir William Penn had been struck by another ferocious attack of gout. He grimaced as he passed on his orders to Harman, nominally the first lieutenant but in practice the flag captain of the *Royal Charles*, and Cox, her sailing master, whom I had encountered when he was master attendant at Deptford yard. Russell listened intently, fascinated by the presence of such great men making such great decisions. He heard the order given for the centre and rear of the Red (for Lawson, in the van, had only just begun his turn) to beat to windward so that Obdam's fleet, now almost through its tack in the north-west, could not take the weather gage away from Prince Rupert and the White.

Russell approached James Stuart, bowed, placed the letter in the royal hand, and watched the heir to the throne read it. 'Captain

Quinton has done well, I think,' the duke said. 'And he has done well by you, lad. He asks that you may remain here, upon my quarterdeck and in my presence, as a reward for your bravery.' By Russell's account, the duke glanced at Falmouth, who seemed greatly amused by the business, and at Monmouth, who nodded gravely, as though authorising what was to be done. 'Very well, then, Mister Russell,' said York, 'it shall indeed be so. We will be up again with the Dutch very shortly, and then it will be truly hot work. See those flashes yonder, hear those guns? The headmost of the prince's ships are engaged again.'

* * *

The next hour was a curious time. The *Merhonour*, now in the wake of the *Royal Charles* and the rest of the Red Squadron – except Lawson's division, out of sight far astern – moved further and further west, to windward, away from the White and Blue, which now formed a barrier between ourselves and the Dutch. We saw the guns blazing between the other squadrons and the enemy. We heard the rolling thunder of the mighty cannonade. Occasionally a mast or yard fell, tearing sails and rigging down with it. We saw Dutch ships repeatedly attempting to punch their way through the new, makeshift line of battle, charging in small groups as they were ever wont to do. Every time, they were repulsed. Yet we ourselves remained apart, well to the west, not firing at all. There was even time to repair rigging and to take some hard Cheshire cheese washed down with some small beer.

This lull was evidently not to the liking of Roger d'Andelys. 'What is this about, *mon ami*? Where is the honour in this? Why do the Red ships of England lie idly, rather than going to the aid of the noble prince and My Lord of *Sans*-Weech?'

I looked about me. I suddenly realised that for the first time, I was seeing the battle as an admiral must see it, not merely as the captain of one ship; as the Duke and Penn no doubt saw it at that very moment upon the quarterdeck of the *Royal Charles*, a few hundred yards ahead of us.

'Do you not see, Roger?' I said patiently. 'By lying here to windward, we deny the advantage to the Dutch. Even if some of Obdam's ships break through the White and the Blue, they cannot weather the entire fleet, for we shall fall on them. And if any of our ships are distressed, some or all of our Red Squadron can fall down at once to their aid. By lying here and seeming to do nothing, in truth we do everything. We make it impossible for the Dutch to win.'

Kit grinned at me: the master was evidently proud of his pupil.

Suddenly there was a cry from the masthead: a cry to look out to larboard. I raised my telescope.

My confidence in the strength of our position had been misplaced, it seemed. There, to the west, was a huge Dutch ship, far larger than the *Merhonour*. She flew the jack of the Zeeland admiralty, and she had the weather gage of our entire fleet. Moreover, she was now bearing down upon the wind. She was heading directly for us.

* * *

The lone Dutch ship came on, seemingly intent on launching a single-handed attack against the entire Red Squadron. 'My God,' cried Kit, 'what bravery! And folly, too, all in one! She's but an Indiaman – a big Indiaman, but still a merchant's hull, up against all this stout English oak!'

A Zeeland captain with the sheer pig-headed stubbornness to put himself up against the whole of the Red. A Zeeland captain with the skill to gain the weather gage, a feat that no other ship in the Dutch fleet seemed able to accomplish. A Zeeland captain in a huge Indiaman, such as the name I had read in the Dutch fleet list: the *Oranje*. I conjured up the face of my good-brother Captain Cornelis van der Eide, and prayed that I was wrong.

Francis Gale, who was better qualified to divine my prayers than any man alive, looked at the remarkably mismatched duel, looked at me, and said, 'It might not be him, Matthew.'

But my guts seemed to be tightening; somewhere, somehow, an instinct was speaking to me. No doubt Ieuan Goch of Myddfai would have had an opinion upon the matter. Indeed, there seemed to be a dreadful inevitability about it all.

She poured broadsides into the first ships to windward of us, but did not tarry. Instead she came on remorselessly, the Zeeland colours streaming out proudly. She fired twice into the *Old James* and was met by a thunderous reply from Lord Marlborough's broadside. Once again the great Dutch ship did not stay and fight. She kept under full sail, intent on passing through the Red and rejoining the rest of her fleet. Or perhaps –

I dismissed the incredible thought that occurred to me in that moment: that the Dutchman was intent on a single-handed attack upon our flagship, against the Duke of York himself. It was too much to believe, and in any case, there was no time for such contemplation. For the mighty Indiaman was now bearing down upon the *Merhonour*.

'Mister Webb!' I cried. The ancient gunner was in the waist of the upper deck, attending to a damaged carriage. He approached the quarterdeck and raised two fingers to his forehead in salute. 'He will likely give us no more than a broadside or two as he passes – to star-board, by the looks of things. Reply as you see best, Master Gunner.'

The old man nodded appreciatively; he was evidently not used to a captain giving him such freedom.

The Dutchman bore down. Her deck was alive with men, most of them armed. What if I was wrong, and rather than contenting herself with a glancing exchange, she mounted a boarding attack upon us?

I had no time to issue new orders. The mighty Indiaman came up with our starboard quarter, perhaps two hundred yards away, and at once began a rolling broadside, bow to stern. Chainshot whistled through the shrouds near to me, severing them. Routledge, one of the master's mates, screamed in agony as canister-shot struck him: I turned and saw him fumbling desperately to hold together the blood-ied remnants of his lower jaw. I ran to him, but as I reached out, his dead weight fell into my arms, his blood staining my shirtsleeves. Yardley stooped down and took hold of this, the most promising of his assistants. Then, without ceremony, he took the corpse to the larboard rail and pushed it over the side. The Christian in Matthew Quinton rebelled at such sacrilege, but the ship's captain in me nodded grimly in approbation. A ship in battle cannot afford to be cluttered with the dead; nothing is worse for a crew's morale than to see the remnants of their messmates laid out in increasingly lengthy ranks upon the deck. Landsmen, safe and warm in front of their hearths, may think this barbaric and my opinion on the matter callous beyond measure. But in my experience battles are determined by the living, not the dead, and the time to mourn is when the fight is done.

Now our decks shuddered as Webb's guns roared out, giving back our own rolling broadside in return. The air was acrid. The smoke from both ships covered us like the darkest of thunderclouds; for some moments I could see nothing at all. The Dutchman's guns fired again. I heard a dreadful shattering of timber well forward. Incongruously, our ship's bell rang and was then silent. As the smoke cleared, I looked forward and saw that much of the forecastle rail was gone, the belfry with it. Ieuan Goch and two of his fellow Welshmen were rushing to attend a blinded man whom I recognised as one of the Londoners. Contorted shapes upon the deck revealed where others had stood only moments before. Ieuan Goch picked up a nearly round, white and red object from near to the shattered belfry; it was only when he elevated it that it became possible to identify the bloodied remnant as a human head. The Welshman contemplated it for a moment, then threw it casually into the sea to swim with the corpse of Routledge.

Sword in one hand and telescope in the other, Giffard and I went down into the waist and picked our way through the carnage, him to larboard, I to starboard. One of the first men I came to was Macferran, slumped against the side of the main hatch; Hitchcock, one of the quartermasters, was pulling a fearsome splinter from his thigh with no ceremony and seemingly no regard for the pain being inflicted upon the young Scot.

'Looks worse than it is, Captain,' he said, wincing. 'Not deep. No need to trouble the surgeon.'

At that the splinter emerged: a five-inch shard of bloodied oak. As Macferran grimaced, Hitchcock wrapped a rag around the wound. 'Lucky Scots bugger,' he said.

'Hitchcock has the right of it,' I said. 'A few inches up and across, Macferran, and you'd never have fathered red-maned bairns upon any Highland lass foolish enough to take you.'

'A good thing, then, Captain!' said Macferran, as cheery as a man in dire pain could be. 'We're but a small clan, and 'tis every Macferran's duty to people it anew!'

As I moved along the deck giving words of encouragement to the men, the great Dutch ship continued upon her course, sailing off to leeward. My suspicion that she aimed to assail the *Royal Charles* and the Duke himself appeared unfounded; instead, she seemed intent upon battering her way through the inner line of the Blue and White squadrons in order to rejoin her fleet. Thus her sternpiece was now visible, and the heraldic decorations carved in the wood enabled Giffard finally to identify her.

'The *Oranje*, then,' he said, although he pronounced it the way the English do when attempting to mimic the Dutch: *Urania*. 'Whoever commands her is a true seaman, by God!'

Indeed he was. For I recalled reading my list of the Dutch fleet, and as I levelled my eyepiece at the quarterdeck of the *Oranje*, I could see the features of her captain clearly. 'And the compliments of the day to you too, good-brother,' I said.

* * *

And thus My Lord returned from his interview, in which he put bluntly to 73.4.28 that which had been sworn to him by Sir Martin Bagshawe. So wrote Phineas Musk all those long years ago, employing cipher lest his words fall into the hands of the great man whose name he dared not record. The ink upon the vellum has faded only slightly as I hold it up to the light; rather, it is my old eyes that have faded. Yet my mind is still sharp, and I realise for the first time that Musk and Lord Percival must have had this meeting almost at the moment that the *Oranje* was making her first pass.

The two men were upon the Bank Side, in the shadow of the ruined theatre, close to where the Lambeth marsh began. There was no other soul in sight; even though the plague was still chiefly across the river and it was long after dawn, the south bank was as silent as the north.

'So he denied everything?' Musk asked gloomily.

'Of course,' said Percival. 'He has a particularly convincing way of making aggrieved denials. And who are we to doubt his word? Thus, whatever we may think, it behoves us still to believe that there is, or might be, a foul conspiracy by twenty captains to betray their king and country.'

Musk was crestfallen. 'And in any case, we've no time to get to the fleet a message suggesting anything contrary?'

'None. Listen, Musk. Tell me what you can hear.'

With the city eerily quiet, it was possible to hear many sounds that were usually masked by the cacophony generated daily by the industries, animals and people of London. With less competition, the birdsong seemed a very crescendo. The Thames water lapped noisily upon the bank. And as Musk listened, there was a sound of distant thunder. Faint indeed, but there it was. Unlike ordinary thunder, though, which brought forth a few rumbles or claps, always getting nearer or further away, this was a constant, its note rising and falling, seemingly always the same distance away.

Musk knew full well what the sound signified, for he had heard it before: twelve years before, to be precise, when the cannonades of the great sea-battles during the first war with the Dutch were heard clearly in London.

'They're engaged, then,' said Musk.

'Engaged indeed,' said Lord Percival. 'So the truth of the conspiracy will already be exposed, one way or another. Let us pray that the god of battles smiles kindly upon Captain Quinton of the *Merhonour* and all our other friends engaged in this business.'

'Amen,' cried Musk with an unusual degree of fervour.

'So, Musk, but one thing remains for us – the final resolution of our other matter. And for that, we must separate.'

'Still to the destinations we discussed, My Lord?'

'Precisely as we discussed. And, Musk, let us trust that this time we have a better conclusion to our efforts!'

As the two men parted, the noise of the distant gunfire increased.

Chapter Twenty

They stab their ships with one another's guns,
They fight so near it seems to be on ground,
And ev'n the bullets meeting bullets wound.
The Noise, the Smoke, the Sweat, the Fire, the Blood
Is not to be expressed nor understood.
~ Marvell, *Second Advice to a Painter*

A little time before the glass turned at eight and the forenoon watch began, the Union broke out once again at the mizzen of the *Royal Charles*. Yet again the entire navy of England tacked in succession from the rear, but now it was under continuous artillery fire – or at least, that was the case with the White and Blue squadrons, those more adjacent to the enemy. This, again, is a tale rather too tall for those young sea-officers of our time who hear me recite it. An entire fleet tacking from the rear successfully, not once but twice, the second time under sustained fire? They cannot conceive of such a thing, for such has never even been attempted again, to this day. But we brought it off *that* day, perhaps simply because the manoeuvre was so very new and thus fear had not yet been instilled into us by those fainthearts who ever dread the difficult and the dangerous. Thus once more the *Merhonour* lumbered around onto the new course to the south-east, almost crashing into the *Leopard* as we did so. Now we were ahead of the *Charles* rather than following in her wake, and with the likes of the *Mary* and *Plymouth* having fallen somewhat to leeward, we were headed only by a couple of the Fifth Rates. The whole affair seemed very chaos upon the oceans. But somehow the fleet completed its turn and fell back into a semblance of a line. Now the business of the day began in earnest. Previously we and the Dutch had passed on opposite tacks, inflicting only minor damage upon each other in so doing. Now, though, we were in parallel to them on the same tack, the very situation that Penn had originally envisaged for his invincible line-of-battle. Surely our superior weight of shot would shatter the weaker, smaller Dutch hulls. It was only a matter of time.

I could just make out Lawson's *Royal Oak* in the far distance. Having been the last to turn when the first great tack of the fleet was made, he was now at the very head of the entire line, the great red flag spilling out from his foretopmast. The broadsides of his division, and of the White and Blue behind him, roared out time after time, returned in good measure by those of the Dutch.

From all of this, the centre and rear divisions of the Red remained apart, still to windward of the main engagement, still waiting to deploy where the need seemed most pressing.

Roger d'Andelys looked out over the scene and mumbled, as much to himself as to me, '*Ce n'est pas juste*. The others yonder, they take all the harm and death, yet here we sit like as though upon a mere summer's cruise. Ah, the poor devils.'

I said nothing, but shared not a little of Roger's disquiet. In Lawson's division, and in the Blue and White squadrons, the casualties were doubtless mounting and good men were surely dying. By now it was noon, and the great cannonade had been going on for four hours;

but the two divisions of the Red, including some of the mightiest ships of Old England, were still lying inactive to windward. I shot many a glance toward the *Royal Charles* and wondered what, in God's name, the Duke was playing at. Or rather what Penn was playing at, for I had no doubt he was the man deciding when, or if, the bulk of the Red Squadron would finally commit to the battle.

Of course, my concern at our inactivity was grounded in my desire to see an English victory, and not at all in a selfish compulsion to obtain glory, honour and prize money. Or so I told myself: those who contemplated my increasingly impatient pacing across the quarter-deck and then back again might have regarded the matter differently. At one point I went down once more into the waist, both to take my mind off our inactivity and to encourage the men. But the exercise was futile. I was met at once by Julian Carvell's typically blunt assessment.

'Captain, sir, we're as idle as eunuchs in a bawdy house. When the fuck will we get the order to attack?'

'Ours is not to doubt the strategy of princes, Carvell.'

'I don't doubt His Royal Highness, sir,' he drawled. 'But as for that fat gouty craven Penn –'

'Thank you, Carvell, that will be sufficient. Unless you wish to see both of us before a court-martial for slandering the Great Captain Commander?'

The Virginian, who had one of the fastest minds of any man I ever met, retorted, 'Don't recall anything about that in any of the Articles of War you keep reading out to us, Captain. In fact, reckon I could call the Lord High Admiral an addled fuckwit, 'cause it don't seem to say that I can't anywhere in the Articles. Sir.'

I laughed. 'All the proud lawyers of the Inns of Court should be grateful you will never enter their profession, Carvell.'

But the men around Carvell were less patient and less witty. They growled with longing to be in battle, some no doubt to bring victory to England, some in hope of prize money, some in the knowledge that a swift end to the war would release them from this floating hell into which they had been thrust unwillingly. Impotent to expedite their ambitions, I retreated once more to the quarterdeck. Kit Farrell had his telescope trained upon the distant *Royal Oak*, perhaps three miles to the east of us and only barely visible through occasional gaps in the smoke and the tangle of increasingly shattered men-of-war. 'Look there, Captain. Lawson is luffing out of the line.'

The old thought of treason crossed my mind again, but even my first cursory look at the *Oak* suggested that nothing could be further from the truth. The great ship was desperately damaged, with much of her rigging shot to pieces and her sails torn. But the same was true of many other ships along the line to leeward of us. Jordan's *St George*, now occupying our old place roughly astern of the *Royal Oak*, seemed in a far worse state than her flagship, yet still she held her position, firing intermittently into the Dutchman opposite her. Something was evidently badly wrong aboard Lawson's command, and word of it came to us soon enough. We saw the *Royal Oak*'s ketch put on sail and weave dexterously through the wreckage and open water that lay between her and our force away to windward. As she passed under her quarter I saw one of her master's mates, whom I recognised from my previous visits to his ship.

'Royal Oaks, there!' I cried. 'What's afoot? How fares it with Sir John?'

The mate almost spat his answer at me. 'Shot through the knee and too hurt to command,' he bawled. 'The master dead, the ship in confusion. It might not have been thus if you had kept station, *Merhonour*!'

I felt the words as a blade in the ribs: surely the man only spoke truth? For my impetuosity in following Prince Rupert into the first tack, a good man – nay, a great man – was perhaps like to lose his life, and the finest new ship in our fleet was maimed so badly that she had to fall out of the fight.

The *Royal Oak*'s boat avoided us in its return voyage, and I only learned later of the message it bore: Jordan of the *St George* to relieve Lawson in command, and thus hopefully to oversee the hasty running repairs of the newer and more potent ship and bring her back into the battle.

Now it was near two, and the issue of the day was in the balance. From our frustrating distance we could plainly see three or four great Dutch ships surrounding Sandwich's *Royal Prince*, endeavouring to hammer that mighty old hull. Sandwich's second, the *Montagu*, came up to her relief but was immediately attacked by the vast Indiaman that I recognised at once as the *Oranje*, the ship that had exchanged broadsides with us so recently. My good-brother seemed deliberately to drive his command into the *Montagu*; even amidst the thunderous crescendo of incessant broadsides, we could clearly hear the impact of timber upon timber as the hulls struck. Through my telescope, I watched Cornelis's men swarm over the gunwales and onto the upper deck of the *Montagu*. It was the Dutch way: charge and board. If they could evade our devastating broadsides and come to close action, as he was doing, the day might yet belong to the Netherlanders.

'Damnation,' I cried, 'the fight will be lost, and yet we still lie here like neuters – what in God's name is that perfidious rebel Penn thinking?'

My answer came at once, fortunately negating my petulant and indiscreet outburst. It took the form of a blue flag breaking out at the mizzen topmast of the *Royal Charles*. It was the signal for the centre and rear divisions of the Red, together with the one stray from the van, to fall down into the melée.

* * *

Upon the *Royal Charles*, young Cherry Cheeks Russell, who recounted the tale to me after the battle, heard the Duke of York order his ships into the heart of the fight. Penn had been for intervening earlier, Russell said, but the courtiers around the Duke, Harry Brouncker the most vocal of them, had urged delay. Surely, Brouncker argued, English arms were so superior to Dutch that the Blue and White alone could defeat the enemy? Surely there was no need to place in harm's way the precious life of the heir to the throne? James Stuart was known to be no coward, but such arguments must have weighed heavily upon him. At last, though, the Lord High Admiral reached his decision, much to Brouncker's apparent dismay, and the fresh ships of the Red fell down against the Dutch. Alas, some did so more swiftly than others. As ever, and despite bearing up her helm and hoisting studding sails, the sluggish *Merhonour* wallowed in the wake of the faster ships (that is, all of them), thus causing her captain to resume his irate pacing of his quarterdeck. Meanwhile, Lord Marlborough's *Old James* made directly for the relief of the *Montagu*, forcing the *Oranje* to withdraw her boarders and to haul away. Cheered by the arrival of the relieving ships, the Blue and White squadrons fell down with the wind to launch headlong attacks against the main body of the Dutch fleet. Almost six hours of relentless bombardment had clearly taken its toll of the smaller, lighter enemy ships; even young Russell, so ignorant of the ways of war, could see clearly that some of the Dutch were starting to give way before the onslaught.

The *Charles* herself made directly for the unmistakeable shape of the *Eendracht*, a long, slender two-decker flying at the maintop the torn but still easily recognisable command flag of Lord Obdam. The Duke of York remained upon his quarterdeck attended by his dog and the little court of Falmouth, Muskerry and Boyle, who laughed easily about the sport they were about to have with the Dutch admiral. Brouncker, unduly affronted by the rejection of his advice (or so it seemed to Russell), had moved away to brood at the larboard rail. Penn sat a little way off upon his chair, in conference with Sir William Coventry; the lookouts, high in the tops of the *Royal Charles*, reported that Obdam was in identical condition to our Great Captain Commander, wracked by gout and seated upon his quarterdeck. The young Duke of Monmouth was further aft upon the starboard rail, earnestly questioning Harman about the progress of the battle.

The two great ships came together, larboard of *Charles* against starboard of *Eendracht*, and their batteries roared out thunderously. Musket fire from the tops raked the decks. Russell looked upon the sight with wonder and turned to make a remark to young Boyle, with whom he had struck up a sort of fellowship in the brief hours that he had been aboard. But as Russell turned, the cannon roared again. He heard a sudden hiss and felt a rush of air pass his ear, bearing something upon it. He felt something strike his face. He looked up, and saw the strangest of sights. The three courtiers, Boyle, Falmouth and Muskerry, still stood there, still stood for the briefest of moments, but they no longer had their heads. Blood spurted from the torso of what until moments before had been the rising royal favourite, Charles Berkeley, Earl of Falmouth. As the three corpses fell to the deck, Russell turned to look at the Duke, whose hat had been blown off, but whose head otherwise remained firmly upon his shoulders. A head and shoulders that were now covered in the blood and brains of his dead friends.

Cherry Cheeks wiped a hand across his face, and as he later said to me, he realised that my nickname for him was more true than ever it was; for he, too, was bathed in the blood of the freshly slaughtered.

The veteran seamen looked upon the scene and retched. Brouncker, the one survivor of the courtiers, vomited long and hard over the larboard rail. Yet James Stuart and young Edward Russell somehow remained serene, looking steadily at each other. The Duke calmly pulled what appeared to be a shard of plate china from a deep cut on his left hand, then took a kerchief from his sleeve and wrapped it round the bleeding wound. It was only when James lifted the shard to inspect it that Russell, and presumably the duke too, realised it must have been part of the skull of one of the dead courtiers.

Russell glanced across at the Duke of Monmouth, standing unscathed on the other side of the quarterdeck. For a moment, just one moment, he could have sworn that the young man's expression twisted into a scowl of disappointment. Then Monmouth rushed solicitously to his uncle's side and assisted him with bandaging his wounded hand.

The Duke of York nodded grimly towards Monmouth and Russell in turn and said, 'The Lord is truly my strength and my shield. Let us give thanks unto Him, for he has preserved us for greater work to come. He has preserved *me*.'

And so He had. The gun crew who fired the fatal shot from the *Eendracht* would never know that if they had aimed just a fraction of a degree differently, they would certainly have changed the entire course of British history: for by not dying that day aboard the *Royal Charles,* James, Duke of York, lived to become His Majesty King James the Second of England, the Seventh of Scots, only to be hounded out of his offended realms within a few dozen months. His son and little grandsons still fester in a palace in Rome, now but feeble pretenders praying every day to reassert the destiny that seemed to have triumphed so manifestly on that third day of June in the year sixty-five.

Perhaps James Stuart foresaw his eventual accession; after all, such dreams and nightmares form the lot of an heir, as I know full well. Perhaps he even daydreamed that one day, he and Monmouth might battle each other for the crowns of Britain, and that the one would order the beheading of the other. But James of York certainly could not have foreseen the consequences for him of God's equally fortuitous decision to spare the lives of Harry Brouncker and Cherry Cheeks Russell.

* * *

The cumbersome old *Merhonour* had lost headway upon the *Royal Charles* as the great ships fell down into the battle. At last, though, we were bearing down upon our own target, a fifty-gun flagship of the Maas admiralty with her mizzen shot away and the mainyard in ruins.

'Perfect,' I said. 'If we hold this course, we can come across his stern and rake him. A fine prize, gentlemen.'

Roger d'Andelys nodded happily, and even the gloomy Giffard grunted in approbation. But Kit Farrell's telescope remained fixed on the Dutchman.

'Bear away, Captain,' he said urgently. 'Bear away *now*.'

'Why, in Heaven's name? We have him, Lieutenant –'

Kit pointed toward the bow of a small ship, emerging from the lee side of the Dutchman that had sheltered her. 'Fireship,' he said simply.

I gave the orders, but sensed that I did not need to: men were already on their way up the shrouds and the helmsman below must have already put over the ship's unresponsive whipstaff, for our bow began to turn away from the oncoming threat almost at once.

The fireship was a converted fly-boat, the only sign of her deadly function being the enlarged sally-port abaft that would allow her crew to escape into the boat secured beneath it. Apart from this, she appeared but an innocent merchantman; yet her main deck would have been converted into a fire-room filled to the brim with deadly combustibles. Through my telescope, I could see concealed grappling irons at the yards and the bowsprit, ready to be secured to our rigging if the deadly craft got close enough.

'Damnation, Mister Giffard,' I cried, 'we need more leeway, sir!'

'Helm's answering fast as it can, Captain. Can't do more, sir.'

In truth, our dash for the exposed stern of the Dutch flagship had literally given us too little room to manoeuvre, especially given the *Merhonour*'s propensity to manoeuvre like a heavily pregnant sow. Barring a miracle, the more nimble fireship would be upon us in minutes.

Calm, boy. I suddenly recalled my grandfather's journal of the Armada fight, and the eternal truth displayed when our own fireships were sent into Calais. Most of the fireship's work is done for it by the dread that its very name and appearance inspires. It is a weapon of terror; thus the way to defeat it is to display no terror in the face of it.

'Mister Webb!' I bellowed at the gunner. 'Larboard broadside to fire at will, as she aims! Mister Lanherne! Thirty men, as many with small arms as can be supplied, with me!'

With Roger at my side, I drew my sword and leapt down the ladder from the quarterdeck into the waist. As our larboard guns opened fire, we ran down the starboard side to the forecastle. Lanherne joined us with a somewhat mixed party that included Tremar, Treninnick, Macferran and a dozen or so of the Welshmen. Oakes, the armourer, had done them proud: they bristled with muskets, pikes, hatchets and *grenadoes.*

'Your orders, Captain?' Lanherne asked.

'We do the thing he least expects. He expects us to be afraid of him. Let's make him afraid of us instead!'

With that I jumped up onto the larboard rail and claimed a few rungs of the foremast shrouds. It was obvious that the Dutchman was heading for our bows, for that was ever the fireship's tactic of choice. The profusion of stays, shrouds and gammoning made it the ideal place to secure his grappling hooks before the crew lit the fuse and made their escape.

Our larboard guns fired again, and at least three balls struck home into the hull of the fireship. Now Lanherne's men joined me at the rail, firing musket-shot and lobbing *grenadoes* at the few Dutchmen visible on deck.

'Come on then, you butterbox bastards!' I shouted, hoping that Cornelia would forgive me. 'You need more of your courage inside you before you tackle the *Merhonour*! Cheese-farters! Hogen-mogen whoremasters!'

Encouraged by their captain, the Merhonours unleashed a torrent of vitriol against the Dutchman, waving their fists, prodding their pikes and firing their muskets at the oncoming vessel. Our defiance must have unsettled the enemy crew. Many great ships had been lost because their men panicked at the very approach of a fireship. The Dutchman must have expected to encounter a similar reaction aboard the *Merhonour*, especially because the element of surprise seemed to have weighed the odds so heavily in his favour. Instead he found our battery intent on hammering him before he could get close, and a gang of raucous, latrine-mouthed, heavily armed men waiting for him at the very point of attack. A couple of the Dutch moved out tentatively onto their bowsprit and made ready their grappling hooks, but Macferran, who had learned shooting by stalking deer and clan feudsmen on the Scottish moors, levelled his musket calmly, fired, and saw his target's torso explode in a fountain of blood, tissue and bone before the Dutchman fell forward into the sea.

That was enough for the Dutch crew. They began to clamber out off the sally-port near the stern just as flames erupted from the chimneys set into the deck. They had fired their deadly cargo without securing to us, hoping that the momentum of wind and tide alone would bring their hull crashing into the side of ours. The updraft from the chimneys carried the flames into the rigging, and within moments almost the whole of the upper deck was alight.

Only one Dutchman had reached the longboat secured alongside his ship before our battery fired again on the downroll. A lucky shot smashed into the longboat, which disintegrated. We were close enough to see the looks of horror on the faces of the other crewmen. The flames were already licking about the foot of the quarterdeck and the mizzen; they knew they were about to be burned alive by their own weapon. A few jumped, but only two heads came back to the surface and struck out for the increasingly distant Maas flagship. We watched in horror as one man ran back up onto the quarterdeck, as though believing the very stern of the ship would be somehow immune from the flames. He caught fire, and ran, all in flames, to the ship's side, throwing himself off into oblivion.

But the danger to the *Merhonour* was still not past. The fireship was still coming on, barely musket range from us now, and would surely strike us amidships –

The *Bachelor's Delight* cut under our stern, turned smartly along our quarter and made directly for our fiery foe. Roberts raised his hand to me in a friendly wave, seemingly without a care in the world. The ketch gathered speed and rammed the fireship forward.

'Magnificent,' said Roger d'Andelys in admiration. 'Now *that* man fights like a Frenchman.'

I did not reply, for I could only stare in horror at the spectacle unfolding before me. To this day, I do not know what Roberts originally intended: whether he somehow hoped that a glancing blow would be enough to deflect the fireship, or whether he hoped to secure a tow-rope and pull her out of harm's way before she ignited properly. But now fate took a hand. The bowsprit of the *Bachelor's Delight* became entangled in the rigging of her opponent. Flames danced along the ropes. A spit of fire caught the ketch's foresail. Within moments, the *Delight* was ablaze from stem to stern.

I thought I caught one final glimpse of the valiant Roberts. I fancied he remained at the helm, the flames consuming him at his post. I felt a sudden and guilty realisation: I had never known the man's Christian name.

* * *

We were well clear of the terrible conflagration. I took a long, welcome draught of bitter Suffolk beer, silently saluting the memory of poor Roberts and the men of the *Bachelor's Delight*. My other officers knew better than to interrupt their captain's anguished contemplation of the sacrifice that had been made to save the *Merhonour* and, with it, the life of Matthew Quinton.

I looked away to the east. We were perhaps a quarter of a mile away from the duelling flagships *Eendracht* and *Royal Charles*, upon their larboard quarters. We could not see what was happening away to the west or east, where the Blue and the White would still be fighting their own battles, but here, at the centre, something of an amphitheatre had formed around the flagships. Individual British and Dutch ships, or small groups of them, were engaged all around, and I had just given the order to go to the assistance of the *Diamond*, to the north, which seemed to be weakening under the onslaught of a large Amsterdammer. Between *Merhonour* and the flagships lay open water, upon which floated broken spars and yards; and, perchance, a few score bobbing, twisted shapes that could only be bodies, or parts of bodies. Oared boats and small craft occasionally braved the murderous crossfire, scudding desperately in search of safe water.

The thunder of gunfire was incessant. Every few minutes, the *Eendracht* would fire a broadside into the *Royal Charles*; and just as surely, the *Charles* would respond in kind. I could see only smoke from the starboard battery of *Eendracht* as she fired, but the Dutch flagship was smaller and lower, so the larboard battery of the Duke's ship was partly visible from our position and I saw the flash of some of her guns as they fired in their turn. The sails and rigging of both ships were torn to pieces. Canvas hung in shreds from yards, broken ropes danced crazily in the breeze. The ensigns of both ships were almost unrecognisable, so many were the shot-holes in them. The Lord High Admiral's flag at the fore of the *Royal Charles,* and the royal standard at her main, were but tattered fragments of their former glory. And yet men were still upon the yards, and through my telescope I could make out other men upon the decks. There seemed to be smoke rising from the galley chimney of the *Eendracht*; perhaps the Dutch were so confident of victory that they intended to take their dinner as they fought.

Scobey brought me another jug of small beer, and I drank it greedily. I rubbed sweat and grime from my eyes and looked again upon the dreadful fight between the two great flagships. Was it my imagination, or was the fire from the *Royal Charles* weakening? What if the Duke and Penn were dead?

The hull of the *Eendracht* broke apart in front of me. I saw it consumed by a vast ball of flame, a sudden and dreadful eruption of reds, whites and yellows followed at once by the greys and blacks of a great smoke cloud. The hull simply disintegrated, huge shards of wood flying in all directions. Great cannon were tossed into the air like children's toys. In the midst of the fireball were the men of the ship. They seemed to swim upon the air, flailing frantically for some refuge that their hands would never find. Many were in pieces, arms, legs and heads all flying off in different directions. Others were ablaze, the flesh melting from their bones as I watched.

A moment later, I heard the explosion. The loudest broadside of the largest fleet was as but a pop-gun compared to it. The blast silenced the battle. Every man's eyes turned to that space where the two flagships had duelled.

But no more. For as the smoke cleared, only the *Royal Charles* floated upon the waters. Her larboard side, the side that had been obscured by the presence of the *Eendracht*, was clear to the view.

Then the truth came to me, all in one with the stench of blood and death.

The *Eendracht* was gone. The Dutch flagship had blown up.

Chapter Twenty~One

Obdam sails in, plac'd in his naval throne,
Assuming courage greater than his own,
Makes to the Duke and threatens him from far,
To nail himself to 's board like a petar,
But in the vain attempt takes fire too soon,
And flies up in his ship to catch the moon.
Monsieurs like rockets mount aloft and crack,
In thousand sparks, then dancingly fall back.
~ Marvell, Second Advice to a Painter

They say that the blast which destroyed the *Eendracht* shattered windows in The Hague. I cannot speak for that, but Cherry Cheeks Russell, aboard the *Royal Charles*, claimed his hearing was not truly right until weeks after the battle. He also told me that the Duke and Penn knew, some time before the explosion, that Lord Obdam was already dead, killed during the cannonade. Penn had just sighted that which I had taken to be galley smoke, and commented to the Duke that there seemed to be some sort of accidental blaze aboard the Dutch flagship, barely moments before that same blaze must have ignited the magazine and blown the *Eendracht* apart.

The sound of the blast brought Francis Gale to the quarterdeck from his station below, where, as was his wont, he divided his time between ministering to the immortal souls of the dying and using his cutlass to upbraid the backsliders among the living. He surveyed the scene, registered what had happened, and made the sign of the cross in the direction of the lost Dutch ship. Then he led those of us upon the quarterdeck in the Lord's Prayer, probably the only words appropriate to the occasion. The *Royal Charles* already had her boats rushing across the water to where the *Eendracht* had been, for even such a conclusive disaster as this had survivors. Five survivors, we later learned. Five from a crew of four hundred. In the moment itself, though, it was impossible to judge the scale of the slaughter. I could see only that we were too far away to be of use, otherwise I would certainly have despatched our own boats to assist. For at the end, when all is said and done, when the kings and the admirals have blustered as they please, we are after all but men cast adrift upon that most unnatural and perilous plane, the sea, and thus united in the common cause of survival.

The loss of Obdam and the *Eendracht* proved the last straw for many of the Dutch, already weakening under the relentless bombardment of our more powerful gunnery. From the quarterdeck of the *Merhonour*, I could see only the clear proofs of victory and defeat. Heartened by the mighty blast, our ships fell about the enemy in furious pell-mell fighting. Broken by the horror that had befallen the *Eendracht*, individual Dutch ships, or small groups of them, turned out of the battle. They cut the lines that secured their boats behind them, hoisted studding sails and every other inch of canvas they possessed, and ran for Holland upon the wind.

'Strange,' said Kit Farrell, who was scanning the scene continuously with his telescope. 'Their dead Obdam appears to have spawned three successors. Look, sir. There – then over to northward, there – and there, fleeing ahead of Rear-Admiral Berkeley's division. Three command flags.'

It was true; it seemed that out of the death of Obdam, no fewer than three new commanders-in-chief had arisen, hydra-like. I learned only much later the cause of this extraordinary confusion. Obdam's second-in-command should have been Evertsen, a Zeelander, so out of its hatred of all things Zeeland, the Admiralty of Holland insisted on installing one of their own, a certain Kortenaer, as Obdam's deputy. But Kortenaer had his leg blown off in the very first pass and lay in his cabin, mortally wounded. His flag captain aboard the *Groot Hollandia* had either forgotten to haul down his flag or kept it flying, presumably on the grounds that if the admiral breathed, he was admiral still; but now the flag captain chose to turn and run, and many of the ships near him, assuming that Kortenaer lived and thus commanded in chief, followed in his wake. Seeing this, Evertsen hoisted the command flag too, thereby hoping to rally the fleet to him for a rearguard action against the oncoming British. But even now, in one of the direst crises ever to face their navy and their nation, the Dutch preferred to play out their little provincial spites. Tromp of Amsterdam, refusing to obey the orders of a Zeelander, hoisted the command flag aboard his own flagship, *De Liefde*. Three flags and three admirals, all claiming to be the legitimate commander-in-chief of the fleet of the United Provinces of the Netherlands: it would have been laughable but for the hundreds, perhaps thousands, of deaths that the confusion towed in its wake.

One ship, and one ship alone, did not join the headlong flight. The *Oranje*, the same great ship that had earlier fought its way through our entire squadron, now veered resolutely into the path of the *Royal Charles* and began trading broadsides with the flagship. My good-brother Cornelis seemed quite determined upon single-handedly changing the outcome of the battle.

The *Oranje* and the *Royal Charles* exchanged a shattering broadside, but Cornelis was clearly intent on more than that. The *Oranje* bore down relentlessly, finally ploughing into the larboard beam of the *Charles* with a resounding crash that visibly shook the hulls of both ships. Dutchmen rushed to their forecastle and climbed into the rigging. A few grabbed ropes and swung themselves across onto the deck of the British ship.

'A brave spirit indeed,' said Francis. 'Refuses to acknowledge defeat. 'Tis easy to tell that he and your good lady are from the same pod, Matthew.'

'He need not be defeated, Francis,' I said in both admiration and trepidation. 'He can win not just the battle but the entire war if he seizes the *Charles* – if he captures the heir to the throne! God in Heaven, can you imagine the sort of ransom the king would have to pay to free his brother from humiliation in a Dutch prison?' The thought that had occurred to me during the *Oranje*'s very first attack upon the Red squadron returned to me, reinforced a hundredfold. 'I think it is what he sought to do before, when he was to windward of both fleets. Run in upon the wind, board and capture the *Charles*, sowing confusion among our fleet. But our press of ships must have been too great for him then – he could not reach her. But now he can.'

Just then, a great gap opened up ahead of us as several of the faster ships of the Red, our line abandoned and all divisions now mingled together, poured past in pursuit of the fleeing Dutch fleet. That left clear water between the *Merhonour* and the *Oranje*; between Matthew Quinton and his wife's brother.

My duty was clear. It was time to put behind me both grief for Roberts and the *Bachelor's Delight* and shock at the horror that had befallen the *Eendracht*. 'Mister Yardley!' I cried. 'A course to lay us alongside the Dutchman, yonder, if you please!'

I took up a voice trumpet and rushed to the quarterdeck rail. 'Men of the *Merhonour*! This is our moment, lads! We sail to save the Duke, for the glory of old England!' I saw Polzeath, Tremar, Macferran and some of the Welsh scowling and hastily added, 'Aye, for the honour of Britannia!'

I was greeted by answering shouts of *Kernow bys vyken*! and *Cymru am byth*! Macferran seemed to be screaming something about a Wallace, or some such name.

The bow of the ancient ship came around into an almost perfect line with the mainmast of the *Oranje*. Cornelis must have realised at once that his design upon the *Royal Charles* was doomed; he veered away and bore down directly toward us upon the other tack, the Dutch red lion figurehead rampant in defiance.

Now the *Merhonour*'s sluggishness was no longer an issue. I could see a grim determination in the eyes of the gun crews on the upper deck, for this would be a duel to the finish, ship against ship, gun against gun. Kit Farrell saluted me and went to his station below, upon the middle gun deck.

'Let us pray,' cried Francis Gale. 'Thou, Oh Lord, art just and powerful: oh defend our cause against the face of the enemy. Oh God, thou art a strong power of defence to all that flee unto thee. Oh suffer us not to sink under the weight of our sins, or the violence of the enemy. Oh Lord, arise, help us, and deliver us for thy name's sake. Amen.'

Solemn amens echoed from all upon the quarterdeck, even from the papist Roger d'Andelys.

As the *Oranje* came alongside, the two ships fired almost as one. Our ancient hull shuddered from the force of our broadside, but almost simultaneously, I felt the blows as the answering fire struck us. I heard screams from our deck and felt the impact of balls striking our hull. The smoke cleared a little, and I saw a terrible scene ahead of me. The *Oranje* was higher out of the water than the squat old *Merhonour*, and Cornelis must have loaded his upper deck guns with chain- and bar-shot, as the Dutch were ever wont to do. The shrouds and stays of our mainmast were in shreds, and the carpenter's crew were already attending to the trunk of the mast; if *Oranje* could bring it down, we would be doomed. The protective fights over the deck were in ribbons. At least a dozen men lay dead or wounded upon the deck, their blood spreading across the planking. I recognised John Tremar, the formidably strong little Cornishman, lying on his back grasping his stomach. He was alive and muttering urgently to the giant Polzeath, who kneeled over him solicitously. I saw the head and trunk belonging to young Castle, my servant. As his remains were thrown unceremoniously over the side, I wondered how, in God's name, I would be able to tell his widowed mother, whose last living child this had been. If I survived to tell her, that was.

Francis Gale ran down into the waist to help with the wounded and to say prayers over the dead. Roger d'Andelys waved his sword at the great Dutch ship in impotent defiance. My warrant and petty officers bellowed orders through voice trumpets, striving to make themselves heard above the roaring of the guns, the pitiful screams of dying men and the rumble of gun-carriage wheels upon the decks as recoiled and reloaded cannon were run back out again.

On the downroll, *Merhonour* fired again, and I saw several of our balls smash clean through the side of the *Oranje*. A merchant's hull, Kit Farrell had said, so thinner than that of any purpose-built man-of-war...

But on the uproll, the *Oranje* fired again.

I heard a scream close to me, and turned to see Roger, staring in stupefaction at the bleeding stump where his left hand had been. 'Ah, *mon dieu*,' he cried in agonised gasps, 'to die will be bad enough, but to die *for England*? No Frenchman deserves that.'

With that he fainted away. Carvell and a couple of the Bristol lads were up to him in a moment, carrying him down to the surgeon's cockpit on the orlop. Perhaps the magic of Ieuan Goch would preserve my friend's life, for I had no faith in our dullard of a surgeon. I fought back the tears. This was living hell, and now it was set to claim the life of one of my dearest friends. I had no doubt that in but a very little time, it would claim my own.

Wind and tide pushed the two ships closer together. The main-yards even touched momentarily, like swordsmen at *prise-de-fer*. Now the musket fire from the tops and upper deck of the *Oranje* began in earnest. Our canvas fights were already horribly torn, the Dutch ship had a much larger crew, and many of her men were soldiers; thus her marksmanship was deadly. I could see plainly the faces of individual Dutchmen as they levelled their muskets.

Yet we were giving almost as good as we got: Macferran and one of the Welshmen, manning a swivel-gun on the rail near me, got off a round of canister shot that scattered its deadly contents of nails and musket balls on impact, decimating a whole swathe of the enemy.

'Good work, Macferran, Prydderch!' I cried.

I drew my own two pistols from my belt and prepared them. I raised a pistol in my right hand and took aim at a tight group of soldiers towards the rear of the *Oranje*'s waist. At that range, I could not fail to hit one of them –

I fired. My arm pulled up with the recoil and the smoke from my shot shrouded me, but cleared quickly enough to see a Dutchman clutch the side of his head, where once his ear had been. His body contorted, and he fell from the rail of the *Oranje* into the sea between the ships. I passed the emptied pistol to young Scobey for reloading, then took aim at once with my left hand and fired again.

I do not know if I hit another of the enemy. In that moment I heard Lieutenant Giffard's shout from further forward. I turned and looked at him, but before he could speak to me a fountain of blood spat from the top of his head and he fell dead to the deck. Almost in the same moment, I felt a sudden sharp pain in my foot, looked down and saw blood seeping over my shoe from a round wound in my instep. I do not know if I cried out or not. Master Yardley dragged me down behind one of the larboard demi-culverins, tore off my shoe, pulled Cornelia's kerchief from my scabbard and wrapped it around the bleeding foot. Poor Cornelia: what torment of mind she would be in if she knew how earnestly her brother and her husband were endeavouring to kill each other, and what far greater torment would overwhelm her if one of us succeeded.

'Lucky, Captain,' he said soothingly. 'A hit from one of the marksmen in their tops. A few inches' difference in his aim and the ball would have gone through the top of your skull.'

Round shot from the *Oranje*'s middle deck smashed through the starboard rail, taking away several feet of the deck where I had just been standing and sending a huge splinter of oak straight through Yardley's stomach. The master looked at me with what seemed to be mild disappointment, his hands gripping the great wooden shard that protruded bloodily through his jerkin.

Scobey and Barcock ran to attend me. My two young servants were still visibly pale from witnessing the death of their companion Castle and the indiscriminate slaughter all around them; now they saw their captain bathed in the blood of Yardley, and momentarily must have thought that I, too, had perished.

'I need reports,' I hissed at them through my pain. 'Reports from all quarters. Order to Lieutenant Farrell. Unman the larboard guns on the middle and lower gundecks and send the spare men up here to replace our losses. Above all, maintain fire on the downroll!'

It took another two or three broadsides for the reports to be brought to me, and it was only Scobey who bore them; Barcock had fallen on the middle gundeck, taken away by a vast splinter that impaled him against a bulkhead. I thought of his father and mother, so well known to me from Ravensden, but now just another set of parents who did not yet know that they ought to don their mourning weeds. Such is war: a time of black drapery.

Our position was evidently desperate. A hundred men, over a quarter of the ship's company, lay dead or dying. Giffard, Yardley and most of the standing officers were gone. That good, honest soul Roger, Comte d'Andelys, straddled the border between life and death. The sails and rigging were in shreds; God alone knew how our masts still stood, but Thurston, our ancient carpenter, seemed to have made it a matter of personal pride that the enemy would not fell our mainmast. He stood by it, oblivious to the carnage all around him, ordering his rapidly diminishing crew to shore up here and hammer some treenails into place there. Through my pain, I tried desperately to conceive of a way in which the captain of the *Merhonour* could extricate the ship and his remaining men from this bloody horror. There was one only that I could envisage: surrender. If *Merhonour* yielded, this would end, and good men would live. My foot screamed at me to haul down the flag; my head, swimming in pain and appalled by the carnage around me, joined it in alliance; but at the last, my heart held out. In a voice all its own, not that of my grandfather or any other of my ancestors, it said simply, 'A Quinton does not surrender.'

But still the guns of the *Oranje* thundered.

It was obvious what Cornelis was about. It was the classic Dutch tactic: weaken the enemy, clear his decks, then close for the boarding. And if it came to that, my good-brother had far more men available to him. Men who would have calculated exactly how much coin the States-General would pay them for taking such a great prize as the *Merhonour.*

We had to do something, *anything*, to hurt the Dutchman. If we were to avoid destruction or surrender, then I had to do something that Cornelis would not expect. Yet unlike me, Cornelis was the consummate seaman, master of the modern arts of war –

The modern arts. But perhaps not of the old ones. 'Scobey,' I said, struggling to my feet and tentatively putting weight onto the wounded limb, 'go down to the orlop and bring up the surgeon's mate, the Welshman. Thence to Oakes, the armourer, with this command…'

Ieuan Goch of Myddfai appeared on deck as another broadside roared out from the *Oranje*, the acrid gunsmoke sweeping across the

Merhonour like a shroud. Once again Cornelis's chain- and bar-shot tore through our standing and running rigging, felling one of the men on the main top but still failing in its main purpose, to bring down masts or yards and thus disable us. The Welshman looked about him with apparent unconcern, as though such slaughter was part of his daily staple.

'Tell me, druid,' I said, 'the Welsh always had a name as great archers – they fought with my ancestor at Agincourt, and did for the French hordes that day. But do your people still train with the bow?'

The Welshman's expression was at once curious and eager. 'Aye, My Lord, we do. Muskets are expensive and clumsy, and though the world cries them up as the only way for modern men to fight, we Welsh still prefer the bow. A good bowman can get off three arrows in the time it takes one of your much vaunted musketeers to fire but one shot.'

'Very well, then.' I grimaced at another jolt of pain from my foot. 'Go through the ship, Ieuan Goch, and find me as many Welshmen as are able to wield a longbow. Then assemble them upon the forecastle, yonder. All speed, man!'

'All speed' to the Welsh seemed to have a different meaning to that taken by the English. Ieuan Goch looked down at my foot and said, 'I will examine that later, My Lord, if you are willing.'

'If you don't get the Welsh to the forecastle, druid, there may be no "later"!'

He nodded, which might or might not have been taken for a salute, but before he moved away he said, 'You should have a crutch, My Lord. Send this infant to fetch you one.'

'Impudent sheep-buggerer,' cried Scobey as the Welshman departed. 'As though I'd do his bidding –'

The hull shuddered as another broadside from the *Oranje* struck home. The unexpected motion sent another bolt of pain through my entire frame. 'I think,' I gasped, 'I think he may have the rights of it, Scobey. Pray fetch me a crutch.'

Amid another hail of musket-fire from the *Oranje*, the fresh men from below arrived on deck, taking cover at once behind the guns or beneath the remnants of the fights. I made my way through them, swinging my newly-acquired crutch and limping to favour my good foot, nodding grimly to each man in turn. The deck was red and sticky from the blood already shed upon it. Once again the *Oranje*'s broadside belched out, to be greeted at last by something like the full broadside of the *Merhonour*. If the Dutch had thought we were weakening, perhaps they were now disabused.

Grimacing through every step, I finally reached the forecastle, where the band of Welshmen was assembled. Their weapons had only just arrived from the orlop and were in canvas bags upon the deck, so they must have seemed a sorry spectacle indeed to those aboard the *Oranje*. The relative positions of our two ships had shifted slightly now. Although both had come to almost a complete stop, wind and tide had moved us a little way, and now, upon the forecastle, I was much closer to my enemy's quarterdeck. As the smoke from another broadside cleared, and the inevitable screams of anguish rose from both ships, I looked up and saw the captain of the *Oranje* at his quarterdeck rail. In that moment, Cornelis van der Eide turned and saw me. His normally imperturbable face fell.

The Welshmen took up the strange weapons that had lain in the armourer's store of the *Merhonour* for decades. Fire-arrows were a common enough weapon aboard ships of that time, but they were large and clumsy affairs, designed for firing from some of the smaller cannon such as sakers or minions. As with all shot fired from cannon, they could be aimed only approximately.

Merhonour carried none of these. But the larger artillery weapon had been based on a much simpler, much older and much more accurate model; and of these, the ancient ship had an abundance.

I looked across to the *Oranje*, to the bewildered face of my good-brother Cornelis. I smiled through the pain from my foot and raised a hand in salute. Then, once I was certain that every Welshman had a bow and a true fire-arrow in his hand, I raised my sword and let it fall.

At such close range, the Welshmen could not fail to hit. The arrows stuck into Cornelis's quarterdeck, his mizzen mast and its sail. The fiery substance immediately behind the arrowheads scattered on impact. Frantically Cornelis turned away, no doubt to order water brought up and for guns to be brought to bear on the extraordinary spectacle on the *Merhonour*'s forecastle. But in that time, my Welsh archers, heirs to those who had decimated the flower of French chivalry at Agincourt, had let loose another volley. In truth, the fire-arrows were merely pin-pricks, igniting small fires and sowing panic on the quarterdeck but not causing much real damage. However to the crew of the *Oranje*, no doubt exhausted from having been at the heart of the fight all day and still being hammered by the battery of the *Merhonour*, they must have been very nearly the last straw.

Very nearly: but not quite the last of all.

Beyond the *Oranje* I caught a glimpse of the masts and sails of another great ship, seemingly floating eerily above the swirling gunsmoke. A torn but still proud plain red flag at the fore identified her. It was the *Royal Oak*. The wounded Lawson and his successor, Jordan, were come to the rescue of the ship that had abandoned her place in line at the beginning of the battle. The suspected traitors had come to the assistance of the man who had been tasked with destroying them. The Commonwealths-men were fighting to save the cavalier.

As the *Oak*'s broadside hammered into her larboard beam, the fire into us from the *Oranje*'s starboard battery weakened correspondingly. I could see Cornelis, still waving his sword, ordering men to put out the remaining fires started by our arrows and gesticulating furiously toward his new opponent. Or rather, opponents: for now the masts and sails of a ship identical to the *Oak* hove into view off her starboard quarter, manoeuvring to take her place alongside the *Oranje*. The blue flag at the mizzen identified her beyond doubt as the *Royal Katherine*, the equally new and mighty sister ship of the *Royal Oak*, flagship of Thomas Teddiman, Rear-Admiral of the Blue.

The appearance of such powerful seconds gave fresh heart to the gun crews of the *Merhonour*. Our rate of fire increased, joined by the fresh battery of the *Katherine* on the opposite side of the *Oranje*. Now, at last, Cornelis's fire began to fall off. At bottom, his great ship was a merchantman, and there was a limit to the punishment she could take; a limit that Cornelis had probably already exceeded, several times over.

The end, when it came, was sudden. The colours of the *Oranje* came down. I saw Cornelis van der Eide, my good-brother, standing at his starboard rail, holding his sword hilt-first toward me. I nodded grimly.

Francis Gale appeared at my side, fresh from his efforts below. No one would have taken him for a man of God: with his torn, open shirt and grimy flesh, caked in the blood of those he had helped, he resembled the roughest tarpaulin.

He surveyed the scene. 'Well, Matthew,' he said with some satisfaction, 'I think I may truthfully report to the Lord Archbishop that the curse of the *Merhonour* has finally been laid to rest.'

Chapter Twenty-Two

The Dutch Urania *fairly on us sail'd,*
And promises to do what Obdam fail'd.
Quinton to the Duke does intercept her way
And cleaves t' her closer than the remora.
~ Adapted from Marvell, *Second Advice to a Painter*

The *Merhonour* now had a respite from the battle, but the occasional thunder of a distant broadside betrayed the fact that our headmost ships were still engaged against the rearmost of the Dutch, who were in headlong flight and apparently entire disarray.

Thus I had an interval in which to entertain Captain Cornelis van der Eide in the remnants of my great cabin; much of the starboard side had been shattered by the guns of the *Oranje*, and our carpenter's crew was busy with running repairs as we spoke. Through the gaping holes that now served me for windows, we watched as his brave ship burned. The *Oranje* had been too badly damaged to save, but we and the other ships around us had taken off as many of her crew as we could and transferred them to some of the attendant hoys and ketches. Some two hundred men survived from Cornelis's ship: barely half the crew. How many of those would survive months of incarceration in a disease-ridden castle was a moot point. That would not be the fate of Cornelis himself, of course: as a captain, he would give his parole and would thus be given a large measure of liberty in an appropriate lodging. It was with some alarm that I suddenly realised where that lodging was likely to be. After all, where could be more appropriate than the home of his dear twin sister, where no doubt they would instantly resume the internecine warfare that seemed to have prevailed between the van der Eide siblings since the day of their birth?

Unsurprisingly, my stocky good-brother, a dour man even when in his happiest condition, was sullen and contemplative. This might have been a consequence of his surrender, or of his wounds – he had a great gash in his head, which had been bandaged beneath his hat, and he had also taken some of our canister-shot in his thigh.

'Bows and arrows,' he said, shaking his head. 'A weapon from another time, Matthias. I had not thought such things still existed, nor men able to use them.'

'Old weapons fired by an old race, good-brother. You had bested almost our entire fleet single-handed, so we were hardly going to stop you with the common weapons of our age.'

'I did my best,' said Cornelis, gloomily. 'I had sworn to take the *Royal Charles*, and my crew gave their all. But none supported us – too many of our captains were cravens and backsliders. And worst of all, good-brother, I think too many would prefer to fight each other than you English. All the hatred between Zeeland and Holland, all the disputes over the command… If we can but resolve that, and find an admiral that all respect, then we will give you English a day to remember, I think.'

'Perhaps, good-brother. If you still have a fleet and a country on the morrow, that is.'

Something of the defiance and undoubted valour of Cornelis van der Eide returned. 'Be not so confident, Matthias. Remember that mighty Spain, with all its bullion and its invincible armies, could not defeat my land in an eighty-year war. Do you really think that you English can do so in a day?'

Just then, Scobey came and informed me that my presence was requested in the cockpit on the orlop deck. I went slowly, leaning heavily upon my crutch and wincing with every step. I also went down with a heavy heart. The summons could surely mean only that Roger, Comte d'Andelys, was on the point of death, and wished to say his farewells...

'Ah, *mon ami*, I give you joy of your victory, Captain Quinton!'

Francis Gale, who was attending the patient, glanced at me and raised his eyes to the heavens. Roger was full of colour, waving his right arm frantically as though to compensate for the immobility of the left, which was splinted and now ended in a tar-cauterised stump.

'My Lord!' I cried joyfully. 'And I give you joy of your recovery, sir!'

'Indeed, indeed. And my recovery is due entirely to your personal sorcerer, here, who provided potions that made the operation bearable.' Ieuan Goch nodded sagely. 'The loss of a hand is inconvenient, of course,' Roger continued, 'but now I think on it, I cannot quite remember what I ever used the left one for. I think I will cope admirably with just the one, Matthew. In truth, perhaps it will make me something of a curiosity at court, for warriors with battle-scars always seem to have a powerful effect on Milady This and the Duchesse de That. Better still, I now resemble a pirate, and I know some very grand ladies indeed whose most secret dream is to be ravished by one such. Who knows, perhaps I shall even invest in a hook?'

'My Lord,' said Ieuan Goch to me, 'it would be best if you took the pallet next to the Gallic count, here. It is time for us to deal with your foot. The longer it is unattended, the greater the risk of the gangrene.'

Craigen, the surgeon, merely nodded in assent; it was clear that authority within the *Merhonour*'s cramped apology for a hospital had passed wordlessly to that elemental force, our own Physician of Myddfai. I would have dissented, as I wished to inspect all parts of the ship and to survey the state of the action from my quarterdeck, but Francis Gale shot me a glance that suggested he would personally strap me down if I rejected the Welshman's advice.

It was Ieuan Goch who sewed up my wound by the light of a solitary lantern, swinging from the bulkhead above. I permitted him to rub the wound with his balms, and I consented to take some mouthfuls from the bottle of excellent French brandy that Roger had evidently produced from one of his dozen or so sea-chests. Perhaps these alleviated some of what I then endured, but it hardly seemed so. Every stitch was agony: the needle pushing through my flesh on the one side, then the briefest of respites before it pushed back up through the other. I desired nothing more than to scream with all my strength, for this exceeded all the pain I had known in my life. But my honour would not permit me to cry out; it was not fit that a king's captain should do such a pathetic thing. Nor, at first, did I permit myself to faint away. Yet at one point I must have been in a kind of delirium, for I seemed to see my grandfather at the foot of the pallet. He was not as I knew him, an ancient man soon destined for the grave, but a young, vigorous figure in the garb of the old queen's time. He seemed to smile at me and said, 'Call that a wound, boy? Wait until you get a Spanish pike in your side.' With that, and another searing pull of Ieuan Goch's needle, shapes and lights swam before my eyes. Still I fought against the faintness, and at last I heard the Welshman's voice: 'All done.' He proclaimed the wound to be clean, the stitching to be good, the prospects for a full recovery and a clean scar both excellent.

With the operation complete and the pain beginning to recede a little, I looked about me. The cockpit was ever a low, dark place, cramped beyond measure, reeking of the bilges beneath. Now it also stank of corruption, of rotting flesh and the discharges from the newly dead. Apart from the usual sounds of timber moving through seawater and the distant rumble of cannon-fire, only groans and an occasional scream interrupted the silence of that awful place. I spied perhaps another two dozen men on pallets or upon the deck, about half of them given up for dead, the others with good prospects of living. I was inordinately pleased to see that one of the latter was Tremar, whose slight frame seemed able to shrug off the most terrible of wounds. He was remarkably merry, given his condition; but then, all of the wounded men seemed remarkably merry. Roger had evidently been typically generous with his private libation.

An hour or so passed before I returned to the quarterdeck, sporting a heavily bandaged foot and a second crutch. The Welshman was furious that I refused to rest for any longer and berated me by relating the dire consequences that had allegedly befallen patients of his whose wounds had reopened. But with the first lieutenant, master and several of the mates dead we had a desperate shortage of watch-keeping officers, and even a wounded and comparatively ignorant gentleman captain was capable of playing that part.

I hauled myself up the quarterdeck stairs and saw Kit Farrell, Francis Gale and my good-brother standing at the starboard rail, looking off toward a group of three desperately shattered Dutch ships with their colours hauled down in surrender.

'Damnable,' said Francis. 'Unchristian. Unspeakable. Un-English!'

'It is against all the laws of war,' said Cornelis. 'Truly monstrous.'

Kit was the first to espy my approach, and turned to salute. 'Mister Farrell, gentlemen,' I said through clenched teeth, fighting back the desperate pain in my foot. 'How stands the battle?'

'The Dutchmen that we catch are surrendering, sir. Like the three yonder –'

'The big Indiaman, that is the *Maerseveen*,' said Cornelis. 'Behind her, *Swanenburg*. To starboard, *Tergoes*, of Zeeland – my friend Kruyningen commands her. They fell foul of each other during their attempted flight. And now see how their surrender is acknowledged, brother!'

At last, I understood the full horror of what was transpiring before me. A small English man-of-war, flying the white flag of Prince Rupert's squadron, was close under the larboard quarter of the *Tergoes*. At first glance I had taken her for one of the sixth rates, presumably closing the Dutchmen to secure them following their surrender. But now, as I saw the longboat pulling away from the stern of our ship and the first flames suddenly spring from her hold, I realised what I was witnessing. She was a fireship. Ignoring the stricken colours, she had fastened herself to the three hopelessly entangled Dutchmen.

'May God grant that the barbarous murderer meets his right end,' said Francis Gale. 'And if the Duke's short of a hangman, I'll gladly play the part.' He gripped the ship's rail tightly, rocking backward and forward in anger.

'Gregory,' said Kit. 'The fireship is the *Dolphin*, so her captain is William Gregory.'

The first flames broke out in the standing rigging of the *Tergoes*. Men ran upon her decks like ants fleeing a disturbed nest. Some attempted vainly to put out the flames. Others leapt into the sea. Yet others attempted to cross onto one of the other ships, the *Maerseveen* and *Swanenburg*, but the flames pursued them mercilessly. Like many of the ships in the Dutch fleets, the three burning men-of-war had cut loose the boats that would normally be towed behind them; and by doing so, they had inadvertently condemned hundreds of men aboard them to a fiery death.

Now the first faint aroma came to us upon the breeze: the stench of burning human flesh. I thought upon poor Roberts and the *Bachelor's Delight*: of all the many ways in which men could perish in battle, this was perhaps the most hideous, and I felt nothing but shame that this atrocity could be committed by an Englishman.

'We should pray for them, Francis,' I said numbly, just as the conflagration took hold of the sails of the *Swanenburg*.

The man who had kept his faith through the notorious slaughter at Drogheda shook his head, and continued to stare at the terror across the water. 'There are no prayers for this, Matthew,' he said, his voice trembling. 'God has no words for such as this.'

The *Merhonour* soon left the dreadful scene astern, but Captain Cornelis van der Eide stayed at the rail, silently watching the blaze recede into the distance. I approached him once, intending some words of comfort, but one look at his face dissuaded me. For in the years I had known him, I had never seen my dour, unemotional good-brother in tears.

* * *

During the remaining hours of daylight, we continued our pursuit of the Dutch. Nine of their ships, unable to flee or otherwise cut off, surrendered to our fleet; nine, that is, in addition to the three destroyed by the foul iniquity of the captain of the *Dolphin* fireship. Four more, that had become impossibly entangled with each other during their headlong flight, were given the chance to surrender by the Duke of York, but valiantly refused the offer and were thus legitimately burned by another of our fireships. We could see the flames in the distance, and heard the blast when one of them blew up. I was later told that this very explosion blew free one of the four, which made its escape to Holland, but that on the remaining ships barely a hundred survived. Such is the fortune of war.

Meanwhile our fleet slowly rearranged itself into a very rough sailing order, returning to our original squadrons. Inevitably, this was a difficult process. Most of our ships were much shattered in their masts and rigging, and we were no exception. Indeed, we were perhaps in a worse state than most, for the antiquity of the ship was all too apparent.

Despite the Dutch propensity to fire on the uproll, aiming for masts and rigging, we had taken at least two dozen shot in the hull, and the consequences threatened to be dire. The water in our hold, never less than two feet deep, was now coming dangerously close to four, and we had crews constantly at the pumps. Much of the beakhead was gone, shattered by the ferocious fire of the *Oranje*. Up above, our sails had been torn to shreds by two hundred or more great shot; barely a rope of either the standing or running rigging survived unscathed. The single most prevalent sound on the *Merhonour*, and across the water upon many of our companions, was that of hammering, as damage was made good, cannonball holes patched and jury masts rigged. My great cabin was slowly rebuilt around me as I rested, my wounded foot elevated to ease the pain. But as we all steered clumsily into something approximating our allocated positions, our ships often came near enough to each other for messages to be bawled through voice-trumpets. Thus by dusk those of us aboard the *Merhonour* were fairly certain of the final butcher's bill upon our side in the great battle that had just concluded. It was said that we had lost over a thousand men; and to them, perhaps, should be added Gregory, captain of the *Dolphin*, who had been placed under arrest pending a court-martial, the verdict thereof being in little doubt.

Only now did I learn of the deaths of the three courtiers aboard the *Royal Charles*, and of the fortunate escape of His Royal Highness. I mourned Charles Berkeley, Earl of Falmouth, less for his own merits – which, in truth, had been invisible to most men – than for the grief that I knew his death would have caused my good friend, his brother. The Earl of Portland, about my age and whom I had known quite well in exile, was dead too, as was the captain of the ship in which he had served: and now I, too, had cause to mourn, for this was the *Old James*. Thus My Lord of Marlborough had fallen in glory, no doubt at the hands of my good-brother's *Oranje*. I had known Marlborough but briefly, yet in the course of my inordinately long life, few men have ever impressed me so much in so short a time. I grieved, too, for Beau Harris, whose *House of Nassau* had disappeared into the midst of the Dutch fleet during the opening exchanges of the battle; not knowing whether he was dead or a prisoner, I decided it would be safer to offer up a prayer for the soul of the departed. Then there were those whom I had known less well, and misjudged so grossly. Sansum, Rear-Admiral of the White, had fallen, as had poor Abelson of the *Guinea*, whose accidental firing into the *Merhonour* I had taken as proof of foul betrayal. Above all, Sir John Lawson, suspected so unjustly of treachery, was badly wounded in the leg, and his life was despaired of. I prayed that he might live long enough for me to pay proper respect to him, to make some amends for the dire error I had made.

Thus it was clear that cavaliers and Commonwealths-men alike had suffered and fallen together in the common cause. There had either never been a conspiracy to bring about a rebellion at sea or else, as the Duke of York had hoped, the sound of the guns of England's enemies put paid to any hint of it. That day off Lowestoft, two mutually suspicious cohorts of men truly came together, forged in the crucible of battle into a new and formidable force: the navy royal of England, at last a reality rather than merely a name.

Our mourning for the dead gave way in surprisingly short order to a growing realisation of what we had done, and of what we were about to do.

We had won a glorious, signal victory.

Disregard the battles won by the false Commonwealth and even the triumph over the Armada, which was in truth more the consequence of a fortuitous Protestant wind; the battle of Lowestoft was by far the greatest victory of the arms of an English monarch since Agincourt or Flodden. We learned later that some five thousand Dutchmen perished in that ferocious fight, perhaps a fifth of their entire fleet. Four of their admirals, Obdam among them, were dead. We did not know all of this that bright June evening, but we knew or sensed enough of it. Yet as we set our course east by north in pursuit of the shattered Dutchmen, putting behind us (as far as we could) the dreadful memories of the battle, of blazing ships and dead friends, we grinned to each other in anticipation of an even greater triumph on the following morning. I dismissed Cornelis's warning; why could we *not* do in a day what the Spanish had failed to do in eighty years? After all, they suffered the inherent deficiency of not being English, and they had never once held the advantage that we possessed on that evening of the third of June, 1665. There was more than sufficient sea-room between ourselves and the shore of Holland. We would fall upon the butterboxes once more and take, sink or burn the rest of their fleet. Then, with no navy to protect them, we would mop up the impossibly rich Dutch argosies as they returned from the Indies. De Witt would be forced to make peace on our king's terms, and those terms would be humiliating. All of the trade of Amsterdam would come to London. All of the trading posts in Asia would come to our East India Company. The fortresses along the Scheldt would come to us, giving us the keys to Antwerp. The world's carrying trade would move from Dutch hulls into English. The mightiest revolution in the affairs of Europe since Luther pinned his theses to the church door; the ultimate triumph of our Britannic realms, which would become the richest and most powerful nation on earth.

Within twelve hours, we would make all of that a reality.

Chapter Twenty~Three

Now all conspires unto the Dutchman's loss:
The wind, the fire, we, they themselves, do cross,
When a sweet sleep the Duke began to drown,
And with soft diadem his temples crown.
But first he orders all beside to watch,
That they the foe (whilst he a nap) might catch,
But Brouncker, by a secreter instinct,
Slept not, nor needs it; he all day had wink'd.
Marvell, *Second Advice to a Painter*

Beneath a brilliant orange dawn, the sea was empty. Of the Dutch fleet, there was no sign.

That could mean only one thing: they had got through the sea-gates. Somehow, we had let them get away.

I had been summoned to the quarterdeck in the middle of the night, at about two in the morning, when the great stern lanterns aboard the *Royal Charles* had flickered the signal that she was shortening sail. I had been in a dead sleep for perhaps three hours, far too little to be properly rested, and had sprung from my sea-bed forgetting my wounded foot, which screamed a reminder to me as it struck the deck. Thus I had limped onto the quarterdeck in a confused state, noted the action of the flagship, relayed its order to my own officers and thus to the hands aloft, who had promptly set about adjusting the clew-lines and the like, and had not really pondered its consequences before returning to my slumber. But when I returned to the deck at dawn, expecting the imminent resumption of the battle, I realised at once that all was wrong – beginning with the assumptions I had made in the middle of the night.

The *Royal Charles* might have ordered a shortening of sail because we were in danger of over-running the Dutch in the night. Well, not so as was now all too evident.

The *Royal Charles* might have ordered a shortening of sail because our scouts had seen the Dutch do the same. Also not so, equally evidently.

The *Royal Charles* might have ordered a shortening of sail because the Dutch had already escaped within their sea-gates, and we were in danger of being blown onto their lee shore. Plainly not so, for we were still too far out to sea and with plenty of sea-room.

Thus either the Dutch fleet had been spirited away by their ally Beelzebub, or, rather more likely, something terribly wrong had happened aboard the *Royal Charles*.

I was fortunate to learn the truth before almost any other man in the fleet, for later that morning, as we despondently sighted the masts of the Dutch safe behind Texel, Cherry Cheeks Russell returned aboard the *Merhonour* and breathlessly recounted all he had seen and heard. Realising the importance of his evidence, I set him at once to write down his account, albeit in his execrable spelling.

Russell had stayed all night upon the quarterdeck (or, as he wrote it, 'kwotadek') of the *Royal Charles*, excited beyond measure by the sights and sounds around him – even by the spectacle of seamen scrubbing the deck clean of the blood of Lord Falmouth and the rest – and eager to catch sight of the Dutch by the first light of dawn. Thus he witnessed the arrival upon deck of Harry Brouncker, evidently intent upon conversation with Captain Cox, the sailing master, who had the watch.

'New orders from His Royal Highness,' said Brouncker officiously to Cox, 'entrusted to me before he retired. He considers it too dangerous for the fleets to engage during the night, Captain, and wishes you to adjust your course accordingly.'

Cox, whom I knew as a capable and quick-witted man, looked at Brouncker suspiciously. 'Adjust my course, Mister Brouncker? But if I adjust my course, every ship in the fleet has to adjust its own, dependent upon the signal from our lanterns.' He looked up at the three huge structures at the stern, in each of which burned a fire that marked the flagship's position by night.

'That is what His Royal Highness means, Captain Cox. The fleet is not to engage by night.'

'Then does he mean for us to shorten sail? Look at all the lights ahead of us, man. Some of them are our scouts, but most are the Dutch. We will be up with them well before dawn unless we shorten sail.'

Brouncker looked about him nervously, or so young Russell thought. 'Well, then, Captain, that is what His Royal Highness means. The fleet to shorten sail.'

Cox stared steadily at him. 'I'll not order such a thing,' he said. 'I need to wake Captain Harman.'

He crossed the quarterdeck, knelt down and shook a bundle that lay between two culverins. The bluff, handsome John Harman, captain of the *Royal Charles*, stirred at once and got to his feet. His own cabin had been given over to Sir William Penn, but even so, Harman had an ample sea-bed awaiting him below; although he wore his hair long and dressed as a cavalier, in times of drama, like many of the true old tarpaulins, he still preferred to sleep on deck under one of the sheets that gave its name to his kind.

In hurried whispers, half-overheard by Russell, Cox apprised Harman of the situation. The two men approached Brouncker, and Harman said, 'To shorten sail, Mister Brouncker? But that risks allowing the Dutch to escape us. You are certain that this is the Duke's intention?'

'I have said so, upon my word,' blustered Brouncker. 'We must not engage in the night. The fleet to shorten sail, if that is what it takes.'

Cox was anxious. 'Perhaps we should wake Sir William,' he said.

Harman frowned. 'We could attempt to wake Sir William, but I doubt if it would do us any good.'

Every man on the quarterdeck, indeed probably every man on the *Royal Charles* – including even young Cherry Cheeks Russell – knew full well that the only way in which the Great Captain Commander could obtain some relief from the gout by night, and thus some precious sleep, was by taking some of the more potent drugs in the surgeon's chest and washing them down with prodigious quantities of the strongest drink on the ship. Thus waking Sir William Penn would be akin to dragging the dead out of their graves before the sounding of the Last Trump.

'In that case,' said Cox, 'surely we should awaken His Royal Highness, to seek confirmation of his intentions?'

Russell saw Brouncker gesticulate angrily at Cox. 'Damnation, man, do you doubt my word? My word as a gentleman? I have told you His Royal Highness's order, sir!'

'Nevertheless,' said Harman, 'it would be best to have the Duke's confirmation –'

'And do you really think he will thank you, Captain Harman, if you wake him and he finds you have done so merely to confirm an order that he has already given through me? What will that do to your prospects of becoming Admiral Harman, do you think?' That struck home; by tradition, the captain of the fleet flagship had the first claim upon a vacant flag, and with Sansum dead, Harman's path to promotion lay open, pending confirmation by the Duke of York.

Yet Cox and Harman clearly remained unconvinced. Russell overheard snatches of their conversation: they were worried by the proximity of the Dutch and the dangers of a night engagement, but equally alarmed at the prospect of slowing the fleet too much and allowing the Dutch to escape.

As the two officers debated, Cherry Cheeks watched Brouncker become increasingly agitated. At last he strode up to Cox and Harman and almost bellowed in their faces.

'Think upon what you do here tonight!' cried the red-faced courtier. 'For all we know, the plague or a fanatic's bullet might have carried away Charles Stuart this day, and the man sleeping beyond that bulkhead might at this very moment be King of England, by the Grace of God! Are you really prepared to deny the will of Majesty, Captain Cox? Captain Harman, are you?'

Cox and Harman exchanged one last, despairing glance. Then Harman said decisively, 'Very well, then. Captain Cox, you will give the orders for the *Royal Charles* to shorten sail. I will see to the transmission of that order to the fleet. May God grant that we do the right thing.'

* * *

Thus we knew how the order had come to be given; but we were still no wiser as to Brouncker's motive. No wiser, that is, until the fleet returned to the shore of England to repair and revictual. The ships were divided, with some going to the Gunfleet, some to the Buoy of the Nore, and others, ourselves included, to Southwold Bay. We were then to return to sea at soon as possible, that being thought the best way to keep the fleet free of the plague. The *Merhonour* thus came to an anchor directly before the town of Southwold, which had been devastated by fire a few years before and which was still only partly rebuilt. I took to our longboat to go across to the *Royal Charles*. I needed the Duke of York's orders for the disposition of the ship; the hull continued to take in water, and Carpenter Thurston was insistent that we should be docked as quickly as possible. I also needed to pay my respects to the duke and belatedly to congratulate him upon his great victory.

I was still on one crutch, and getting down into the longboat secured alongside the larboard entry port took not a little effort and a considerable amount of pain. In the end, I was effectively manhandled down into the boat by Polzeath and Carvell, who commanded the oarsmen.

'Putting on weight, Captain,' said Carvell, his broad grin belaying any suggestion of insolence.

'I'll thank you to keep such an opinion to yourself, Mister Carvell,' I said, although I found it difficult to suppress a smile.

We cast off, oars dipped into war, and at a steady pace we moved across the calm sea toward the unmistakeable bulk of the fleet flagship. She flew a new royal standard and Lord Admiral's flag, but at the stern, her torn and barely recognisable ensign was still that which had flown during the battle. Like *Merhonour* and most of the ships in the fleet, the *Royal Charles* bore the tell-tale signs of war: the fresh timbers, still not painted, that filled the gaps where the old had been blasted away by the *Eendracht* or the *Oranje*; the indentations caused by the impact of round shot; the canvas temporarily replacing glass in some of her stern windows. And we were the victors.

As we neared the *Charles*, I spied a boat casting off from her, pulling toward the shore. In the stern was the unmistakeable figure of Harry Brouncker. He saw me, raised his hat in salute, and smiled. I did not reciprocate, pretending instead not to have seen him.

'Damnable man,' I hissed, more to myself than to my crew. 'Why in God's name did he transmit that order…'

Carvell looked at me quizzically. 'Thought you knew, Captain.'

'Knew, Mister Carvell? What is there to know?'

The black man shrugged. 'It's been all over the lower deck these last few days. Every lower deck in the fleet, probably. Expect someone on the *Charles* told someone on one of the victualling hoys, who spread the word to the cook's crew on the next ship, and so on.'

I must have looked startled, but probably should not have done: I had already served for more than long enough to realise that the most detailed knowledge of everything that transpires aboard a great ship is usually to be found upon her lower decks, rather than in her officers' quarters, and that even aboard a fleet at sea, word could get round even faster than in the frenetic hubbub of Whitehall.

Carvell said, 'Word is that Mister Brouncker, there, was only doing the bidding of the admiral's lady – the Duchess of York, that is. They say she'd told him to make certain the duke came back alive. They say Brouncker took fright after the narrow squeak the duke had, so first chance he had, he concocted an order to make sure there'd be no more fighting the next day.'

'Aye,' piped up Polzeath in his gruff Fowey tones, 'and the duke ain't likely to punish him, is he, if he was only doing his wife's bidding, else he'd have to answer to the duchess. Seen her, I did, when we was last at 'arwich. Wouldn't like to be on the wrong side of that 'un, I tell thee, Captain.'

We were nearly alongside the *Royal Charles*, but I remained frozen to the gunwale. I could barely take in what my men had told me. It was incredible – simply unbelievable. The greatest victory England might ever know, denied because of one woman's fretful obsession to keep her husband safe at all costs? Because a foul, idle pimp of a courtier sold his soul to do her bidding? Surely they would not have done such a thing without –

At all costs, preserve the life of His Royal Highness, my son-in-law.
In that moment, the words of the Earl of Clarendon came back to

me. Then I remembered the night of the state reception at the Banqueting House, when the Chancellor, his daughter the Duchess and Harry Brouncker had all been in conclave with each other. And with another, too. Another who was surely more likely to have insinuated some malicious intent into the easily deluded mind of her plaything, the vapid Brouncker –

Perhaps, after all, the lower deck did not know quite as much as it claimed to.

I saw the flagship's boat making for the shore. I saw Brouncker's smug face. In my mind's eye, I saw him escorting the Countess Louise that night at Whitehall, and recalled the boast to be bedding her that he had made at Sayes Court. I imagined the conversation that might have passed between Louise, Brouncker and the Hydes, father and daughter. I imagined what my good-sister might have said to her lover when she came to the fleet at Harwich. I was furious with rage on behalf of a thwarted fleet and nation. I thought upon Lawson, Marlborough and all the valiant dead or dying souls who seemed to cry out for an avenger. Perhaps I was also consumed by the growing suspicion that our victory had been snatched from us by the machinations of the Countess of Ravensden.

I still shudder at the recollection of what I decided to do next, in thrall to that flood of emotions. Turning to my right I said, 'Mister Carvell, we will come about and follow the *Charles*' boat, there. Ten shillings to each man in the crew if we can overtake her before she reaches Southwold quay.'

* * *

It would be a suitable place to die, I thought as I looked about me. I stood atop a great cliff looking down upon Southwold, or Sole, Bay. The fleet stretched away before me: there was the *Charles*, there the *Prince*, and there the *Merhonour*. The crumbling ruins of a church stood a little to the north, precariously close to the cliff edge. Inland, what had once obviously been a monastery was now a farm; hummocks and indentations in the earth marked where houses had once stood. This, then, was Dunwich, the great lost city that the relentless sea had reclaimed inch by inch over the centuries.

'One good foot,' said Cornelis. 'One foot, good-brother, and yet you challenge a man to a duel. I do not relish informing my sister that her husband died in such a fashion, Matthias.'

My paroled good-brother was my second in the encounter to come, although there had been no shortage of candidates for that position. Indeed, Roger d'Andelys had offered to take my place, although he was arguably even more hurt than I was; ultimately only a direct order kept him aboard the *Merhonour* to continue his recuperation. Kit Farrell inevitably had to remain aboard ship in acting command, but Ieuan Goch accompanied me to act as surgeon, and Francis Gale attended in full canonicals to say prayers over the dead if required.

My honour demanded it, I had announced when I explained what I had done to an incredulous dinner gathering in my cabin aboard *Merhonour*: I had waited for Harry Brouncker to step ashore (my boat's crew having amply earned their reward) before slapping the incredulous courtier with my glove. Despite Brouncker's enraged protestations of innocence, a time and place had been fixed. Almost every man present at dinner attempted to dissuade me. There would be no dishonour in withdrawing because of my wound, Francis averred. The challenge could be put down to a temporary light-headedness brought on by the pain, Cornelis suggested. Roger made his gallant offer to take my place. Any other captain in the fleet could justifiably have called Brouncker out, he said, so why, by Saint Denis and Saint Jeanne d'Arc, did it have to be Matthew Quinton?

Only one of those present actually nodded in agreement with what I had done: ironically, the one to whom gentlemanly honour was a new and entirely alien notion. Kit Farrell had a quiet word with me before I went ashore to take the field.

'God be with you, Captain,' he said. 'Your cause is just. That man betrayed us all, so I'll pray your sword strikes home.'

'And God be with you, Lieutenant. This might be the final lesson that I ever teach you, so heed this well, my friend – this is where honour can lead you. And if you think there must be a mighty fine distinction between honour and folly, then I think I'll concur with you.' I smiled, but my voice was breaking. 'If I don't return, Kit, see my ship safe into harbour.'

'Aye, aye, Captain Quinton.'

We shook, and I took my leave of my good and honest friend.

As Brouncker and his party of fashionable, sneering young men approached along the cliff-top, much of my fragile confidence evaporated. My foot throbbed. I could manage without a crutch, but only barely. I moved with the grace of a carthorse. What supreme arrogance had brought me to this? What lunatic notion of honour had made me assume I should take up the sword on behalf of an entire navy? And after all, what evidence did I possess against Harry Brouncker, beyond the report of a thirteen-year-old drunk, the tittle-tattle of the lower deck and my own suspicions of an unheard conversation spied across a crowded room in Whitehall?

Francis brought the two combatants together. The courtier had been happy with my suggestion that my chaplain should act as our arbiter; despite his closeness to me, who could be more neutral than a man of the cloth? Thus we saluted each other and took our guards.

Brouncker began with a dainty little feint, accompanied by an extravagant flourish. I parried easily, but this first pass made two things immediately evident to me. First, Harry Brouncker was no swordsman. He had learned enough from the training manuals to essay the odd flamboyance that might impress a court lady or two, but of real fighting he evidently knew next to nothing. In ordinary times, Matthew Quinton might have toyed with him a little and then either placed a scratch wherever he willed or else despatched him to his maker, depending upon the seriousness of the affair of honour. But this was not an ordinary time. Even the easy step required to parry Brouncker's first attack had sent jolts of agony from foot to brain.

Brouncker was not such an ignoramus that he could not see at once both the weakness and the strength of his position. He could not stand directly in front of me, exchanging thrust for thrust, always within easy striking distance of my blade; wound or no, that gave me all the advantage, for he would have realised at once that I was a serious swordsman. Thus he began to circle me, lunging only when I was turning or slightly off balance. He was not aiming for flesh: not yet. He did not need to. For by forcing me to turn quickly, to step forward or back to parry his attacks, he was inflicting almost as much pain upon me as any actual stab-wound.

I cursed my damnable pride. As metal struck metal, my own always defending, my head saw countless ways through his guard, endless openings to disarm or finish my opponent, and yet my body simply could not respond. My breath became shorter and faster. Sweat ran into my eyes. Oh God, for two or three pain-free steps, just two or three –

Brouncker knew I was tiring. Indeed, he was counting on it. Once again he sprang to my right, forcing me to put my weight upon the damaged foot as I turned. This time, though, he attacked at once, and vigorously, with more than his customary one or two tentative thrusts, seemingly intent on ending it there and then.

Over-confidence is always the enemy of the swordsman. I parried Brouncker's attack with ease, observed his slowness at resuming his guard, and in the same moment shifted onto my good left foot and thrust directly at his head.

'For the fleet you betrayed, and the honour of England!' I cried as I lunged.

Alas, fortune favoured the rogue, who moved his head aside just before my sword could bury itself in his skull, but he cried out in anguish as my blade nicked his right cheek.

Francis stepped in. 'Honour is satisfied –'

Brouncker reached up to the wound with his left hand, stared in amazement at the blood upon it, and looked at me in fury. 'Honour be fucked!' he cried. He sprang toward me, slashing furiously and without method. I backed away before him, although every step was purgatory – if I was fit, I could have exploited the frantic nature of his onslaught and easily struck a mortal blow, but all I could do was defend for grim life –

As I backed away, I tripped over a low ridge that had once been the base of a wall. I fell to the earth, brought up my sword barely in time to deflect away Brouncker's exultant slash toward my shoulder, but knew at once that I would be able to do nothing if he followed up with a quick thrust at my legs or groin –

I heard the hooves of the Four Horsemen, felt their thunder upon Dunwich cliff, and knew that my time had come. Ridiculously, I thought upon the disgrace of dying at the hands of a fop like Harry Brouncker, and wondered what my father and grandfather would say when I met them shortly –

Cornelis's sword came up, parrying Brouncker's blade and then coming down to knock mine to my side. We both looked at him quizzically, and in Brouncker's case angrily too, but as I got to my feet, Cornelis merely nodded toward the approaching party of horsemen, galloping toward us across the heath. There were rather more than four of them: perhaps twenty or more, all heavily armed, all in burgundy uniforms, and at their head was a familiar figure, the most natural and splendid horseman I ever saw in all my days, resplendent in a huge befeathered hat after the old fashion.

It was His Highness, Prince Rupert of the Rhine.

* * *

Brouncker had retired in disarray, for the prince was no friend of his, and His Highness's reminder to us of the king's many injunctions against duelling had been delivered with a stern ferocity that made us both exchange sheepish, ashamed glances.

Rupert's face was no less serious when he took me a little way off from my bemused companions, into the ruins of the church upon the cliff-top.

'So, Matthew Quinton,' he said, 'you considered it incumbent upon yourself to right the wrong that Brouncker committed?'

Those words, coming from the greatest cavalier of them all, made me feel pitiful, and ashamed of my folly.

'I – I acted on the spur of the moment, Highness. For the honour of all in the fleet.'

'Ah, yes, the honour of the fleet. And who exactly appointed you to be the guardian of the honour of the fleet, Matthew Quinton?'

I looked out, through the gaping hole where the east window had been, toward the ships at anchor in the bay beyond. 'No man, Your Highness. I beg forgiveness for my presumption and pride.'

Rupert nodded. '*Ja.* Presumption and pride indeed. That you, a wounded man incapable of moving and wielding his sword properly, should have reached Brouncker before any of the three army officers, outstanding swordsmen all, whom I had assigned to different quarters of Southwold, with my direct – but naturally unwritten – orders to ignore my cousin's injunctions and challenge the accursed fellow at the first opportunity… As it is, Quinton, you have deprived me of the pleasure of seeing one of my men's blades lodged in Brouncker's ribs, and you almost lost your own life to boot. You are a damnably impetuous young man.'

And then Rupert of the Rhine did something that I had never witnessed before; indeed, I believe there were very few who ever witnessed the sight that I now beheld.

His face broke into the most radiant, boyish grin.

'Yes,' he said, 'damnably impetuous. As I was, once. And then, your conduct in the late battle was outstanding – your ship's resistance to the *Oranje* was quite glorious, Captain. You probably saved the *Charles* and thus my cousin, the Duke. But for my part, I was more impressed by the initiative you showed in turning out of the line to follow me.' Rupert's uncharacteristic smile broadened. 'Which is what I had hoped for when I recommended you for this command.'

'*You*? You recommended me, Highness?'

Rupert nodded sharply in the Teutonic fashion. 'Who else? James was reluctant to commission a man who had so offended his brother the King, but I am beyond such sensibilities. Your conduct and loyalty during these last years made me certain you were the man to watch Lawson and the rest if they proved treacherous. You have much of your father in you, Matthew Quinton, and he was one of the best men I ever knew.' The prince sighed. 'I have been a warrior for thirty years, and have been responsible for the deaths of more men than I can count. Not only my enemies, but too many of my friends. And I regret no death for which I was responsible more than that of your father. You know it is twenty years, to this very day, since the Naseby fight?' I felt a sudden shock: I had quite forgotten the anniversary of my father's death in the battle where this prince, standing so few feet from me, had won and lost a war in the space of an afternoon. 'Twenty years, but I still see it as though it were yesterday. Still I mourn the men who fell, and the cause that was lost. Thus to honour the memory of your father, and to acknowledge your own courage and other merits, I pledge that henceforward I will be a true friend and patron to you, Matthew Quinton.'

With that, Rupert, Prince Palatine of the Rhine, extended his hand toward me. In those days the gesture was still rare; coming from this man above all others, it was doubly unexpected.

Twenty years to the day. Time to close the chapter. I reached out and shook the royal hand.

Chapter Twenty-Four

[Lawson] led our fleet that day too short a space,
But lost his knee, died since in God's grace;
Lawson, whose valour beyond fate did go
And still fights Obdam through the lakes below…
[Falmouth's] shatter'd head the Duke disdains,
And gave the last – first proof that he had brains.
Berkeley had heard it soon and thought not good
To venture more of royal Harding's blood…
With his whole squadron straight away he bore,
And, like good boy, promis'd to fight no more.
~ Marvell, Second Advice to a Painter

When I finally got aboard the *Royal Charles*, the Duke of York made
no mention of my duel with Brouncker, although he must have been
fully aware of it. But Sir William Coventry, at his side, smiled broadly
throughout the interview, and at its conclusion, he winked happily at
me; evidently the Lord Admiral's secretary thoroughly approved of my
conduct. The duke himself was businesslike, enquiring after my wound,

my casualties and the state of my ship. He listened intently, and when I had finished my account, his orders to me were brisk and categorical. The *Merhonour* to proceed at once to Chatham, there to be docked pending survey and – if repair proved uneconomical, as all expected – to be condemned as unfit for further service. Captain Quinton to be granted leave to recover from his wound, and (at Captain Quinton's private request) to attend to his own personal affairs ashore. Captain van der Eide to be sent to the *Royal Charles* so that the duke could compliment him in person upon his outstanding conduct during the battle, and to entertain him in his retinue for a time; indeed, the heir to England spoke of my good-brother with almost reverential awe and admiration. Roger, Comte d'Andelys, to be permitted to return to France in the train of the ambassadors, there to continue his recuperation; it being an unspoken understanding that the Battle of Lowestoft had put paid to the duc de Verneuil's embassy, and by so doing had increased that the likelihood that France would declare war on Great Britain in belated compliance with its treaty obligations to the Dutch.

Thus the week or so that we spent at anchor at the Buoy of the Nore, off Sheerness, awaiting suitable tides to take us up the Medway after sailing down from Southwold Bay, was a time of leave-taking. Roger's departure was accompanied by drums, trumpets, and the finest choir of Cornish and Welsh voices that the *Merhonour* could provide. The Comte d'Andelys, still nursing his damaged left arm in a sling, took a final look around the upper deck and then lifted his hat to me.

'Captain Quinton,' he said, 'I give you thanks, sir, for your hospitality to me upon this voyage. You know that you and your dear wife are always welcome at the chateau of Andelys, and you will always be welcome aboard any ship of mine.'

I responded in an equally formal manner. 'Your presence aboard has honoured us, My Lord. I wish you well for your return to France, sir.' And then, rather less formally – 'Let us pray it's not to be war between us, Roger.'

'Ah, there can never be war between us, my friend. Between our kingdoms, perhaps. Between your ship and mine, quite possibly. But never between friends.'

A day later, Cherry Cheeks Russell left us. A letter had recently come to me from the Earl of Bedford suggesting that the boy's voyage with us had not been as entirely with the concurrence of his family as he had claimed, nor of the headmaster of his school, the same one that I had attended but a few years before. No concurrence whatsoever, to be precise. Thus it was a somewhat chastened and unusually sober young man who was rowed ashore to Queenborough Quay, there to be collected by one of the retainers from Woburn Abbey. Young Russell waved from the boat, and as I returned the gesture I turned to Francis Gale, alongside me on the quarterdeck, and remarked, 'Well, our duty is done in his regard, Francis. But I doubt that young man will ever amount to very much.'

I did not know then how wrong it is possible for a man to be. That thought struck me those few months ago when I saw this same Edward Russell buried; not in some obscure corner of the churchyard at Woburn, but in Westminster Abbey, replete with all the honours that our land could bestow. As Garter King of Arms recited the titles, my thoughts wandered back to that summer of sixty-five and to the snot-nosed, drink-addled boy who had grown to be the Most Noble Lord Edward, Earl of Orford, Viscount and Baron, Admiral of the Fleet, First Lord of the Admiralty no fewer than three times; the victor of Barfleur and La Hogue, the twin battle that constituted an even greatest victory than Lowestoft, a colossal naval triumph unlikely ever to be surpassed or forgotten; sometime the joint chief minister of England; aye, and one of the 'immortal seven', those who signed the letter inviting William of Orange to invade this realm, thus bringing about what some still call 'the Glorious Revolution'. Or so he liked to believe.

In the year ninety-two, the exiled King James the Second watched from a clifftop in Normandy as Admiral Edward Russell's ships destroyed the French invasion transports that were meant to restore him in triumph to his Britannic thrones. Although I was not there, I have thought upon that beautiful irony many times. I have wondered whether, as the French ships burned in the bay of La Hogue, both the king and the admiral thought back to that day in June 1665: to that moment when they stood together upon the quarterdeck of the *Royal Charles* and a shot took off the heads of the men next to them, rather than their own. The chance of a moment, a stroke of luck, divine pre-destination, call it what you will – *that* is what makes history.

As it was, to the end of his days Edward Russell could spell barely a word, ever kept a bottle close at hand, and always had to bear the embarrassment of his first captain greeting him as 'Cherry Cheeks'.

* * *

There was one call of duty that had to be made before I could return to London and attempt to get to the bottom of the strange conspiracy, if so it truly was, that seemed to exist between my wife, my uncle and Phineas Musk. Once the *Merhonour* was safely docked at Chatham, I took horse, crossed Rochester Bridge and so rode on to Gravesend and Greenwich. There I dismounted before a goodly house of three stories, making my way up the stairs through a throng of concerned seamen (Will Berkeley at their head), tearful servants and grieving kin to the deathbed of one of England's fallen heroes.

'Matthew Quinton,' said Sir John Lawson in a weak voice. 'I had not expected to see you here.'

The wound in his knee had turned gangrenous, and the stench in the room was truly dreadful. As I stood before his bed and looked upon the pale, sweating face of the recumbent Yorkshireman, I came to a sudden and discomfiting realisation: I did not have the slightest idea of what I wished to say to him. 'I – I have come to apologise, Sir John. For ordering my ship out of its rightful place in the line.'

He fixed me with a quizzical stare. 'You have come to say that to me? Father of Heaven, you are indeed a curious young man.' He coughed, then laughed the thin, bitter laugh of the dying. 'You did the right thing, Quinton. When I saw the prince tack, I thought as you must have done – do I follow him? And when you turned, I thought once again – does that young blade have the right of it?' An old nurse stepped forward, mopped Sir John's brow and glowered at me for taxing him, but he waved her away. 'But you see, Quinton, I served under the generals-at-sea, Blake, Deane, aye, and the Duke of Albemarle as now is. Army men all, and under them, obedience to the command flag was paramount. Initiative was frowned upon – unless they were the ones displaying the initiative. So when you and the prince tacked, my heart told me to go with you. But my head was still filled with the dictums of a dozen years past. No signal from the flagship, so hold your course, John Lawson. And if all had done as I did, we would surely have lost this battle and perhaps this war. So you do not need to apologise to me, Matthew Quinton.' He coughed long and hard.

'I thank you, Sir John,' was all I could find to say.

'Aye, well. Nor do I blame you for your part in that business of the twenty captains. After the *London* blew up, I made some enquiries of my own to discover whether it could have been sabotage, and learned of the rumour at that time. And of a strange, dark creature said to be involved with it in some way. A creature going under the name of Lord Percival.' *Percival?* But that was the name Lady Louise had uttered when she and I were alone at Ravensden – 'Twenty traitorous captains,' said Lawson through a coughing fit. 'A monstrous slander against our honour. An unfounded rumour started God knows where – perhaps by this very Percival – to discredit we who had served the Commonwealth, yet somehow it was elevated by the black arts of the king's ministers into the grandest of conspiracies. So we all fell under suspicion, and we Englishmen nearly defeated ourselves as a result.' He reached out and pulled me down, close to him, so that the others in the room could not hear. The smell was almost unbearable, yet his words were even heavier upon my heart. 'I tell you this, Quinton. I have been loyal to England until this, my dying day,' Lawson whispered. 'I have been true to Proverbs Three, Verse Three, as have the others. We have all been loyal. But the foulest treacheries are always those that grow closest to home – the betrayal of a cheating wife, or the disdain of an unfeeling child.' The great admiral coughed, speckling his chin with blood. 'And there is the irony, is it not? England was not betrayed by us, the old Commonwealths-men. England was betrayed by one of your own kind, Matthew Quinton. Betrayed upon the idle whim of a great lady.' He coughed again. When he spoke once more, his words were barely audible. 'That is the truth of your new cavalier England. I am glad to take my leave of it.'

I left Sir John with a heavy heart, for I knew he had only spoken the truth.

Will Berkeley took me to one side. 'I'm grateful to you, Matt. It was good of you to come.'

'You'll stay with him, Will?'

'To the end. He was a great man – our greatest seaman of all, I think.' My friend seemed troubled by more than the imminent death of Sir John Lawson, and I asked him the cause. 'My conduct is condemned, in the streets and already in pamphlets that are about London. In short, my friend – I am denounced as a coward.'

'A coward? But dear God, man, you did what all the rest of us in the Red did!'

'Aye, and there's the rub. What *did* all of us in the Red do, Matt – apart from Lawson's division, that is? Might not those with a mind to censure contemplate the fact that we all lay apart from the battle for hours, and judge that the Red Squadron contained a pack of cowards?'

I was stunned, and I suspect my face betrayed it. 'But that was *strategy*, Will – the duke's orders, no less! To lie to windward that the

Dutch could never weather our fleet, then to deploy where and when we were most needed –'

'All well and good, Matt, but tell that to the roaring boys in the alehouses who think that the only proper conduct for an Englishman in battle is to lay about the enemy furiously and constantly, even if he loses his life along the way.' Berkeley shook his head sadly. 'They cannot attack the Duke directly, of course, and although they whisper against Penn, he is too close to the Duke to criticise openly. Lawson, the vice-admiral, was always in the heart of the battle and will die a hero of the nation. So they censure the rear-admiral as a proxy for the apparent inactivity of those greater than myself. Accuse Will Berkeley of cowardice, and by implication you denounce His Royal Highness' conduct of the battle. And thus, by yet further inference, you censure the entire royal government of England.' My friend smiled wanly. 'It is the humour of the times, Matt, and of our English propensity always to tear down those who have risen faster than the common herd think is fitting, for that is how they see my poor dead brother and I. But I think I can bear it better than the loss of the dear friend dying over yonder.'

We embraced, and I promised I would do all in my power to clear the name of Sir William Berkeley. Thus we parted, and Will returned to the deathbed of the man who had been his patron and so nearly his father-in-law.

I descended the stairs with a heavy heart. Consumed in my own thoughts, I did not pay full attention as I opened the door and stepped out into the street. Thus I collided heavily with the next visitor who had come to pay his last respects to the dying admiral.

'Y – Your Grace,' I stammered, rapidly bowing my head to the dark young man who stood in the doorway. 'I am most profoundly sorry –'

'Captain Quinton,' said the Duke of Monmouth. 'As well that you steered a truer course during the battle.'

'As you say, Your Grace.'

'I had been hoping to get the chance for a word with you. All men speak highly of your conduct in the battle, and although I usually avoid the common herd, on this occasion I happily concur with its opinion.' The Duke smiled pleasantly. He was ever an easy man to like, and was very aware of the fact that he could generate such liking in almost anyone he met; a trait which proved ultimately to be his fatal weakness. 'I will be going directly to court, and to my father. I will be certain to speak to him on your behalf, Captain Quinton.'

To the best of my knowledge I was still anathema to His Majesty, so the prospect of an intervention on my behalf by Monmouth, the son on whom the king doted, was something to be snatched at with both hands. 'Your Grace is most kind,' I said. 'And if I can ever be of service to your Grace…'

I left the sentence unfinished, for it was intended as no more than a conventional pleasantry, but Monmouth seized upon it. 'Yes, perhaps so. One day, perhaps you may indeed be of service to me, Matthew.'

It is said that words return to haunt us, and I have learned the truth of that saying many times. But never was it more apposite in my life than in the case of that exchange between James, Duke of Monmouth, and myself, on a street in Greenwich in the summer of 1665.

$$* * *$$

'Cornelia!'

I called out for the twentieth time, but still there was no answer. Our rooms in Hardiman's Yard were deserted. The conviction that she must have gone to Ravensden Abbey to escape the plague grew upon me; and yet she had left no word, which surely she would have done. Despite the risk, I opened a window to let some air into our stiflingly hot and musty home. Outside, the streets were all but deserted; it seemed that the door of every other house was marked with a red cross. The smell of death, the same as that present in Sir John Lawson's chamber, was upon the air, and with it a faint whiff of the lime-pits that had been dug in Aldgate and elsewhere to consume the ever-multiplying legion of plague corpses. I had to get out of London before I was infected. I had run enough of a risk by riding brazenly through the streets from London Bridge; isolated aboard the fleet, I had not realised how terrible the contagion had become. Few men were abroad, and those who did risk the streets were muffled against the poisonous air around them. Behind countless doors, I could hear muffled sobs and screams. It was a veritable city of death.

The court had decamped long ago to the palace of Hampton Court, but finding that to be still too close to the tentacles of plague, it was now removing itself all the way to Salisbury. The navy would be safe as long as it kept at sea, but with the *Merhonour* too shattered to go anywhere but the dry dock at Chatham and Captain Quinton on leave pending a new command … well, then, to the abbey it would be. Musk had to be there, too: he was certainly not at Ravensden House, which bore suspiciously little sign of recent building work – and if Tris was back at Oxford, as he surely was by now, it would be an easy matter to override my mother's objections and bring him to the Abbey. There, surely, all matters could finally be resolved.

I was almost out of the door when I spied the letter, resting on the top of a small chest. It was addressed to me, but was not in any hand I recognised.

My dear Matthew,

I trust that you receive this upon your return from sea. I have despatched copies to Chatham and Harwich in the hope that these words reach you before it is too late.

The plague being so prevalent in London, I have invited your whole family to my estate at Lyndbury, it being more removed from the likely spread of foul air than Ravensden and also more convenient for the court while this tarries at Salisbury. Thus your dear mother and Cornelia are here with me.

I was astonished. For my mother to have travelled so far was inconceivable; for Cornelia to have done so without sending me word was, if anything still more fantastical. Something about the whole business, about this very letter, was not right.

It is convenient that we should all be here, Matthew, and that you should join us as quickly as you are able. Poor Charles is here also, and alas, his health deteriorates daily. I fear that the end might not be far off. Thus it would only be fitting for you, the new Earl of Ravensden, to be present to say your farewells to the old.

I am yours, good-brother, in love and in sadness,

Louise Ravensden

I was on the road to the south-west within an hour, my head filled with terrors and anxieties. Thus, at last, the man who might already be Earl of Ravensden set out to confront his destiny.

Chapter Twenty~Five

Nothing, thou elder brother even to Shade,
Thou had'st a being ere the world was made,
And (well-fixed) art alone of ending not afraid...
The great man's gratitude to his best friend,
Kings' promises, whores' vows, towards thee they bend,
Flow swiftly into thee, and in thee ever end.
~ John Wilmot, second Earl of Rochester, *Upon Nothing*
(published 1679)

It was already the middle of the afternoon when I galloped out of London upon a good steed from my brother's stable. My road took me past the incomplete shell of Clarendon House, and I reflected briefly upon all that had passed since I was summoned within its walls. At first I was determined to ride through the night, but I knew within an hour that to attempt it would be folly; my foot, which I had foolishly believed to be largely healed, was in agony as every equine movement pushed it hard against the stirrup, and to attempt to change horses at two or three in the morning would have risked bringing upon my head the righteous wrath of some disgruntled ostler, torn unwillingly from his bed. Moreover, Charles might already be dead; if he still lived, he would either survive until after my arrival or not. (The fatalism of my wife's Calvinist faith was somewhat infectious, and perhaps it had been reinforced by my recent experience of the senseless, random nature of human dying.) Above all, I suspected that I would need all my faculties about me on the following day. Thus as dusk fell, I halted at a mean inn in the shadow of the ruins of Basing House, the mighty palace blasted to pieces by the rebels during the late wars, and there snatched a few troubled hours of sleep.

I pressed on at dawn upon a new steed hired from the inn's stable, and reached Lyndbury late in the afternoon. The countess's deceased second husband, Major-General Gulliver, had evidently been something of a favourite of the Lord Protector, for he had been granted a truly lavish property. The seat for four hundred years of a once-mighty dynasty that had been impoverished and then extinguished by the civil wars, Lyndbury was a lofty castle after the Gothic manner, partly rebuilt with larger windows and more capacious rooms in Queen Elizabeth's day, but dreadfully shattered when Gulliver's own men had besieged it. Most of the north side lay in ruins, as was evident to me even as I approached from the east.

I rode into the cobbled courtyard and dismounted. There were no servants anywhere in sight, but I had the unsettling feeling that several pairs of eyes were fixed upon me. I made my way to the obvious entry into the main building, a grand arched doorway at the top of a sweeping flight of stairs, pushed the door, and found myself at the bottom of a dimly lit stairwell. I ascended. The room on the first floor must have been the great hall of the original castle; it was a cavernous, vaulted chamber, but it was completely empty. Upward, then. Through the half-open door onto the next floor, I glimpsed lush tapestries and the movement of a woman's skirts. I pushed open the door and entered.

The tableau before me was astonishing. Cornelia sat opposite the doorway, and although she raised her eyes at sight of me, she did not spring up and embrace me passionately, as was her wont. Instead she appeared dejected, and did not even manage a smile. Off to the right, near the fireplace, sat my mother, who gave the merest nod to acknowledge me. Further right again, beneath a fine Tudor window that looked out over the parkland beyond, sat my brother, Charles, Earl of Ravensden, his head resting upon his hand, looking deathly pale. And beside him, proud and exultant, clad in an extravagant scarlet gown, stood the Countess Louise.

'Matthew!' she cried. 'You have made excellent time. Splendid. Now, at last, we can all conclude our business here.'

'Business, My Lady? What business is this?'

'We are prisoners,' said Cornelia bitterly.

'Oh, guests, Cornelia, not prisoners!' said the countess, airily. 'A pleasant family gathering, is it not? Nought but a summer sojourn away from the plague-ridden city. What a thoughtful hostess, to offer such hospitality!'

Cornelia scowled. 'The woman is insane, husband –'

'Insane, Cornelia?' snarled Lady Louise. 'Ah well, there we shall have to agree to differ. For is it insane to bring out the truth? That is what I am about, you see. The truth that your family has hidden for nearly forty years.' She moved across the gallery toward me. I rested a hand on the hilt of my sword. 'Your weapon can stay sheathed, Matthew. The castle is filled with my men. Several are just beyond that door, in the antechamber. And I have no doubt that you are curious. It would be such a shame to strike me down before you learn what your mother and brother have concealed from you throughout your life, would it not?' Her tone was almost playful, taunting me; for she knew that her words struck home. I looked at Charles and at my mother in turn. The earl's eyes were blank; my mother's were tearful, and tears from the Dowager Countess were nearly unknown. 'And with you and your dear Cornelia to witness the depositions that they will shortly sign, all will be legal and indisputable, you see? Proof that will stand in any court of law, and proof that demands to be trumpeted to the world. Proof positive of the great lie that the House of Quinton has inflicted upon England.'

She was close to me now: I could easily have drawn my sword and struck her down. But I did not doubt the truth of her words about the men in the antechamber, and could not bring down their inevitable vengeance upon my family.

'What are you about, madam? What is it that you *want*?' I demanded angrily.

The countess stared at me quizzically, and for just one fleeting moment, I thought I saw an unspoken answer in her eyes: that what she wanted was the man standing before her. As it was, her answer was provided by my wife.

'Power, husband,' said Cornelia, 'power and money. All that has ever mattered to this murderous whore. She hoped that allowing the king to father an heir to Ravensden upon her would elevate her into His Majesty's principal mistress, ousting Lady Castlemaine.'

'But even His Majesty proved more discriminating,' said my mother, harshly. Tears and criticism of the Lord's anointed: this was indeed a day of unexpected glimpses of a very different Anne Quinton to the one I had known all my life.

'And as our king's fleeting interest in her vanished, so her use to the French king diminished in turn, and with it the pension that allows her to maintain all of this,' said Cornelia. 'So she had to find a new way to make herself indispensable to King Louis.'

'Crudely put, Cornelia,' said the Countess Louise, 'but not entirely wide of the mark.' Her eyes were very strange now: ablaze with emotions that might have been exultation, or scorn, or fear, or a little of all of them. 'What could be more valuable to France than proof of a dark secret of state, of knowledge that can be used against Charles

Stuart if he strays from policies favoured by King Louis? Can be used, indeed, to force him to abandon his present policy that so offends the Most Christian? Do you not think that the agent who uncovered such knowledge would have proved herself worthy of France's continuing gratitude and beneficence?'

I went to Cornelia and stood alongside her chair. She placed her hand in mine and gripped it tightly.

'You speak in riddles, madam,' I said. 'What policy? What secret? Be direct, in God's name.'

'The policy you know, Matthew. You were at the reception of the ambassadors. I seek merely to further their purpose, although by rather different means.'

I recalled the night of the great state reception in the Banqueting House of Whitehall: of the grand entry of the Duc de Verneuil, and of my sight of the Countess Louise's agitated conversation with Monsieur Courtin.

'France wishes England to withdraw from this war with the Dutch,' I said slowly, piecing together the implications in my head. 'If we do not, King Louis' treaty obligations to them will force him to enter the war on their side. And that does not suit the purpose of the Most Christian, who wishes England and Holland neutered so he can pursue his ambition to conquer Flanders.' I looked at her and nodded with what might even have been a hint of respect. 'The embassy failed to achieve its end, but perhaps you yet may, Madam, if whatever secret knowledge you think you hold against the king is so truly heinous that it compels him to change his policy and end the war.'

'Bravo, Matthew!' cried Louise admiringly. 'You should become a statesman, methinks. And the knowledge is heinous indeed – a secret able to halt a war or topple a king. Very well, then.' She turned and faced my mother directly. 'Time to tell your son the truth that you have hidden from him and the world, My Lady.'

My mother seemed incapable of speech. Her eyes were focused on the unlit fireplace, not blinking, seemingly lost in a far distant place and time. Charles shifted uncomfortably in his chair and said, 'I will say it, to spare our mother.' His voice was thin and broken, bearing the weight of illness and of the ages. 'It is – it is possible that my father was not James Quinton, Earl of Ravensden.'

Not James Quinton. Not our father – *my* father.

As I struggled to take in the enormity of the impossible words that Charles had uttered, I thought back to the conversation I once had upon a Scottish moor with a great general, a man with barely days to live, and to my subsequent interview with his lover Henrietta Maria, Queen Mother of England. Now, at last, the pieces all fell into place.

'It was the king,' I said, staring at my mother. 'You were King Charles' lover.'

Charles Stuart, the First of that name. A man revered as a saint and martyr, a man whose spotless private life was held up as an example and indictment to his son. My mother's guilty eyes spoke the truth of the assertion. I recalled all the candles she lit every thirtieth day of every January, the anniversary of the king's execution. I remembered the fanatically devoted way in which she venerated the dead king's memory. At last, it was all clear to me: the Dowager Countess was mourning her lost lover.

In that same moment, I realised one of the two chief consequences of this terrible new truth. Proof that the royal martyr had betrayed his queen and fathered a bastard would be utterly devastating for the cavaliers, who had built an entire religion upon his memory and a potent romantic myth around the loving, doomed marriage of a king and a queen. It would be a mighty weapon in the hands of the malcontents who sought once more to bring down the entire edifice of monarchy, restored so very recently and still so fragile; as, indeed, the whole business over the twenty captains had so recently proved to me. England was a powder keg, and it would take only one small spark to blow it all to kingdom come. Moreover, possession of the House of Quinton's fateful knowledge – categorical, legally proven knowledge, not the ordinary tittle-tattle of rumour and slander that ever swirled about the court and the streets of London – and the threat of trumpeting it to the world, would have given King Louis an almost irresistibly powerful hold upon his English cousin. Perhaps even a hold powerful enough to compel Charles Stuart to withdraw from the war and to be in thrall to King Louis ever after; such had to be the calculation made by Courtin and executed on his behalf by the Countess Louise with this desperate throw of the dice, detaining us all in this grim ruin until she achieved her purpose. It would matter not a jot that the depositions she wished my mother and brother to sign were made under duress, for upon such evidence ever rests a large part of English law.

In any case, how could my brother and mother deny testimony that was essentially true?

With the words spoken, a great weight seemed to lift from the dowager countess. She looked at me directly, and said, 'I loved him, and I loved your father. Equally, for those few heady months in the year twenty-seven, when the world was new and all seemed possible. Buckingham loved the Queen of France, Campbell of Glenrannoch loved the Queen of England, so why could I not love a king?' For the briefest of moments I caught a glimpse of the bold, lively young woman that my mother must once have been. 'Your father came back from campaign, and he was different. Changed. Distant. I loved him still, and we lived conjugally, as man and wife ought – but the king was kind, attentive and understanding. He craved a woman's company, a woman who could show him the way to make his wife love him.' Her eyes seemed lost in that long-dead past, at once desperately happy and yet so utterly painful to recall. 'So I cannot be certain, Matthew. I cannot say who fathered your brother.'

'Perhaps that is so, madam,' said the Countess Louise. 'I sympathise, as one's king's whore to another.' I bridled at that and even reached for my sword, but Cornelia restrained me. Strangely, though, the remark seemed not to offend my mother in the least. 'But that is not what you will depone before the lawyer waiting in the antechamber,' the countess continued. 'You will testify that you were the mistress of the first King Charles, and that the man who calls himself Charles, Earl of Ravensden, is in truth the bastard son of that king.'

Then the second terrible consequence of this revelation struck me. If Charles was not the son of James Quinton, then he could not be the Earl of Ravensden. I was. I had been since the age of five.

There was a strange silence. None moved. My mother still seemed far away, lost in the memories of her dream-time; my brother stared feebly out of the window toward the green acres of Lyndbury. The Countess Louise stood in the centre of the great gallery, seemingly revelling in her triumph. My heart pounded, and my thoughts raced.

Strangely, Cornelia seemed impassive. Indeed, after a few moments she did the strangest thing. She smiled. At first, I thought this must be her reaction to the realisation that she might now be the rightful Countess of Ravensden; in contrast to the ambivalence I had always felt toward the prospect of succession, she positively relished it. Swiftly, though, I realised that her reaction betokened something else. I was tense and perspiring, yet Cornelia seemed strangely relaxed. She no longer seemed to be a prisoner; she had the confident air of a gaoler.

'Well, husband,' she said, 'now you have heard. This Jezebel has condemned herself from her own mouth, and you can testify to it.'

For the first time, the Countess Louise seemed nonplussed. 'The only testimony given here will be that which I dictate, Cornelia!'

'Oh, I rather think not,' said a new but familiar voice. 'The game has altered, My Lady.'

The door to the gallery opened. Framed within it was the wizened form of my uncle, Doctor Tristram Quinton. He entered the room, thus enabling Phineas Musk to make his own entrance behind him. But Musk was not alone. At his side was a young woman of eighteen or so. Her hair was as raven-black as that of the Countess Louise, but she was perhaps half a foot shorter. Her face was pinched and her complexion pallid; the girl had not lived well, I thought. I did not know then that her face looked remarkably well, considering how recently she had recovered from the plague.

Her eyes fixed upon the countess.

'Hello, mother,' said Madeleine Lugg, alias De Vaux.

Chapter Twenty-Six

Be not too proud, imperious Dame,
Your charms are transitory things,
May melt, while you at Heaven aim,
Like Icarus's waxen wings;
And you a part in his misfortune bear,
Drown'd in a briny ocean of despair.

~ Thomas Flatman, *The Defiance* (published 1686)

Lady Louise stared in stupefaction upon her daughter. She did not greet her; she did not embrace her. Instead, she suddenly looked away, toward the door of the antechamber, and screamed, 'Sleep! Hughton! Baines!'

Tristram shook his head. 'All below, My Lady, along with all your other men. It is as well that this place was built with most commodious cellars. If you look out of the window, you will see that we have secured it all around with a troop of Wiltshire militia.'

She went to the window, satisfied herself of the truth of Tris's words, then turned back at last to face us.

'You have no authority here,' said the countess, still seemingly serenely confident. 'You cannot give orders to the militia! You do no man's bidding but your own, Tristram Quinton!'

'Not so,' said Charles mildly. He was still seated in his chair near the window, still the very image of a man at death's door. 'All that has been done here, and will be done, is at my bidding.'

She turned on him furiously, but could only stare incredulously at him. '*Your* bidding, husband?' She nearly spat the words at him. 'Not even your own body obeys your bidding, Charles.'

He smiled; and a smile from Charles Quinton was as rare as snow in summer. 'My dear Louise,' he said, 'you should never have essayed the part of a spy. You are too gullible, for you trust appearances and letters recounting the movements of a sickly husband rather too readily, madam.'

Then Charles did something unexpected. He lifted himself from his chair and drew himself up to his full height, an action that always pained him. He turned to my uncle, and his face was suddenly as hard as gunmetal. When he spoke next, his voice was deeper and stranger; the voice of an actor. Or of a man who had learned the art of actors.

He said, 'Do you know me, Tristram Quinton?'

My uncle smiled complicitly as he recited the ancient passwords. 'Yes, My Lord, I know you now.'

'By what name do you know me?'

'You are Lord Percival.'

I felt a shock in my heart, and knew at once that it was not the single shock of my brother's revelation: for I stared at Cornelia, and saw plainly that for her, this was merely prior knowledge.

Lord Percival. To my surprise, I found myself grinning in belated realisation. For I recalled at once how my brother was always much taken with an old book by Chretien de Troyes, the *Percivale*. The tale of a valiant, pure knight who grew up not knowing that he was the son of a king.

Lady Louise stared open-mouthed at her husband: at Lord Percival. 'You? But I first heard that name months ago from – from an agent of the Most Christian –'

'As the man who was intent on bringing you down, and obstructing all the machinations of France in this land. Intent upon exposing you for what you are, Louise. And now you have done so quite thoroughly, by your own admission before us all – a French spy, a traitor who seeks to blackmail the king, and so much more besides. As we shall shortly hear.'

She looked desperately around the room, as frantic as a cornered animal. At last her eyes settled upon Phineas Musk. 'You lied to me, Musk!' she cried. 'You told me that Percival was an alias of Mordaunt's! You *showed* me Mordaunt, garbed as Percival, at the conventicle in Barking! You swore upon oath that Earl Matthew told you he knew his grandson was spurious! And you swore never to betray me to one named Quinton –'

'Many better people than you have come to grief by actually believing what Phin Musk told them, My Lady,' he growled. 'If the late earl knew anything of My Lord's paternity, he certainly never revealed it to me – truth to tell, our discourse rarely extended beyond "Musk, you poxed fustilarian, where the hell are my boots?" But otherwise I kept my word, in a sense, and never betrayed you to one named Quinton. By your own logic, My Lord's real name is Stuart, is it not?'

Louise stared at him open-mouthed; that a mere servant might have been better versed than she in the principles of Machiavelli seemed genuinely shocking to her.

'And as for My Lord Mordaunt,' said Charles, 'let us say that he was perfectly happy to play the part I assigned to him, as he did so often in the past. He relished the opportunity to play the man of action again, rather than the role which he usually plays in public these days – the disillusioned and idle bore. Yes, a good man, Johnny Mordaunt. My man.' Charles was relentless now, moving toward his wife and circling her without the trace of a limp. 'It took many months to assemble the evidence against you, Louise. Almost as many months as it took Matthew, Cornelia and Tris to convince my mother and I that you were indeed the harpy that they took you to be from the first. You covered your tracks well, but not well enough.' He nodded toward the impassive figure of Madeleine De Vaux, who had not taken her eyes off her mother. 'As in the case of your daughter, here. Sent to a convent in France, I believe you said? I think not.'

'Convent, My Lord? Aye, some convent,' said Madeleine. Her voice was harsh, a cynical, world-weary London accent. 'A whorehouse, more like, when I was but six. At least the old bitch Anderson had the grace not to put me with the customers for a few years afterwards. Not that it would have mattered to you whether she did or not, would it, mother? But I remembered you, the proud Lady De Vaux. And I remembered what you screamed at me, that day you left me behind.' The girl's eyes welled with tears. 'That my being born had done for your womb – that you could never bear children again, and it was my fault...'

Lady Louise moved toward her, hand raised, but Charles reached out and grasped her wrist. 'You have committed enough violence, madam,' he said.

'These are *lies*!' screamed the Countess of Ravensden. She released herself from Charles and backed toward the window. 'You have bought this girl's testimony – I have never seen her before –'

'We have evidence,' said Cornelia. 'The ledger of Goodwife Anderson, for instance. Which names you, My Lady, as the – the depositor, let us say, of this child with her.'

'Of course,' said Charles, 'it would have been mightily inconvenient for you to admit to the king or I that you could not bear children – not when your first scheme depended on you being able to convince both he and I that you could provide an heir to the earldom. His Majesty does not take kindly to being lied to, madam.'

Aye, I thought, a strange paradox, that: for Charles Stuart had no compunction in lying to men's faces if so doing ensured his survival upon the throne.

'Nor does this family take kindly to your lies,' said Tris. 'Your assumed interest in the earlier generations of Quinton history – that was but a ploy to conceal your real target, the evidence of Her Dowager Ladyship's liaison with the late king, was it not?' Louise stared at him, her eyes a curious meld of fury and fear. There was something about Tristram's words, something about Tristram himself, that unsettled her more than the condemnation of her own husband. 'And then there is the question of your origins. Oh, you must have thought that tearing from the parish register the page recording the entry of your marriage to Sir Bernard de Vaux – an entry giving your place of birth – would keep that information safe from all mankind. It took some considerable time to locate the Reverend Tobias Moon, the man who conducted your marriage. He had been deprived of his parish at the Restoration and forced to seek a living in the New World, chiefly because of your evident and relentless persecution of him – is that not so?' She made no reply. 'But finally we located him, in some foul and distant fastness within the Commonwealth of Massachusetts, as that remote place terms itself, and he sent us the piece of information that you had sought to conceal. Tell me, My Lady,' said Tristram, 'what do you know of a place called Chaldon Worgret, in the county of Dorset?'

'I – I have not heard such a name –'

'Really, My Lady? How strange. For that is where you were born and christened as Louise Lugg, was it not? A remote place, cradled within the broad downs where Dorset comes down to the sea. The sea whither your Spanish father came, and whence he swiftly returned, or so the goodly folk of the place tell me. For I have been there, you see. I have even fought something of a battle there. And although you claim to have forgotten it, there are many still alive in that place who recall your birth, and your childhood. Aye, and many who remember who and what your mother was.' Tristram smiled. 'It must have been some-what uncomfortable, growing up in the knowledge that your mother had given birth to you and was then immediately burned as a witch.'

Then, and only then, did Louise, Countess of Ravensden, break down. Her entire frame shook, and she sobbed pathetically. When she looked up, it was toward me: her one remaining hope of a sympathetic hearing in that place. But I could not meet her eyes, and looked away.

'No child should suffer for the sins of its parents,' said Charles, looking significantly toward our mother, 'but equally, no king is likely to want to take as his mistress – or a royal duchess to take as her boon companion – the offspring of a condemned witch, and a mother who pimps her own daughter. Nor a murderess, in truth.'

'*I did not kill my husbands –*'

'Frankly, madam, it does not really matter whether you did or not.' This was a Charles Quinton that I had never seen before: a decisive, even brutal, man of action. But then, I reflected, this was not really my brother at all. This was Lord Percival, and he was clearly a very dif-ferent creature to the cultured, ascetic, sickly tenth Earl of Ravensden. 'Enough of the world believes that you did – and if it does not now, then it certainly will after Lord Percival disseminates the rumour. A pam-phlet, I think, from one of those infernally persistent printing presses in London that our ministers and intelligencers singularly fail to shut down. One of the better writers, perhaps Dryden or Marvell. The child of a witch and a papist enemy of England, her own child condemned to a brothel, the murderer of two husbands, an agent of the hated French, who tried to ensnare an earl, a duchess and a king with her wiles… We will rewrite history, of course, to ensure that the king and I appear as all-seeing and all-knowing, humouring your schemes until the moment came to strike you down. That is the good thing about history, I find – it is so easy to alter it entirely with a stroke of a pen, particularly in these days when mankind as a whole is so remarkably gullible.'

'And with your own daughter swearing to the truth of this account, what will be left for you, mother?' said Madeleine bitterly. The Countess Louise gave her a look that seemed to encompass the rage and hurt of a mother spurned, but perhaps something else, too: a pride that her child had inherited her steel.

'There is one thing more,' I said. 'Something that your chosen writer will find irresistible, brother. Paint her as the dark power that prevented her country's navy winning this war.'

Despite reeling from the onslaught against her, the Lady Louise still managed an incredulous laugh. 'Dear God, you as well, Matthew? I thought you had better sense than all these who seek my ruin. Well, then, what did I do to prevent your precious fleet's victory? Hold back your ships through witchcraft inherited from my mother, perhaps?'

'I fought a duel with Harry Brouncker, lady. Brouncker ordered our fleet to shorten sail in the night after the battle. Now where do you suppose he got that idea, My Lady? From Clarendon and the Duchess of York, desperate to preserve the life of the Duke? That is the tale currently favoured in the fleet and the city. But Brouncker was your lover – your puppet. When you came down to the fleet at Harwich, was it not to perfect the scheme that you had hatched with Monsieur Courtin? Brouncker to do all he could aboard the flagship to prevent the fleet gaining too crushing a victory, for an English navy unchallenged at sea would be utterly contrary to King Louis' interests?'

'With the poor duped Duchess as your scapegoat should the scheme misfire,' Charles added.

'Aye,' said I, 'for how many hundreds would have seen her with you and Brouncker at the reception for the ambassadors? A wife's natural concern for the life of her husband, translated into an order to Brouncker to keep him safe at all costs – both of them little realising that they were truly serving the cause of King Louis.'

Framed against the window, the Lady Louise finally recovered some of her fight. 'Damn you all to Hell! You talk of the judgement of history upon me? Well, then, let history judge this, Matthew Quinton

– which of us strove to stop a war and preserve the lives of thousands, you or I?'

The barb struck home. In a sense, I felt more pain in that moment than I had when the Dutch musket ball struck my foot; for was not this but the plain truth?

Tristram was unfazed. 'My Lady, King Louis' peace has another name to it. That word is slavery. Yes, it suits him at this present moment to have peace between England and the Dutch, but only so that he may eventually achieve his real aim – and that, My Lady, is to rule over us both.'

She stared at him, that same strange expression upon her face. 'Tristram Quinton, my most inveterate enemy of all. And I know why, Doctor Quinton – I know the role you play.' She looked around the room, her eyes ablaze. 'You can accuse me all you like,' she said bitterly, 'but I know the truth of you Quintons now – of the secret that you have tried to hide all these years. I will take it with me to France, and denounce you all, and your foul hypocrite of a king, from there!' She was exultant now. 'Aye, none of you can touch me! I will walk from here a free woman, for I am under the protection of France!' she spat. 'Of France, I say!'

'No longer, madam.' This voice was the least expected of all. I turned, startled beyond all measure, to look upon my mother. She was smiling; and in recent times, I had known my mother to smile only when a particularly large dissenter congregation was arrested. But the revelation of her extraordinary past had seemingly liberated the Countess Anne. 'King Louis was susceptible to your reasoning once, perhaps,' she said. 'But now, My Lady, he takes the counsel of others. Recently, he has been particularly receptive to the arguments of his aunt, Queen Henrietta Maria. My dearest friend. Arguments that I provided her with, before she left this shore for the last time.'

The Dowager Countess of Ravensden raised herself from her chair.

My brother might have feigned his pain, but my mother clearly did not; yet she intended to bring down this interloper, who had deceived her more thoroughly than any of the rest of us, by confronting her face to face.

The Countess Anne walked slowly, painfully, across the great gallery, and stood at last in front of her daughter-in-law.

'You may ruin my name,' said my mother. 'It is of but little concern to me now. But you will not ruin the sainted reputation of the Queen Mother with malicious accusations about what passed between her and Colin Campbell, and you will not sully the name of the King and Martyr whom I loved.' The dowager countess was almost spitting her bile at her good-daughter. 'It would be impossible to proceed against you here, in England. We have such inconveniences as a rule of law, with juries, a need for evidence, and other such troublesome barriers to the execution of justice. But they are not so particular in France, and for all your bluster, you are now an embarrassment to that state and its king, good-daughter. The French have a device called the *lettre de cachet*, which permits indefinite imprisonment under royal warrant and without trial.' She reached within her sleeve and produced a small, folded piece of parchment, sealed with wax. 'A letter such as this one.'

'It need not be so,' said Charles, 'depending upon –'

But it was too late. Louise Quinton ran to the wall near where Cornelia and I were, lifted the tapestry over her, and disappeared. Musk tore the tapestry from its hangers, revealing a concealed doorway. Despite the pain from my foot, I was the first to reach the opening and the spiral staircase behind it. Drawing my sword, I took the steps two at a time. I could hear Louise's steps high above me. Below, Charles, Tris, Musk, Madeleine and Cornelia followed up the stairs in their turns, for this was a particularly narrow spiral which must have survived from the earliest days of the castle.

At last there was some light upon the stair – the roof had to be near –

Out, and onto a broad crenellated platform with fine views of the wooded countryside all around. She stood there, before me, pressed against the battlements.

'Louise,' I said, 'I beg you, there is no need for this – I will mitigate their wrath –'

My brother stepped out onto the roof behind me, followed in short order by the others.

'Damn you,' she hissed. 'Damn you all, you so-mighty Quintons! What did I do? *What did I do*? All I sought was to end a war – is that so very wrong? And Harry Brouncker ensuring sail was shortened, saving thousands more lives – can that be a crime?' She looked at me imploringly. 'True, I also wished for the best life I could have – to be a great lady – I saw the coach of the Lady Bankes once, when I was a child in Dorset – aye, a child living with the stigma of having a witch for her mother – the coach came through our village, and I thought, *one day that will be me* – oh yes, but that which in men is called ambition, in women is called whoring and witchcraft. Sweet Mother of God, *is all I have done so very wrong?*'

'Wrong indeed, if at the expense of the lives of your husbands and your daughter!' cried Cornelia.

'And of your king,' said Tris, coldly.

'Oh, Tristram Quinton,' she said mockingly. 'See yourself now, sir, as I see you. A fine, rational man of science. Master of an Oxford college, member of the Royal Society. But what has it been, your pursuit of me, if not that of a witchfinder hunting his witch?'

I had never seen my uncle flummoxed and wholly at a loss for words: never until then.

'It is over, madam,' said Charles firmly. Then his voice changed; no longer was he Lord Percival. 'Come, Louise. We need not employ King Louis' letter – quiet exile will not be so bad, if you will but agree to it –'

Louise was flushed and increasingly hysterical. 'You think I believe that, Charles? That you and your harridan of a mother will trust me to keep the secrets I now know? And even if I trusted the House of Quinton, do you really think I trust Charles Stuart? Do any of you?'

'I give you my word,' said Charles Quinton. 'The word of the Earl of Ravensden.'

'And is that really a word you can give, husband? You, who might be a king's bastard instead? And in any case, would it truly be your word, or that of Lord Percival? For I would not trust him in a century of Sundays.' She laughed bitterly. 'Ah, perhaps I might trust the word of an Earl of Ravensden, after all. But only of one.'

At that, she stared directly upon me. As she did so, she moved along the wall until she was framed directly in the embrasure, her back to the open air.

I stepped forward. 'Louise,' I said, 'you have my word – in the name of God, come away –'

'Too late, Matthew. Too late for all, now. You will not parade me to public scorn, as you did my mother. You will not burn me as you burned my mother!'

With that, she turned, gripped the battlements, stepped up and flung herself into space.

I was the first to reach the wall, and was thus the only one to see the mortal form of Louise, Countess of Ravensden, strike and break upon the ground far below. To this day, I can recall the expression on her face in that last moment before her head snapped forward on impact with the earth. I will go to my grave convinced that she was smiling.

Tris gently moved me to one side and looked down upon the grim sight. 'A singular woman,' he said. 'Singular and unsettling. Her entire life was a lie, and yet at the end it brought her to a clear vision of the truth. Disturbingly clear.'

My brother looked down upon the remains of his wife, watching as Madeleine came out from the castle, knelt down by her mother's body, and began to weep. Charles was silent for some moments, but when he spoke again, it was with the voice of Lord Percival. 'Musk, attend to the body. She will be buried with all the honours and respect that befit a Countess of Ravensden.'

'As you say, My Lord.'

As Musk retired, I went to Cornelia and took my shaking wife into my arms. 'You called her Louise,' she said, half quizzically and half accusingly.

I looked out, far beyond the walls of Lyndbury Castle. A small black cloud upon the horizon seemed to presage a distant storm.

Epilogue

We boys are truly loyal,
For Charles we'll venture all,
We know his blood is royal,
His name shall never fall!
[Chorus]
Fill the pottles and gallons,
And bring the hogshead in,
We'll begin with a tallen,
A brimmer to the king!
~ Anon., *The Courtier's Health, or The Merry Boys of the Times*
(popular royalist song of the 1670s)

The court and government of Charles the Second had descended upon Salisbury like a plague of locusts. The population almost doubled overnight; the cesspits and the old-fashioned water channels that flowed in the midst of every street could not cope. The rooms of the antique low-roofed inns of the town were suddenly crowded out. It was said that at the Haunch of Venison, two baronets and a viscount shared one garret, while the King's Arms was so full of young ladies of dubious reputation that it was newly by-named Signor Dildo's Convent. The butchers, bakers and brewers were confronted by at once the greatest opportunity and the greatest nightmare of their lives, for the insatiable needs of the royal purveyors and the countless lackeys placed intolerable demands upon their supplies. Within days, courtiers and men of Sarum alike were grumbling at this singular choice of a royal refuge. What was wrong with Oxford, the old cavaliers complained, which was good enough for this king's parents, the royal court and the entire royalist army in the civil war? Plenty of rooms in the Oxford colleges, they said, and spacious quadrangles for perambulation. Ah, said the more knowing, but Oxford is not My Lord of Clarendon's city. Hereabouts are the village where the Chancellor was born and the ruined palace from which he takes his title. The graves of Salisbury are full of dead Hydes. Most of the butchers, farriers and vintners are kin to the Hydes. Such economy of effort on the part of the Chancellor, who could thus attend to his estates, the enrichment of his friends and neighbours, and the governance of England without needing to move an inch! And so the capital of England had decamped to this peculiar little provincial town, beneath the shadow of the cathedral's lofty spire, simply because it was convenient for His Eminence, England's secular Richelieu.

The king had installed himself in a fine new house close to the cathedral, a square, grey-stone pile with a multiplicity of south-facing windows. It was there that my brother and I found him, looking for all the world like a lofty attendant to the far grander personage in his company, the Earl of Clarendon himself.

King and Chancellor began by congratulating me on my efforts in the *Merhonour* – heroics, Clarendon said – during the late battle. The king demanded a detailed account of the action, clapping his hands with glee at the account of the *Eendracht*'s destruction. Only that morning, he had learned that Obdam's family had invoiced the

States-General for all the silver cutlery, extravagant tablecloths and other personal effects lost when the ship blew up.

'And that, of course,' said King Charles, 'is why the Dutch are destined to lose this war. Mean, avaricious penny-pinchers, all of them, who can think only of their balance sheets! Whereas our true and honest Englishmen serve for honour, not for base coin.'

Which is as well, I thought, given how tardy this king's treasury proves in actually paying any of the moneys now long overdue to the same true and honest Englishmen, the captain of the *Merhonour* among them.

Clarendon was clearly bored during my discourse of the battle; his entire lack of interest in naval affairs could not be shaken even by the tale of England's greatest victory by sea. As soon as he decently could, he changed the topic of conversation to his perennial and most pressing concern, the security of the crown – that delicate euphemism for the continuation in power of the Earl of Clarendon.

'As you know, sirs, the business of the twenty captains was seemingly a canard, a mere fiction,' said the Chancellor. My brother and I glanced at each other complicitly. The great Clarendon was clearly not as all-knowing as he assumed, for in this matter he had been well and truly gulled. 'The invention of a disgruntled Middlesex magistrate and some of his circle of fanatics and malcontents, who turned the ordinary murder of a poor wretch into the basis of a great conspiracy. They sought to spread dissension and uncertainty within our fleet, hoping thereby to bring about a Dutch victory –'

'Which would encourage all the sectaries to rise up and send me packing,' said the king, with equal complicity. 'To think there are those within my realms who would revel in an English defeat.'

'A plot defeated chiefly by the guile of that dark and mysterious creature, the Lord Percival,' said Clarendon, smiling and nodding toward my brother, who reciprocated. 'Let us be thankful for his unexpected and timely reappearance.'

The Earl of Ravensden smiled and bowed. It was still strange to see him as he really was, this feared and indomitable bulwark of the realm.

On our journey to Salisbury, Charles had told me something of his alternative identity. He first adopted it in Cromwell's time, initially as a way of protecting his family and estates from the wrath of the Protector.

'Gradually, I came to realise that the disguise was far more potent than plain Charles Quinton,' he said, taking me fully into his confidence for the first time in our lives. 'A man whose face is concealed and whose true identity is unknown strikes fear into the hearts of the credulous, who see in him all their nightmares of wraiths and phantoms and the like. With the playhouses closed, my theatrical friends had ample time on their hands to train me in acting a part and convincing an audience. Soon, Lord Percival had a small army of agents at his disposal, with Phineas Musk at their head.'

The idea of Musk alongside my brother at the heart of royalist intrigues – aye, as a cavalier hero, no less – was more than a little disconcerting. 'Then why did you not recruit me, Charles, or at least confide in me?' I demanded.

'Come, Matt, you remember how dangerous the times were. One of us could play the spy, but for the good of the house of Quinton – and our mother's peace of mind – it was better that the two of us did not lay our heads upon the same block. And if you were ever arrested by the Puritans and their lackeys, you could legitimately deny all knowledge of this Lord Percival.'

As we rode on, Charles explained that he believed the Restoration would be the end of his days as an intelligencer: there would a new era of peace and contentment under our rightful sovereign, and the Earl of Ravensden could devote all his efforts to the recovery of his ancestral estates. 'But by last autumn, it was apparent that plots against the king were multiplying faster than rabbits in a warren. And if truth be told, Matt, I was most dreadfully bored by the endless ledgers, the disputes over rentals, the discussions upon wheat… Christ God, spare me from wheat… It needed only a catalyst to revive the dark spectre of Lord Percival. A catalyst that you provided.'

'That *I* provided, brother?'

'Of course – your exposure of my wife as a French agent, Matt. Oh, I was already convinced of her duplicity, and regretted my weakness in allowing myself to be persuaded to the marriage by our mother and the king. But I had thought of the marriage as a penance for my many sins – as a cross I would have to bear for as long as I lived. Your intelligence of her true nature made me realise that I had an alternative. Thanks to my unnatural marriage, I had been presented with incomparable access to one of King Louis' most important agents in England – an opportunity that I simply could not pass over, brother.' Almost as one, our steeds jumped a shallow gully. 'I approached the king, Clarendon and Arlington. With the fanatics restless and a war imminent, they were more than enthusiastic to recall the most successful royalist agent of the late troubles, if I may so immodestly term myself. Thus was Lord Percival reborn.' Charles smiled. 'The preachers say that rebirth in Christ makes a man new again. I won't gainsay that, but the rebirth of Lord Percival certainly remade Charles Quinton. I had been sick, weary of my old wounds, weighed down by the doubts over my marriage. I would probably have been a dead man within months.' We rode through a stream, scattering some ponies that were drinking a little way downstream. 'But the moment I resumed the identity of Lord Percival, I felt as though a surge of new blood had been pumped into me. I felt a thrill that I had not known since the Protector's dragoons were in pursuit of me across the fields of Northamptonshire. This was what I was born to do, Matt.'

This, and not the part of the Earl of Ravensden? It was a question that I could not ask; nor did I feel inclined to raise the allegations of the late countess. But Charles himself must have sensed my predicament. We reined in amidst the ruins of Old Sarum, on the bleak hill above Salisbury, looking down to the lofty spire of the cathedral in the broad vale beneath.

'It tormented father, you know,' he said, suddenly and evidently regretfully. '*Your* father. He told me of it, the day he rode out before Naseby. I think he had a sense that he would not return – indeed, I have often wondered whether he did not truly care if he lived or died in the battle, whether his charge into the midst of Parliament's army was the fulfilment of a death wish. Mother has blamed Rupert all these years, but I think that has been only a way of assuaging her own guilt.' He looked into the distance and shook his head sadly. 'I had to succeed to the title. You realise that? To proclaim myself both illegitimate and the king's son would have bestowed the entire Quinton inheritance upon a five-year-old in the midst of civil war, when it urgently needed a steady hand to hold it together – and God, what would Cromwell and the Parliament-men have done with intelligence that the king had a bastard?'

'When did the king know?' I asked. 'The present king.'

'His father told him when they, too, parted for the last time. I think it had caused less anguish between the king and queen than it did between your father and our mother. After all, Matt, it is expected of men, and perhaps of kings especially – but as my late wife rightly said, in women it is called *whoring*.'

'And are these, then, the deep secrets of the House of Quinton, that you once swore upon our sister's grave to reveal to me one day?'

My brother – maybe my half-brother, for all we and our mother knew – looked at me, looked away over the ruins of Sarum and to the cathedral spire beyond, then smiled and turned back to me.

'One of them, Matt. But only one, and perhaps not the greatest. That day of revelation is still to come.'

So we rode down into Salisbury, and despite Charles Quinton's enigmatic prevarication, at last I knew the truth of his unlikely friendship with Charles Stuart.

Genesis Four, verse Nine.

They were each their brother's keeper.

* * *

'I wouldn't have forgiven you if you'd killed Harry Brouncker,' said King Charles the Second, a little later. 'Damn difficult these days to find good opponents at chess. But then, if I'd suspected him of giving the order to shorten sail I'd probably have run him through myself. Wouldn't you say so, My Lord Clarendon?'

The Chancellor, who was suspected by many (Matthew Quinton at their head) of having played a part in that perfidious order, seemed momentarily discomfited, but quickly recovered his customary arrogance. 'As well, then, Your Majesty, that the incident seems to have been but a misunderstanding between tired men, all numbed by the shock of battle.'

So this was to be the new truth; and Clarendon's daughter, gulled by the Lady Louise, was hardly likely to dispute it.

The king sent for wine, and we drank cheerily. Strangely to my mind, there was no mention at all of the late Countess of Ravensden. But then, Charles Stuart presumably did not wish to be reminded of the fact that he, too, had been gulled by that lady, and wished even less to be reminded of the fact that he, the king, had been wrong about her, and that I, plain Matt Quinton, had been right. In my experience, those with divine right have some difficulty admitting to their earthly wrongs.

At length Clarendon withdrew, pleading some urgent business of state; we were, after all, at war, although it was easy enough to forget that amid the cloistered serenity of Salisbury. With him gone, the three men left behind could turn at last to the matters known to them alone.

'I still feel like a naughty child when I dissemble before My Lord of Clarendon,' said the king. 'But it is better that he believes your story of Bagshawe's guilt, Charles, rather than the truth – especially as Bagshawe lies in a damned convenient plague-pit and cannot disabuse him.'

Charles had told me the truth of the 'twenty captains' at Lyndbury, but I still found difficulty in believing it. The story was indeed a canard, as Clarendon had said, but it was certainly not a canard of Sir Martin Bagshawe's making.

'*Arlington*,' my brother had said, as we stood alone in the half-ruined chapel of Louise's home, keeping vigil over her coffin. 'It was of his devising, although of course he denied it to my face when I visited him and presented him with Bagshawe's testimony – the testimony of the man whom Arlington had bribed and browbeaten into instigating his scheme. Bagshawe had too many dubious friends among the fanatics, and had incurred too many debts. Arlington could at once intimidate him into doing his bidding while also buying his silence – or at any rate, could do so until the plague condemned Bagshawe to death and thus destroyed his hold over him.'

'Arlington?' I was incredulous, yet perhaps not quite as incredulous as I might have been; for I recalled Arlington's behaviour toward me at Clarendon House and his insistence upon the reality of the 'twenty captains' in the face of Clarendon's scepticism. 'In the name of dear Heaven, Charles, why would Arlington concoct such a tale – spreading suspicion and discontent in our fleet just as we were about to face the Dutch?'

'Precisely for that reason, Matt. Create suspicion of the old Commonwealth captains and what might be the outcome, especially if our fleet did not obtain a decisive victory, thus seeming to give credence to such doubts?'

I recalled the council of war at which His Grace of Buckingham had demanded a command; and in those days, Buckingham was ever the staunch ally of My Lord Arlington. 'A wholesale purge of the old captains,' I said slowly, the realisation seeping into my veins, 'and only cavaliers to be entrusted with commands.'

Charles nodded. 'Aye, and more, I'd say. I'll wager Arlington intended to use the tale as an excuse to attack the man who advocated commissioning those old captains in the first place.'

'The Duke of York! And if Arlington undermines York –'

'He undermines York's father-in-law.'

I was incredulous. 'He would play such games when the kingdom is at war? When so much is at stake?'

My Lord of Ravensden smiled. 'I know Arlington better than you, Matt. Have known him for many years. I think he would say that the highest stake of all is to be the supreme authority in England, beneath the king; that the war will not be prosecuted vigorously while Clarendon holds the place; that Clarendon will never act firmly enough against the dissenters and malcontents; that Clarendon, at bottom, is simply not Arlington.'

'Surely the king will dismiss him for this?'

'Dismiss him? Lord, no. His Majesty has precious few clever men about him, and none are cleverer than Arlington, for all his faults. And he is hardly likely to dismiss a man for advocating the promotion of ardent royalists.' Charles shrugged. 'The king will rebuke him, I have no doubt, but it suits him well to keep Arlington and Clarendon in balance. Without the one, the other becomes too powerful.'

But it is better that he believes your story of Bagshawe's guilt, Charles, rather than the truth. So it had transpired as my brother predicted. Arlington remained in office, with the truth of his conspiracy concealed from his rival Clarendon – concealed, no doubt, so that the king could dangle it like a sword of Damocles over the Secretary of State's head, a sword to be unsheathed whenever it suited the royal purpose. But as we stood there, alongside the coffin of the Countess Louise, I began to wonder whether Arlington's dark scheme had one other ingredient to it. Prince Rupert had recommended me for the *Merhonour*, I now knew, but he had no say in where that ship would be stationed in battle. Instead, I recalled the Secretary of State's words to me at Clarendon House: *we have prevailed upon His Royal Highness to place you directly behind Lawson's new flagship, as his second.* A callow young gentleman captain, promoted to command a ship far too large for him, his head filled with a great statesman's insinuations of a plot: might not such a captain perhaps rashly open fire upon the wrong ship at the wrong moment – at such moments, say, as the *Guinea's* misfired broadside, or when the *Royal Oak* failed to tack and follow Rupert – and thus trigger the very dissension in the fleet that Arlington wished to engender?

Thus it was that summer of 1665 in England. Plague, war and death cast their dark shadows over the land; the rulers of the kingdom made shuttlecocks of the lives of a thousand score of men, Matt Quinton among them, simply to further their own petty interests; and a witch's daughter did all in her power to fulfil the comet's dire prophecy, and to bring the fourth horseman to England's fragile shore.

* * *

Charles Stuart had refilled his glass, but was contemplating the object intently. 'Finest Venetian, this,' he said. 'Unexpected, in Salisbury. Better than any I have at Whitehall, I'll wager. My Lord Chancellor does have expensive tastes, does he not?' He turned to me suddenly. 'Well then, Matthew Quinton,' said the King, almost as though he were contemplating me for the first time, 'so now you are privy to one of the deepest secrets of the state.' I was still thinking of the machinations of My Lord Arlington, but the king evidently had another matter upon his mind. 'The human weakness of my late father – although of course, I would be the last man on earth to condemn him for that.' The *fornicator immensus* of our times smiled. 'So, Matt, does the knowledge crush you?'

'As you say, Majesty, they were but very human weaknesses, and a very long time ago.'

'True, but with very urgent consequences in our own time, I think.' The king's face clouded, masking in an instant his previous good humour. 'For instance, Captain Quinton, have you considered how it was that the late countess suddenly discovered that her new family might be harbouring some great secret that could be of considerable embarrassment, or worse, to the crown of this realm?'

The directness of the king's question took me aback. I had never given it a thought. 'No, Sire. The chatter of servants, perhaps?'

'Not so, Matthew Quinton. It was you.'

Me? I could say nothing: the king's simple words, and his stern, dreadful face, stunned me into silence and despair.

My brother looked at me dispassionately and said, 'It seems you have an enemy, Matt. A most influential and inveterate enemy, who has lately been taking a particular interest in the history and connections of the House of Quinton. An enemy who, shall we say, rather took my wife under his wing and introduced her to his close ally, Ambassador Courtin. He passed on to her various tales about our family that are mentioned within the King of France's secret archives. Rumours about the fate of Earl Edward, for instance – so she could feign an interest in that story, the better to conceal her sponsor's true target, the liaison between our mother and the king.'

'Montnoir,' I said in horrified realisation. 'Gaspard de Montnoir would go to such lengths to wreak revenge upon me, and upon England?' The memory of the black-cloaked Knight of Malta and envoy of the French king, who had clashed with me during a previous voyage, still came to me in nightmares. I had defeated and humiliated Montnoir, but I had known full well that he was the sort of man who would one day seek vengeance.

'Quite so,' said Charles Stuart. 'All kings are troubled by factions in their realms, trying to pull them this way or that, and my cousin Louis is no exception. I am vexed principally by fanatics, dissenters, republicans and all their strange kin. His chief burden comes from extreme

Papists, those who believe even the present Pope to be too liberal and daily endeavour to persuade Louis to herd all his Protestant subjects onto bonfires. For such men, even a King of England who is remarkably tolerant to Catholics and seeks to be a good friend to France is considered a damnable heretic. It seems that your foe is one of the principal voices within this camp – that is, when he is not scouring the Mediterranean in his galley, looking for Mahometans to kill.' The king sniffed. 'So it seems, Matt, that I have you to thank for interesting this Seigneur de Montnoir in my affairs.'

'Majesty,' said my brother, 'I feel certain that both Captain Quinton and Lord Percival will do their utmost to protect both you and the House of Quinton from Montnoir's infernal machinations.'

'I will hold you to that,' said Charles Stuart. It was impossible to tell whether he was jesting or in earnest. 'But, gentlemen, perhaps the Frenchman and the late countess have actually done us a great service. When all is said and done, they have brought us finally to confront a great issue that should have been resolved many years ago.' The king looked at me with what for him approximated an expression of kindness. 'By the admission of your mother, Matt, it is entirely possible that the Earl of Ravensden, here present, is the son of *my* father, not yours. He certainly bears no resemblance to your father Earl James, nor to your grandfather. I remember them both well.' The king stepped very close to me, that vast, bulbous nose only inches from my own. 'So we have to consider the possibility that a grave injustice has been done to you all these years, Matthew Quinton – that since the age of five, you have been the rightful and legitimate Earl of Ravensden. You would be entirely justified if you sought to assert your rights. So, gentlemen, what to do?'

I had thought long and hard upon this during the ride from Lyndbury from Salisbury, for I knew full well that the question was bound to be asked. My brother looked keenly at me, and then at the king; the man who was, perhaps, his other brother.

'Majesty,' I said slowly, 'there is no certainty that Charles and I did not share the same father. My mother's opinion is but that – it is not fact.' The thought of my ancient, crabbed, righteous mother as a nubile young courtier, betraying her husband with no less a lover than the King of England, was still truly shocking to me. 'And faces can disappear in families for generations, then suddenly reappear in a newborn. So we also have no certainty that Charles does not resemble some long-dead Quinton whose portrait was never made.' Charles Stuart, whose entire lack of resemblance to both his parents was a byword, nodded thoughtfully. 'This being so, it seems to me that Charles is as likely to be the rightful Earl of Ravensden as I am. And this being so, then Earl of Ravensden he should remain, for to take any other course would be to do the work of Montnoir and Lady Louise for them.'

And with that, my lifelong fear – the dread of inheriting the earldom – fell away like a redundant husk. For I *had* inherited it, twenty years before; and now I had made my one and, I prayed, only decision as the rightful Earl of Ravensden.

Charles Stuart scrutinised me closely, as though searching for any signs of doubt or falsehood in my statement. Then he drew himself up and grinned. 'Truly noble! Aye, truly noble indeed! A credit to the House of Quinton, which has always been one of the staunchest bulwarks of my ancestral throne. So, Charlie – Earl of Ravensden you remain.'

My brother came to me and embraced me warmly. 'I am forever in your debt, Matt.'

Making that statement was evidently a deep embarrassment to this most guarded of men. Fortunately, King Charles began circling us, talking almost to himself.

'But we have to consider the other case,' said the king, 'which is the possibility that a very great wrong has been done to you all these years, Matt Quinton. Now, one of the more pleasurable aspects of kingship is that God has bestowed upon us a certain ability to right wrongs.'

Thus Charles Stuart resumed the royal 'we', transforming himself by that simple grammatical act from a devious rutting mortal into a kind of demigod. 'In this case, it is easier to justify because of the manifest merit that you have displayed in our cause, most recently by your bravery and good conduct during the late battle of Lowestoft, and the most earnest solicitations on your behalf by our cousin, Prince Rupert, and our son James of Monmouth.' He stopped before me and smiled broadly. 'Your sword, Matt.'

Scarcely believing what was happening, I drew the blade that had belonged to my grandfather.

'Well, bow, man!' laughed Charles Stuart, taking the sword in his hand. 'We're the same height, after all, so if you don't lower yourself, I'll probably decapitate you!'

I bowed deeply before the king, felt the blade touch my shoulders, and heard the four words that I had dreamed of all my life.

'Arise, Sir Matthew Quinton!'

HISTORICAL NOTE

Much of the action of The Blast That Tears the Skies *is based on the actual historical events before, during and after the Battle of Lowestoft (3 June 1665). Like so many battles of the age of sail, this was a confusing encounter, and several of the contemporary accounts contradict each other; this is only to be expected, as there were over two hundred ships fighting simultaneously in a sea area up to ten miles long and several miles wide, with thick clouds of gunsmoke and the profusion of sails and hulls often restricting vision to the immediate area around each ship. However, some modern accounts of the battle overstate the confusion and present a distorted impression of the action. Although there remains some doubt about the preliminary manoeuvres, several of the key elements are beyond dispute: notably the British fleet's two tacks from the rear (a feat never again accomplished in the entire era of sailing navies); the fumbled hoisting of the signal flag aboard the flagship, the duel of* Royal Charles *and* Eendracht *leading to the destruction of the latter, the heroics of the* Oranje; *the confusion over the command and provincial jealousies within the Dutch fleet; and the pursuit of the Dutch. The Battle of Lowestoft was arguably the worst naval disaster ever suffered by the Dutch navy, certainly the worst of its magnificent 'golden age' that stretched for roughly a century from 1572 to 1688, and it has been reconstructed accurately and in some detail in both Frank Fox's superb study of the second Anglo-Dutch war,* The Four Days Battle, *and in my* Pepys's Navy: Ships, Men and Warfare 1649–89.

The rumour that twenty former Commonwealth captains intended to defect to the Dutch during the first battle of the war was reported confidently at the time, notably in the despatches of the Venetian ambassador. The Duke of York's narrow escape when the three courtiers nearest to him were killed, and the presence of his dog aboard the flagship, are well documented, as is the mysterious shortening of sail after the battle. There was a strong contemporary rumour alleging that Henry Brouncker had been carrying out the Duchess of York's instructions to preserve her husband's safety at all costs; this formed the basis of Andrew Marvell's vitriolic attack in the Second Advice to a Painter *and underpinned the parliamentary enquiry into these events in 1668. Brouncker's own account, previously unknown but which I discovered in the British Library a few years ago (Additional Manuscript 75,413), suggests that the disastrous decision was probably based on an unfortunate series of misunderstandings. There was no ship called* Merhonour *in 1665, although a man-of-war of that name had served with distinction between 1590 and 1650. I have drawn aspects of the fictional story of Matthew Quinton's* Merhonour *from the histories of several real ships of the period. Similarly, the loss of the* House of Nassau *during the battle is based upon the almost identical fate of Captain Robert Wilkinson's* Charity.

In order to accommodate the timescale of the plot, I have modified some of the chronology of 1665 to a certain extent. The London *blew up on 7 March, rather than somewhat later as implied here; the Duchess of York's visit to the fleet at Harwich took place rather earlier than I have set it. The most significant change has been to bring forward the worst effects of the plague by a couple of months. The court did not leave London until the beginning of July and went initially to Hampton Court, then to Salisbury and eventually to Oxford. The comet at the beginning of 1665 (there were actually two) and the dire predictions that followed in its wake are recorded in Pepys and many other contemporary sources. Pepys also chronicled the unfounded rumour that De Ruyter had instigated a massacre at Guinea, the catalyst for the attack upon Cornelia on London Bridge; this canard excited popular sentiment to such an extent that a guard had to be placed around the Dutch ambassador's residence. I have taken a slight liberty with the composition of the council of war, in order to enable Matthew to attend it. In this period there were actually two councils, an 'elite' one comprising the flag officers alone and a council of all captains, the former meeting more frequently; but to have replicated this pattern exactly would have been to overburden the narrative, and I needed Matthew present at the meeting (actually held on 12 April 1665) when the Duke of Buckingham petulantly demanded a place by virtue of his rank.*

Sir William Coventry did indeed possess a circular desk of his own devising; this was satirised mercilessly by Buckingham, his arch-enemy. The widespread belief that Coventry sold naval offices for his personal profit eventually led to a parliamentary enquiry, which exonerated him. The accounts of Clarendon House, the destruction of the London *(together with the presence of women and many of Sir John Lawson's relatives aboard her), the rise of the Earl of Falmouth, Lord Arlington's scar, the Duke of Monmouth's presence in the fleet and the French embassy of the duc de Verneuil and Courtin are also drawn from the historical record. Both the membership of the Royal Society and the experiment undertaken by Tristram Quinton are based closely upon fact; variants of the latter were actually undertaken by Daniel Coxe on 19 April and 3 May 1665, as recorded in Pepys's Diary. My descriptions of the plague in London are also based principally on Pepys, together with various modern accounts, Defoe's* Journal of the Plague Year, *and 'fieldwork' at the plague village of Eyam. Defoe's most famous work,* Robinson Crusoe, *was first published in 1719; the 'first English novel' swiftly became a runaway bestseller. Francois-Marie Arouet, alias Voltaire, lived in exile in London from 1726 to 1729, during the time when 'old Matthew' would have been writing his journals.*

Admiral Edward Russell, Earl of Orford, is not known to have served at sea until the year after the events described in this book. But his subsequent career developed exactly as Matthew describes it, except for the slight dramatic licence that I have taken of having him buried at Westminster Abbey, rather than in the Russell family mausoleum at Chenies where he lies to this day. The nickname of 'Cherry Cheeked Russell' was contemporary: the extant portraits of him display the characteristic clearly enough, even if he had not been the man responsible for the creation of 'the largest cocktail in history' (a historical phenomenon described in minute detail on many websites). His atrocious spelling is apparent in all of his extant letters. John, Viscount Mordaunt of Avalon, is another character drawn directly from history; he was one of the leaders of the 'Sealed Knot', the secret royalist organisation of the 1650s. Other real characters appearing in this book include Sir John Lawson, Sir William Penn, Sir William Berkeley, the Earl of Marlborough, Sir William Petty, and of course John Evelyn and the Pepyses. Although I have invented the character of Ieaun Goch, the legends of the derfel gadarn *and of the physicians of Myddfai are well known in Welsh folklore, and the dubious nature of many of the Welshmen recruited for the fleet during the Anglo-Dutch wars is confirmed in contemporary reports.*

Unlike both his sons, the famously moral and monogamous King Charles I did not father a brood of illegitimate offspring. Nevertheless, several potential bastards of his, albeit markedly implausible ones, have been suggested over the years: these include John Wilmot, second Earl of Rochester, the notorious poet and rake, and, more plausibly, Joanna Bridges, who was living at Mandinam near Llangadog, Carmarthenshire, in 1648. Joanna was said to have been the daughter of Charles and the much older Duchess of Lennox; she subsequently married the noted churchman Jeremy Taylor. Her story, along with the alleged affair of the Duke of Buckingham and Anne of Austria from The Three Musketeers, *provided the inspiration for the story of the uncertain paternity of Charles Quinton, Earl of Ravensden.*

Finally, I am aware that I have done a grave disservice to the memories of Bastiaan Senten, the true captain of the Oranje *at the battle of Lowestoft, and of the officers and men of the* Mary, *which played the part in the saving of the* Royal Charles *that I have assigned to the* Merhonour *(and which suffered even more terribly for so doing); like Matthew Quinton, her captain, Jeremy Smith, was knighted for his efforts. Senten's ship behaved almost exactly as described in this book, earning her crew the profound admiration and respect of her opponents, and very nearly changed the course of the action by so doing. It is therefore particularly ironic that 'Senten', who died about half an hour after receiving the personal approbation of the Duke of York, was probably an expatriate Scot, originally named Seaton. I hope that this book will honour both his memory and that of the thousands who fought, suffered and perished on both sides during the Battle of Lowestoft.*

Acknowledgements

I first began studying the age of the Anglo-Dutch wars, including the Battle of Lowestoft, thirty years ago, and it would be impossible to enumerate and thank all those who have contributed over the years to improving my knowledge and understanding of the events recounted in this book. Some of the greatest debts are to those who died well before my time. For example, the first detailed account of the battle that I read (and which still stands up well) was in *The Navy of the Restoration*, published in 1916; its author, Arthur Tedder, went on to become a Marshal of the Royal Air Force and Eisenhower's deputy supreme commander, thus proving that turf wars and cutthroat denigration of those in differently coloured uniforms need not always characterise inter-service relations. Sir Peter Lely (1618-80) painted a series of portraits of the British admirals who commanded during the battle, and standing before the 'flagmen of Lowestoft' in the Queen's House at the National Maritime Museum, Greenwich, provided much of the inspiration for my pen-portraits of the likes of Sir William Penn and Sir John Harman (although sadly, the museum no longer displays the entire series).

Returning to the more immediate and specific debts I incurred in writing this book: Frank Fox provided me with much valuable information about the battle of Lowestoft and in particular about the loss of the *London*, giving me an early sight of his excellent paper on the subject which is intended for publication in the *Transactions of the*

Naval Dockyards Society (www.navaldockyards.org). Thanks, too, to Dan Snow and Richard Endsor for a lively discussion about the presence of women aboard the *London* at the time of her destruction. Gijs Rommelse of the Netherlands Military Institute provided me with useful material on the Dutch aspects of the battle. As usual, David Jenkins ensured that my ships did not behave in impossible ways. Finally, once again I owe great debts to my agent, Peter Buckman, to my publisher at Old Street, Ben Yarde-Buller, and to my partner Wendy, who fights the corner of the female characters in the series with a tenacity that would have done credit to Cornelia Quinton.

J. D. Davies
Bedfordshire
'Gowrie Day' 2011